D0540614

The Fledging of
Az Gabrielson

The Fledging of Az Gabrielson

THE CLOUDED WORLD: BOOK I

Jay Amory

Gollancz

LONDON

Copyright © Jay Amory 2006
All rights reserved

The right of Jay Amory to be identified as the author
of this work has been asserted by him in accordance
with the Copyright, Designs and Patents Act 1988.

First published in Great Britain in 2006 by
Gollancz
An imprint of the Orion Publishing Group
Orion House, 5 Upper St Martin's Lane, London WC2H 9EA

A CIP catalogue record for this book is available
from the British Library

ISBN 0 57507 878 2 (cased)
ISBN 9 780 58507 878 9 (cased)
ISBN 0 57507 879 0 (trade paperback)
ISBN 9 780 57507 879 6 (trade paperback)

1 3 5 7 9 10 8 6 4 2

Typeset by Deltatype Ltd, Birkenhead, Wirral

Printed in Great Britain by
Mackays of Chatham plc, Chatham, Kent

The Orion Publishing Group's policy is to use papers that are
natural, renewable and recyclable products and made from wood
grown in sustainable forests. The logging and manufacturing
processes are expected to conform to the environmental
regulations of the country of origin.

www.orionbooks.co.uk

CHAPTER I

The Groundling Exhibit

The airbus touched down outside the Museum of Arts, Sciences and History and opened its door to let out thirty students from High Haven senior school. Some of them rushed straight for the museum entrance, propelling themselves with quick, eager thrusts of their wings. They couldn't wait to get started. Others were less keen. They couldn't think of anything duller than spending the day looking at stuffy old exhibits and listening to lectures from droney-voiced curators. They drifted across the landing apron using the bare minimum of effort to stay aloft. A few even walked, to show just how unenthralled they were.

Last to step off the airbus was Az. He, too, walked, but not because he was trying to look cool and nonchalant. He would gladly have flown, had the option been open to him. Shoulders slumped, hands in pockets, Az dragged his feet all the way to the building entrance, where Miss Kabnielsdaughter, the form teacher, was marshalling her pupils and counting heads.

'Quizzes!' Miss Kabnielsdaughter announced, and began doling out mimeographed sheets of paper. A groan rippled among the students. 'Well, you didn't think I was just going to let you dawdle around aimlessly, did you? I know you lot. Given half a chance you'd sit in the museum café all day drinking coffee, or else sneak off to hang around in the Seven Dreams Mall. Whereas I expect you to make good use of your time.'

'Hanging around in the mall *is* making good use of our time, miss,' said one joker.

Students laughed but Miss Kabnielsdaughter ignored the

wisecrack. 'Now, you'll find fifty questions relating to items in the museum. Simple observation will provide the answers, though be warned – I've thrown in a couple of tricky ones to keep you on your toes. Azrael?'

Miss Kabnielsdaughter handed Az his sheet.

'You do as many as you feel able,' she said in a slightly lowered voice.

Az narrowed his eyes. 'I can manage, miss. I don't need special treatment.'

'Even so. Unlike at school, the museum isn't adapted so that you can get around easily. I'll understand if you can't cover quite as much ground as the others.'

'I can manage,' Az repeated firmly and stuffed the questionnaire in his back pocket. 'I'm not a *completely* hopeless case.'

Miss Kabnielsdaughter debated whether to scold him. She didn't mind wit but normally she would not tolerate backchat from any of her pupils. With Az Gabrielson, however, you had to make allowances. Though she did her best to treat him the same as everyone else, she couldn't help feeling sorry for the poor kid.

'Off you go,' she said to the whole class. 'We rendezvous on the mezzanine at lunchtime. That's one o'clock sharp.'

The students flowed through the arched entrance portal and dispersed in groups of three and four. Brushing past Miss Kabnielsdaughter, Az set off on his own.

Spherical in shape, the Museum of Arts, Sciences and History was divided into ten levels. Each hoop-like floor ran around a cylindrical atrium which was capped at either end by a vast circular window made up of concentric roundels of glass. The museum's upper levels were devoted to technology and culture while the lower levels dealt with famous events and figures from the Airborn race's past. Most of Az's classmates rose through the atrium to view exhibits such as the Casmaronson brothers' prototype biplane and the waxwork effigy of the celebrated concert harpist Talia Israfelsdaughter.

Az, however, gravitated in the opposite direction. There was a narrow, zigzagging staircase at the rim of the atrium for the benefit of the elderly and infirm. Az followed it downward until he could go no further.

Few visitors ever bothered with the bottom floor. Today, in fact, Az was alone there apart from a middle-aged man clad in black, who was wafting around on the far side.

From a previous trip to the museum with his family Az knew that this floor dealt with the earliest days of the Airborn – the period immediately following the Great Cataclysm when the survivors of that worldwide disaster built the sky-cities and moved up into them in order to escape the shadow of the cloud mass which was slowly blanketing the planet's surface. Various models and dioramas showed how the sky-cities were constructed, a feat of engineering as brilliant as it had been rapid. Architects had innovated and labourers had toiled, all of them inspired by the urgency of the crisis to find solutions to monumental problems and work like they had never worked before. Columns had risen from the ground at impossible speed; cities had branched out at the top, each different in design, each unique, some functional, some bizarre, some perched on a single column, some on several.

But there was one particular exhibit that Az remembered from before and was drawn to now. It was a scene depicting how life must have been for those who hadn't migrated into the sky-cities, those who'd remained below. The Groundlings.

It consisted of a replica of the interior of a small wooden shack, home to a family of four. The furniture was crude, little better than nailed-together planks, and the sole source of heat and light was an open hearth that fed up into a brick chimney. Flames made of orange silk fluttered above a heap of fake coal and licked around the base of a copper cauldron suspended from a hook. Through an open doorway a landscape backdrop could be glimpsed, an artist's impression of dense, damp forest beneath a menacing overcast sky.

The family themselves were waxwork representations of a father, a mother, a teenage daughter and a very young son. The father was sharpening the blade of a wood-chopping axe with a whetstone, the mother was cooking, the daughter was teasing wool from yarn on a spinning wheel, and the son was playing with a furry four-legged animal which, according to the information caption in front of the exhibit, was a domestic pet called a 'cat'. All four were dressed in rags and looked weary and malnourished. The parents looked especially haggard. Their troubled expressions seemed to say they knew what the future of their race was going to be, as if they had some inkling that this harsh, gloomy, primitive existence of theirs was going to wear them out and grind them down and that the coming generations would dwindle and decline and soon there would be no more Groundlings left.

Az felt pity for them, but more than that he felt a terrible, aching pang of empathy.

Because the Groundlings were wingless.

That was what fascinated him about the exhibit. That was why he stood now with his thighs touching one of the sections of velvet rope which cordoned off the exhibit; why he stared at the detailed tableau of Groundling domesticity, absorbed, transfixed. The waxwork Groundlings resembled the Airborn in every respect but one. They had arms, legs, heads, torsos – no wings. They looked normal yet incomplete. They looked, in short, like Az.

Lost in contemplation of the exhibit, Az forgot about everything else, including Miss Kabnielsdaughter's quiz. He became so oblivious to his surroundings that he didn't hear the other person on the floor, the black-clad man, float up behind him on slow, stealthy wingbeats. He didn't even realise that the stranger was hovering at his back, close enough to whisper in his ear, until the man did just that.

One word.

Softly spoken.

A single syllable.

'Freak.'

CHAPTER 2

The Man With The Crimson Spectacles

Az almost jumped out of his skin. He whirled round to face the stranger.

The man was small and slender but well-proportioned; handsome, if a little hawkish-looking. The dark suit he was wearing appeared tailor-made and expensive. The feathers of his wings were combed into neat, almost obsessively neat rows. The most striking thing about him, however, were the crimson-tinted spectacles which perched on the bridge of his nose. Behind the lenses his eyes shone like a pair of setting suns.

'What did you just say?' Az demanded. His body was tingling all over with shock. And with anger.

'You heard,' the man replied.

'Say it again.'

'Very well. Freak.'

The man smiled as he said this, revealing thin, sharp teeth.

'You've got a nerve,' Az said, jabbing a finger at him. 'What gives you the right to go around calling someone else a freak? What gives you the right to criticise anyone's appearance – *four-eyes?*'

'I'm merely stating something I see through these very useful spectacles of mine, which correct a small defect in my vision,' the man said, unflustered, 'and what I see through them is a young man with a very *large* defect. Namely no wings. I presume you were born this way.'

'So what if I was?'

'You didn't lose them in some dreadful accident?'

'No, I did not,' Az said with an aggressive sigh. 'But it's got nothing to do with you anyway, so why don't you just pluck off and leave me alone!'

The man smiled again, briskly and without warmth.

'How interesting, then, that you should be standing here,' he said, 'looking at an exhibit about Groundlings. A boy born without wings looking at a lost race of people also born without wings. Perhaps ... perhaps you're wondering if you might be related to them.'

'We're all related to them. The Airborn were Groundlings once. We evolved to suit our new environment.' Az said this as though he were explaining it to a simpleton.

'Except you didn't. Does that make you a throwback maybe? Is that the word to describe you? No, all said and done, I think I prefer "freak". Much more straightforward and to the point.'

That did it. Az had had as much as he could take. A few jibes and taunts he could handle. He was used to it. Kids his own age could be unthinkingly cruel. So could some adults. But this man was being deliberately malicious, and Az was not going to stand for it.

He did something he knew he would regret but had to do anyway. He balled his hand into a fist and took a swing at the stranger ...

... who avoided the punch as if he had known Az was about to hit him even before Az did. A single forceful pulse of his wings drove him backwards out of Az's reach.

Az blinked, then lunged at the man.

The man darted sideways with effortless ease.

Az stumbled forward and recovered his balance just in time to catch a blow from the man's left wing. It wasn't especially hard – little more than a swat. Still, it had sufficient force to knock him to the floor. Stunned, he staggered to his feet. The side of his head smarted, but he ignored the pain, more determined than ever to inflict some kind of reprisal on the man.

He had been thrown close to the Groundling exhibit. His gaze fell on the axe being sharpened by the waxwork father, but he knew it was just a flimsy confection of wood and paint.

However, the short brass poles which held up the lengths of velvet rope in front of the exhibit looked sturdy and useful. Az snatched up the nearest one, twisting it at the same time so that it unhooked itself from the loops at the ends of the ropes it was attached to. Then he turned towards the man, brandishing the pole like a club.

'Oh really!' the man snorted, as if he couldn't believe his opponent would stoop to such a low tactic. 'I thought this was going to be a fair fight.'

'It is now,' Az said. 'I'm the one without wings, remember? This evens things up.'

The man's crimson-shaded gaze flicked from Az's face to the pole and back again. 'You could break a bone with that.'

'You could break one with your wing.'

'I bet you wouldn't dare, though.'

Az gritted his teeth. 'Try me.'

The man barked a laugh. He was hovering half a metre off the floor. He could swoop at any moment. Az tightened his grip on the pole.

'Azrael Gabrielson!' said a loud, shocked voice, echoing across the atrium. 'What in the name of all that's high and bright are you up to!?'

Miss Kabnielsdaughter flew across the open space to land near Az and the man. She had three students in tow, all of them front-of-the-classroom types, teacher's pets. They looked smirkingly amused at Az's plight, whereas Miss Kabnielsdaughter was just plain aghast.

'Defending myself,' Az said. 'This bloke attacked me. I didn't do anything to him. It was entirely unprovoked.'

'Is this so?' Miss Kabnielsdaughter asked the man.

He alighted on the floor and dipped his wings in a gesture of humility. For some reason Az thought the man would admit the truth and back up his version of events. How could he not?

But in the event, perhaps unsurprisingly, he didn't.

'Of course not, madam,' he said. 'What a ridiculous story! There I was, minding my own business, enjoying the many

7

delights of the museum, and all of a sudden I find myself viciously set upon by this ... this hooligan.'

'You – you plucking liar!' Az burst out. '*You* started it. You know you did.'

'Az!' snapped Miss Kabnielsdaughter. 'Language!'

The man shrugged at her, as if Az's swearing simply proved his point. Az was clearly an out-of-control teen thug with no manners and no respect for his elders.

'But this isn't right,' Az protested hotly. 'What he said didn't happen. He's just trying to shift the blame. He—'

'He, Az,' said Miss Kabnielsdaughter, cutting in, 'isn't the one waving a piece of museum property around in a threatening manner, which inclines me to put more store by his claims than by yours.'

'But – but—'

'Put the pole down, Az. Put it down now and apologise to the gentleman.'

'No.'

'Do as I tell you.'

Sullenly Az let the brass pole drop onto the floor. It made a satisfyingly loud, resounding clang. 'I won't apologise, though.'

'Do you want a Censure?'

'Don't care.'

Miss Kabnielsdaughter studied his expression and knew he meant it. The threat of a black mark on his report card, along with a note to his parents, really didn't bother him.

She let out a sigh. 'I am sorry, sir,' she said to the man. 'Azrael can be one of our more difficult pupils. He has his unruly moments. If you wish, you may file a complaint with our principal, but I'm hoping you'll be good enough to over-look the whole episode.'

The man deliberated, then nodded. 'Consider it forgotten, madam. After all, I was a hot-headed, impulsive lad myself once, believe it or not. I understand that some youngsters aren't always in control of their emotions.'

'I'm most grateful to you. And so should you be, Az.'

'Huh,' said Az.

'As a matter of fact,' the man added, 'I'd ask you to be lenient with him. Don't punish him on my account. No harm's been done, after all.'

'If you're certain.'

'I insist on it.'

'Very well,' said Miss Kabnielsdaughter. 'All the same, Az, I feel the only way to ensure you stay out of trouble is if you don't leave my sight for the rest of the day. Have you even started on your quiz? Because it looks to me like that piece of paper hasn't left your back pocket since you put it there.'

Az wanted to protest some more. He didn't want to be cast as the villain here. Fine if he had done something wrong, but he hadn't. Quite the opposite. He was completely innocent. It was all so unfair! And the man's patronising forgiveness only made it worse.

But Miss Kabnielsdaughter's stern expression brooked no further argument. She had made up her mind about the situation and nothing was going to change it.

The teacher's pets tittered as Az tugged out the quiz and sidled over to join them at Miss Kabnielsdaughter's side. With a further, final apology to the man, Miss Kabnielsdaughter led them off in a group, making for the staircase.

At the last moment Az turned and fixed the man with a fierce, glowering glare.

In return the man with the crimson spectacles gave a sly wink.

To Az, still fuming with the injustice of it all, the wink seemed like an insult but also, somehow, a promise.

It seemed to say: *You and I haven't seen the last of each other*.

Az, though, firmly hoped they had.

CHAPTER 3

The Ultimate Pulling Machine

Michael picked Az up after school.

Az's brother was ten years older than him and worked as a test pilot for Aerodyne Aeronauticals over on the west side of town, not far from Valhalla Mansions, where he lived in an all-mod-cons bachelor pad. The job was a prestigious and demanding one, but nevertheless Michael made a point of leaving the research and development hangar mid-afternoon, whenever he could, in order to collect Az from outside the school gates. That way Az was spared from having to use public transport for the journey home. The other children could fly to wherever they needed to go, if they wanted to, but for Az there was always the long wait at the airbus queue and then the embarrassment of having to sit with all the infants and old people on the bus, surrounded by mothers with squalling, barebacked babies and by pensioners with wrinkled faces and grey feathers and weakened wing muscles. And the stares. Inevitably, whenever he was in public, there were stares.

Whereas travelling with Michael was always a hoot, not least because Michael was a helicopter fanatic. He got through them at a rate of knots, one every six months, always purchasing the newest sports model when it came out and selling off his old one second-hand. Helicopters were where most of his spare money went, and he usually bought Aerodyne because of the employee discount, but not always. It depended on the specifications – airspeed, power-to-output ratio, manoeuvrability and, above all, looks.

For Michael, a 'copter had to look good. It had to be sleek, trim, with fins and ailerons in all the right places, with rotors that shimmered as they spun. And it had to turn heads, especially girls' heads. Girls were Michael's second main interest. They were where the rest of his spare money went. In fact, he got through girlfriends at an even greater rate than he got through helicopters. His relationships with two-seater, rotor-powered aircraft invariably outlasted his relationships with members of the opposite sex.

Currently Michael was piloting the latest offering from Aerodyne's main rival marque, the AtmoCorp Dragonfly 750. The open-cabbed Dragonfly afforded near-silent flight thanks to its razor-thin blades and shrouded tail rotor. It was stream-lined to within an inch of its life, had an iridescent indigo paintjob, and danced in the air as lightly as a dust mote. It was, as Michael put it, 'the ultimate pulling machine', and this was no idle boast. He had owned the helicopter for less than a month and managed to date three different women during that period, two of them simultaneously.

For a while, as he and Az darted through the ups and downs and sidelongs of the city, they chatted about jetball. Their team, the Stratoville Shrikes, was doing very badly in the league, and both brothers feared relegation at the end of the season. The thought of the Shrikes lapsing from Division One to Division Two was almost too depressing to contemplate, and the brothers agreed that the blame for the team's present losing form could be laid at the feet (and hands, and wingtips) of Iaoth Zeruchson, the Shrikes' upper forward, who was failing to score even when the most glaringly basic opportunities presented themselves.

'That featherbrained moron,' Michael said. 'All those sponsorship deals have gone to his head. Thinks he's too good for the game now, that's his trouble.'

'Yeah,' said Az. 'Last week against the Cumula Collective Harpies he was worse than useless. Neriah Tenth-House had him marked from first whistle to last. She was on him like a tattoo.'

'She *is* pretty lethal. Anyone who says women can't play

jetball has obviously never seen Neriah Tenth-House in action.'

'But then what about that vertical toss that Zeruchson missed? Finally he manages to slip past Tenth-House for a moment, there's an open frame, it's a sitter – and he still misses! Even *I* could do better than that.'

'You know what? I reckon you could and all.' Michael thrust the joystick down, and the Dragonfly fell into Anvilhead Avenue with giddying, stomach-churning speed, missing a gyro-cab by inches. The gyro-cab's pilot flipped Michael the bird, and Az chortled, and so did Michael. In a helicopter Az came as close as he would ever get to true flight, and his brother always did his best to make the experience as exhilarating and breakneck as possible.

'In fact,' Michael continued, as they straightened out along broad, four-lane Sunbeam Boulevard, 'I think we should get a surgeon to transplant Zeruchson's wings onto your back, and you can show him a thing or two about jetball.'

'I wish, Mike,' said Az, with feeling. 'I really do.'

Michael glanced over at his little brother. 'Sorry, that was stupid of me. I was only making a point.'

'No, no, it's not that.' Az knew Michael wouldn't have dreamed of saying anything deliberately to hurt him. 'I'm just a bit sensitive at the moment. Something happened on our trip to the museum today. I was standing at this exhibit and then ...'

'Then what?'

Az realised he didn't want to rake up the whole episode with the man with the crimson spectacles again. He had only just got over his feelings of anger and humiliation and he was enjoying the flight with Michael. Why ruin it?

Instead, he changed the subject slightly.

'Groundlings,' he said. 'That's what's on my mind.'

'Oh ho,' said Michael. 'You were down on the bottom floor of the museum again, weren't you? Looking at those wax-works. I remember this from last time. That exhibit put you in a funny mood all day, and it's done it again.'

'Well, maybe. It just got me thinking. I mean, who were they? Groundlings? What were they like? And what happened to them?'

Michael looked askance at Az, then threw the Dragonfly into a tight turn around a corner, pitching the helicopter over almost onto its side. When they righted, he said, 'You know as well as I do. They died out. That's what the historians say. They stayed down below to oversee the machines that gather the essential raw materials and feed them up to the sky-cities, but after a while they realised that the machines run themselves. There was nothing more for them to do. So they just sort of ... faded away.'

'We know that for certain?'

'Yes. No. Sort of. Put it this way, we don't know any differently, and there's no way of checking since no one can go down below the cloud cover. You'd die if you tried. You can't fly through it. On your own or in an aircraft, you'd get shaken to pieces by the turbulence. But it's pretty obvious that nothing can have survived on the ground. It's all lightless and poisoned down there, and ... oops, hold on.'

Michael decelerated sharply, having just spied a member of the Alar Patrol on traffic duty at a six-way intersection ahead. He gave the Patroller a wry salute as the Dragonfly buzzed past at precisely 1 kph below the speed limit. The Patroller's reaction was unclear, because his face was hidden behind his helmet visor. However, he clenched his lance a little more tightly and shook his wings, making the broad gold hoops that pierced their upper arches flash in the sun. The action implied that he had spotted Michael going too fast but was prepared to let him get away with it this once.

'And you know where you can stick that lance of yours, my friend,' Michael said through a cheesy grin, hardly moving his lips. The moment he was out of the Alar Patroller's sight, he throttled forward again, pushing the Dragonfly back up to its previous velocity.

It was clear that he considered the earlier conversation finished, and Az let it lie. Michael, much though Az loved him, was not a great thinker, not prone to dwelling on the big issues the way Az did. Sometimes Az envied him for that.

For the remainder of the journey Az leaned his head out from the cockpit and peered at the cloud cover below, wondering. It wreathed the planet, this layer of vapour. It hid sky from ground and ground from sky, a permanent white nebulous shroud, the aftermath of the Great Cataclysm, that time of terror when fire fell from the sky and the whole world shuddered.

The cloud cover never broke, never parted. Occasionally it was smooth and flat, more usually it was whipped and tormented. At night you might see dim flashes of light flickering within it – electrostatic discharges – and hear the faint rumbles that accompanied them, like the gurgling of a hungry stomach. The cloud cover was perpetually present, the base of the Airborn realm, and nothing penetrated it except the gigantic stems of the sky-cities, on which the automated supply elevators forever rose and fell.

Generally among the Airborn there was the feeling that they should be grateful for the cloud cover's existence. It meant they never had to view the ground beneath, never had to be exposed to the ugliness that must lie down there. The cloud cover was like a bandage over a wound.

That day, though, Az would have given anything just to be able to peel it back for a moment and take a peek beneath – see what was under it, see *who* was under it maybe.

Just to know. Just to be sure.

CHAPTER 4

Serena, Lady Aanfielsdaughter

It was widely agreed that the smallest of all the sky-cities was also the most beautiful. More ornate than Pearl Town, more dazzling than Prismburg, the Silver Sanctum was a miracle of structural whimsicality and extravagance. Its every tower was festooned with a dozen lesser towers. Its every stained-glass window was an intricate, brilliant mosaic of colours. Building was linked to building by a network of bridges and walkways, and every building within was a maze of corridors and pillared rooms, each grander and more imposing than the last.

There was no traffic in the Silver Sanctum. You winged your way around, or walked. Nor was any business allowed to be conducted inside its limits. There were no shops, no bars or restaurants, no commercial premises of any kind. The Silver Sanctum was the administrative headquarters for the entire Airborn race, and a place for thought and contemplation and sober decision-making. It was home to people who preferred to live without any distractions and superfluous demands on their time. Only the wisest heads dwelled there, the clearest minds, the sharpest intellects.

Serena, Lady Aanfielsdaughter, certainly fitted that description. Hailing originally from the city of Zenith, born of fowl-farming stock, Lady Aanfielsdaughter had never had any ambition in life but to join the ranks of the great and good who circulated through the Silver Sanctum's halls and debating chambers. From a very early age she had known that she was destined to govern, and at the first available opportunity she had left Zenith and begged a lift to the Silver Sanctum, where she had thrown himself on the mercy of the first resident she met.

This happened to be Asmodel, Lord Urielson, and Lord Urielson happened, by immense good fortune, to be in need of a new permanent secretary, his previous one having recently left in unfortunate circumstances (pilfering from petty cash, a minor crime but even the smallest misdemeanours were frowned upon at the Sanctum). Recognising something in Serena, an alertness, a special quality of keenness, not to mention a bewitching charisma, Lord Urielson offered her the position; and from there, through diligence and obvious talent, the girl had worked her way up through the hierarchy of power until, eventually, indeed inevitably, she reached the top.

Now in her mid-sixties, Lady Aanfielsdaughter was regarded, by all who knew her personally and by any who knew *of* her, as the cleverest and subtlest-minded of the Silver Sanctum's inhabitants. The Silver Sanctum was run by committee, or rather by numerous committees and subcommittees, so there was no such thing as an absolute ruler, no single person to whom everyone else deferred. But had there been such a role, Lady Aanfielsdaughter would undoubtedly have filled it. She was the one whose opinion always counted, the one to whom the serious political issues were always brought for consultation. If Lady Aanfielsdaughter suggested something, even hinted at some idea, it was invariably considered official policy and put into effect. A simple yes or no from Lady Aanfielsdaughter could affect the lives of nearly three million people.

What this great woman had learned over the years, however, was that with increasing responsibility came increasing uncertainty. For all that she appeared a confident and authoritative leader, Lady Aanfielsdaughter was actually anything but. Within her roiled a confusion of doubts and fears. The more she had found out about the workings of the world during her rise to prominence, the less contented she had become. There were days, now, when she sat alone in her lavish apartment and looked back on her childhood at the fowl farm and wept.

If someone had told her she could return to Zenith tomorrow and pick up exactly where she had left off, she would have jumped at the chance. Mucking out the chicken coops, fending off the geese who always came at you hissing viciously when you entered their pens, putting up with racket of the peacocks wailing in their cages all day and night – she wouldn't have minded one bit. Give up all this luxury and splendour for the stinky, impoverished lot of a fowl farmer? In a flash she would have, if she could.

This morning Lady Aanfieldsdaughter knew she had to keep such remorseful thoughts at bay. There was a crucial decision to be made today and, in order to make it properly, she needed to be as untroubled and unpreoccupied as possible. At first light, she went for a soar around the Silver Sanctum's topmost pinnacles. There were few better methods for de-cluttering one's brain and reinvigorating one's heart than to loop and swoop for half an hour above this most majestic of sky-cities, especially when the rays of the rising sun were striking it from the side and giving its metallic surfaces a burnish of glowing pink. A flock of swifts joined her for a while, swirling around her and chirping. She laughed as they zoomed playfully close then darted away again.

She then spent the breakfast hour engaged in debate with a dozen of her juniors, discussing some fine point of legislation. The purpose of the debate was not to settle anything but simply to hone their thinking skills and keep hers in trim. Cerebral gymnastics.

Next, she went for a wander through the city, meeting groups of colleagues along the way and dipping in and out of their conversations. This was an opportunity for her to gauge the mood among her peers, and the results, she was unsurprised to find, were not encouraging. There was a distinct atmosphere of unease. Everyone in the Silver Sanctum was aware that an awkward situation was developing, a volatile and very possibly dangerous situation. Even when no one was mentioning it directly, it lurked behind what they were saying. Lady Aanfieldsdaughter had taken it upon herself to resolve the crisis if she could. In the eyes of everyone she spoke to she saw a gleam of hopefulness, directed at her. They wanted her to succeed. How they wanted her to! For if she failed ...

But the consequences of failure were too terrible to imagine.

Finally, around the middle of the morning, Lady Aanfielsdaughter flew to her office for a scheduled appointment which she was both looking forward to and dreading.

Her personal assistant, Aurora Jukarsdaughter, informed her that her emissary had already arrived and was waiting for her. Aurora held open the door which connected the antechamber to Lady Aanfielsdaughter's office with the office itself, and Lady Aanfielsdaughter strode through.

The emissary rose to greet her.

'Milady,' the man said, with a bow and a smile. A brief, sharp-toothed, and not very engaging smile. His eyes flashed like rubies behind his crimson-tinted spectacles.

'Mr Mordadson,' said Lady Aanfielsdaughter. 'Tell me, what have you discovered?'

CHAPTER 5

The Only Candidate For The Job

'The boy,' said Mr Mordadson, 'is a loner. That much I could gather from the fact that he was on his own when I accosted him at the museum, and background enquiries confirm it. This, of course, is likely to be a consequence of his, for want of a better word, condition. He feels different from his peers and therefore, by choice, sets himself apart from them.'

Lady Aanfieldsdaughter had stationed herself at the office windows, which were tall and opened out onto a broad balcony. Her hands were behind her back, her wings crossed and furled. Her gaze was fixed outward, on the far horizon. From this angle and altitude you could see nothing but a perfect blue firmament, an azure eternity.

'Milady?'

'Go on. I'm listening.'

'Right. Well. I have to admit that, in person, I found him quite hard to "read". So much of our body language is conveyed through our wings, isn't it? All those little physical tics and mannerisms which we give as a matter of course, without even thinking about it, he can't. All the same I received a clear impression of a high degree of intelligence coupled with a strong-mindedness bordering on wilfulness. There appear to be discipline issues.'

'Discipline issues. Is that how the educational establishment refer to bad behaviour these days?'

'Apparently so. Again, this is something I dug up with a little surreptitious snooping around. It seems Az has had more than his fair share of Censures and detentions over the course of his academic career. Nothing too serious, scuffles in the schoolyard now and then, the occasional flunked exam. But again, I'd say his winglessness was probably at the root of it.'

'No run-ins with the Alar Patrol?'

'Oh no, nothing like that. He's not one of those juvenile delinquent types. Just a very troubled teen.'

'And you pushed him, in order to see how he would respond?'

'I did indeed. I provoked him verbally. I was, as a matter of fact, somewhat unkind.'

To judge by the casual smile that accompanied the remark, Mr Mordadson didn't seem any too troubled by his actions.

'And he stood up to me,' he went on. 'Didn't bat an eyelid, and full credit to him for that. There aren't many his age who would have done the same, shown that kind of backbone, especially to an adult. Eventually I goaded him to the point where he came at me with a right hook. It would have been quite a good punch, too, had it connected. And he'd have done a lot worse, had he had the opportunity. Aggressive tyke, he was.'

'And you believe this to be a good thing?'

'Naturally, milady, yes. He'll need to be tough and assertive. Very much so. It's a valuable trait for him to have if we're going to use him for what we want to use him for. Nevertheless ...'

Lady Aanfielsdaughter looked round. 'Nevertheless what?'

'Milady, it isn't my place to query your judgement. Far be it for me to suggest that your plan won't work. However, I do think—'

'You have a better plan?' Lady Aanfielsdaughter said brusquely.

Mr Mordadson's smile this time was a quick, nervous one. His wings drooped a fraction.

'Not as such,' he replied. 'It's merely – in my view, this is a significant burden to be placing on such a young pair of shoulders. Not to mention the potential physical risk to the boy himself.'

'You yourself just said that he's tough and assertive.'

'Correct. But he's only sixteen. You're asking a great deal of a sixteen-year-old.'

'And he can always refuse to do what we ask of him, or his parents can on his behalf. I don't expect him to take part in the mission unless he volunteers to. I can't force him. I won't.'

Lady Aanfieldsdaughter then turned and made her way to the centre of the room, where an ancient teak desk resided, an object that was huge and dark and heavy and in every way redolent of the ground. Seating herself behind it, she picked up another gift of the ground, a multifaceted chunk of amethyst that served as a desk ornament. She hefted it in her hands, watching mauve and lilac highlights play across its surfaces.

'The thing is, Mr Mordadson, we don't really have a choice here. There's no one else we can ask. The boy isn't simply the most suitable candidate for the job, he's the *only* candidate. I know there's that other person similarly afflicted, wingless, the one who lives over in the Cumula Collective, but she's how old? Eighty?'

'At least. And frail as a twig.'

'Exactly. She wouldn't last a minute, and even if she was in good health, that Cumula lot are so ferociously independent, they probably wouldn't agree to allow her to go.'

'Quite. But still, milady, we could keep searching. We may turn up someone else. Maybe a double wing amputee. You never know.'

'No,' said Lady Aanfieldsdaughter with finality. 'We don't have the time. Like it or not, we're going to have to go with this lad. So it's up to you now. I want you to pay a call on him at home and convince him to come and meet me.'

'That may be tricky. I left him with a distinctly negative impression of me. Perhaps if *you* were turn up in person ...'

'Not an option. We need to keep this operation as low-profile as possible. If I were to appear on his doorstep and someone spotted me and recognised me, there'd be talk. Neighbours would want to know what Lady Aanfieldsdaughter was doing in the area. Tongues would wag, rumours would start, and we can do without that. No, I'm afraid it's down to you, Mr Mordadson. I need you to bring him here. However you manage it, get me Azrael Gabrielson.'

CHAPTER 6

A Familiar Visitor

The model of Troop-Carrier *Cerulean* was taking shape. Az and his father, mainly his father, had been busy constructing it over the course of several weeks, off and on. The balsa wood framework was complete, and today they were pasting sections of light blue tissue paper over the largest part of the model, its balloon. The tissue paper emulated the canvas covering of the real *Cerulean*'s balloon. Attaching it was a delicate, painstaking process, like fitting skin to a skeleton.

'Easy with the glue,' Gabriel Enochson warned his son. 'Too much and that bit of paper will go soggy and rip.'

Az wiped off the excess glue with a cloth, then passed the piece of tissue paper to his father, who laid it over the airship's nosecone and gently tamped it into place.

They paused a moment to admire their handiwork. The balloon was covered on one side. The model was really starting to look like the military vessel it copied, or at any rate it was really starting to look like the picture of Troop-Carrier *Cerulean* which was tacked to the wall next to the workbench.

'We can start painting the control gondola when this is done,' Az's father said. 'Then the next job's putting together the propellers, although those are going to be fiddly, I warn you. So is the Prismburg insignia on the tailfins. That's going to be pretty hard to get right. I'll do a few preliminary sketches first, for practice.'

'Good idea, Dad.'

'You could have a bash at it yourself, you know, Az.'

'I could,' Az agreed without enthusiasm, 'only ...'

'Only this is very boring for you, isn't it?' said his father.

'Come on, be honest.'

Reluctantly Az nodded. 'I enjoy spending time down here with you and everything. Really. I'm just not ...'

'Not twelve years old any more,' Gabriel Enochson finished for him. 'I know. And I know you're helping me make this model just to indulge me. I tell myself it's for you but really it's for me.'

'Well, a retired man like you has to have little hobby-type projects to keep you busy.' Az pointed to the tools that could be found in their dozens around the basement workshop, racked on the walls, and the various items of equipment – a lathe, a vice, a band-driven jigsaw – the legacy of his father's long career as a maker and mender of clocks. 'Otherwise all this stuff would go to waste. Like Mum says, "Gabe, you need to be doing something, otherwise you'll be under my feet all day and annoying me."'

Az's mimickry of his mother's fruity tones drew a furtive smirk from his father. Gabriel Enochson glanced upward.

'Let's pray she didn't overhear,' he said. 'You still like *Cerulean*, though, don't you, Az? I'm not wrong about that, am I? That hasn't changed.'

'Oh yeah. *Cerulean*'s pretty cool.'

'And here's me under the impression that the young are always into whatever's now and newfangled and "in". Michael and his helicopters, for example. And yet you're fascinated by a big old obsolete airship. Why is that?'

Az peered at the picture of the lighter-than-air military vessel. From the moment he first learned about *Cerulean* he had felt a strange affinity for her. She seemed at once so grace-less and so fragile, with her massive balloon and her helium-filled gas cells and her propellers on their spindly mountings. She had no wings. She looked like something that couldn't – shouldn't – fly. And yet she did. Beautifully.

Also, she was the only one of her kind. Every other military vessel like her had been decommissioned and broken down for parts years ago, after the signing of the Sky-City Pact of Hegemony, part of a worldwide demonstration of abhorrence for war and the vessels of war. *Cerulean* alone had been spared that fate and was now a museum piece, a tangible reminder of an age when the sky-cities used to fight among themselves. She was unique, the last survivor of a time gone by.

A lumbering, ungainly, wingless thing which defied appearances by being able to fly – yes, Az could certainly relate to that. Troop-Carrier *Cerulean* was both something he understood and something he admired.

But he felt a little foolish trying to put this into words, so all he said in answer to his father's query was: 'I just like her, that's all.'

The old man gave a wry, quiet grin, in a way that suggested he knew what Az had really meant to say. 'Maybe one day we should go and take one of those tourist trips in her.'

'Maybe,' Az said.

His father had made the offer many times before, but Az invariably wriggled out of accepting it. He feared they would go to Prismburg and take a short flight on board *Cerulean* and it would be a letdown. It wouldn't measure up to how he imagined. She wouldn't be all he thought she was. Perhaps it was better simply to dream about *Cerulean* and never have that dream dashed.

They had just resumed work on the model when the doorbell rang upstairs. Both of them cocked their heads and listened out. Michael had promised to drop by this evening for supper, but it was still a bit too early for that. Most likely it was one of Az's mother's friends, or else a door-to-door sales rep, of which High Haven seemed to have an endless supply. They hawked everything from floor-mops to life insurance, encyclopaedias to toothpicks, and somehow made a living at it, even though no householder was glad to see them.

Az's mother went to open the front door, her footfalls passing directly overhead on the hallway floor.

The voice that issued down from the front doorway was courteous and soft. It was a man's voice, and Az heard his mother being addressed with full formality – forename (Ramona), maiden name (Orifielsdaughter), then married surname (Enochson). The visitor was evidently keen to make a good first impression.

A sales rep then, as he had suspected. One of those rare ones who did their homework before calling by.

As Az continued to listen, however, it dawned on him that he knew that voice. He couldn't quite place it, but he was sure he had heard it before, and just recently.

The man had a lot to say to Az's mother and was hardly allowing her to get a word in edgeways. He apologised for disturbing the lady of the house and wondered if he might beg a few moments of her and her husband's time.

Az felt the hackles on the back of his neck rise. Who *was* this? Why did the voice make him feel so uneasy?

His mother called out, 'Gabe? Would you come here a second?'

Az's father shrugged. 'Coming, dear!' To Az, he added softly, 'Wonder what this is about.' With a couple of flap-thrusts of his wings, he rose to the trapdoor in the basement ceiling. He hovered there, wings beating, as he undid the latch. Then he hauled himself through and closed the trapdoor behind him.

A low, muffled conversation followed between Az's father and the visitor, and it was while this was going on that something clicked in Az's head. He remembered where and when he had last heard this visitor speaking. It had been just a couple of days ago.

The man at the museum. The man with the crimson spectacles.

Az went to the ladder which was his means of getting out of the basement, and clambered stealthily up and put his ear to the trapdoor so that he could hear more clearly.

'... talk with your son on a matter of the utmost importance,' the man was saying. 'I can't put it any plainer than that. Perhaps if you could see your way to inviting me in ...'

'Gabe?' said Az's mother. 'What do you think?'

Az heard his father ruffling his wings. 'Maybe if the gentleman were to show us credentials of some sort ...'

'Oh, but of course. Silly me,' said the man. There was the sound of pockets being patted. 'I have something ... yes ...

here. I assume that will do.'

Az's mother gave a small gasp, then said, 'Come on through to the living room.'

'And the young man himself? I take it he's home,' the visitor said, as the front door was closed behind him.

'He's downstairs,' said Az's mother. 'Let me give him a shout. Az!'

Az waited a moment, so that it wouldn't look as if he had been eavesdropping, then levered open the trapdoor and climbed the last few rungs of the ladder, emerging into the hallway.

'Az, there's someone here to see you. He's—'

'I know who he is,' Az said, eyeing the man coolly. 'We've met.'

'Really?' said his father. He was puzzled by his son's obvious hostility towards their guest. 'Why didn't you tell us about this, that you'd met someone so prestigious?'

Az hadn't mentioned anything at all to his parents about his encounter with the man at the museum. Once he'd calmed down about it, he had decided he just wanted to put the whole matter behind him. He counted himself lucky not to have got a punishment. He was in trouble at school often enough and one less Censure for his parents to fret about was no bad thing.

'He didn't seem very prestigious at the time,' he said. 'And I'm not sure he is.'

Gabriel Enochson's puzzled expression deepened. 'Well, you're wrong. See?'

He held up a small leather wallet to show Az. Within the wallet was set a silver badge, a feather overlaid on a circle. The circle represented the world and had several dozen tiny embossed dots on it, representing sky-cities.

Az recognised the emblem. Who wouldn't?

The seal of the Silver Sanctum.

'My name, Az, is Mr Mordadson,' said the man, 'and I come on urgent business. Azrael Gabrielson, the Airborn race needs your help.'

26

CHAPTER 7

Face-off In The Living Room

Oh please, Az thought. *This is a joke. This is ludicrous.* How could the man sitting opposite honestly expect him to agree to go to the Silver Sanctum with him? Without explaining exactly *why* he should go with him?

'You'll have to take it on trust,' Mr Mordadson said, looking very comfortable in the family's best armchair. 'In matters of state, one must take great care what one does and doesn't say. In this particular instance, I'm afraid I'm forbidden to reveal anything specific. The whole issue is far too delicate. What I *can* tell you is that our future – all of our futures – may well depend on your agreeing to participate. I'm asking you, Azrael, and you, Mr and Mrs Enochson, to consider what's good for all of us.

'I appreciate,' Mr Mordadson continued, focusing on Az, 'that you and I got off on the wrong foot. I'd be grateful if you could erase that incident from your memory and we could start anew. I am, I hope you'll soon come to see, not a needlessly unpleasant man. I had a job to do then. I have another job to do now.'

The smile he gave desperately wanted to be likeable, but it was all too reminiscent of his other, charmless smiles.

'How *can* I trust you?' Az retorted.

'Now, Az,' said his mother, 'he's carrying the Silver Sanctum seal. I don't know what went on between the two of you before, but the seal gives Mr Mordadson absolute governmental authority.'

'Yeah? For all we know he stole it, or it's a fake.'

'Az!' said his father. 'How can you say such a thing!'

'No, no, it's quite all right, Mr Enochson. Perfectly understandable, under the circumstances. I was testing young Azrael the last time we met, to see what stuff he's made of. What I did wouldn't have endeared me to him in the least. On the plus side, it proved to me that he's up to the task we have in mind for him. It proved it to Lady Aanfielsdaughter as well.'

'Lady Aanfielsdaughter,' breathed Az's mother. 'You work for *her*?'

'Indeed I do, madam. Directly answerable. I am, you might say, milady's strong right arm.' Mr Mordadson bent forward and took a sip from the cup of fragrant tea which Az's mother had prepared. The gesture implied a casualness about his close professional relationship with that most august and revered personage, Serena, Lady Aanfielsdaughter.

'But – well – Az, there's no question, then. You must do as Mr Mordadson says. You must go with him.'

'Must I? Why?'

'I'm sorry, Mr Mordadson. This attitude of his … he's a stubborn one sometimes.'

'Stubborn is fine, Mrs Enochson. Don't apologise. At the heart of a stubborn person lies a strong spirit.'

'Does this,' said Az's father, 'this "task" you have in mind for Az – does it by any chance have to do with Az being different from other kids the way he is?'

Mr Mordadson nodded gravely. 'Let's just say it requires someone with his special talent.'

'Special talent!' Az snorted. 'Huh! Why not just come right out with it: you want me to do something for you because I'm wingless.'

'It is, yes, because of your unfortunate lack of wings. More than that, though, I'm not at liberty to divulge.'

'It's because I'm a – what's that word again? – freak.'

'As I explained—'

'Darling,' Az's mother cut in, 'put aside your feelings for the moment. Regardless of what happened earlier, Lady

Aanfieldsdaughter herself has summoned you. You simply cannot refuse.'

'Can't I?' said Az, and stood up. 'I think I can, and I will.'

'I was afraid of this,' said Mr Mordadson, standing up too. 'Azrael, if you won't come with me of your own accord, I regret to say that I'm going to have to make you. I was hoping we could do this without resorting to physicality, but apparently not. Most regrettable.'

So saying, he reached across to grab Az. Az yanked his arm out of Mr Mordadson's grasp. Mr Mordadson made a second lunge, which was thwarted by Az's father placing himself in between them.

'That's enough, Mr Mordadson. You've crossed a line. Seal or no seal, you can't just saunter into my house and abduct my son. I won't have it.'

'Oh yes?' sneered Mr Mordadson. 'And what are you going to do about it? Are you going to stop me, *old man*? I doubt it.'

It was a harsh jibe but true. Az's father was not in the prime of life, and his health was not brilliant. You could tell by the state of his wings – the yellowness of their plumage, the missing feathers (gone like much of the hair from his head). His joints often ached, and he moved slowly and found it an effort to fly any great distance.

He was, in other words, hardly a match for someone like Mr Mordadson. If it came to a tussle between them, there was no question who would win. Both knew it.

Still, Az's father did not budge. He glared defiantly at Mr Mordadson, who peered sneeringly back through his crimson spectacles. Each man waited for the other to make the next move. Tension crackled in the air.

Perhaps they would have stood there for ever, holding each other's gaze. Perhaps the situation in the living room would have remained as perpetually static and unchanging as the tableau of Groundling life at the Museum of Arts, Sciences and History: Az's father and Mr Mordadson facing off against each other, Az hunkered behind his father, Az's mother frozen with anxiety in her chair.

Then someone entered the room and broke the spell.

'Hello, hello,' said Michael, sauntering in. 'What's going on here then?'

CHAPTER 8

Journey To The Silver Sanctum

High Haven fell away behind, diminishing into the distance. Bent round in his seat, Az watched it recede. The roughly dome-shaped agglomeration of buildings, which seemed huge and pulsing with life when you were in it, shrank and shrank until he could block it from view just by raising a hand. From afar the city, balancing on its quartet of supporting columns, looked like a tiny paper sculpture, extraordinarily delicate.

Then it was gone, swallowed in sky haze.

Az turned forward. Ahead, Mr Mordadson's monoplane was making its way sedately along the airlane. It was a Metatronco Wayfarer, a boxy little thing, the kind of vehicle that accountants and office managers flew, a reliable, unexciting ride that got an excellent kilometre-per-litre ratio but was dull in every way, right down to its name. It wasn't a patch on Michael's Dragonfly for speed and elegance, and Michael soon became impatient with having to tootle along in its wake.

'Come on, Az, let's have a little fun,' he said, with a wicked look on his face. 'Let's show our friend Mr Mordadson what a *real* aircraft can do. Buckle up!'

Az was already strapped into his seat but he tightened the belt anyway in eager anticipation.

Michael checked that the airlane ahead was clear, then poured on speed till the helicopter's nose was right up to the Wayfarer's tailfins. He made sure Mr Mordadson had seen them in his rearview mirror. Then he abruptly cut power to the rotors so that the Dragonfly plummeted.

Az's stomach rose into his throat as they free-fell. Fifty metres down Michael re-engaged the rotors and soared up under the

Wayfarer. At the same time he stamped on the anti-torque pedals, spinning the Dragonfly on its vertical axis so that it was facing the other way round. He re-entered the airlane in front of the Wayfarer, hurtling along in reverse. They were travelling at the same speed as Mr Mordadson, so for a while the Wayfarer and the Dragonfly were nose to nose. Az could see Mr Mordadson through the plane's windscreen. He was gesticulating wildly, flapping a hand at Michael to get out of the way, and beeping his horn. Michael waved cheerily back, and Az followed suit. Both brothers were laughing hard.

They laughed harder when Mr Mordadson attempted to overtake. He pulled to one side, and Michael steered the same way, blocking his path. He pulled to the other side, and again Michael matched him.

Finally, infuriated, Mr Mordadson hit the flaps and reduced speed almost to a standstill – any slower and he would have been in danger of stalling. Seeing this, Michael decided to perform one final stunt, the kind only a experienced test pilot would dare attempt. He throttled forward, and the Dragonfly dipped its nose and aimed straight for the Wayfarer. At the very last second, when it looked like a midair collision was inevitable, he flipped the helicopter upside down and shot over the plane. The rotor blades were mere centimetres from the Wayfarer's cockpit canopy.

Michael righted the Dragonfly and fell in behind Mr Mordadson again. For a while both aircraft droned slowly along, until finally Mr Mordadson understood that Michael was finished with his fun and games. The Wayfarer accelerated till it was at cruising speed once more, and every so often its driver shot a scowling glance in the rearview, to let Michael know what he thought of *that* kind of behaviour.

'Serves you right,' Michael said, as though Mr Mordadson could hear him. 'Shouldn't fly such an old piece-of-guano junker, should you?'

Apart from this little episode, the five-hour flight to the Silver Sanctum was uneventful, and Az had plenty of time to think about things.

Above all he wondered what would have happened if Michael had not turned up early for dinner. Would Mr Mordadson have got into a fight with Az's father? Would he really have forced Az into his plane and flown him to the Silver Sanctum against his will?

Az feared the answer to both these questions was yes, and this led him to think that whatever situation it was that required his services, it must indeed be a dire one if Mr Mordadson was prepared to use extreme measures like assault and kidnap in order to get hold of him. He could not for the life of him fathom what Lady Aanfielsdaughter wanted him for, and this uncertainty made the prospect of meeting the great woman, which would otherwise have been a thrill and an honour, somewhat daunting.

Michael had truly arrived in the nick of time, and it was lucky he had. Mr Mordadson had backed off the moment Michael came into the room. Clearly it was one thing to threaten an old man, quite another to tackle a young, fit, well-winged fellow like Az's brother. With Michael's arrival the balance of power in the living room had undergone a subtle but significant shift, not in Mr Mordadson's favour.

Az's mother had quickly filled Michael in on what was going on. In response, Michael had said, 'Az isn't going anywhere, not if he doesn't want to. I mean it.'

'Perhaps,' Mr Mordadson had replied, 'we could come to some sort of accommodation …?'

'If it involves you getting straight out of my family's house, then fine, I don't have a problem with that.'

'No, what I meant was, perhaps Azrael might be able to see his way to accompanying me if he were to have a chaperone.' He gestured to Michael. 'Yourself, for instance.'

There had been some discussion amongst the family, and eventually it had been agreed that Az should journey to the Silver Sanctum, but only on condition that Michael went with him every wingbeat of the way, to look after him.

Az himself had been able to overcome his reluctance because, with his big brother beside him, he felt there was very little

33

that could go wrong.

Three hours into the trip they made a scheduled stopover at a waystation, a vast snowflake-shaped structure which was kept aloft on a cushion of air generated by a half-dozen horizontal fans. They docked at one 'arm' of the snowflake and an attendant in overalls came out to refuel both aircraft and polish the windshields. Michael expressed dismay at the price the waystation was charging for aviation fuel, and the attendant shrugged and said there had been problems with deliveries. He hoped it would sort itself out quickly, but in the meantime there was no alternative: prices had to go up.

It became a moot point anyway, thanks to Mr Mordadson's Silver Sanctum seal. He showed it to the attendant, who studied it and then said, with a wince of reluctance, 'Right. The Sanctum. Well then, consider the bill settled.'

'Not bad, this working-for-the-government lark,' Michael commented to Az as they went inside the waystation to buy refreshments and visit the toilets. 'Flash that seal and it's freebies all round. Unlimited everything. I could get used to it.'

In front of them, Mr Mordadson overheard. 'Mr Gabrielson, the chance of someone like you ever qualifying to join the Silver Sanctum is, I'd say, somewhere between remote and impossible.'

'Ooh!' Michael said. 'Snarky!'

'Simply being honest. And while I'm about it, no more antics when we get back in the air, please.' It was half request, half warning. 'You have a valuable passenger on board, remember.'

Michael chuckled, unabashed. 'Fair enough, Mordy. On condition that you admit that top-prop beats front-prop any day.'

'But helicopters are so much more costly to run than planes.'

'But so much more agile in the air.'

'But they reek of frivolity and waste, and they— Oh, never mind. Why am I wasting my breath? If it'll satisfy you, I'll say it. Top-prop beats front-prop.'

'Good man,' Michael said, and patted Mr Mordadson's wing in a manner that was calculated to irritate, and did.

Az was elated by the lack of respect Michael was showing Mr Mordadson. It made him feel far less intimidated by the man, almost to the point where he could forgive him. Almost.

A couple of hours after that, the Silver Sanctum hove into sight.

Pictures Az had seen did not prepare him for the breath-taking loveliness of the place. Unlike other sky-cities, which were often sprawling and unruly creations, the Silver Sanctum was small and self-contained. It was virtually a single edifice, a shining vision of metalcraft and spires, a work of art.

The beauty of the Silver Sanctum, however, did not make Az any less nervous about his upcoming meeting with Lady Aanfielsdaughter.

CHAPTER 9

The Belvedere Vineyard

They were met on the Silver Sanctum's perimeter landing apron by Aurora Jukarsdaughter, Lady Aanfieldsdaughter's personal assistant. Aurora had long, curling, black hair, and the swan-whiteness of her wings contrasted exquisitely with the darkness of her complexion. She was more than attractive, she was glorious, and Az could tell that Michael was smitten by her. As soon as Mr Mordadson introduced them to each other, Michael dropped his voice and did a certain trick with his eyes, making them go wide and limpid. This, as he had often told Az, never failed with the ladies.

It did with Aurora, though. She seemed more amused than impressed by Michael's attempts to charm her. When he arched his wings slightly, to give himself more height and show off the blue-black magpie feathers that were stitched into his plumage, a laughing look came into Aurora's eyes, suggesting she didn't think much of fashion statements like that. When he oh-so-casually asked her if she had ever flown in a Dragonfly, she looked as if she was trying to stifle a yawn.

Az knew her indifference would only make Michael more determined than ever. Aurora was now a challenge, and he wouldn't stint in his efforts to pursue her.

In the meantime, however, there were more pressing matters to be attended to.

'Lady Aanfieldsdaughter is expecting you,' Aurora said. 'She's up in the Belvedere Vineyard. I'll show you the way.'

Michael scooped Az up in his arms. Aurora took flight, and Michael followed. Mr Mordadson fell in behind. In procession they dived through a round gateway and followed a twisting, turning, circuitous route between various buildings. A team of window washers, suspended in midair from helium balloons, waved to them as they went by. They gained height till they were near the summit of the city, passing over tower tops and spires. Michael kept pace with Aurora the whole way. Although he had the extra weight of Az to carry, he was doing his best to make it seem as if this was no effort.

They arrived at a tower which was capped by a hexagonal area of grass crisscrossed with trellises. Leafy vines swathed the trellis wires, and Az saw grapes hanging in thick, ripe clusters.

Someone was standing alone in the midst of this garden. She was a tall, slender, aristocratic woman with a mane of white hair and a long, tapering nose. As Aurora led the three of them – Az, Michael, Mr Mordadson – down to land, the woman did not rise up to meet them. This would have been the polite thing to do, but instead she remained firmly footed on the grass. Az wondered why, then realised that Lady Aanfielsdaughter (for that was obviously who the woman was) was staying put for his benefit. By making a point of not flying, she meant to set Az at his ease.

Michael lowered Az to the grass. Lady Aanfielsdaughter strode forward.

'Azrael Gabrielson, it's a pleasure to make your acquaintance.'

They shook hands, and Az noticed that Lady Aanfielsdaughter had eyes of the purest, most piercing blue. *Stratospheric blue*, as it was known.

Lady Aanfielsdaughter turned. 'And you are …?'

'His brother,' said Michael.

'Ah, of course. It's Michael, isn't it? Here to keep an eye on him, I take it. Doing your fraternal duty. Most commendable.'

Michael was thoroughly disarmed. Az had seldom seen his brother stunned or lost for words, but he was now. Lady Aanfielsdaughter knew his name and had complimented him.

Michael's mouth gaped and he looked like he might need to sit down.

'Now then,' Lady Aanfielsdaughter, turning back at Az, 'may I say how grateful I am that you agreed to come, Azrael. I've heard many good things about you. If it's not impertinent, I'd like to ask a couple of questions.'

'No. I mean, yes. I mean, it wouldn't be impertinent. Fire away.'

The corners of Lady Aanfielsdaughter's mouth twitched. 'Fire away I shall. Firstly, you've never had wings, correct?'

'Never.'

'Any idea why?'

Az was surprised to find that he wasn't peeved by this line of enquiry, as he might have been. It was the way Lady Aanfielsdaughter was asking the questions – she wasn't prying, she was curious, genuinely interested to know the answers. Compare and contrast with Mr Mordadson's approach at the museum.

'Our parents are pretty old,' Az said. 'My mum was well into her forties when she had me, my dad just fifty. The doctors think that had something to do with it. Kids of older parents can be born with illnesses, defects, that sort of thing. Quite often they're born dead, so I suppose I should consider myself lucky.'

'You're normal in every other way?'

'Yeah, I think so. I've been to see all sorts of specialists. I have the nubs on my back. Pinfeathers should have sprouted from those when I was a baby. They just … didn't, and none of the specialists could figure out why.'

'Do you miss not being able to fly?'

'I don't know. I don't think "miss" is the right word, because to miss something you have to have had it and lost it, don't you? I'd love to be able to fly, of course I would. But I can't, so that's that. I did once, actually. Sort of.'

Lady Aanfielsdaughter raised her eyebrows. 'How so?'

'Well, my dad, he used to make and fix clocks for a living. He's very good with his hands. He can build stuff, invent stuff

– and one day, for my fourteenth birthday, he made me a pair of wings. He put together this kind of backpack, a harness with these wings attached on armatures. The wings were made out of metal. Copper. Every joint, every feather – copper. So, as you can imagine, the whole contraption weighed a tonne, and he stuck it on my back, strapped it on, and the idea was that I would put my hands through these loops on the underside of the wings and flap them and fly. Only ...'

The wings had been too heavy. Far too heavy. Az recalled very clearly his father and Michael tossing him out into space, and then moments of plummeting, a sickening vertiginous downrush, the terrible sense of being out of control, utterly helpless. The weight of the wings had rolled him over onto his back, and he had plunged face upwards, down past his house, down into the street below, then further down, falling, falling, nothing to be done about it, buildings hurtling up past him, traffic, people, the city letting him slip through its gaps ...

Above him, Michael shouting: *Go limp, Az! I'm coming for you!*

Michael swooping, his arms outstretched, his wings pressed flat against his back.

'... only, it all went a bit wrong,' Az resumed. 'Michael managed to catch me in time. If he hadn't, well, I'd probably have gone through the cloud cover and ended up splatted on the ground.'

'A hair-raising experience,' said Lady Aanfieldsdaughter.

'Just a bit.'

'I imagine it might have put you off the whole idea of flying.'

'It put it into perspective. I'd like to be able to fly, just not in that way. I'd like it to be on my own terms. But' – he shrugged – 'it's not going to happen.'

'And you don't resent your father for building you the wings?'

'Oh no. He did it because he loves me and because he wanted to grant me my greatest wish. He did me a favour, in

39

fact, since now that wish isn't nearly so important to me any more.'

'Do you think, Azrael...'

'Call me Az. Nobody calls me Azrael unless they're cross with me or I don't like them.' He said this while flicking a glance in Mr Mordadson's direction.

'Az it is then,' Lady Aanfielsdaughter said. She had spotted Az's glance and who it was aimed at. 'Do you think, changing the subject a little, that on the whole you're happy with your lot, Az?'

'On the whole, yeah. Sometimes it gets me down but mostly – mustn't grumble.'

'Because, now that I've met you, I'm firmly convinced that there's a reason you were born as you are. I don't mean a medical reason. A higher purpose. Let me explain ...'

CHAPTER 10

Wine And Soil

Lady Aanfielsdaughter laid an arm across Az's shoulders and drew his attention to the vines all around them.

'These are some of the finest grapes around,' she said, 'and they produce a most excellent wine, which we make here in the Silver Sanctum ourselves. It's a hobby of ours, something to while away an idle hour. I myself, when I have the odd spare moment, come up to this garden to do some pruning or picking. Others do the pressing, the distilling and the bottling, and then we all enjoy the fruits of our labours over an evening meal. Delicious, I promise you. I might even go so far as to say ambrosial!

'This is the Silver Sanctum's own small version of the cultivation areas you'll find in every sky-city – the orchards, the nurseries, the greenhouses, the crop plazas. And what are the essential ingredients that keep plants alive? Sunlight, of course, which we have a constant supply of, and water, which our vaporisation vats furnish us with. But also earth. Soil.'

She bent down to the roots of one vine and dug up a handful of earth, then let the brown granules trickle through her fingers.

'Soil, though, doesn't last for ever.' She brushed her hand clean. 'Its nutrients are soon used up, and we can fertilise it with guano to extend its life but that's not enough. So we need to import fresh soil, which of course comes from the ground. All this is somewhat obvious, Az, I know. I can tell by your expression that that's what you're thinking. "What *is* the old bat wittering on about? I learnt all about it in Biology ages ago."'

Az shook his head, but he was blushing. Lady Aanfielsdaughter had read his mind.

'I'm telling you all this, Az, to illustrate the fact that we Airborn rely on what we can get from the ground. Not just soil, but other raw materials. Fossil fuels, ores, you name it. The copper your father made those wings out of. We live up here in these magnificent, lofty sky-cities, three, four kilometres high, but we're far from self-sufficient. The ground supports us in more ways than one. We need its natural resources.

'But this is a fact which we're apt to forget. We're not directly involved in the gathering of the raw materials. We rather take it for granted. Seldom do we think about where the natural resources come from and how they get here, and indeed I'd go so far as to say that most of us never think about it at all, because we never need to.

'Unfortunately, we're going to *have* to think about it, Az. It's a truth we're going to have to confront, all of us, and soon.

'Because, you see, there's a problem.'

Lady Aanfielsdaughter paused to allow her words to sink in. She was no longer genial. Her face was now utterly serious, her mood deadly earnest.

'A problem?' said Az.

'With the system of supply. There have been disruptions. Shortages. Deficits. Nothing to get alarmed about, at least not yet. You yourself may well not have noticed. It's unlikely anyone in the general population has.'

Az thought of the raised price of aviation fuel at the waystation.

'So far the trouble appears to be confined to here in the Central Sector of the Western Quadrant,' Lady Aanfielsdaughter continued. 'It hasn't spread any further than this region. Still, the data is worrying. We in the Silver Sanctum have collated statistics from the supply-arrival depots at every sky-city in the Sector, and the conclusion is unavoidable. Sporadically, we have not been receiving as much from the ground as we should.'

'What is it, a fault with the machines?'

'It could be, it could be. We've not yet been able to pinpoint the cause. Nor do we know yet whether this is a temporary glitch or something more sinister. We simply don't have enough information to work that out. Only when we do will we be able to formulate a response strategy.'

'And how do you plan to ...'

Az's voice trailed off. All of a sudden everything was beginning to make sense. Mr Mordadson's remarks to him at the museum. His winglessness. Why Lady Aanfielsdaughter had summoned him.

Lady Aanfielsdaughter was scrutinising Az's face. She could see Az putting two and two together.

'You want me,' Az said slowly, 'to go down there, don't you? You want me to travel down to the ground and find out what's happening. That's it, isn't it?'

Serena, Lady Aanfielsdaughter, gave a sombre nod. 'That, Az, is it. We believe that you, out of the entire Airborn race, are the one person who might be able to survive on the ground. Owing to your unique attributes, you are the only one of us who could stand a chance.'

'But I'm Airborn, like anyone. The only difference is I don't have wings.'

'True, true, but you're accustomed to moving without flight and to operating in two dimensions rather than three. Not to put too fine a point on it, you're to all intents and purposes a Groundling. That aspect of our racial heritage has come to the fore in you.

Throwback, Mr Mordadson had said.

'In physiological terms,' Lady Aanfielsdaughter continued, 'it's unlikely there's anybody more suited to surviving conditions on the ground than you.'

'But,' said Az, 'if it's as toxic down there as everybody says it is ...'

'You wouldn't be expected to stay down there for long. Just long enough to reconnoitre and build up an impression of the situation, then report back.'

'And I'm not a machinery expert ...' A practical talent with

43

machines was something Az had not inherited from his father. Something *else*, along with wings.

'Az, these are valid objections and you're entitled to raise them. I'm not ordering you to do anything. I'm *asking* you to. I'm asking you at least to consider it. I don't expect you to give me an answer straight away. Go off and mull it over. Discuss it with your brother. You're under no pressure whatever, and nobody will think any the less of you if, after thinking about it, you come back and say no. Please believe me when I say that. What I would like, though, is a reasonably quick decision. By tonight, say?'

Lady Aanfielsdaughter instructed Aurora to escort Az and Michael to the Silver Sanctum's guest quarters. Az's brain was in a whirl as, cradled in Michael's arms, he was borne aloft from the Belvedere Vineyard. So much was happening at once. There was so much to think about.

A decision by tonight?

For all his bewilderment, Az already had an inkling what his choice was going to be.

CHAPTER 11

A Brief Dialogue

Mr Mordadson sidled over to Lady Aanfielsdaughter.

'Forgive me, milady,' he said, 'but I couldn't help noticing that you were somewhat *selectively* honest with the boy.'

Lady Aanfielsdaughter let out a rueful sigh. 'I had to be. I told him as much of the truth as I dared, but I had to withhold a few salient details.'

'Why? I would have thought that, if he's to make an informed decision, he ought to know everything.'

'That would have been fairer on him, yes. But frankly, the less he knows, the better. He needs to go down there with an open mind. It could be what will save him if he gets into difficulties. That and his own resourcefulness. Besides, with his brother standing there I couldn't just blurt out everything. The fewer people who are in on the secret, the more likely it is that the secret *stays* a secret.'

'It's your call, milady.'

'Yes, it *is* my call, Mr Mordadson.' Lady Aanfielsdaughter was irritated. 'And I'd appreciate it if you'd remember that. You may not realise this, but it's far harder to give orders than it is to take them.'

'I apologise.' Mr Mordadson flattened his wings.

'No, I'm sorry too. I shouldn't have snapped. It's just – this whole business is so trying.' Lady Aanfielsdaughter rubbed her temples, wincing as though in pain. 'What the old adage? "Uneasy lies the head that wears the crown." That's never felt truer than now. After all, I could well be about to send a teenager to his death.'

'Let's hope not.'

'Let's. But do you want to know a funny thing? I like Az. I like him a lot. He reminds me of myself at that age. Bright and full of fire, and just needing something to channel it into, a focus for all that restless inner energy. Misgivings aside, I don't think we could have asked for a better recruit for the job. I think he'll perform it admirably.'

'Assuming he agrees to do it.'

'If I've read him right,' Lady Aanfielsdaughter said, 'then I don't think we need have any worries on that score.'

CHAPTER 12

Another Brief Dialogue

'She's crazy about me,' Michael said, after Aurora had left the room. 'I can tell. She's giving me all the signals. Crazy.'

Az hadn't noticed any significant change in Aurora's attitude towards Michael while they were on their way over to the guest quarters, but he said nothing. If she *was* crazy about him, she was disguising it well.

'What should I do, Mike?' he said, crossing over to the balcony. From here the view of the Silver Sanctum was spectacular: gleaming canyons of streets, with wrought metalwork everywhere, so intensely detailed that the eye could scarcely take it all in. Two birds of paradise flapped by, looking utterly at home with their extravagant plumage of velvety golden heads and long, swooping pink tails.

'Do?' Michael had decided to try out one of the twin beds in the room. He flumped into it face-down. The mattress nearly swallowed him. 'Now that's what I call soft,' he said in a muffled voice. He rolled over. 'Well, what do you want to do?'

'Obviously I want not to have to visit the ground.'

'Fine, then you don't. Just like Lady Aanfielsdaughter said.' Michael paused, shaking his head. 'Lady Aanfielsdaughter. We were just talking to Lady Aanfielsdaughter! Can you believe it, Az?'

Az smiled indulgently at his brother. 'No, you're right, I don't have to. Except that I do.'

Michael looked up with a frown. 'Eh? I don't get it.'

'You heard her. She said it was my … my higher purpose. My destiny, almost. It's why I don't have wings.'

'Uh, well, maybe. I thought that was a bit highfaluting of her, myself. You know politicians. They can get very flowery sometimes, especially when they're trying to convince somebody about something.'

'I know. But look at it this way, Mike. You're not me. With the best will in the world, you have no idea what it's like to be me. If I can do something useful, if I can find some virtue in the fact that I don't have wings, then really I should. I must.'

'But there are risks …'

'There are risks all the time for me. My whole life is a risk. I could fall off a pavement by mistake, any day of the week, and that would be that. A single misstep, and 'bye-bye.'

Michael hopped up off the bed and came over to Az.

'So you're sure about this, little bro.'

Az forced a smile. 'Not really, no.'

'But …'

'But it's got to be done.'

Michael reached out and engulfed him in a huge hug.

'You're a brave little plucker, you know that, don't you?'

'… crushing me, Mike … can't breathe …'

'Oops.' Michael let go. He stepped back, and a musing look came over his face. 'And it's good that you're so brave, because it's going to make me look even better in Aurora Jukarsdaughter's eyes, isn't it? The hero's big brother.'

'Well, as long as *you* get something out of it,' Az said, with a lopsided grin.

Michael cuffed him with a wingtip.

What Az nearly said then, but didn't, was that an idea was forming at the back of his mind. It was, as yet, the merest glimmer of a suspicion, but it seemed valid and plausible. Lady Aanfieldsdaughter had kept something from him, some crucial piece of information. And if it was what he thought it was, then a trip down to the ground would make sense of many things and, from his own personal point of view, be more than a little interesting.

Assuming he survived the conditions down there, or even the journey.

CHAPTER 13

The Astral Dome

The refectory was lit by what appeared to be a million candles. Their glow reflected off the mirror-bright metallic panelling on the walls, so that the whole of the chamber was ablaze with illumination, right up to the vault-ribbed ceiling. The dazzle took some getting used to. For the first minutes of the meal Az found himself having to squint, but eventually his vision adjusted.

They ate butter-laced asparagus stalks for starters, followed by pigeon pie and then a second main course of swan steak served on a bed of spicy rice. Az and Michael were in the privileged position of having seats at the top table, where the seniormost residents of the Silver Sanctum sat. Around them were Lord this and Lady that, a plethora of grey-feathered nobles whose names Az had forgotten almost as soon as he had been told them. He managed to hold his own in conversation with them, but sometimes the talk at the table turned to arcane political matters which he couldn't follow, so he kept quiet then and sipped his wine. The wine was, as Lady Aanfieldsdaughter had promised, ambrosial, and after a couple of glasses of it everything took on a warm fuzziness. A trio of harpists were playing in a corner, providing background music, and to Az, as he got tipsy, the rippling ebb and flow of their arpeggio notes became lullingly hypnotic.

Finally dessert came, nectarine soufflé, and after that Lady Aanfieldsdaughter stood up, thanked the assembled worthies for their company at their meal, and invited Az and Michael to accompany her to the Astral Dome. The three of them walked out of the refectory, and as they went Az sensed that every eye in the room was on him. People were watching him go past, some of them trying to disguise it, some not. He felt an incalculable weight of expectation pressing on him. This helped sober him up.

The Astral Dome lay at the top of a tower to the north of the city. Its walls and ceiling were a hemisphere of transparent crystal, and the moment Az stepped into it he felt he was actually part of the heavens. Star clusters glittered brilliantly around him. It seemed that there was nothing to stop him reaching out and running his hand through the universe as though it were an upturned pool of water.

Then Lady Aanfielsdaughter switched on a series of lights recessed in the dome's base. All at once, through a trick of refraction, numerous sets of lines appeared overhead, flaws deliberately introduced into the crystal. They formed an array of irregular geometrical patterns which linked the stars together in their constellation shapes. Powered by an immense, hidden system of clockwork, the dome revolved slowly in time to the turning of the heavens, and its angle could be adjusted by means of gimbals, so that the lines and the stars always corresponded.

Az passed several happy minutes identifying constellations by name. He recognised Agor the Vulture and Tift the Bat, and there was the Huntsman, Jophiel, with his falcon on his wrist, and there was the pilot Metatron. The dim, pale band that traversed the sky was the wake of Metatron's aircraft, a cloudy furrow which this mythical entity renewed every night as he crossed east-west from horizon to horizon. He navigated by the True Star, the bright, sparkling scintilla of light that remained constant at the apex of the firmament, the fixed point around which all the other stars pivoted.

'Now, Az,' said Lady Aanfielsdaughter, breaking in on his heaven-gazing reverie. She switched the lights off and the stars reverted to their natural randomness. 'I really need to know. I've been patient all evening, but … an answer. Yes or no?'

Az turned to her and gave an emphatic nod.

'You're aware of the dangers? The possible consequences?'

Another firm nod.

'Very well.' Lady Aanfieldsdaughter looked gratified, although not wholly glad. 'Then tomorrow you'll be travelling to Heliotropia.'

'Why Heliotropia?'

'That's where the supply disruption has been worst. Might as well send you into the heart of things, where the problems will be at their most apparent.'

'And will you be going there with me?'

'Unfortunately not. There's no escape for people like me. Government is a prison sentence!' She laughed. 'But we'll meet again when you return, Az. Have no doubt about that. You'll be brought straight to me to report what you've found out.'

They shared a firm handshake.

'Best of luck.'

'Thank you,' said Az, hoping fervently that he wouldn't need it.

CHAPTER 14

Heliotropia

The holiday resort of Heliotropia was one day's journey away. They travelled there in convoy with Mr Mordadson. Aurora joined them on the trip, which Michael was delighted about, but she flew with Mr Mordadson in his Wayfarer, which he was less delighted about. There was, of course, no room in the Dragonfly for her, unless Az gave up his seat, and Michael wasn't going to ask him to make that sacrifice. Nevertheless, Michael would dearly have loved some time alone in the helicopter with Aurora so that he could continue to, as he put it, 'work his magic' on her.

Heliotropia perched atop a single column and was designed along the lines of a flower, with dozens of flat radial arms arrayed like petals around a disc-shaped hub. Each 'petal' was a strip of hotels, while the hub contained souvenir shops, swimming pools, funfairs, cabaret theatres, and casinos, plus a few nightclubs, many of them with a rather risqué reputation. Heliotropia, being the highest of the sky-cities by a margin of nearly a kilometre, was also the coldest, but what it lacked in ambient temperature it gained in proximity to the sun. For anyone wishing to get a tan and not waste time about it, this was the place to come. After just quarter of an hour shivering semi-naked on a sun lounger, you'd be browner than if you had spent a couple of hours doing the same at a lower, milder clime.

Az and Michael had no opportunity to sample any of the recreational delights on offer in Heliotropia, however. No sooner had they arrived than they were being shown into the city's underbelly.

'Huh, brings back memories,' said Michael as they descended beneath the streets via an access shaft. 'Six months working the supply elevators. I really felt like I'd done my bit for society after *that*. You've got all this to look forward to when you turn twenty-one, Az.'

Az, in Michael's arms, nodded, thinking that his winglessness would probably excuse him from his mandatory stretch of community service – and then thinking that he might not even reach twenty-one, if something went wrong today.

He was starting to get anxious, for the first time since agreeing to Lady Aanfieldsdaughter's request. He had been able to put it out of his mind before, but now it was hitting home. The ground. He was about to travel down to the ground. His mouth felt dry and his stomach had tightened into a hard, painful ball.

Michael sensed the tension in his brother's body. 'You can pull out any time, little bro. It's never too late. Just say the word.'

'I'll be fine,' Az replied, although he wasn't sure whether he was trying to convince Michael or himself.

At the base of the shaft, a tunnel led off at right angles. It was dimly lit and not much broader than the average wingspan. From far off came a thrumming sound, vibrating along the tunnel's length.

'Now then, you probably should put these on.'

This was said by the supply-arrival depot supervisor, who had led Az, Michael, Aurora and Mr Mordadson down here. The 'these' he was referring to were sets of zip-up gauze wing covers, which he produced from a wall locker.

'One size fits all,' the supervisor went on. 'They'll keep the dust and grime off your feathers. None necessary for you, of course,' he said to Az.

Az would have come back with some smart-alec retort, but he was too preoccupied to think of one just then.

Everyone who had wings sheathed them in gauze. Then they trooped off along the tunnel on foot, the supervisor leading the way. The further they went, the louder the thrumming sound became, until soon it was like a bass note on a concert organ, deep and resonant.

'Don't remember there being this much noise,' Michael commented to Az.

The supervisor overheard. 'That would be because Heliotropia has all its supply elevators confined to one spot. Since the city has just a single column, all of its elevators – a hundred or so – are grouped around it. The mechanism to run that many of them is, as you can imagine, of a pretty considerable size, hence the noise. You'll see for yourselves in a moment.'

They did. The tunnel terminated, and Az found himself entering the biggest room he had ever been in. It was cylindrical, and he estimated that at least three jetball hoopdromes could have fitted comfortably inside it, one on top of the other. The ceiling was so high up as to be all but invisible. The opposite wall looked impossibly distant.

At the centre of the room – although *room* seemed much too diminutive a word to describe this place – there was a raised area, circular in shape and buttressed with girders. It took Az several moments to work out what he was looking at. This was the summit of Heliotropia's column, the point on which the entire city rested.

Even as he assimilated *that* fact, his eye was drawn to the complex arrangement of pulleys and cables that filled much of the open space above the raised area. Huge wheels revolved, suspended in an intricate steel framework. Counterweights the size of airbuses rose and fell. It was a gigantic spiderweb of mechanical activity, all to facilitate the raising and lowering of the elevators on their tracks spaced around the circumference of the column.

'Remarkable, isn't it?' the supervisor said, with a gloat of professional pride. 'The sky-cities' designers certainly didn't think small. The elevators work on a gravity-driven system. One descending helps another rise. It's the closest thing you'll ever get to perpetual motion. And you know what? Right up above us, over our heads, tens of thousands of holidaymakers are gadding about, having fun, enjoying themselves, none of them caring a jot about any of this. Nobody gives a hoot what goes on right beneath their feet. Makes you think, eh?'

Mr Mordadson, for one, didn't seem to be in the mood for rumination just then.

'What about all those workers?' he asked, pointing to clusters of men and women dotted around the supply-arrival depot floor, near the elevators. 'It doesn't suit us to have them around. We don't need any witnesses.'

'They'll be going off-shift quite soon.' The supervisor consulted his watch. 'Couple of minutes' time, in fact.'

'Not exactly doing a lot of work, are they?' Michael observed.

The workers were dressed in olive-green overalls and had wing-covers on. The majority of them were just sitting around, apparently waiting for something to do. Each time an elevator arrived, they glanced at it, then resumed their lounging.

Not all of them were idle, however. Az spotted two people in flight, daubing grease on the pulleys. He saw another at the controls of a hover-lifter, practising how to manoeuvre the little vehicle. There was an unladen pallet on the hover-lifter's forks, and the worker was trying, with great care, to lodge it into a distribution bay in the wall, a couple of hundred metres up off the floor. The 'lifter's fans swivelled this way and that as he tried, and kept failing, to insert the pallet correctly.

'Well, that's because nothing's coming up right now, is it?' said the supervisor. 'There's nothing to unload. We have periods like this, when the elevators keep turning up with empty pallets and everybody just has to twiddle their thumbs. Only, I have to say, it's been happening rather a lot lately. Whole shifts will go by, and no coal, no crude oil, no timber, no soil, nothing. Heliotropia has enough to be getting by with for now. Our stockpiles are OK, and there's plenty of money in the city coffers to buy in anything we're running low on. Still, it's a bit worrying. But of course, that's what you've come here to—'

A klaxon sounded, and the workers immediately took to the air and swarmed towards a far-off exit.

'Right-ho,' said the supervisor. 'We've a few minutes before the next shift comes on. Changeover's always slow. Let's get this lunacy over and done with, shall we?'

CHAPTER 15

Departure

One after another, in sequence, the elevators heaved up through apertures in the floor and rolled their doors open, revealing dark, featureless interiors. Up close, Az noticed that their metal sides were covered in patches of rust, and here and there the corrosion had eaten through, leaving small jagged holes. He noticed, too, that many of the elevators creaked and shuddered as they moved.

None of this made him any more thrilled at the prospect of travelling in one.

'Downward journey time will be best part of an hour, by my estimate,' said the supervisor. He was talking to Mr Mordadson. 'That's only an educated guess, though. Could be a great deal longer. Then you want to allow him how long to look around? Two, three hours?'

'That would seem adequate,' said Mr Mordadson.

'After which he can come right back up. So a six-hour round trip, let's say. Seven, to be on the safe side.'

'And you'll be here all the time? Outside the elevator?'

'All the time,' the supervisor confirmed. 'The moment he resurfaces, I'll whisk him out of sight before anybody spots him. That's as long as he comes up on the exact same one. You think you can do that, boy? Come back on the same elevator?'

'Yeah,' said Az drily, 'I reckon I can manage that.'

'And we,' said Mr Mordadson to the supervisor, 'will wait for you and Azrael up in your administrative offices. I don't need to remind you, do I, that the Silver Sanctum is counting on your discretion in this matter.'

'You don't.'

'Or that a good turn done for the Silver Sanctum is always reciprocated.'

'Just pleased to be of service, that's all,' said the supervisor, although it was obvious he didn't mind the Silver Sanctum being in his debt. It might come in handy someday, to be able to call in that kind of favour.

'Good, good,' said Mr Mordadson.

'The lad ...' The supervisor eyed Az. 'He does understand that the ground isn't a healthy place for a human to be? I mean, he's clear on the fact that *you just don't go down there*, right? Not and live.'

'He is,' Az said, who was fed up with the way the supervisor kept talking about him in the third person, as if he wasn't even there. 'He's also clear on the fact that he's going to chicken out if we don't get on with this right away.'

'Yes. OK. Fair enough.' The supervisor brisked his palms together. 'Here we are then, next elevator in line to arrive, coming up. Doors'll remain open till I release this lever here. The lever re-engages the drive ratchet, and descent commences. If you've goodbyes to say, now's the time to say them.'

Az turned to Michael and was alarmed to see that his brother was struggling to hold back tears.

'You're coming back,' Michael said, with conviction. 'Seven hours' time, we'll be seeing your ugly mug again.'

'Count on it,' said Az.

'Go on then. Stop faffing about. Sooner you leave ...'

'... sooner I return. Mike, if anything does go wrong, you should tell Mum and Dad—'

'Nothing's going to go wrong.'

'Still, you should tell them I love them and they're not to blame. For anything. They carry this guilt around with them, guilt about me. They don't ever say anything about it but I know they do. And they don't need to. There's no reason to.'

'Tell 'em yourself, squirt.'

'All right. I will.'

Aurora Jukarsdaughter leaned close and gaze Az a peck on

the cheek. She even smelled beautiful, the scent of her skin like lilacs. 'Good luck, young man.'

Az couldn't resist a chance for mischief. 'You realise my brother fancies the socks off you, don't you?'

'Az!' hissed Michael, exasperated.

Aurora's teeth sparkled as she laughed. 'I had noticed. He's not subtle, is he?'

'Not very.'

Michael buried his face in his hands. 'I've changed my mind, Az. *Don't* come back. Ever.'

'Azrael?'

Now Mr Mordadson stepped forward. He looked oddly hesitant, ill at ease with his emotions.

'Be careful,' he settled for saying. 'And be observant.'

'Will do.'

'You're not alone,' Mr Mordadson added, his eyelids closing behind his spectacles in a slow, meaningful blink.

'Uh, right,' said Az, thinking that the last thing he needed right now was a heartfelt expression of moral support like this from Mr Mordadson.

Or was he trying to imply more than that?

This wasn't the time to dwell on it. Az about-faced. The elevator had risen and halted. An empty pallet had rolled out of it and now the elevator was waiting, doors agape. From within, a dark, burnt odour drifted out, the smell of functionality and necessity.

He stepped forward.

'Ready?' said the supervisor, hand on the lever.

Az swallowed and nodded.

'Then here goes.'

Az entered the elevator.

The lever fell with a clank.

The doors trundled shut with a clunk.

The elevator gave a groan and started to sink.

CHAPTER 16

Down

Through a rust hole in the elevator's roof, Az watched Heliotropia recede above him.

The sky-city's underside was veined with sewage pipes and garbage conduits, like some complex, interlocking tubular puzzle. It was possible to discern a pattern, however, and the pattern became clearer the further Az descended. Everything ultimately led towards the column, fed into it, and continued down inside. The column served as a gigantic waste disposal chute, along with its many other functions.

Gradually Heliotropia darkened, until soon it had become a silhouette against the firmament, a vast black flower, and Az couldn't make out details any more. He found another rust hole, this one at chest height in the right-hand-side wall of the elevator. Through it he could see the cloud cover. The sun was low, and the cloud cover, where it wasn't in Heliotropia's immense lengthening shadow, had started to take on evening hues. Soon the peaks would be pink, the troughs purple. After that its surface would become a uniform dark grey.

The cloud cover was still some way below, but rising fast.

Az was alone.

The feeling swamped him – *engulfed* him. Everything he knew, everyone he loved, was up there. Up in Heliotropia, up in High Haven. Up in the world of the Airborn. He was beneath them, and getting further away with every passing second. He was separated. Isolated.

Then came fear.

There was no way out. He was trapped in the elevator till

it reached the ground – and then what? What awaited down there?

He fought the urge to scream and hammer at the doors of the elevator. As if there was someone outside to hear him and let him out!

The elevator gave a sudden, heart-stopping lurch, then continued as before. That put paid to any ideas Az had about pounding on it. He lowered himself into a corner and sat there with his knees to his chin, keeping himself small and still. He didn't want to do the slightest thing to interfere with the elevator's progress. He knew that it must have made the trip up and down the column a million times without a hitch, but what if this was the occasion when it finally malfunctioned? What if, by a stroke of appalling misfortune, it got stuck, or even broke free of its track and fell?

A long time passed before Az's thoughts settled into any semblance of order again. There was no point in panicking. It was far too late for that. He might as well try and enjoy the ride, even if it turned out to be the last ride he ever took. No, *especially* if.

By that point the elevator was drawing level with the cloud cover. Carefully Az got up and pressed his eye to the chest-high rust hole again. This close to, the agitation of the cloud cover was clear to see. Wisps of vapour twisted upward from the surface, forming spirals and cones that dissipated rapidly. Deeper down, the clouds flurried and swirled. Currents were visible, surging powerfully around in immense streams and eddies.

It swallowed him suddenly. One moment, Az was beginning to wonder if the elevator was ever going to reach the cloud cover. Next moment everything outside went hazy, then blank grey.

The air turned clammy, so that Az could see his breath. The interior of the elevator darkened, the air got clammier still, and then the elevator started to shake. Winds had begun to batter it, hurling themselves at it from front and sides. The doors whumped inward every time a particularly powerful gust struck. The floor under Az's feet juddered. It seemed such a frail thing, this metal box he was in. Too frail to withstand the cloud cover's fury. If it wasn't wrenched loose from its tracks, it might just get crushed to pieces.

Fear returned, and Az resorted to prayer. He didn't believe in God. Who did? A few strange folk who gathered in community halls to hold hands and mumble about a Superior Being, that was who. A tiny minority of superstitious weirdos who clung to the notion that Someone watched over the Airborn race from on high and looked after them, whereas anybody with an ounce of sense knew that the Airborn were clever enough and organised enough to look after themselves, thank you very much.

For all that, Az had always been intrigued by the notion of God. He wanted to believe that his being born without wings was part of some divine master plan, that there was a meaning to it, it wasn't just a random genetic accident. Lady Aanfieldsdaughter, perhaps knowingly, perhaps not, had touched on this hope of Az's when she had referred to Az having a 'higher purpose'.

Everyone wanted to feel special, didn't they?

So, silently, he prayed. Eyes tight shut, he strung together a few rambling, desperate pleas, as the elevator trembled and rattled in the cloud cover's tempestuous grasp.

Please let me live.

Please, if you're up there, let me live.

CHAPTER 17

Groundfall

A while later, the shaking stopped and calm was restored.

Az opened his eyes and found himself in darkness. He groped his way to the rust hole. Outside, all was murk and gloom. He couldn't tell how high he was. He had no idea how long he had been in the elevator. It would take an hour, the supervisor had said, to get to the ground. But the supervisor had just pulled that figure out of thin air. He didn't actually know.

Az felt as though he had been in the elevator for ever and would always be in it. The journey was an eternity.

He noticed that he was feeling slightly dizzy but he put it down to the trauma of going through the cloud cover. It wasn't a wholly unpleasant sensation and a couple of deep breaths were enough to clear his head.

Then, below, he spied lights.

There was just a handful of them, a smattering. It was as if he was looking down at a lone constellation, a group of stars on the ground. For a brief, exhilarating moment he thought he might even be going up again and the lights were real stars. Somehow he had managed to avoid visiting the ground. A reprieve!

But of course this wasn't so. He was still travelling downward.

What were they then, those lights?

As he got nearer to them, he perceived that they were scattered across the surface of a dark, looming structure of some kind, and that they shone with an uneven flicker.

Nearer still, he realised that the lights were glows from the mouths of several tall chimneys. There were furnaces burning down there and the lights showed where the furnaces were being vented. Above each glow a thick black plume of smoke arose, churning up into the air.

As for the structure, it was an agglomeration of buildings that spread around the foot of the column and outward, visible to Az as a jumbled mass of roofs, some curved, some jagged, plus those chimneys. It was hard to make out the structure clearly by the uncertain orange light of the furnaces, but even so Az had never seen anything so haphazard before, so apparently thrown together. The whole thing looked as if it had grown rather than been constructed, as if it had sprung up around the column's base like some kind of fungus.

The elevator seemed to be moving faster. Maybe this was just an optical illusion as the ground came closer, or maybe gravity's hold on it was stronger here. Whichever, Az felt it rushing to complete the final section of its journey. The last few minutes of the descent were a swoop, a throat-tightening plunge.

At the back of Az's mind was the thought that he should not inhale, or at least should inhale shallowly. The smoke from those chimneys. Poisoned air. Toxic.

But no. There was nothing he could do about that. He was either going to die now or he wasn't.

The elevator sank into the structure, entering some sort of shaft. The sounds it was making changed, becoming at once confined and echoey.

Then it started to decelerate, easing itself bit by bit to a stop.

When it finally did halt, Az felt distinctly unsteady on his feet. Inside, he was still going down. He had been in the elevator for so long that his body had adjusted and now needed to *re*adjust. It had to get used to the idea of being motionless once more.

The doors divided, rolling open to reveal ...

... an empty pallet, hurtling along rails, straight towards Az's shins.

CHAPTER 18

Going Through The Motions

He leapt aside just in time. The pallet slammed home inside the elevator. Had Az reacted a split-second more slowly, it would have pinned him against the back wall, crushing his legs.

He scrambled out of the elevator and scanned frantically around. Where there had been one hazard, there might be others.

In every direction he saw machinery. He was in a chamber that was not unlike the supply-arrival depot. It wasn't quite as vast, and the level of illumination was dim to the point of being nonexistent, coming as it did from a set of skylights located way up in the ceiling. But there was the same impression of constant mechanical commotion, and here the noise was even louder and more disorientating than above, at Heliotropia. In fact, the racket was such that Az's ears could barely take it. Things were working – ponderously, repetitively working. Pistons thump-whumped. Flywheels whirled. Gear chains as thick as a man's torso went scrolling through systems of cogs. Great pendulum-like weights shot downward and slowly rose. And everywhere, pallets were shuttling around, either rolling along rails or else being plucked from one spot and transported to another in the jaws of cranes, which glided along tracks mounted on the ceiling joists. There were squeaks of metal grinding on metal, sudden eruptions of steam from valves, the occasional shower-burst of sparks – all of which added to the near-deafening din.

Az thought two things. First of all, that his ex-clockmaker father might feel right at home here. It was like being inside an enormous timepiece. And second of all, that he himself wanted to get out. The dizziness from earlier had returned, worse than before, no longer pleasant in any way, and even if the cacophony around him wasn't the cause, it definitely wasn't helping. He needed to find a quieter spot if he could.

He staggered away from the elevator, which had closed its doors and was ascending back towards the ceiling. He made a mental note of its location within the chamber, hoping against hope that when the time came he would be able to find it again. In an odd way he felt an affinity for that particular elevator, over all the others. After all, it had got him here safely, more or less. He owed it a debt of gratitude for that.

Fighting the dizziness, he ventured through the – what would you call this place? Supply-departure depot? Somehow, because it was automated, it didn't seem to merit a name. He threaded a wary path between the various devices. A pallet came swinging towards him, hoisted by a crane. He ducked and it passed over his head. A jet of steam nearly scorched his backside. A piston thrust itself out at him unexpectedly.

If he hadn't known better, he would have thought the machinery had taken a dislike to him and was on the attack.

Eventually he reached the sanctuary of the chamber's outer wall. Three metres up there was a gantry, which could be reached by a metal ladder. Connected to the gantry by a door was a room with a row of viewing windows – some kind of monitoring gallery. Once, long ago, the Groundling equivalent of the supply-arrival depot supervisor might have looked out from that gallery to observe the machinery as it laboured away. Now no one did any more.

Az climbed the ladder and took a breather, leaning on the gantry's safety rail and watching the vista of robotic industry in front of him. From this vantage point he could see more clearly than ever how the machines weren't achieving anything. They were meant to be filling the elevators with essential supplies for Heliotropia but there were no raw materials anywhere to be seen. The pallets were conspicuously bare. Yet still the machines went through the motions, loading the elevators with nothing.

It was a starkly depressing sight, a vision of mindless futility. All that effort and energy, to no end.

The dizzy spell finally passed. The door to the gallery was made of steel and secured by a heavy lever-type handle. It was hard to open, much as you might expect of a door that hadn't been used in centuries. Az grappled with the handle, which was stiff to the point of being almost unmoveable. He pushed down on it with all his might, and in the end, with a sharp, protesting screech, it shifted. He pushed again, grunting with the effort, and all at once the handle gave, the door sprang open and he tumbled through. He closed it behind him, relieved to be able to shut out the deafening ruckus in the chamber.

Inside the gallery were banks of consoles with levers, dials, switches and gauges on them, an array of instrumentation glinting faintly in the gloom. Az pictured Groundlings manning the consoles, perhaps touching a knob here, a lever there, with the growing realisation that what they were doing didn't seem to make any difference. The machinery on the other side of the windows went on regardless. The Groundlings must have sensed they were becoming redundant.

Mustn't they?

A race that had collectively lost the will to live. Was it possible?

Az was beginning to wonder.

Another steel door led out from the gallery. Reasoning that the interruption to the flow of supplies must be occurring somewhere further up the production line, Az knew he had to delve further into the building to investigate.

This door opened far more easily than the last, and he found himself in a passageway that was bathed in murky red light. As his eyes accustomed themselves to the crimson glow, it occurred to him that this must be how Mr Mordadson viewed the world through his tinted spectacles: everything blood-coloured.

Not nice.

It also occurred to him that the lighting must be for somebody's benefit. If, as he and all the other Airborn had been led to believe, there were no Groundlings any more, wouldn't the bulbs have burned out long ago and not been replaced? So far Az had seen nothing but abandoned automation. However, his half-formed suspicion – the one he had refrained from voicing to Michael – was still there, and the presence of the working lights helped give it strength. It was gradually coalescing into a conviction, although as yet he lacked absolute, clinching proof.

He headed off along the passageway. The dizziness returned briefly. His brain woozed and the walls of the passageway flexed and pulsed around him. He halted. But as before, the sensations passed and he felt OK again. Perhaps Lady Aanfieldsdaughter was right. Physiologically he could cope with the rigours of being on the ground in a way no ordinary Airborn person could.

The passageway turned a corner, and not long afterward Az emerged into a chamber of similar dimensions to the first one but far quieter. Here, there was only a distant rumble to be heard, emanating from the other chamber. In this chamber nothing was moving. What apparatus there was stood inert. Huge pieces of machinery hulked to the rafters but were inactive.

This appeared to be the place where items were deposited onto pallets and transferred by conveyor belt through a connecting conduit to the chamber where the elevators were. And if nothing was operational here, then here, logically, was where the problem lay. Here or in the conduit.

Az strode into the room, flooded with a sense of satisfaction. Mission not quite accomplished but almost. He couldn't believe it had been so easy. (Well, perhaps not easy, but straightforward.) All he had to do was check around, identify where the hold-up was, then head back to the elevator and report to Lady Aanfieldsdaughter. After that, it was up to Lady Aanfieldsdaughter and everyone else at the Silver Sanctum to sort things out somehow. Az would have done his bit. The problem would be someone else's.

He explored the chamber thoroughly, examined every machine, but was unable to find anything obviously awry. There wasn't a jam anywhere in the system. None of the machines appeared to have broken down. They just weren't *on*.

Maybe the power was out. There was power elsewhere but maybe a fuse or a circuit-breaker for this particular chamber had blown.

Further investigation brought Az to an exit at the far end of the chamber. He took it. He was starting to feel bold. He would have some stories to tell Michael and their parents when he got back!

He was in another red-lit passageway. Right or left? He chose left.

The passageway twisted around several right-angle corners. Az came to a T-junction and went left again. He knew he must be careful not to lose his bearings. He promised himself if he arrived at another junction he would turn back. This place was a maze.

An entrance appeared. It consisted of two doors, each adorned with a set of designs. Etched steel panels depicted arrows pointing upward and an Airborn figure, wings and arms outstretched, gazing serenely down.

What did that signify? Why Airborn?

Intrigued, Az nudged one of the doors open and went in.

There was no light in the room apart from the faint red illumination borrowed from the passageway outside. Az glimpsed vague shapes – something like a bed in the middle of the room and a large square portal with an ornate frame set into the far wall.

On the bed there was a man lying down.

Az froze.

The man didn't stir. Either he was fast asleep and Az's entering had not woken him, or ...

Gradually Az's eyes adapted to the dim light. He could see the man was on his back and naked except for a white loincloth. His hands were folded across his stomach and his wings lay flat, forming the outline of a heart around him. Az looked for the rise and fall of the man's chest. There wasn't any.

The awful truth dawned. He was looking at a dead body.

CHAPTER 19

Anatomy Of A Dead Man

Steeling himself, Az went further into the room. He didn't want to examine the corpse more closely, and yet he knew he had to. His curiosity must be satisfied, even if it meant going to within touching distance of death.

He tiptoed up to the bed, which he could now see was not a bed at all but a kind of gurney, similar to the ones that sick people were moved around on at a hospital. There were castors on the ends of its legs.

The man was very skinny. His face was whiskery, his hair was thin and lank, and the veins were prominent through his pale skin, twisting around his bones like vines around posts. He was old, or rather had been old when he died.

Who was this? Was he perhaps Az's predecessor, someone who had come to the ground before him to investigate and had not returned? Lady Aanfielsdaughter hadn't mentioned sending anyone else on this mission first, but then why would she? It would hardly have helped her cause if she'd told Az, 'In point of fact, the last chap didn't make it back alive. Still willing to go?'

The explanation didn't quite hold water, though. It failed to account for why the man was lying there on the gurney, quite clearly having been placed in that position. And his wings. His wings were strange. The way they sat so flat on the gurney – it just didn't look right. There was no thickness, no solidity to them.

Squinting, Az studied the wings and realised that they weren't actually wings at all. They were just feathers arranged around the body to resemble wings. An assortment of feathers, too, not uniformly white. There were grey ones, half-white half-brown ones, even a few black ones. They'd been placed on the gurney in such a way to make the man look as if he was Airborn.

And yet he was not.

Groundling.

Had to be.

'Yes,' Az hissed to himself.

So there *were* Groundlings after all. His suspicion had been correct. Contrary to popular Airborn belief, they hadn't died out. This one might be defunct, but someone else had placed those feathers around him, therefore the race as a whole remained alive. And that fact was common knowledge to those in the upper echelons of Airborn life. Lady Aanfielsdaughter knew it and Mr Mordadson had hinted at it with his 'You're not alone' remark, a kind of oblique warning to Az, a way of preparing him for what he might find down here.

While Az was coming to terms with this, the dizziness returned with a vengeance. All at once his head was reeling. His stomach was churning greasily. Nausea rippled through him in waves.

And then from the passageway outside came the sound of voices.

Too dazed and disorientated to know what else to do, Az scanned about for somewhere to hide. He didn't want to be caught with the body. Whoever these people were, if they found him peering at the dead man, what would they think? What would they *do*?

A hasty hunt around the room revealed a closet. There were clothes hanging inside – robes of some sort – and bottles on a shelf containing a clear fluid. Az crawled in and tugged the closet door shut. The catch slipped and the door swung open, though only a little way. He didn't have time to try and shut it properly again. He heard a switch being thrown. Bright light flooded the room. Two men had entered.

CHAPTER 20

Archdeacon Corbelgilt

Az peered through the open crack of the closet door. His head was swimming and he felt on the brink of passing out. Still, he couldn't help but gaze in amazement at the two arrivals. Living Groundlings, in the flesh.

Both of the men were clad in robes, just like the ones hanging above him in the closet. The robes were black with symbols embroidered on them in scarlet and gold. One of the men had more symbols on his robe than the other and, where the other had just a plain skullcap, he wore an ornate item of headgear. It was a tall arch-shaped hat with a golden arrow on the front, pointing upward like the arrows on the door.

This man was clearly the more important of the two. The other man addressed him with deference and, Az thought, with a certain amount of fear. The more important man was also the fatter of the two, by quite some margin. He was, indeed, obese. His body was a massive quivering sphere, his head was as round as a jetball, and he wheezed as he walked, his stubby little arms working hard to keep him balanced. If he had been Airborn and winged, he might well have been too heavy to fly.

'Your grace,' the second, much thinner man was saying, 'everything is prepared. The body is feathered, as you can see, and the mourners will be arriving shortly.'

'Have they paid tribute?' the obese man with the ornate hat enquired. He spoke through his nose, with a haughty air, as though it was beneath his dignity to discuss such mundane, practical matters.

'Naturally, your grace. A tithe of the deceased's estate, such as it was, has been presented to the Chancel actuaries.

Unfortunately, of course, the obligatory bodyweight's worth of offerings has *not* been provided. The family were unable to obtain anything suitable. I'm assured they tried, they made every effort, but...'

'The pickets.'

'Indeed, your grace, they were hindered by the pickets. Nothing is coming out of any of the local commercial premises unless it can be guaranteed that it's going to the people and not to here.'

'This blasted industrial action, Deacon Shatterlonger,' the obese man said with a heartfelt, contemptuous sigh. 'When is it going to end? It cannot be allowed to continue much longer. Do the people not realise the danger to their souls?'

'I wish I could give you an answer, Archdeacon Corbelgilt. All I can say is, the militancy out there is getting worse by the day. Wretched Humanists! Stirring up trouble wherever they raise their heathen heads. One can only hope that common sense will soon prevail.'

'*Faith* and common sense.'

'Yes, your grace, that's what I meant. Faith and common sense will prevail. Otherwise...'

'Otherwise we're damned, all of us,' said Archdeacon Corbelgilt. 'No salvation, no life after this life. The disfavour of the heavens will be upon us. We shall none of us rise to join the Ascended Ones.'

Deacon Shatterlonger's face was a picture of misery, mirroring the sentiments of his superior. 'Perhaps if your grace were to deliver one of your trademark rousing sermons at the ceremony ...'

'Already composed.' The Archdeacon tapped his temple. 'Memorised and ready. Usually I would be wary of intruding on the grief of mourners, but today I cannot allow myself such niceties of conscience. The situation demands that the Chancel restate its case in the strongest terms possible. The people *must* be told that the Humanist cause is wrong and insupportable, and they must be encouraged to carry that message out into the community.'

Az struggled to make head or tail of what he was listening to. It didn't help that he felt close to fainting and that there was a buzzing in his ears which made the conversation seem as though it was coming from a hundred metres away. Also, the men spoke with a thick accent which stretched some words out and shortened others. For instance, *raring* sounded like it had at least three R's in the middle of it, while *encouraged* came out as *incard*.

Mainly, though, Az didn't get certain references. Humanists? Salvation? Chancel? Ascended Ones? It was like a whole new language.

'Ah, here we are,' said the Deacon. The sound of shuffling footfalls could be heard in the passageway outside.

'Your grace,' he added softly, pointing to Corbelgilt's hat. 'Your mitre. A tad lopsided.'

Archdeacon Corbelgilt hurriedly straightened the hat, then composed himself, putting on a polite, pleasant face.

More Groundlings filed into the room, thirty or so in all, and Corbelgilt greeted each with a handclasp and a condescending tilt of the head. There were men and women of all ages, and a few children, and the majority looked sombre and sad. One elderly woman, whom Az took to be the dead man's widow, was especially distraught. Her eyes were red-rimmed and she was barely looking where she was going – a couple of younger relatives had to guide her by the elbows. When she caught sight of the body on the gurney, she burst into fits of sobbing. The archdeacon moved to comfort her, whispering something reassuring in her ear.

The mourners took their places in the room, lining up facing the body. Deacon Shatterlonger moved to a position close to Az's hiding place. Archdeacon Corbelgilt, meanwhile, stationed himself next to the gurney.

He raised his hands.

'Let us begin.'

CHAPTER 21

The Ceremony Of Ascension

The next few minutes were a blur for Az. He tried to keep up with what was going on but there were shooting stars exploding across his vision and the buzzing in his ears had become a deep drone. It was all he could do simply to stay conscious.

Archdeacon Corbelgilt intoned long sentences, punctuating them with formal hand gestures. He was talking about the dead man, describing his life, saying he had been a good person and a hard worker, and anyone who was good and worked hard would deserve a place in the glorious hereafter of the skies.

Then came something he called the Rite of Unction. The archdeacon signalled to Deacon Shatterlonger, and the latter turned and opened the closet door.

Az looked up blearily, expecting Shatterlonger to catch sight of him and let out a yell of surprise.

In the event, the Deacon didn't spot him on the floor of the closet, half-obscured by the hanging robes. Instead, intent on his task, he removed a bottle from the shelf and shut the door.

As before, the catch didn't hold and the door swung silently ajar.

Archdeacon Corbelgilt took the bottle, which was small and made of frosted glass. He unstoppered it and poured a quantity of oil into his cupped hand. He drizzled this over the dead man's chest in a pattern – an arrow shape, Az thought – at the same time uttering some phrases about 'fragrant smoke' that would 'transport the body to its new and better incarnation' and be 'favourable to the noses of those whose company the deceased is to join'.

In the meantime, Deacon Shatterlonger slid open the portal in the wall, exposing a chute. Distantly Az heard a sound like an immense fire.

Furnace, he thought.

Then there was singing. The archdeacon led the mourners in a cyclical, lugubrious melody, the lyrics of which reiterated much of what he had already said. Each verse ended with the lines:

> This is our one intention –
> To rise in true Ascension

The song concluded, and a solemn Deacon Shatterlonger took hold of the gurney and rolled it over to the chute. He undid a latch and, with the archdeacon's assistance, raised one end of the gurney's top section. It came up on a hinge until it reached a steep enough angle, whereupon the dead man slid off, disappearing down into the chute head first, feathers and all.

As the body vanished, the man's widow let out a despairing wail and sagged. If not for the relatives on either side of her, she would have collapsed.

The gurney was restored to its original position. The portal was closed. Archdeacon Corbelgilt then announced that, before he gave everyone his blessing to depart, he had something to say concerning the current 'undesirable industrial situation'.

This would have marked the beginning of his rousing sermon, if Deacon Shatterlonger hadn't at that moment re-opened the closet door to return the bottle of oil to the shelf.

Unlike before, this time the Deacon *did* spot Az.

The cry of surprise he let out was girlishly high-pitched, and was accompanied by a crashing and a splattering as the bottle of oil slipped from his fingers and shattered on the floor, releasing a cloyingly pungent reek.

'What is it?' Archdeacon Corbelgilt snapped.

Deacon Shatterlonger didn't have a chance to reply. Az, summoning all the strength and speed he could muster, leapt from his hiding place, darted around the Deacon's legs, and made for the exit. He veered between the startled mourners, while behind him Archdeacon Corbelgilt shouted, 'Who is that boy? What was he doing in there? Stop him! *Stop him!*'

Az hurled himself through the double doors and dashed off along the passageway.

He didn't know which direction to go in. He couldn't think straight. His only thought was: *escape*.

He ran.

Along red-lit passageway after red-lit passageway.

Ran and ran.

Hoping he was headed towards the elevators.

Ran and ran and ran.

CHAPTER 22

In The Shadow Zone

Den Grubdollar's voice crackled through the speaker tube.

'Bless my bum, Cassie! You'm asleep up there, girl?'

Cassie's head twitched and she straightened up in her seat. Not asleep, no, but she had fallen into a daze. It had been a long, hard outing, and she'd spent all of it at the controls of the murk-comber. She was exhausted.

She snatched the speaker tube off its hook to reply: 'Wide awake and grinning, Da.'

'Then hit full floods. It'm nearly duskfall, in case you hadn't noticed.'

'Hitting full floods, straight up.'

Cassie reached above her head and clicked a series of switches. Outside, the Shadow Zone was in gloom – not the usual gloom but the deeper, denser gloom that showed the day was nearly done. With each switch she threw, a floodlight on *Cackling Bertha*'s hull came on, injecting a cone of yellow brilliance into the greyness. Through the windscreen well-defined shapes appeared, their outlines flat like stage scenery. Here, a gnarled, stunted tree. There, an outcrop of rock. Cassie could no longer see as far as she could with her naked eye, but everything in the immediate vicinity of the murk-comber was much more clearly visible.

The floodlights put an extra demand on *Cackling Bertha*'s batteries, and her engine automatically stepped up its output to compensate. The noise she made went from a throaty chugging to a higher pitch, from *hughh-hughh-hughh* to *hehh-hehh-hehh*. This pattern then began to break up, becoming irregular. A faulty drive piston, which no one had never been able to fix properly, threw the engine's timing out whenever there was a strain on the system.

All at once *Bertha* was making her signature sound, that wheezy, broken, choking rhythm that resembled an old woman's laugh.

Cassie sat back in the driving seat, comforted by what she was hearing. She had grown up with *Bertha*'s cackle. It was music to her. She had spent all her life near, on, or in the murk-comber. A foetus in the womb, listening to its mother's heartbeat, could not have been as soothed as Cassie was by the stuttering, on-off exclamation of glee that came from *Bertha*'s engine when under pressure. The massive, caterpillar-tracked vehicle beneath her seemed perpetually eager to work. There was nothing *Bertha* liked more than to have to make an effort.

Cassie grasped the dual control sticks and steered around the rock outcrop. Then she huffed into the speaker tube's mouthpiece and demanded a status update.

From their observation nacelles on each corner Cassie's family responded one after another, in order of seniority – first her father, then her brothers, Martin, Fletcher and Robert. Nothing to report. No bounty visible. It looked like they were going to return home empty-handed.

'Keep she steady, Cass,' Den warned. 'Ground gets soft round here. There'm boggy patches that could swallow we up without so much as a burp.'

'Don't worry, Da. Eyes is peeled like grapes.'

'Mind them is.'

Cassie stifled a huge yawn and blinked several times owlishly. Her stint at the controls had lasted nearly eight hours, the longest uninterrupted period of driving she had ever done. The effort of staying focused and alert for all that time was taking its toll on her, but she refused to give in and ask for a rest. One of her brothers would have gladly taken her place – but she was the best driver in the family. Her father said so. They all knew it. And there was no way she would give any of them an excuse to think otherwise. She had that special touch with *Bertha*. Maybe it was a female thing, all girls together.

The terrain ahead undulated. This was, as her father had just reminded her, one of the Shadow Zone's most treacherous regions. There were swamps that looked like solid ground – lakes of mud with a crusty, dried surface which would crack like an eggshell beneath the fifty-tonne weight of a murk-comber. It was said that the swamps could be up to two kilometres deep, but this was highly unlikely. Fifteen metres was nearer the truth. Even so, *Cackling Bertha* would still disappear without a trace in fifteen metres of mud, and the Grubdollar family with her. Cassie could not afford to lose concentration.

It was a mark of the family's desperation that they were in the area at all. But after several days on the trot without so much as a glimpse of an item of salvage, the Grubdollars had to go where few others of their kind would dare. Murk-combers didn't run on thin air, and neither did the people who owned and operated them. The Grubdollars needed money – for fuel, for food – and when the pickings got as slim as they had recently, that meant taking risks.

In the distance Cassie spied the lights of the Chancel, where all salvage went to, if salvage could be found. The Deacons paid well but only for results. They didn't extend credit. If you failed to come up with the Relics they were after, you didn't receive a penny.

She entertained some very uncharitable thoughts about the Deacons, and about Archdeacon Corbelgilt in particular. Cassie wasn't a Humanist herself, far from it, but she could see that the Humanists had a point. For all these centuries the Deacons had held sway over everyone. Tucked up in their Chancels, they were keepers of the key to the next life. They had used and abused that position. They were rich and powerful, and jealously guarded their wealth and their dominance. You couldn't—

Bertha gave a sudden, sickening lurch to the left. Cassie, with a curse, slid the control sticks into neutral, and the murk-comber halted. What had she been thinking? She had let her attention drift. Idiot!

'What were that?' said her father. 'Cass?'

Not answering, Cassie peered out. She couldn't tell if *Bertha* had run into a soft patch or just a ditch of some sort. The ground look pretty firm. She hoped—

Bertha lurched again, and Cassie knew her hope was in vain. A soft patch! Swamp!

Immediately, she slammed both control sticks into reverse. It was an instinctive reaction but, as it happened, the wrong thing to do. *Bertha* let out a steep roar and Cassie could feel through the left-hand stick that the track on that side was not gripping. A jet of mud squirting forwards into her line of vision confirmed it. *Bertha* slewed round clockwise, her right-hand track propelling by itself, the left one useless.

Cassie thrust both sticks into neutral and *Bertha* stopped turning.

For a moment nothing happened. Then, with an almighty *gloop* from outside, *Bertha* began to list to the left. She was side-on to the swamp, half in it, half out. And she was starting to sink.

Panic seized Cassie. She shot a glance at the roll meter mounted on the dashboard – a ball, marked off in five-degree increments, housed in a water-filled glass globe. It was reading 10° off the lateral plane. 15° now.

Bertha was going down, tipping to the left with steady, ponderous inexorability. It wouldn't be long before she over-balanced and rolled onto her side, or perhaps even further than that, onto her roof. And it was happening too quickly for the family to evacuate. If *Bertha* went under, the Grubdollars would go under with her, and then all that would be left for them to do was wait as the mud oozed in through chinks in her bodywork. Wait to drown, if they didn't suffocate first.

Cassie heard Robert yelling, 'Do something, sis! Get we out of here!'

But Cassie didn't know what to do. She could only stare helplessly at the roll meter, while leaning rightwards in her seat to stay vertical. The roll meter was reading 20°, edging towards 25. All her brothers were shouting into their speaker tubes.

'Shut up, you lot!' their father ordered.

They shut up.

'Cass,' said Den Grubdollar.

'Da.'

'Listen to I. Listen to my voice. Keep cool. Focus. Us doesn't have traction on the left but us still does on the right. Use that.'

'How?'

'Go forwards with the right track, reverse the left.'

'But that'll spin *Bertha* back the way she came and us'll just end up nose-first in the—'

'Not if us is lucky. There might be enough grip on the left to push we halfway clear, and then, at the crucial moment, when I tell you, you hit both sticks full into reverse. Got it?'

'All right, Da. I'll try.'

'Good girl. You can do this.'

Cassie manipulated the sticks as advised. *Bertha* responded with a gutsy rumble and began to pivot round anticlockwise. It was slow, slippery going. *Bertha* slithered constantly, shuddered, threw up a huge splattering plume of mud ... but gradually she was hauling herself out of the swamp, her left track digging into increasingly solid ground.

'Come on, good lady,' Cassie murmured, 'my dear, my lovely, come on, come on, come *on*.'

Then, abruptly, *Bertha* was free of the mud, both tracks in full contact with terra firma – and straight away she began to rotate into the swamp again, this time angling her right flank towards it.

'Now, Cass!' shouted her father.

Cassie thrust both sticks against her knees and *Bertha* skidded backwards, fishtailing like crazy, then gained traction, reversing smoothly. Cassie watched the swamp recede into the distance, its churned-up edge already flattening out, soon to form a fresh dry crust and pose a hazard to the unwary once again. She braked only when she had put several hundred metres between it and *Bertha*. Then she sat and took several big, deep breaths to calm her racing heartbeat.

Her brothers started jabbering, all three of them at once, veering between relief and rage.

Den told them to be quiet, then asked his daughter how she was doing.

'I be fine,' Cassie replied.

'Good. It were a near thing but you came through.' The praise was cautious and reserved. Cassie knew she would be in for a stern talking-to later, but for now her father simply wanted his children to understand that the crisis was past and they were safe and sound. 'Maybe you'm done enough driving for one day, girl. Martin and you swap places.'

With mixed feelings Cassie vacated the driver's pod and elbowed through the murk-comber's crawl-ducts to the rear right observation nacelle. She met Martin coming the other way. All he did was give her a sarcastic wink as he squeezed past.

The wink said that none of her brothers was going to let her forget this. They'd be ragging her about it for some while. She probably wasn't going to be allowed to drive again for some while, either.

She resigned herself to that.

'Head for town, Mart,' said Den, with a sigh. 'Let's call off today as a bad job.'

Martin brought *Bertha* around and started homeward at a stately trundle.

Cassie, glum in her observation nacelle, stared dully at the retreating landscape. Not even *Bertha*'s cackle could console her at this moment.

That was when she saw him.

Flickering into and out of the beam of a floodlight.

A boy.

At first she thought she had imagined him. Must have.

But there he was again, further away now, running in a line perpendicular to *Bertha*'s course. And then Cassie spotted a series of pale, skulking shapes loping along after him, a couple of hundred paces behind.

Verms. Verms on the hunt.

'Da,' Cassie said into the speaker tube, urgently. 'Da, us has to stop. There be someone out there, and him's in trouble.'

CHAPTER 23

Verm Attack

What they actually were, verms, remained open to debate. The creatures they most resembled were rats – large, hairless rats with puckered little slits where there had once been eyes, till nature decided these were surplus to requirements. At the same time, they grunted like pigs and worked in packs like dogs. Their blindness, and the fact that they lived in underground burrows, made everyone think they must somehow be related to moles. Their large, semi-translucent ears suggested there was bat somewhere in their family tree.

It could be that they were some ghastly hybrid of all these species, misbegotten things, grotesque evolutionary fusions.

Whatever their origin and ancestry, though, verms were uniquely suited to life in the Shadow Zones. They didn't require light to see by, they thrived in dirt and sogginess, and they were very unchoosy about what they ate. In fact, when there was no other source of food available, quite often they ate each other.

Of all the many hazards you might encounter in a Shadow Zone, a pack of hungry verms was by far the worst. They mostly stayed clear of the main roads to the Chancels because the noise of traffic hurt their sensitive ears. But step off the road, venture out onto the open plain, travel across a Shadow Zone on foot, alone, without the protection of a murk-comber around you – you were asking to become verm dinner.

As, it seemed, this boy was.

To Cassie, now ensconced in one of the front observation nacelles, the boy didn't even realise he was being stalked. Nor did he understand that *Cackling Bertha* was a potential source of safety. He was blundering and stumbling heedlessly along, while the verms were gaining on him with every second. If he had known they were on his trail, he would surely have been running. Not that anyone could outrun verms once those creatures accelerated to top speed.

Martin had spun *Bertha* around and locked her on a course that would intersect with the boy's, as long as the boy kept going in a straight line. Robert and Fletcher, meanwhile, were down in the loading bay, kitting themselves out in retrieval suits. Cassie wanted to do something more than simply sit there like a useless lump, so she clambered back through the murk-comber and hauled herself up into the roof turret, where she found her father hunched at the controls of the javelin launcher. He had the verms in his sights and was swivelling the barrel of the launcher in order to keep them there. His thumb was over the trigger, but he would take the shot only if he had to. Javelins were expensive and the Grubdollars couldn't afford to deploy one unless it was absolutely necessary.

'What be him up to anyway?' Den said, glancing over his shoulder at Cassie. 'Out taking a nice evening stroll?'

'How should I know, Da?'

They both heard Martin let out a hiss of exasperation. 'Him's only gone and turned the wrong way. Back here, you bugger! *Towards* we, not away!'

The boy had veered off to the side, having suddenly noticed *Bertha*'s approach and taken fright. The verms, sensing his panic, picked up their pace. Ordinarily they would have been scared off by a murk-comber coming so close to them, but bloodlust overrode their natural caution. They were thinking about their prey, nothing else.

Cassie could hear them even above *Bertha*'s engine. The verms were squealing and yipping in their excitement. There were at least two dozen of them and they moved flowingly, the whole pack operating like a single organism, twenty-odd animals thinking as one. Now they were mere metres from the boy, and they broke into a sprint, a last burst of speed before the fatal pounce.

'Da…'

'I know, Cass.'

Den took careful aim and fired. The javelin sailed straight and true, spearing the verm who was running at the head of the pack. The creature somersaulted forwards and tried to get up, but the javelin had impaled it through the ribcage, the barbed tip poking clean out the other side. The verm was already dead, it just didn't realise yet. It snapped its jaws uselessly at the protruding haft of the javelin, then rolled over and lay still.

The effect on the other verms was instantaneous. They swarmed around the corpse of their fallen packmate and began devouring. The boy was temporarily forgotten. The verms had been distracted by the scent of blood from a fresh kill.

'That should hold they,' said Den, 'for a bit.'

Cassie, without needing to be asked, selected a new javelin from the rack behind her and slotted it into the groove of the launcher, while her father primed the air-pressure pump for the next shot.

With the verms otherwise engaged for now, Martin was able to put *Bertha* between them and the boy, using her bulk to block him from their view. By this time Robert and Fletcher were ready. The loading bay hatch went up with a clang and they emerged from the murk-comber's belly in their padded retrieval suits, with their helmets and their chainmail gloves on. They made for the boy as quickly as the cumbersome suits would allow, wading through the air like it was water. As they caught up with him, he turned and stared, apparently unable to comprehend who or what they were. Then, just like that, he keeled over. Fletcher caught him before he hit the ground, hoisted him over his shoulder, and began lugging him back to *Bertha*.

Cassie checked on the verm situation and was appalled to see that they had finished feasting and were on the prowl again. All that was left of their dead packmate was a few bloodied bones and some twists of intestine. With gore-smeared chops the verms picked their way anxiously towards *Cackling Bertha*. Their snouts were up and sniffing. They were back on the boy's scent.

'Dammit, look at that,' said Cassie's father. 'Them's gone separate ways.'

Some unguessable instinct had prompted the pack to split into two and go around *Bertha*. They were still keeping a wary distance from the murk-comber but they were close enough to make a clean shot difficult. The angle from the roof turret to them was too steep.

'Electrify *Bertha*'s hull?' Cassie suggested.

'Thought of that,' said her father, 'but them'd have to be a whole lot nearer. Touching her, in fact. Nope, there be nothing else for it now. It'm up to those two lads. Them needs to get a wiggle on.'

Robert and Fletcher were certainly heading for the murk-comber as fast as they could. They knew they were in danger, but perhaps not how much danger. They certainly had no idea the verms would be coming at them from two directions at once.

Cassie had an urge to hammer on the glass of the roof turret and yell at her brothers to hurry up. With their helmets on, however, they would never hear her. They probably wouldn't see her either, since the helmet visors gave them such a restricted view.

There must be *something* she could do.

Decisively, she spun round and hurled herself down the ladder that led from the turret to the loading bay. Above, her father shouted, 'Cass, where'm you off to? No!' But it was too late. Sliding down the uprights rather than using the rungs, she reached the foot of the ladder in an instant. Crossing the loading bay, she grabbed the first pair of chainmail gloves she could find and shoved them on. Then she headed for the open hatchway, just as Robert and Fletcher came staggering up to *Bertha*'s side.

The dank, foetid stink of the Shadow Zone filled her nostrils as she leapt to the ground.

'Cass!' Robert cried, voice muffled by the helmet. 'What'm you doing? Get back inside!'

'The verms!' she replied. 'Them's going to—'

All at once, her warning was redundant. The divided verm pack appeared, half of them to the front of *Bertha*, half to the rear. With a rush the two half packs converged on the group of humans at *Bertha*'s flank, yelping with ravenous glee.

Robert lunged for the loading bay, Fletcher following with the boy.

Then Fletcher tripped. His foot struck a rock and he crashed to one knee. The boy tumbled from his arms.

Fletcher was back on both feet almost straight away. The brief hiatus, however, nearly cost him his life. He bent over to scoop up the boy, unaware that there was a verm just a metre or so away from him. The creature's hindquarters were coiled. It was tensed to jump.

And jump it did. It sprang at Fletcher's neck, jaws wide, fangs bared, and would have torn his throat out …

… had Cassie not thrust a chainmailed fist in the way.

The verm clamped its mouth shut on her hand. The pressure was immense. Her hand was bring crushed. She could feel the small bones in there grinding together. The verm was hanging off her arm by its teeth, gnawing at the chainmail, desperate to bite through. It was grunting with effort and frustration. Grey slobber leaked from its mouth onto the glove. The stench of its breath! Like rotten meat and rancid vegetables and wounds gone gangrenous.

Cassie was repulsed, nauseated. She had to get the verm off her any way she could. She shook her arm violently, but the verm held fast. She punched the side of its skull with her other fist. That nearly did the trick. The verm yowled in protest, but still would not budge.

Nothing else for it.

Cassie jabbed a rigid index finger into its ear.

The verm quivered in agony. Cassie dug her finger further in. The verm shrieked in pain and indignation. Hooking the finger, Cassie wormed it around in the creature's ear canal, using the chainmail to scrape and scour the delicate inner tissues.

At last the verm let go, falling to the ground and writhing there, helpless with agony. Blood was streaming out of its ear. Blood was also dripping from Cassie's finger, along with scraps of flesh. Fighting her disgust, she looked up. Her struggle with the verm had lasted just a handful of seconds, although it had seemed much longer. Robert was leaning out of the loading bay and Fletcher was passing the boy to him. Fletcher then leapt aboard *Bertha* and stretched out a hand to Cassie.

'Come on, Cass. Quick!'

Cassie took a couple of steps towards him. Then her father appeared in the hatchway, brandishing a javelin.

'Duck,' he said, in a tone of voice that didn't expect her to disobey.

She didn't. She ducked.

The javelin shot over her head, and she heard a shrill howl behind her. She didn't look round. There had been a verm at her back, about to attack. Now it was an ex-verm. Good. She leapt for the hatchway. Robert and Fletcher grabbed her wrists and she went flying into the loading bay, crash-landing on her chest. There was a huge, resounding *clunk* as the hatch came down. This was followed by a series of slobbering, snacking sounds from outside as the verms turned on another dead packmate, as before, and feasted.

'Be you OK, kids?' Den asked.

Robert, Fletcher and Cassie all announced that they were fine.

'Cass,' said Fletcher, 'I owes you one. Thanks, girl. That verm'd've had me, straight up, if not for you.'

Nodding, Cassie removed the gloves and began massaging her mauled hand. It ached and was reddened in that way that promised bruises later. But that didn't matter. What mattered was that she had saved Fletcher's life. By doing so, she also felt she had redeemed herself after nearly killing the whole family earlier. Her father, at any rate, was looking at her forgivingly – as forgivingly as someone with Den's craggy, grizzled features could. He was perhaps even proud of her, although he was never the kind of man to say such a thing.

He grabbed a nearby speaker tube. 'Martin? Us is all aboard, safe and sound. Let's go.'

As *Bertha* started to move, Den turned and peered at the boy. 'So who be this then, what'm caused us so much trouble?' He nudged the sprawled, unconscious body. 'Dead to the world. But breathing still. Wet through, too. Grab a blanket for he, will you, Cass? There'm a girl. Cover he up and keep he warm. Can't have the lad perishing of rattle-lung. And once us is back in Grimvale, us can look for somebody who might know who him be.'

CHAPTER 24

Waiting

In the administrative offices of the supply-arrival depot at Heliotropia, a clock ticked slowly. Distressingly slowly, as though seconds here took ten times as long to pass as they did anywhere else. Michael sat, stood up, paced, sat down again, went outside for a breath of air, came back in, sat, tapped his teeth with his fingernails, tried to amuse himself by reading documents on the supervisor's desk (till Mr Mordadson told him to stop it), spent a few minutes de-fluffing his wings, another few minutes picking at a loose bit of cuticle on his thumb, another few minutes thinking about work and the fuselage stress-fracturing problem that was giving the Aerodyne design team so much grief on the new model ...

None of it made the time go any more quickly. Michael, not a naturally patient person, hated waiting, and this wait was especially difficult. It was nearly eight o'clock. Az was due back around midnight. What if he didn't come back? How was Michael supposed to break the news to their parents? They hadn't a clue what Az was doing, why Lady Aanfieldsdaughter had wanted him. If it all went wrong, if Az failed to make it back, Michael would not only have to cope with that fact, but he would have to return to High Haven and explain everything, and then his mother and father would no doubt want to know how he could have let it happen, how he could let Az, his own brother, their only other son, travel down to the ground. They would be angry. They were likely to blame *him* rather than anyone else.

Aurora Jukarsdaughter intruded delicately on his thoughts. 'Maybe we should go and get something to eat. Michael?'

'Hmm?'

'Something to eat?'

'But—'

'Don't worry,' said Mr Mordadson. 'I'm not hungry. I'll stay here. You two go off.'

In a restaurant somewhere along one of Heliotropia's garish main avenues, beneath the flashing, cascading brilliance of a multiplicity of coloured lights, Michael shared a meal with Aurora. At any other time, under any other circumstances, he would have been overjoyed and would have been chatting her up for all he was worth. Now? He toyed with his food, and his conversation with the beautiful girl across the table was desultory at best.

Still, somehow he managed to glean a little bit about her. She was exceptionally intelligent, having graduated top of her year at Cloud 9 University, with honours. The Silver Sanctum had recruited her straight from there, and she was evidently on the fast track to the highest levels of government. Otherwise, why would she be Lady Aanfielsdaughter's personal assistant?

Next to her, Michael felt like an underachiever and a bit of a dimwit. After all, what as he? A test pilot, yes. And it was a glamorous occupation but it hardly required much use of your brain and it had a limited career span. You couldn't stick at it much past 35, when your reflexes started to slow. And then what? You were too young to retire and too old to start again from scratch. You were washed up. Weren't you?

'I think that's the first glimpse I've had of the real Michael Gabrielson,' Aurora said as he outlined these doubts and insecurities. Her smile was nothing short of dazzling. 'I think I like him. Much more than the Michael Gabrielson you normally present to the world.'

The remark buoyed Michael up considerably. He felt, at that moment, that he could have flown even if, like Az, he'd had no wings.

The recollection of his brother dampened his spirits again. Az, down there on the ground, alone ...

'Cheer up,' said Aurora, gently patting his hand. 'He's going to be fine.'

Some dreadful gut instinct, however, was telling Michael otherwise.

CHAPTER 25

Grimvale

Rain had set in by the time *Cackling Bertha* reached Grimvale – the kind of creeping, insidious rain that was going to last all night and probably well into the next day, rain that fell without hurrying, a humid seep from the sky.

In Grimvale Forest the boughs of the thin, scraggly pine trees sagged and dripped like the limbs of exhausted, sweaty labourers. *Bertha* trundled along an old, paved road, her track links clanking. The route took her past several lumberyards, and outside the entrance to each there was a Humanist picket. The Humanists didn't look very happy to be there in this weather. Gathered round blazing braziers, they stood with hunched backs, warming their hands. Some had waterproofs on, others had draped tarpaulins over their shoulders. By the light of the braziers Cassie saw eyes staring out from beneath hoods, aiming surly looks at the murk-comber. The Grubdollars were not breaking the goods embargo; they weren't transporting materials to the Chancel. They were, however, employed by the Deacons to scavenge in the Shadow Zone, and so in principle they weren't on the picketers' side.

Or so the picketers thought, till Martin hooted *Bertha*'s horn in a show of solidarity. Then there were raised hands and clenched-fist salutes around the braziers, as the picketers saw that this wasn't just any old murk-comber but *Cackling Bertha*, and were reminded that at least one person aboard her was sympathetic to their cause.

Each time Martin hit the horn, Den shouted at him to pack it in. But Martin would not be stopped, and Fletcher backed him up, arguing that it was his right to support the picketers if he wished.

'This be a family after all, Da,' Fletcher said, 'not a dictatorship.'

'I'll dictate *you* in a minute,' their father growled. The threat didn't make any sense but it was menacing nonetheless. 'Straight up, if your ma were alive today to see two of her boys showing Humanist tendencies ...'

'Be'n't she alive, Da?' said Fletcher, as sarcastically as he dared. He wouldn't have been so bold if his father had been directly in front of him, rather than at the other end of a speaker tube. 'Be'n't she watching down on us from above the clouds as one of the Ascended Ones, in her new body, with her new wings?'

Whatever Den might have replied to that, was lost beneath another blast on *Bertha*'s horn. Now Martin was sending a friendly message to a picket outside a coalmine which stood on the fringes of Grimvale Township itself. In response he got a low, ragged cheer from the picketers.

A short while after that, the Grubdollars arrived home.

The property consisted of a large courtyard where they could park *Bertha*, with just enough space on every side to allow maintenance and repairs to be carried out on her. Her loading bay hatch opened directly onto a raised concrete dock, which extended out from a storage area where tools and spare parts were kept and where, also, salvage was stockpiled before being taken to the Chancel.

While Robert closed the huge portcullis gate that secured the courtyard, Den carried the still unconscious boy across the dock. He took him up via a spiralling iron staircase into the family's living quarters, which surmounted the storage area, and there, in the lounge, stripped off the boy's damp clothes, leaving just his underpants on. He laid the boy's semi-naked form out on the creaky-springed couch and got Cassie to fetch a fresh, dry blanket for him. Then he spent several moments peering down at the youngster with a puzzled frown.

'It'm odd,' he said, scratching his stubble-covered chin.

'Him just doesn't look like him's from around here. Doesn't look rough enough around the edges, if you see what I mean. Delicate, kind of. And those clothes as well. Them's decent clothes, more decent than you usually see. Likely as not him's come from the Chancel or some such. But that still begs the question: what were him doing out in the Zone?'

'What about a doctor?' Cassie asked. 'Shouldn't us get him medical attention?'

'At this time of night? You'd be lucky. Besides, doctors costs money. If the lad takes a turn for the worse, then I'll think about it. But otherwise us can look after he, don't you think?'

Cassie didn't answer that. She had a feeling only one of the family would be doing any looking after, and it would be her.

'Now, how about some supper?' said her father. 'Can't speak for anyone else but I be famished.'

Cassie heated up some Last Chance Stew, which was an accumulation of leftover bits and pieces from previous meals that she couldn't afford to throw away and couldn't think of anything else to do with. Her verm-gnawed hand ached, so she had to do the work single-handed in more ways than one. She set bowls of the stew before her father and brothers at the kitchen table and watched them slurp it down so fast they barely seemed to taste it. They shovelled in mouthfuls of bread and butter at the same time, and glugged down pint-pots of beer. There was no conversation till the meal was finished and bellies were full, and then Martin broke the silence by letting out a long, resonant belch.

'Not bad,' he said, smacking his lips. 'Gets better with every warming, in fact. It'm got kind of a more *lived-in* flavour now.'

Cassie knew this was the nearest thing she would get to a compliment on her cooking. Mostly her family took her culinary efforts for granted. Never a word of thanks escaped their lips for the time she put in at the stove, although she was sure that if she served them up something truly disgusting they wouldn't hesitate to tell her what they thought about *that*.

'Now Fletch,' said her father, as he sat back, loosening his belt a notch, 'you happens to notice something about that lad next door when you was carrying he?'

Fletcher looked puzzled. 'What do you mean, Da?'

'Well, maybe it be as I don't knows my own strength, but it seems him don't weigh nearly almost anything.'

'Can't say as I were in a way to notice such a thing,' Fletcher said, 'on account of there were a pack of verms snapping at the seat of my trousers at the time. But now's you mention it ... him weren't what you might calls heavy.'

'It be a mystery all right,' Martin said, although his tone of voice suggested it wasn't a mystery that intrigued him much. With a quick glance at Fletcher, he shoved back his chair and stood up. 'Da, OK if me'n Fletch heads off to the pub? I mean, if there'm nothing you needs us for ...'

Den Grubollar's eyes went hard and narrow. 'The pub, eh?'

'Yeah, Da,' Fletcher said, standing too. 'Just for a pint or so, like.'

'Any particular pub in mind? You wouldn't be heading down to the Logger's Head, say, by any chance?'

Cassie watched her two brothers exchange a furtive look.

'Well, might be the Logger's Head, might not,' said Martin, airily. 'Can't say as us has decided.'

'Sounds to me like you has. And this'm be the Logger's Head where it just so happen them Humanists is holding a rally this evening?'

Again a furtive look, although both brothers were wearing guilty expressions now.

'Go on then,' their father said with an irritated growl. 'You be old enough to know your own minds, even if you be'n't old enough to know better. Them's a dangerous lot, them Humanists, I'll tell you that. Trying to upset the status quo, them are, and it'm be the ruin of us all if them succeeds. There'm a balance in the way things are. Be'n't perfect, but it be a balance nonetheless, and it'm lasted this long because it works. You go about upsetting that at your peril. But why listen to your old da? What's *him* know about anything? Only raised you all on his tod, him did. Only ...'

Martin and Fletcher, by this point, were long gone. Den's voice trailed off as he acknowledged that he was delivering his lecture to a pair of empty chairs.

Cassie looked over at Robert, who had his head down and was subjecting the surface of the kitchen table to intense scrutiny. Neither of them knew what to say. Their father hated the fact that his two older sons had fallen under the Humanists' sway, and there had recently been some savage rows between him and them on the topic. He understood that the family was going to stay together only if Martin and Fletcher were allowed the freedom to pursue whatever political beliefs they wanted. Equally, those beliefs could end up tearing the Grubdollars apart anyway. Sooner or later Martin and Fletcher might come to the conclusion that murk-combing on the Chancel's behalf was not compatible with Humanism, and would refuse to carry on working in the family business.

So Den was in a no-win position, and that pained him.

'If their ma could see they ...' he said finally, with a sigh. And that was that. Subject closed.

For now.

CHAPTER 26

The Humanist Rally

'Half,' said Alan Steamarm. 'One half. One half of everything we dig out and chop down and drill for and smelt and refine. One half of it goes up in those elevators. One half of our worldly goods disappears into the clouds. And what for? What do we get in return?'

He paused, allowing the questions time to echo around the room. The rally was extremely well attended. The function room upstairs at the Logger's Head was packed, and there were people on the landing outside, craning their necks to get a view through the doorway. Not only that but there were people downstairs in the bar who hadn't been able to get up to the first floor at all. Steamarm planned to chat with them later, informally. He made a mental note: *next time, arrange a bigger venue.*

'I'll tell you what we get in return,' he said. 'Nothing. Absolutely nothing. Nothing but false hopes and empty promises. The Deacons tell us that making these sacrifices is the only way to guarantee our passage to the next life. They insist this is true. They've been insisting it since time immemorial. But then, they would, wouldn't they? They're no fools. Their position, their status, depends entirely on them being intermediaries between us and what's up there.'

He made a gesture that was a parody of a Deacon's blessing – hand held loosely open, a skyward flourish. It got a ripple of laughter, the audience marvelling at his nerve.

'And they make sure they get their cut from us. A tithe from us when we die. And in return for ten per cent of our savings, ten per cent of our worldly goods, plus a bodyweight's worth of supplies – in return for this *taxation*, there's no other word for it, this *taxation* – they carry out their mumbo-jumbo with the oil and the feathers, and up in smoke we go … and then they go back to sitting snug and smug in their Chancels and laughing at us behind our backs. Mocking our gullibility. They can't believe we keep falling for it, and yet we do. We want to believe in a next life, we want to become Ascended Ones, we want to ensure this for ourselves and our kin, and that's what they take advantage of. That's how they've been exploiting us for centuries. Centuries! And do you know what I say?'

Steamarm raised his voice, and also a fist.

'I say, "No more!" I say, "Enough!" It's time we stopped letting them get away with it. It's time we kept everything that's ours for ourselves and stopped giving half of it away. The ones who are up there above the clouds – let them fend for themselves. Let them go without. I, for one, don't want to join them after I die, assuming that's what actually happens. Not if it means I buy my next life at the expense of people in *this* life. That's not fair. It's never been fair.'

The crowd were grumbling and chattering indignantly now. Steamarm had them in the palm of his hand. He could feel his rhetoric spreading through them, one to another, like a flame, firing up their resentment, igniting dormant grudges. It was a delicious sensation, this ability to motivate audiences, to rouse them to anger. Steamarm was becoming quite addicted to it.

'Brothers, sisters,' he said, bringing his speech to a conclusion, 'the hour is almost upon us. I've been touring the region, and I've been keeping in touch with my fellow Humanist leaders, and let me tell you, there's a groundswell building up. All across the Westward Territories, we're mobilising, and it won't be long before we're taking assertive action. Pickets are just the start. The next step is insurgency. I invite you, I *urge* you, to join me in the struggle. Together, united, we can overthrow the tyranny of the Deacons. We can expose their religious so-called orthodoxies for the lies they are. We can usher in a new age – a fairer, wealthier, more rational age. And we can all be happier and freer as a result. What's ours should be ours. That's the Humanist motto, the movement's call to arms. What's ours should be ours. Let's make that statement come true. Thank you.'

Tremendous applause followed, whistles and foot-stamps adding to the deafening din of handclaps. Steamarm accepted the ovation with a reluctant bow, as if he wasn't – OK, he *was* worthy of it. Before the applause could die down completely he made his exit, passing through the ranks of the audience. By the time he reached the door his back was sore from all the slaps it had received.

Downstairs, Steamarm mingled with the Humanist supporters who hadn't managed to attend the rally. There was no shortage of offers to buy him a drink, but as it happened, his beers were on the house tonight. The pub landlord was doing a roaring trade thanks to all the extra customers whom Steamarm's presence had attracted. The least he could do in exchange was give Steamarm free booze.

Steamarm was accosted by a couple of young men, brothers, who introduced themselves as Martin and Fletcher Grubdollar and said how sorry they were that they hadn't got the chance to hear him speak upstairs. They'd arrived at the pub too late. They wanted him to know, however, that they were ardent Humanists. They said they felt that in this day and age there was no worthier cause a person could follow.

'Us deals with them Deacons on a daily basis pretty much,' said Martin. 'Right bunch of stuck-up ponces them is, too. It'm like, sometimes you gets the feeling them's doing we a favour just speaking to we.'

'Wouldn't mind seeing that lot out of a job,' added Fletcher, 'even if it means us is out of a job too. Us can always find something else to do. It'm the principle of the thing, be'n't it?'

'You work in transportation, then? You'm ferrying stuff to the Chancels?' Steamarm wasn't ordinarily the sort to use grammar like *you'm*, but he had learned long ago the value of careful mimickry. In one-to-one conversations people responded well if you met them at their own verbal level.

'Nope, not transportation,' said Martin. 'Murk-combing.'

'Really?' All at once the two Grubdollar brothers had Steamarm's undivided attention. He wasn't just making polite chitchat with them any more. 'That's a tough business to be in, straight up. Those Shadow Zones are pretty perilous places.'

Fletcher gave a manful shrug. 'Hard work but it pay the bills.'

'You must be fascinated by some of the items you retrieve. Pieces of machinery, detritus from above ...'

'Relics, as the Deacons calls it.'

'Indeed.'

'It'm fallen a long, long way. Most of it gets mashed up on impact. But still, us has seen some strange bits and bobs, hasn't us, Fletch? Like, pages from books. Shoes. A saucepan.'

'Pair of lady's undergarments,' said Fletcher. He and Martin sniggered at the recollection.

'And perhaps a body or two?'

'That us has, Alan. By the way, I can call you Alan?'

'Of course you can, Fletcher.'

'Yes, us has retrieved bodies,' Fletcher went on, 'although there never be much left by the time us finds they. Verms has gnashed most of the tasty parts. But the Deacons pays top whack even for a broke-up skeleton. Then there was that time us hauled part of a car, or something like, out of a soft patch.'

'Some kind of flying vehicle, it were,' Martin chipped in. 'Got a tidy little sum for that, us did.'

'So it'm a funny old game, murk-combing, but us likes it enough. Though not so much as us couldn't live without it.'

'It doesn't trouble you, then,' said Steamarm, 'that we live in a world where objects fall out of the sky on us and we're supposed to treat them as holy artefacts?'

'Earns we a wage, them objects,' said Martin. 'But now you mention it, yeah, it do trouble we. Which is why us is all for Humanism. You know, because why should us have to put up with being the underlings? The underclass? Them's what gives so much and gets back the privilege of living in' – he searched for the right word – 'somebody else's trash bin?'

'I couldn't have put it better myself. "The privilege of living in somebody else's trash bin." I shall use that phrase in a future speech, Martin. Thank you.'

Martin preened with pride.

'So you own your own murk-comber, I take it.'

'Yes. Well, sort of. It'm our da's, and it were his da's before him. But us all works with it, the whole family, so I suppose you could say it belongs to all of we.'

'That's good, that's good.' Steamarm was studying both brothers with avid interest now. 'Boys, how are you off for drinks? You seem thirsty. Let me get you something. And then I think us needs to talk, us three. Us needs to sit down in a quiet corner and have a good long chinwag ...'

CHAPTER 27

Housebound

Cassie wasn't sure why she volunteered to watch over the boy. She was bone-weary and her nice, warm bed was calling to her. It seemed like the right thing to do, however. If the boy came round in the middle of the night, in a place that was unfamiliar to him, it would help if there was a friendly face beside him. She realised, too, that if she didn't play nursemaid, nobody else was going to.

She drew up an armchair next to the couch, huddled under a blanket, and promptly fell asleep.

She was roused, briefly, by Martin and Fletcher returning home in the small hours. They were drunk, to judge by the way they yelled at each other while clearly under the impression that they were whispering.

She sank into sleep once more, assuring herself that if the boy woke up, she would sense it and wake up too.

Then: daybreak. Outside the lounge window the sky was brightening to its customary hazy grey pallor. It was still raining. Droplets rattled softly against the panes. Cassie hauled herself from the chair and stretched various kinks and knots out of her body. She flexed her injured hand and found that it was in better shape than she'd expected. Overnight, bruising had formed, U-shaped purple patches on the back and palm denoting the pattern of the verm's teeth, but the hand was functional and didn't ache too badly any more.

The boy remained comatose. Cassie prepared toast and tea for everybody, and there was the usual groggy breakfast around the kitchen table. Martin and Fletcher were obviously hungover, and their father commented on this, saying he hoped they were feeling rotten because they deserved to. Neither of them could muster a comeback, but Cassie did catch Martin firing a surreptitious grin at Fletcher, which Fletcher returned. She said nothing, but it was clear the two brothers were sharing some kind of secret.

'What be us up to today?' she asked her father. 'Off into the Zone again?'

He nodded yes. 'Got to keep trying. Our luck'll surely turn soon. Except that you, girl, be'n't coming with we. You be staying at home today.'

'What!' Cassie couldn't believe her ears.

Her father jerked his head in the direction of the lounge. 'Someone has to keep an eye on that boy till him recovers. You'm best qualified for the job.'

'But – but—'

'Going to leave he to the tender mercies of one of your brothers, eh? Don't think so. Sorry, lass, no arguments. You be staying and that be final.'

Cassie bristled at the injustice of this. She couldn't help but think she was being punished in some way for the near-disaster yesterday.

Her sense of outrage was not at all lessened by Fletcher saying, with a smirk, 'Better you in charge of he than in charge of *Bertha*.'

'Yeah,' Martin chimed in, 'though likely as not you'll kill he just like you nearly killed *we*.'

'Buggers! Buggers the lot of you!' Cassie yelled, and stormed out of the room.

After *Bertha* left with the four male Grubdollars aboard, Cassie sulked in her bedroom, refusing to pay attention to the boy. Since he was the source of all her woes, she got a petty satisfaction out of ignoring him. But eventually the novelty of sulking wore off, so she went round the house tidying up and putting away. The only rooms she left untouched were her brothers'. Being young men, they appeared to enjoy living in squalor, surrounded by a knee-deep debris of unwashed socks, dirty teacups, and worse. Every so often one of them would complain about his own mess, as though it was someone else's fault. Seldom did the complaint lead to positive action, however.

Her father was a different story. Cassie didn't mind cleaning up after him. Not only did he at least make some effort to keep his room in order, but as a widower there was a helplessness about him when it came to domestic matters. The wife who should have been looking after him was not around to do so any more, and Cassie could tell that he still missed her, even after twelve years. In so many ways he missed her.

While she was straightening the counterpane on her father's bed, Cassie's gaze fell on the framed picture of her mother that sat on the dressing table. It was a mezzotint etching which had been commissioned by her mother's parents, Cassie's grandparents, as a gift to her on her twenty-first birthday.

Orla Grubdollar had been a very pretty woman. Not beautiful, but she had a kindly face and a mischievous twinkle in her eyes, which the artist had skilfully captured. It was often remarked how like her Cassie looked, but Cassie couldn't see the resemblance herself. Mirrors showed her a slightly chunky girl, round-faced, with a tendency to frown and with a crop of wayward hair that didn't fall in an elegant sweep like her mother's in the picture. She would have liked to look like her mother but doubted she did or ever would.

Rattle-lung had taken Cassie's mother when Cassie was just three years old. Within a week of contracting the disease, Orla Grubdollar was dead. Cassie could remember nothing about this, and very little about her mother in general. She had no visual memories of her to fall back on, just a collection of faint, non-visual impressions. A voice, trilling a song. A certain fragrance. The enfolding embrace of two warm arms. And the only reason she even knew that these were impressions of her mother was because whenever she thought about them she felt a deep, sharp pang of yearning. If not for that, she would have assumed they were things her imagination had conjured up to fill the space where her mother should have been.

For better, for worse, Cassie was the mother in this family now ...

A creak of couch springs roused her from her reverie.

The boy was lying in the lounge with his eyes wide open, staring around. How long he had been like this, awake, Cassie had no way of knowing.

She stifled her resentment of him just enough to sound civil. 'Oh, hello there. Hungry?'

The boy frowned, puzzled. He let out a cracked, dry sound from his throat. Some kind of question, but Cassie couldn't make sense of it.

The boy tried to frame the question again, but it was no good. He was too hoarse.

'Thirsty?' Cassie asked.

He managed a nod.

She brought him a glass of water and tipped it up to his lips.

'Just sips,' she said, but the boy seized the glass and gulped the whole lot down.

Next thing Cassie knew, he was puking on the floor.

'I said just sips,' she sighed, and went to fetch a cloth.

By the time she got back, he had lapsed into insensibility again. She mopped up the vomit, glowering at him all the while.

A little later, he came to again, and she tried him with the water again. This time he sipped, as instructed, and was able to hold it down. She reheated what remained of the Last Chance Stew and fed him a few spoonfuls. This, too, he held down. She didn't try to engage him in conversation; it seemed he hadn't the energy for that yet, and she had no great urge to chat with him anyway. She concentrated solely on helping him get his strength back. The sooner he recovered, the sooner he would be out of the house and not her problem any more. Then life could return to normal. The boy was an imposition and she wanted him gone.

He slept once more. It was midday, and by now Cassie was beginning to get a little stir-crazy, so much so that she decided to launder the boy's damp clothing, just for a distraction.

As she rinsed out his shirt in the sink, she remembered her father's remark about the boy's clothes. 'More decent than you usually see,' he had said, and he was right. The stitching on the shirt was finer than any Cassie had ever beheld, and the cloth it was made from was glossily smooth and had a good, tight weave. The clothes which she and her family and everyone she knew wore were much coarser. Only someone with money could afford a shirt like this, which gave credibility to her father's assumption that the boy came from the Chancel. But there weren't children at the Chancel, were there? The youngest age at which a novice could join was twenty-one. The boy was a good half-decade shy of that.

She held the shirt up to the window to get a better look at it, and noticed something odd. In the back of it there were two long slits which had been sewn up, starting from where the shoulderblades sat and going almost the whole way down to the shirttail. The stitching there was not the same as everywhere else: it had been done with a different thread, and by hand rather than by machine.

Why would you alter a shirt this way?

No, that was the wrong question.

'Why would you *make* a shirt with two long slits in the back?'

Cassie asked herself the question aloud without realising it. She also answered it aloud.

And her answer stunned her, and at the same time raised a host of fresh questions.

'For wings,' she said. 'You'd make it like that to fit wings.'

CHAPTER 28

Genesis Of A Revelation

'*Somebody's* responsible for this!' snarled Michael. 'And I know who!'

'Calm yourself, Michael,' said Mr Mordadson. 'Please. There's no need to go flying off the handle.'

'No need? *No need?* Pluck you!'

Red-faced, wild-eyed, Michael lunged for the Silver Sanctum emissary. He couldn't see straight. He was blind with distress and anger.

With a flicker of his wings, Mr Mordadson darted out of Michael's way. As Michael hurtled past, Mr Mordadson grabbed his wrist and his wing root. *Flip, shove, thump* – Michael was on his belly on the floor, with Mr Mordadson on his back, holding him down. Michael squirmed, but the combination of arm-lock and wing-lock was unbeatable. For all that Mr Mordadson was slender and none too tall, he possessed a surprising strength and nimbleness.

'Combat and self-defence training,' he said to Michael. 'I was in the Alar Patrol before I joined the Sanctum. I have the hoop scars in my wings to prove it, in case you doubt me.'

'Let me up, you four-eyed bustard!' Michael snarled.

'I will if you promise to be a good boy and behave yourself. You're upset, and I quite understand why. Believe me, I'm as concerned about Azrael as you are.'

'Az is dead! He should have come back twelve hours ago, and he hasn't, and he's dead!' Tears sprang to Michael's eyes, and all at once he was sobbing helplessly, burying his face in the administrative office's carpet. 'My ... little brother ...'

'Michael,' said Aurora, kneeling beside him, 'no one meant

for any of this to happen, but there were risks. Az knew that. We all knew that.'

'Easy for you to say ...'

'No, not easy, Michael. Not in the slightest. But still, it has to be said. And Michael ... there's something else.'

Mr Mordadson levelled his gaze at her. 'No, Aurora. I don't think we should tell him.'

'And I think we should. It's only fair.'

'Tell me what?' said Michael.

Aurora, still holding eye contact with Mr Mordadson, said, 'There's a very good chance Az isn't dead.'

'Huh?'

'It could be that he's been ... detained somehow.'

'Detained? What are you talking about, detained?'

'Mr Mordadson's going to release you, and you're going to sit down quietly, and I'm going to explain something to you. All right? And you're going to listen, that's all you're going to do. No histrionics. No fisticuffs. Do we have a deal, Michael?'

'... Yeah.'

Moments later, Michael was in a chair, rubbing the arm which Mr Mordadson had twisted behind his back, and Aurora was speaking to him, and what she had to say astonished him and dispelled the weariness of a sleepless, fretful night, and cut through his grief, and even gave him grounds to be slightly optimistic.

'There are Groundlings?' he said at the end. 'Still?'

'There are. There always have been. It's just been convenient for us to forget that fact.'

In hindsight, the revelation wasn't as shocking to Michael as it had first seemed. Somewhere deep down, on a subconscious level, he had known it all along. Yes, automation could account for the flow of supplies to the sky-cities. It *could*. It was plausible enough. But it didn't really stand up to scrutiny. Machines, unattended, left to themselves, couldn't do everything. They needed overseeing, maintenance, human involvement. As someone involved in aeronautics Michael understood that as well as anyone, if not better than most.

'So it's all just some lie we've been fed,' he said. 'A Silver Sanctum conspiracy. "The Groundlings died out." So that we don't have to think about them, don't have to remember all the time that there are people down there beneath the cloud cover...' He shuddered. 'What can it be like down there? I can't imagine.'

'You're looking at it from the wrong perspective,' Aurora said. 'It isn't a conspiracy. It isn't a case of government influencing public feeling. It's a case of public feeling influencing government. What came first was the Airborn race gradually forgetting about the Groundlings. They slipped from our memory. Whether it was deliberate or not, we stopped being mindful of them.'

'Aurora used the word "convenient",' said Mr Mordadson, 'and that's it in a nutshell. It didn't sit well with people, thinking that there were other people slaving away on their behalf, down below in constant twilight, after the Great Cataclysm. So it became easier – preferable – *convenient* – to imagine that they weren't down there, to say it was machines doing the work and the people themselves had died out.'

'Life up here is wonderful,' Aurora said. 'We have everything we could need, and more. We have luxury. Perpetual sunshine. We work and play, sleep and love, blithely, almost without a care in the world.'

'The Airborn are happy,' said Mr Mordadson. 'We don't even wage wars any more. We seem to have progressed past that, finally. The last conflict between sky-cities was nearly half a century ago, wasn't it? And it was over in seven days and all but bloodless.'

'The Week's War.' Aurora and Mr Mordadson had fallen into a pattern of taking it in turns to speak. 'And there's been peace ever since.'

'And the Silver Sanctum's job is to make sure that state of affairs remains. But it's also to make sure that the Airborn continue their lives of, well, of blissful ignorance.'

'So, while the Sanctum doesn't actively promote the story that the Groundlings are extinct, it doesn't actively deny it either. It lets people continue to believe what they wish to believe. It allows the collective amnesia about the Groundlings to persist because there's nothing to be gained by dispelling it, nothing except distress and disharmony.'

'It's official now, of course. Places like the Museum of Arts, Sciences and History state as fact the myth that there are no more Groundlings, and their exhibits foster the impression of a backward race of beings, not quite sophisticated enough to survive. We choose to let this inaccuracy go uncorrected.'

'In fact, outside of the Sanctum itself, the continued existence of Groundlings is a complete secret.'

'But it's not a conspiracy,' said Mr Mordadson, reiterating Aurora's earlier remark. 'The term suggests a policy of actively hiding the truth, whereas it's actually a policy of passively allowing the truth to fall into disuse. Not the same thing.'

'You see, Michael?' Aurora said. 'And now you're in on the secret, and now you understand why it's possible that Az is still alive.'

'The Groundlings,' Michael said, tonelessly. 'The Groundlings have him.'

'They may well do.'

'Well, what …? I mean, if they do, then … then what can we do about it? Can we get him back?'

Suddenly he shot to his feet.

'The elevators!' he exclaimed. 'I'll go down and look for him.'

'No, Michael,' said Mr Mordadson.

'Just try and stop me.'

'Oh, I will if I have to.' The smile Mr Mordadson gave then was profoundly unnerving, not unlike the leer of a skull. 'And you know I can. I used minimum force to restrain you last time. You wouldn't want me to resort to maximum force. Trust me on that.'

Michael eyed him, weighing up the options. Male pride growled at him not to back down. Common sense, however, gently suggested that he would be wise to heed Mr Mordadson's warning.

'All right.' He resumed his seat. 'Why not, then? Why can't I go down?'

'Several reasons. First and foremost, you have wings. You'd stand out a mile. You'd perhaps make a target of yourself. Az's lack of wings is a sort of camouflage, enabling him to merge with his surroundings. He could pass for a Groundling, you could not. And we can't allow the Groundlings to know yet that we Airborn are interested in them and what they're up to.'

'Because ...?'

'Because, Michael,' said Aurora, 'if you think about it, why are supplies being disrupted? If it isn't a mechanical break-down ...'

Michael made the leap of logic. 'It's the Groundlings. Doing it on purpose. They're angry.'

'Angry, and worse. Possibly mutinous. Possibly starting a rebellion.'

'Rebellion,' said Michael tonelessly.

'We spoke of war a short while ago,' Mr Mordadson said, 'and of our half-century of peace. We're very much afraid, at the Silver Sanctum, that that period may be about to come to an end. In the most devastating manner imaginable.'

CHAPTER 29

Flight

It all seemed like a dream, a sequence of events he had no control over and just had to go along with. At times it wasn't even a dream, more like a nightmare, and there was nothing he could do to snap himself out of it. A nightmare that was actually happening.

As he fled from the room where the Ceremony of Ascension was being held, Az's main impulse was to get back to the chamber with the elevators and jump aboard the first one that opened its doors to him.

He was disorientated, however. His brain felt clogged and muddled. He took a wrong turn. Several wrong turns, indeed. Next thing he knew, he was stumbling through a set of rooms that were sumptuously furnished and decorated. There were marble floors, rich red velvet curtains that hung in opulent swags and were trimmed with gold tassels, oil paintings in beautiful frames, gleamingly polished wooden chairs and tables, teak-cased mantel clocks that would have made his father's mouth water, and shelf upon shelf of leather-bound books. One room led to another, and each was grander than the last. Az found it hard to reconcile all this luxury with the functional, machinery-filled areas he had seen elsewhere in the building. It didn't make sense, having industry and elegance in such close proximity ... did it?

By the time he reached a fourth room, it dawned on him that he wasn't getting any nearer to his destination going this way. He backtracked dazedly. Sometime later he was in a corridor and realised he had no memory of how and when he had got there. He must have faded out for a while and kept going through sheer instinct alone. There was a vibrant hissing sound in his ears. He couldn't tell if it was real or imagined, coming from outside him or within. His vision was filled with blotches of light that swelled and popped like soap bubbles. At the back of his skull a low ache had set in.

'There! There he is!'

The voice that barked these words belonged to one of the two men from the ceremony, the thinner one, Deacon Shatterlonger. Accompanying him were two more Deacons. Shatterlonger was pointing, straight-armed, at Az.

'Stop right there, whoever you are. The Archdeacon would like a word with you. Why were you eavesdropping on us? How did you get in here?'

Az began backing away. He didn't fancy having 'a word' with Archdeacon Corbelgilt. Not in the slightest.

'I told you to stop!' Shatterlonger motioned to the other two Deacons. 'Well, go on. What are you waiting for? Get him.'

The two Deacons moved towards Az. They were neither of them especially big men but their robes lent them a sinister, crow-like look, and they strode with menacing purpose.

Az turned and ...

Another fadeout. He was on a raised steel catwalk. That hissing sound from earlier was now a surging. On either side of him were arrays of huge sealed metal vats, each with the words SEWAGE TREATMENT painted on the side in bold capitals amid streaks of rust. About three metres below him there was a brick channel, like a large half-drainpipe, through which a torrent of brownish water sluiced. He was aware of a rotten odour in the air, and dimly his brain deduced that this was where the waste-water downflow from Heliotropia ended up.

Then he realised that the three Deacons were closing in on him along the catwalk, Shatterlonger coming from one direction, his two colleagues from the other.

'Chase over,' said Shatterlonger, who was looking flustered. There were spots of bright pink in his sallow cheeks. 'We've got you now. Just come quietly. I swear no one means you any harm, boy.'

Az would have liked to believe this but somehow couldn't.

He was cornered. There was no escape route. Or was there?

He pictured himself clambering up onto the catwalk handrail.

No, that's crazy, don't do it.

He pictured himself swinging over and dangling off the other side, above the brick channel.

You don't know where it goes.

He pictured himself letting go and dropping.

It was only when he hit the water below that he realised he hadn't imagined this feat. He had actually done it.

The torrent snatched him like a fist and whisked him along with it, away from the Deacons. They shouted at him but he could barely hear above the liquid tumult engulfing him. He tumbled, sank, rose again, somersaulted, flailed, fought to keep his head above the surface, choking on the water's brackish stink, gasping as it sluiced sickeningly down his throat ...

All at once everything went dark. The channel had become a tunnel, a full pipe. In the enclosed space the surging of the water took on a roaring echo. Az truly believed he was going to drown. He could no longer tell which way was up. He sped along helplessly in the torrent's clutches. Each time his arm happened to strike the side of the tunnel he grabbed out in the hope that there might be something to cling on to, but there was just brickwork. It was slippery-slimy and there were no fissures in it nor any projecting bits, nothing that might serve as a handhold.

The tunnel appeared to be angling downward, getting steeper; the torrent was getting faster.

Then Az was falling.

A huge *splash*, and he was underwater, completely immersed and plunging deeper and deeper, still being rolled this way and that by currents which seemed to take a cruel pleasure in toying with him. He kicked with his legs, lashed out with his arms ... and gradually the water relaxed its grip and stopped tossing him about. He rose as fast as he could, but not fast enough, it seemed. Air. He needed air.

He broke surface, and heaved in a lungful of air.

... fadeout ...

He was slogging through muddy shallows, wading up onto dry land. He could barely see a thing. The darkness around him was total. There was perhaps a vague distinction between the ground underfoot and the sky above – the latter marginally less black than the former.

The ground.

He registered that he was outdoors, down on the very ground itself, out in the world beneath the Airborn's world. But it was a fact he would have found difficult to digest even if he had been in good shape, and he was in anything but good shape. He had a pulsing headache, and somehow he couldn't catch his breath. He was soaked to the skin and starting to shiver with cold. All in all, just keeping walking was the most he could manage. He was down to the core of himself, a creature operating almost solely on instinct.

Walk. Move.

The ground had pebbles that rolled treacherously when trodden on. It had unexpected clefts and cracks that tripped you. It had roots that snagged at your ankles.

Where are you going?

No idea.

The ground had noises, too.

Footfalls. Like a crowd of people, running shoeless, softly.

People ... or animals?

And a deep, reverberating rumble ... like someone chuckling very hard?

And sudden, sharp, blinding lights.

And creatures that looked like men but with thickset bodies and no faces. A pair of them, coming towards him, haloed by the fiercely bright lights. Creatures with metallic hands that reached out and—

Nothing.

Blankness.
Afloat.
Numb.
Voices.
Mumbling.
Silence.
Calm.
Soft.
Light.
Face.
Girl.
Speech.
Enquiry.
Water.
Sick.
Sleep.
Wake.
Girl.
Food.
Doze.
Awake.
Room.
Girl.
Girl talking.
Talking to him.
Girl in room, talking to him.
'Nice to see you again. Back with we. Who'm you be then?'

CHAPTER 30

Not A Very Good Spy

Az tried to clamber off the couch.

'Have to ... Have to go. Get to ...'

A wave of light-headedness washed over him and he sank back onto the cushions.

'Rest, be what you has to do,' said the girl, drawing the blanket up to his chin. 'Lay still and rest.'

'But—'

'But nothing. You'm in no fit state to go gallivanting about.'

Az acknowledged it with a feeble nod. 'What's wrong with me? I feel terrible. I've felt like this virtually since I ...' He was going to say *since I arrived in the elevator*, but amended it to: 'Since I don't know how long.' Lame, very lame.

'Well now,' said the girl, 'I be'n't no doctor, but it may have to do with you being out in the Shadow Zone, wandering around all soaked through. Recipe for catching rattle-lung, that be.'

Az struggled to make sense of what she was saying. Her dialect and thick accent weren't helping matters. 'Rattle-lung?'

'Everyone knows someone who knows someone who caught rattle-lung and died. You do, on account of you's met I.'

'Oh yeah, rattle-lung,' Az said, pretending he understood now. He added, 'I misheard, that's all. Thought you said something else.'

'Be the dampness, you see. The clammy air.'

'Yes. Obviously. And someone you know died of it?'

'My ma.'

'Oh, I'm sorry.'

'It'm all right. I weren't much more than a nipper. Don't hardly remember she at all. So, you be having a name?'

'Hmmh?'

Az had been studying the girl. So this was what a proper Groundling looked and sounded like. Not one of those Deacons, who were clearly an elite – privileged members of the species. Here was the authentic version, the real deal.

She was brown-haired and dark-eyed, although her complexion was contrastingly pale, her skin so white that in places the veins showed through. She had a sturdy build, with strong arms and a chunky jawline. In spite of that she wasn't in any way unattractive. In fact she was rather pretty.

Her clothes were plain: a suede jerkin over a shirt made of some rough material, and a pair of leather trousers cross-stitched down the sides. (In that respect, at least, the curators at the Museum of Arts, Sciences and History had got their facts right. Groundlings did favour simple dress.)

Age-wise, Az put her at sixteen, same as him. She seemed far more forthright than the sixteen-year-old girls he was familiar with, however. *Those* girls were all secrets and giggles, and made out they were more grown-up than they were. *This* girl didn't seem to have time for that sort of behaviour.

'A name. I asked what you'm being called. Come on, it be'n't a difficult question, surely.'

Az debated how much he could reveal without giving away that he was an Airborn spy. Probably it would be OK to tell her his name. There would be nothing suspicious about that. Besides, he was still too foggy and fuddled in the head to come up with a convincing alias.

'Az.'

The Groundling girl's forehead puckered into a frown. '"Ash", did you say?'

'No, Az. Az Gabrielson.'

She laughed. 'Az Gabrielson? What kind of name be that?'

Az offered a noncommittal shrug. 'It's the one I was given. And you're ...?'

'Cassie Grubdollar.'

He couldn't keep his eyebrows from rising a centimetre or so. 'Well, you're one to talk. What kind of a name is Cassie Grubdollar?'

'Nothing wrong with it,' Cassie Grubdollar replied with a haughty glare. 'Be a good, traditional Westward Territories name, it be. Straight up.'

Az said, 'Well, anyway, now that we've established that we both have funny names ...'

'No, *you* does.'

'I'm trying to change the subject. You said you found me in ... the Shadow Zone?'

'Yup. Ambling around, you was, like some kind of sightseer or something. Didn't seem to realise you had a pack of verms on your tail.'

'Verms.' Az tried to make it appear as if he recognised the word, hoping Cassie would go on to explain it, unprompted. He didn't think he was making a very good job of this spying business. Then again, nobody had seen fit to inform him that there would be people down here and that he might have to concoct some sort of cover story for himself.

'Yes, verms. Me and my brothers, and our da, we saved you from they. You'd have been verm dinner if not for we.'

'Then I'm very grateful to you. Thanks.'

'And us has been looking after you ever since. Or rather, *I* has.'

'Again, thanks.'

A teasing note entered Cassie Grubdollar's voice. 'I's got to say, Az Gabrielson, you doesn't speak like someone what comes from round hereabouts.'

'Oh?'

'No, more like someone what comes from quite a ways away. And here's I, mentioning rattle-lung and verms and that, and there you be, looking just as like you never heard of such things.'

'I have. Honestly.'

'Don't lie. Want to know what I think? Actually, it be'n't

123

what I *think* so much as what I *know*. I *know* what you be, Az Gabrielson, and where you be from.'

Az felt a peculiar blend of anxiety and relief. 'Really?'

'You be one of they.'

'One of ...?'

Cassie gestured upwards. 'They up there. The Ascended Ones. Although, why you's here and where your wings be – that'm a puzzle. A puzzle which maybe you wants to clear up for I, yes?'

CHAPTER 31

Not Such A Bad Spy After All

Az considered clamming up. It would certainly have been easier to do so, but it would also have been pointless. Saying nothing was tantamount to admitting everything. Cassie Grubdollar had seen through his paltry efforts at bluffing. Admittedly he had underestimated her. He had thought that someone whose grammar was so muddled must be muddled in the head as well, but that was clearly not the case.

In any event, he was left with nothing to fall back on but the truth.

It couldn't be the whole truth, though. He couldn't, for instance, tell her he was a spy. If he did, she would no doubt hand him over to the Groundling authorities. She would feel duty-bound to, because that was what you did with spies, wasn't it? Turned them in, let whoever was in charge deal with them. Weak as he was right now, there was no way he could stop her doing that if she felt like it.

'Can I trust you?' he asked.

Cassie cocked her head to one side. 'No idea. Can you?'

'I don't suppose I have a choice, under the circumstances.'

'No, I don't suppose you has.'

'OK then. I *am* from "up there".'

She nodded with the satisfaction of someone proved correct. 'But you doesn't have wings.'

'No, I doesn't – I *don't*.'

'Why's that? Them fall off or something?'

'No, nothing like that.'

'An accident, then.'

'Accident of birth. I was born this way. I'm not the only person

I know of who was, but we're exceptionally rare. Everyone else is winged. I just got unlucky, I guess you could say.'

'You'm got no wings and you live way up high up there. Be'n't that a bit scary?'

'Certainly is. I've got used to it, but sometimes – quite a lot of the time, in fact – I have to be careful what I do. One mistake, and it's a long way down.'

'So what be it like up there? I mean, the Deacons tells we there be these amazing, beautiful cities, and there'm dazzling sunshine all the time, and people is as kind and friendly as can be. Be it like that?'

'More or less, yes. We don't all get along constantly. Wouldn't need prisons and the Alar Patrol if we did. It isn't perfect. What is? But there haven't been any wars, not lately. And the sky-cities – well, they are beautiful, most of them, there's no denying that.'

'Tell me about they.'

He gave a verbal sketch of his hometown High Haven – the bustling central avenues, the quieter outer suburbs, the way the buildings all latticed together, over, under, around.

'A three-dimensional town,' said Cassie. 'Imagine that. And so this all balances on, like, the columns?'

'Cantilevers arch out from the tops of the columns, and they support some buildings, and those buildings support other buildings, and so on. A big framework, branching out. Somewhat like a tree. Although most of the cities have more than one column, so a tree with several trunks.'

'Yeah, that'd be sort of how I pictured they. And open sky above?'

'Blue sky.'

'Blue sky,' she echoed wonderingly. 'And you see the sun? I mean, properly. It'm more than just this pale circle? And the moon too?'

'And stars.'

'Stars.' It was almost a sigh. 'The Deacons, them talks about stars now and then. Bright twinkles of light, like sparks from a furnace. Oh, it'm true. It'm all true. Tell I more.'

He told her more. He described school, jetball, his brother's helicopter – all these everyday things which to Cassie seemed impossibly exotic.

'Now, your turn,' he said. 'What's life like down here?'

'You's seen, hasn't you?'

'Some of it. Not much.'

'It be grey. Always grey. Sometimes lighter grey, sometimes darker. But always grey. The clouds is always there, like a lid over us, and it rains a lot, like it'm raining now.' She shrugged. 'I don't know what else to say. It be'n't great. But this be just the first life. There'm the next life waiting for us up above, and if us is good and us sacrifices materials and keeps the Deacons pleased, us'll get there after we die.'

'You'll' – what was the phrase he had overheard in the Chancel? – 'Ascend?'

'Straight up.'

'How does that work, exactly? Ascension? The Deacons burn your bodies and ...'

'... and the smoke rises and what happens then is Reconstitution, it'm called. The smoke enters the womb of a pregnant lady above, mingles with the foetus what be growing inside her, and that be how you gets born again. With wings. *Not* with, apparently, in your case. But usually with.'

Az pondered this. It didn't strike him as very plausible. Perhaps, at a molecular level, it was conceivable that a few atoms of smoke from a cremated Groundling cadaver could form part of an Airborn foetus's makeup, if, say, the expectant mother happened to inhale them. But that was assuming the smoke even got that far and wasn't dissipated in the cloud cover.

No, frankly the whole idea seemed bogus. A con, perpetrated by the Deacons on ordinary people. A way of manipulating the existing situation to their advantage.

'It'm faith, see,' Cassie said, perhaps sensing what was going through Az's mind. 'You has to believe in it. You has to believe you'm going to become Ascended when you die. It'm what makes life, and death, bearable. Otherwise ... Well, there be'n't no "otherwise", really. Although there is according to them Humanists. Them argue that us doesn't Ascend and become Reconstituted, that that be all a load of Chancel baloney, and that you lot up there's just people like we – with wings, but just people – and you doesn't think about us or care about we one little jot. But that be'n't' true, right?'

'No,' said Az, lying (convincingly, he hoped). 'No, we're concerned about you. We think about you a lot.'

'That be why you'm down here then?'

He hadn't anticipated this particular question, although perhaps he should have. So far, he felt he had been doing pretty well. He was actively gathering information. He was learning about Humanists and Deacons and suchlike, and it would all be of immense interest to Lady Aanfielsdaughter if – no, when – he managed to get back up above the cloud cover. He was, in short, making a better job of being a spy than he had initially thought.

He stalled for time. 'Me? Erm ... What do you mean?'

'You'm down here 'cause you'm concerned. Be that it?'

'I'm ... down here ... because ...'

Think, Az, think!

'Because I was curious. Look at me. I have no wings. I'm like one of you. So I wanted to see ... to see if I might fit in down here. Fit in better than I do up there.'

His speech gained momentum. Here, at last, was his cover story.

'I sneaked onto an elevator. Strictly forbidden, of course. I could have got into terrible trouble. But I had to take a look. I had to see for myself. Often I've felt that I don't belong in a place where everyone else can fly and I can't. Whereas down here, maybe I could belong.'

Yes, that was it. Good work.

'And?'

'And what?'

'What conclusion has you come to? Does you?'

'Belong? Not sure yet. I've hardly had a chance to look round and see the place. You're the first person I've actually spoken to. But now that I have, and given how you've taken care of me …'

She smiled.

He smiled back.

It seemed, in that moment, that they shared something, that something passed between them, although Az could not accurately interpret what it was. An understanding? Or was it something more than that?

It occurred to him that this girl, Cassie, might have taken a shine to him. To her, after all, he was an ordinary boy. Up in the world of the Airborn, girls seldom gave him a second glance, and when they did it wasn't so much second glance as double take. *Oh look, he hasn't got any wings*. And then they would either ignore him or subject him to stares of embarrassed pity.

Whereas down here he was outwardly no different from anybody else. He wasn't abnormal. He was equal.

Therefore, down here, might he not have a similar effect on the opposite sex as Michael did up there? Might he not be as irresistible to Groundling girls as Michael was, usually, to the Airborn variety?

It wasn't beyond the realms of possibility.

CHAPTER 32

A Human Relic

Had Az known what was actually going through Cassie's head, he would have been considerably crestfallen. She wasn't entertaining romantic notions about him at all.

Basically what she was thinking could be boiled down to a single word.

Relic.

Not to put too fine a point on it, Cassie was thinking money. She was looking at Az, not as a boy, but as a transferable cash asset.

The Grubdollars had found him in the Zone, after all. They had scavenged him fair and square, in accordance with the Code of Murk-Combing.

How much would the Chancel pay for him? Not just any old Relic from above, not some random scrap of debris, but a living, breathing person. A genuine, honest-to-goodness Ascended One, in more or less perfect condition. What kind of sum might *he* fetch?

A small fortune, she thought.

Truly, the family's luck *had* turned.

For the rest of the day she tended to Az solicitously, without a hint of resentment any more. She spoon-fed him more stew. She brought him a basin of warm water and some soap so that he could wash himself. She presented him with his clothes, laundered and pressed, and waited outside the room while he put them on.

She wasn't simply nursing him, of course. She was guarding him as well, like a security man outside a bank vault.

By mid-afternoon Az had regained some of his strength. He

no longer complained of dizziness and there was colour back in his cheeks.

'Think I'm safe from rattle-lung?' he asked at one point.

Cassie said she reckoned so. 'Though you was courting it, slopping around in the wet in the Zone like that.'

'The Zone. The Shadow Zone. What *is* it exactly?'

'Well, it be where us works, for one thing.'

'Doing what?'

'Us, me and my family, us is in the murk-combing biz. Us and *Cackling Bertha*.'

'Who's she?'

'Strictly speaking her be an it, but her's a she to we. Our murk-comber. That big damn vehicle us was in when us found you. Us trawls around in the Zone in she, looking for Relics.'

'Relics being ...?'

'Stuff that falls from above. Bits and bobs. Anything.'

She could see Az thinking hard about that. 'And what do you do with these ... Relics?'

'Sells they to the Deacons. Us pays for a licence to go in the Zone, and in return gets the privilege of the Deacons buying off we whatever us finds there. It'm not a great living but it'm what us does.'

'And then what happens to the Relics?'

'Deacons stores they away in their Reliquary. All goes in there.'

'And you can only sell it to the Chancel? No one else?'

'Against the law to. And against the Code of Murk-Combing. The Deacons gets it all.'

'Bit of a cartel, isn't it?'

'You mean unfair? That be'n't the half of it. You can only buy one licence, and the Chancels is very strict about their territory. You can't play one Chancel off against another to get a better price. Be all sorts of trouble if you tried. Lose your licence, apart from anything.'

'So I'm sort of ... a human Relic, you might say.'

Cassie was startled. Had he guessed what she was planning for him?

'You might,' she replied, buttressing the words with a light laugh.

'Huh.'

The idea seemed to amuse him, but nothing more. Cassie was relieved. But there was also a first small stirring of guilt inside her.

Around teatime Az said he felt well enough to brave a few tentative steps. Although the effort left him weak and breathless, he was delighted, and Cassie echoed his delight.

A tour of the Grubdollar abode followed, and was necessarily brief, because it wasn't a very big house. In essence, it was a first-floor flat, its rooms hunkering under the roof.

Az summed up the place – décor and layout – as 'simple'. He meant this as a compliment, and Cassie took it as such, although she felt he was being slightly patronising.

He spent some time scanning the world outside through the windows, although there wasn't much to see, in the event. The rain had stopped but a mist had set in, shrouding everything in a haze of white. The courtyard below was visible, and next-door's slate-tiled rooftop, and the unlit gas lamp out in the street, but that was all.

Then, worn out, Az hit the couch again and collapsed into a deep slumber. The chuntering return of *Bertha* failed to wake him. Cassie, on the other hand, sprang to her feet the moment she heard the murk-comber's engine, and scurried downstairs to greet her family.

Four glum expressions told her it had been another fruitless day in the Zone.

Never mind. The news she had would cheer everyone up.

'Da? Boys? I's got something to tell you.'

Her father's immediate response, once Cassie revealed what she had discovered about the boy, was to purse his lips sceptically and suck his front teeth, all three of them.

'Bless my bum, him's been spinning you a yarn all right, girl. A neat one too. But where'm the proof?'

'Proof? Da, you should hear he. The sky-cities and that – nobody could make it up. Not in so much detail.'

'But the *proof*, lass. What's to say him's not just some nutter with a head full of fantasies about the Ascended Ones? Being as the lad was out there in a Shadow Zone, all on his own-some, I'd say "nutter" be a pretty fair description for he. And nutters make up stuff all the time, and they be convincing with it too, 'cause them's believing in it whole and full.'

'What about the weight of he, Da?' said Robert. 'You your-self said as how him be far lighter'n you expected. Now, if him comes from up there, where everyone flies, be'n't it likely that them'd have to not weigh as much? You know, like birds have hollow bones, or, not hollow, but what be the word? Porous.'

'No wings, Robert. That be what it comes down to. Where's the wings?'

'Come and see his shirt,' Cassie said. 'There be your proof.'

The Grubdollars went upstairs and tiptoed single-file into the lounge. Az, fortunately, was sleeping on his front, so that to expose his back all Cassie had to do was gently peel the blanket down to his waist.

Everyone took a good look at the sewn-up slits on the back of the shirt, then withdrew quietly to the kitchen. There, Cassie's father sat and ran a hand back and forth across his chin stubble, his eyes unfocused. You could see him slowly, slowly going over things in his head. Den Grubdollar was a man who seldom came to snap-decisions.

'Well now,' he said eventually, 'I be'n't saying you'm right, Cass. But I be'n't saying you'm wrong any more, either.'

'Reckon the Deacons will want he?'

'Maybe.'

'It'd be good money.'

'Maybe. But the lad be'n't just something for they to store in their Reliquary, if you take my meaning. He be'n't some mangled hunk of metal or the like. And us can't treat he as if him were. Not proper, that.'

'But what else is us to do with he?'

'There, Cass, you'm asking a fine question.'

Had Cassie been looking at one of her brothers just then,

instead of concentrating on her father, she might have seen a strange light enter that brother's eyes.

Martin Grubdollar had had an idea.

No one else might know what to do with the boy, but Martin certainly did.

CHAPTER 33

A Day In The Life Of A World-Changer

Steamarm's plan had been to spend just twenty-four hours in Grimvale before moving on. Events, though, were racing ahead, requiring the plan to be revised.

The strength of pro-Humanist sentiment he had encountered in the township was extremely gratifying to him. What surprised Steamarm was just how widespread it was. It seemed that virtually everyone he met was a supporter of the movement, from shopkeeper to schoolteacher, from road-sweeper to notary. Even on the municipal council there were people with Humanist leanings, although being professional bureaucrats they couldn't simply come out and admit it. Instead, a delegation of councillors invited Steamarm to visit the town hall and, over lunch, expressed their approval for his aims in a coded fashion, by means of vague statements such as 'Far be it from us to stand in the way of your endeavours' and 'The public is free to demonstrate its will'.

Above all, Steamarm was aware of a definite restlessness in the air. The township was bristling with agitation, ready to take the next step, just awaiting the word *go*.

He had been scheduled to travel to this next stop on his itinerary, Darkham Crag, by overnight train. However, he sent a telegram to the local movement organisers there, tendering his regrets and saying he had been unavoidably detained. He then sent another telegram, this one to his colleagues at the Central Office of the Popular Movement For Radical Secular Change, a.k.a. Humanism HQ, in the regional capital, Craterhome. It read:

SEEDS SOWN IN GRIMVALE BEARING FRUIT AND
RIPE FOR CULTIVATION + STOP + METHOD OF
COVERT INGRESS ACQUIRED + STOP + STRONGLY
URGE BRINGING FORWARD TIMETABLE FOR ACTION
+ STOP + CONFIRM + STOP +

The clerk at the telegraph office did not charge Steamarm for sending the telegrams.

'What'm ours should be ours,' she said to him, brightly. She was a delightfully pretty, petite young thing, and she wore her hair in a tidy plait, which was just how Steamarm liked girls to wear their hair.

'The time is now, sister,' he replied, and beamed charmingingly at her.

The clerk blushed and giggled, and Steamarm was tempted to invite her out for a meal, give himself a little treat. No, duty first. He couldn't allow himself to be distracted, not when the situation was reaching such a critical juncture.

'There'll be a reply to that second telegram,' he told her. 'Can you have it delivered to my hotel? I'm staying at the Pithead Inn.'

'Run it over there myself, I shall. Straight up.'

'Thank you, my dear.'

Next, Steamarm toured the local pickets and gave a speech of encouragement to the men and women standing there valiantly in the drizzling rain. It was the exact same speech at each picket, although there was no way the picketers could know that, especially as Steamarm recited it each time as though he was coming up with it on the spur of the moment. This was one of his many talents, making well-rehearsed words sound fresh and new to every pair of ears that heard them.

'... the hour is at hand ... overthrow the monopolistic tyranny of the Deacons ... the Chancels everywhere will fall ... days numbered ... twice as much wealth for the people ... casting off the shackles of moral oppression ...' And so on and so forth.

Back at the Pithead Inn, Steamarm found the reply from Central Office had been slipped under the door to his room.

On the envelope containing the telegram, the clerk had scribbled a note. It said, 'Sorry I missed you, XXX'.

The telegram itself read:

```
TIMETABLE    AMENDMENT   APPROVED   +    STOP   +
ACTION COMMENCES NIGHTFALL TOMORROW + STOP
+ FIRST BLOW TO BE STRUCK AT CLIFFSIDE CITY
CHANCEL + STOP + FURTHER ACTIONS TO FOLLOW
DEPENDING  ON  LOCAL  CONDITIONS  +  STOP  +
OPERATE AT OWN DISCRETION + STOP + WHAT'S
OURS SHOULD BE OURS + STOP +
```

Steamarm couldn't help grinning.

Down at the Logger's Head he assembled a small group of men, hardcore Humanists, the loyalest of the loyal. He plied them with beer and rhetoric, and watched them get drunker and more belligerent as the evening wore on. At the precise moment when they were still sober enough to take in and re-member instructions, but not so sober that their consciences were functioning properly any more, he revealed what he wanted them to do for him.

To a man, they agreed.

Steamarm left the pub and wended his way back to the hotel. The rain had eased off and a chilly mist billowed through the streets of Grimvale, but he was warmed by a inner glow of tri-umph. As he walked he got glimpses through windows, hazy snippets of the domestic lives of the townsfolk. Families were preparing for bed. Parents were kissing children goodnight. Faces were being washed, teeth brushed, curtains drawn, lan-terns snuffed. Hearth fires were banked up, their final flames flickering down. Grimvale was slowly closing its eyes and going to sleep, little suspecting the tumultuous events which lay in store just a few hours from now.

In his hotel room, Steamarm climbed into bed and willed himself to sleep too. He needed his rest. He had a very early start tomorrow.

He sank into slumber, and dreamed of a new world.

CHAPTER 34

Visitors At Dawn

Den Grubdollar, in a quandary as to the best way of dealing with the boy, determined that he would sleep on the matter before deciding. So Cassie spent another night in the armchair, keeping vigil over Az. This time she didn't nod off straight away. Her conscience plagued her. Was it right to try and sell Az to the Chancel? She looked at his prone, snoring form, outlined by the dim glimmer coming in through the window from the streetlamp. He seemed so ... frail. She hated the thought that he had put his trust in her and her immediate response had been to think of a way of exploiting him for money.

Money, though, would come in very handy indeed. The Grubdollars' outgoings were substantial, not least their diesel bill for *Bertha*, whose fuel tank was seemingly bottomless. Replacement parts for a murk-comber as old as *Bertha* was did not come cheap either. Right now, the family was deep in debt to several businesses in the township. The credit they were getting would not be extended indefinitely.

Guilt and self-interest warred within Cassie, until finally she reached a truce with herself. She would leave it up to her father. Whatever solution he settled on, she would go along with.

After that, she was able to sleep ...

... at least until shortly before dawn, when the entire household was woken by a strident hammering from outside. Somebody was thumping at the portcullis gate, hard.

'Who'm the hell can that be?' Cassie heard her father roar. 'Doesn't the idiot know what time it be?'

'I'll go see, Da,' Robert called from his room.

'Already on it,' said Martin, and there was the sound of his feet clattering down the spiral staircase, shortly followed by voices out in the courtyard and then the rattle of the portcullis gate being raised.

'Cassie, what's going on?' said Az in a slurred, sleepy fashion.

'Don't know. Visitors, seems like. Odd, though, at this hour.'

Out in the hallway Cassie found her father standing in his longjohns. He was stretching his arms and in the throes of a yawn so enormous it threatened to split his head in two.

'Martin's let they in, whoever them be,' she said. 'Must be someone him knows.'

Her father's face creased into a scowl. 'I's not liking this, Cass. Maybe you should—'

The sentence terminated there, incomplete, as Martin came back up the stairs. With him there were a half-dozen men, locals. Cassie knew two of them by name – Fred Tollbeam and Lawrence Brace – and recognised the faces of the rest. They were all large, burly types, hard workers, lumberjacks, miners, quarrymen, pillars of the community. What did they want?

Behind them, someone else came into view, someone Cassie didn't recognise. He was definitely *not* a local. Tall and lean, he was smartly dressed and well groomed, patently the sort of man who took great pains over his appearance. He was clean-shaven, his teeth were white, and his fingernails were clipped and buffed to perfection. He must have been fiendishly handsome when he was young. Not so young any more, he did everything he could to maintain his looks, even to the point of dyeing his grey patches of hair. The brown at his temples did not match the brown on the rest of his head.

Cassie's immediate impression, apart from his looks, was that there was something slightly disdainful about him. He considered himself a cut above.

'Aha,' the man said to Cassie's father as he reached the top of the stairs, 'Mr Grubdollar I presume.'

'And who in the name of all that's bright and high be *you*?' was the growled response.

'Da,' said Martin, 'this'm a friend of mine and Fletch's.'

Fletcher, who had emerged into the hallway a moment earlier along with Robert, nodded. 'Good friend of ours,' he said.

'Friend?' said their father. 'Oh, don't tell I. This'm some ruddy Humanist, right? Them all is Humanists. Yes, of course them is. Now I see. Fred there, you'm notorious for having those tendencies. And this here clean-cut Mr Fancypants, him's the ringleader of the bunch. Got a name, sir, has you? I'd very much like to know it.'

'Steamarm,' said the well-dressed man. 'Alan Steamarm.'

'Good. Thanks for that. I always likes to know the name of the person whose face I be about to rearrange.'

So saying, Cassie's father drew back his hand, balling it into a fist.

The burly Humanists immediately closed ranks around Steamarm to shield him.

'Fred,' Den growled. 'Lawrence. All of you. I'll say this just once. Out of the way. I'll fight you all if I has to, but I won't have Humanists in my house.'

'Da, please,' Martin said. 'Nobody wants any trouble. Alan and the lads—'

Den rounded on his son. 'Shut up. I's going to deal with you later, you and Fletcher both. But first off I's going to show these here gentlemen what I thinks of their sort. Coming barging into a man's home like that ...'

'I let they in, Da,' Martin said.

'I be well aware of that, more's the pity.'

'Mr Grubdollar, there's no need for threats,' said Steamarm from behind his barricade of thick torsos and muscular arms. 'In any case, you're outnumbered, and my colleagues won't think twice about—'

'Grraaarrghh!'

Cassie's father charged at the Humanists, barrelling into them like a bowling ball. The speed and ferocity of the attack caught them off-guard. He got in two good blows before they could muster a retaliation. Fred Tollbeam was decked by a single punch to the jaw. Another of the Humanists staggered backwards clutching his nose, from which blood was spurting freely. He caught himself on a small side-table, which collapsed under his weight. The sudden loss of support sent him sprawling to the floor amid wooden shards and splinters.

Even when the Humanists collected their wits and fought back, there seemed to be no stopping Den. He lashed out in all directions, catching one of the men under the chin with an uppercut and knocking the wind out of another with a jab of the elbow. He was rage incarnate, a force of nature.

Robert joined in the fracas, but was soon sent reeling and banged his head against a wall with concussing force. The impact dislodged a nearby embroidery sampler, whose stitched letters read 'HOME SWEET HOME'. It fell from its nail and hit the floor with a crash, frame splintering, glass shattering.

Den, meanwhile, for all his fury, was rapidly succumbing beneath sheer weight of numbers. After much grappling and struggling, two of the Humanists succeeded in pinning his arms behind his back. Then Lawrence Brace stepped forwards, fists clenched.

'Den,' he said, 'you'm a decent man, but you know what your problem be? You'm no friend of the modern age. You need to move with the times.'

So saying, he thumped Den in the gut, once, twice.

That was when Cassie finally roused herself from the state of horrified paralysis that had seized her. As Brace brought back his arm to punch her pinioned father a third time, she hurled herself at him. Leaping on him from behind, she wrapped an arm around his throat and squeezed with all her might. Brace, choking, flailed at her and swung around wildly, trying to dislodge her. Cassie clung on grimly, her only thought being to throttle the life out of this man who was hurting her da.

Eventually hands grabbed her and prised her off him. She kicked and shrieked in protest.

'Be still, Cass,' hissed a voice in her ear. Fletcher's voice. 'You'm only making it worse for everyone.'

'Traitor! Bloody buggering traitor! Let me go!' Cassie squirmed in her brother's grasp but couldn't break free.

'Everyone! Everyone! Please!'

This was Steamarm speaking. He lofted his hands in a peacemaking gesture.

'Please! This is all so unseemly. We mustn't fight one another. We're all on the same side here, united against a common enemy.'

'I be'n't on any side of yours,' gasped Cassie's father. A trickle of blood was flowing down from the corner of his mouth. He strained against the men holding him, but to no avail.

'Believe me, Mr Grubdollar, you are. Humanism is on the march. We're preparing to strike a blow for liberty. All across the world a revolution is starting. And whether you like it or not, you're a part of that.'

Den spat a wad of blood-flecked spittle at Steamarm's feet. 'What'm you wanting here anyways? Your lot's already poisoned the minds of two of my sons with your nonsense. You's taken *they* from me. What else of mine is you after?'

'Isn't it obvious?'

'Not to me it be'n't.'

'Well, if you can't work it out, you'll know soon enough. And after tonight you'll understand everything very clearly. After tonight, Mr Grubdollar, we're going to be living in a different world.'

'Alan?'

Steamarm swung round.

Martin was standing in the doorway to the lounge. Cassie hadn't realised but he had slipped out of the hallway when the fighting started. Now he was back, and he had Az with him. Holding Az by the shoulders, he thrust him forward to show him to Steamarm.

'Who's this?' said Steamarm quizzically. 'I thought you said you only had two brothers, Martin.'

'This'm no brother of mine,' came the reply. 'Remember

how I mentioned that kid we found in the Zone, day before yesterday? This be he. And guess what? Turns out him's one of them. Him's Ascended.'

'What? No. Surely not.'

'Surely yes.' Martin was grinning at Steamarm, gleefully, ingratiatingly, like a student with an apple for teacher. 'Bit of a prize, eh? Might come in useful. And him's yours, Alan. All yours.'

CHAPTER 35

Aftermath

Cassie, Robert, and their father were locked in their father's bedroom and one of the Humanists was posted on guard outside the door. Steamarm told them this was for their own good, to keep them out of harm's way. He insisted they shouldn't regard themselves as prisoners, but that was certainly how it looked to Cassie.

Her primary concern, though, was Robert. He was semiconscious from the bang he had received on the back of his head. She got her father to place him on the bed, where he lay burbling incoherently, like someone in the grip of a fever.

'His brains is all shook up,' her father observed.

Cassie fetched a damp washcloth from the basin on the dressing table, folded it into a roll, and draped it across Robert's forehead. Its coolness soothed him and he soon went quiet.

'Reckon him'll be OK,' she said. 'Him's breathing steady. Going to have a mighty headache when him wakes up, I reckon, but that be all. Now Da, what about you?'

'Fine, lass. Don't worry yourself about I.'

He wasn't fine, however. His lip was starting to swell, there were abrasions on his face, and every time he moved he winced. To judge by the way he held himself, his stomach was very tender where Lawrence Brace had punched him.

'Can't I just give you a quick look-over?'

'What for? It'm only bumps and bruises. Them'll heal. I's fine, I tells you!'

'No need to get shirty. I were only trying to help.'

'Yes. Sorry, girl.' Den turned down his mouth at the corners. 'Look, I'll be all right, honest I will. I been hit far worse in the past. Brace weren't really trying, I doesn't think. His heart weren't in it. What hurts the most be …'

He couldn't finish what he had been going to say.

'Martin,' said Cassie. 'Fletcher.'

'Yes. They. Can't bring myself to speak their names, I can't. Not now. But how could them do this? My own flesh and blood. It'm hard to believe.'

'Maybe them—'

He cut her off, jabbing a finger at her. 'Don't, Cassie. Don't say it. Don't even think about coming up with some excuse to justify what them did. There be'n't none. Them's brought shame on this household with their behaviour. As of now, I has two children only. Do you hear I, girl? Two children only. You'm forbidden from ever mentioning them other two again.'

With that, Den stalked off to a corner of the room and leaned against the wall, resting his brow on his forearm and staring morosely at the floorboards.

Cassie turned back to Robert. She sat on the bed beside him and stroked his arm. Poor Robert. Perhaps if she had got involved in the fight sooner, instead of standing there like a scared rabbit, Robert would now be all right. No, it wouldn't have made any difference. Probably *both* of them would have got hurt rather than just him. Besides, everything had happened so quickly. From start to finish the fight couldn't have lasted more than half a minute.

As she replayed the events over in her mind, she found herself wondering what the answer was to the question her father had asked Alan Steamarm: *What'm you wanting here anyways?* It wasn't Az, that was for sure. Steamarm hadn't known who and what Az was till presented with him by Martin. So, if that wasn't the original reason for the visit, what *had* he come for?

The answer popped into her head at the exact same moment that a roar of engine ignition came from down in the courtyard.

CHAPTER 36

Captive In The Larder

They hauled Az through the still-misty predawn streets of Grimvale Township. Gripping his arms, two of the Humanists frogmarched him across cobbles and flagstones, past houses whose darkened windows stared out like blind eyes, past shopfronts with metal shutters closed to protect the wares inside, across a humpbacked bridge that traversed a stream of running water, down an alleyway so narrow that the buildings on either side appeared to touch heads. Everything seemed unreal to Az through the thickening and thinning of the mist, provisional, as though at any moment it could all fade into nothingness. A dirty twist of rag in a gutter – unreal. That long-tailed animal scampering for safety beneath a gate (from the Groundling exhibit, Az recognised it as a cat) – unreal.

Finally they arrived at a two-storey cottage with a whitewashed exterior and a sagging, deep-eaved roof. One of the Humanists escorting Az was called Lawrence, and this, apparently, was where Lawrence lived. Inside, the cottage consisted of small, dingy rooms with beamed ceilings. The doors had lintels so low that both Humanists had to duck to go through them.

Az was taken to a back room, a larder. It had a brick floor and a single, diamond-paned window set high up in the wall. The window lacked a handle and was sealed fast, never intended to be opened. Its purpose was to let in a wisp of light, not air, and its dimensions were so small that even if Az smashed out the glass he couldn't possibly squeeze himself through. Cobwebs hung over it like a net curtain, studded with fly husks.

There was no furniture in the larder apart from shelves

which held jars of dried food and preserves and assorted items of grubby crockery, some of them greened with mould. In one corner of the floor there was a scattering of what looked like black grains of rice. Had Az known what a mouse was, he would have recognised these as mouse droppings.

The door slammed behind him, a key turned, and that was that for the next few hours. Az was left alone in the larder with nothing to do except squat cross-legged on the cold, bare floor and wonder what was going to happen to him. In an instant, his situation had gone from hopeful to dreadful. He despaired of ever being able to return to his own world. High Haven, home, his parents, Michael – all these seemed impossibly remote now, like a life that he had once imagined, a dream he had once had before waking into this harsh, grey reality. He hated the ground. He hated the people here, and he hated himself for ever having agreed to come down here. This was a ghastly place: no sunshine, everlasting gloom, everything damp and dank, and with a population who squabbled amongst themselves and double-crossed each other all the time.

As best he could judge, he had met just one halfway decent Groundling so far, and that was Cassie Grubdollar. One, out of who knew how many. And even her he wasn't completely sure about.

It might have been midday when someone finally came to look in on him. 'Might have been', because although Az was convinced that several hours had elapsed, the sky outside the tiny window didn't look a whole lot brighter than it had been at daybreak. The key clunked in the lock, and into the larder stepped the well-presented man who'd been giving the other Humanists their orders at the Grubdollars'. Az had overheard his name. Was it Alan Steerarm? Steelarm? Something like that. Groundling names were hard to get a grasp on.

'Good day to you, young man,' the man said to Az. 'Apologies for leaving you so long. I had things to attend to. Busy chap, you know.'

Az, out of a combination of stubbornness and apprehension, said nothing.

'Look, let's not be like that, shall we?' said the man. Steamarm. Yes, that was it. His name was Alan Steamarm. 'I'm here for a friendly chitchat, that's all. A little heart-to-heart. Because, as you know, the rumour is that you're an Ascended One, or at any rate you come from where the Ascended Ones live. Now, I've always been led to believe that to be an Ascended One you need wings. It's a basic requirement of "membership". Am I mistaken on that front?'

Az stared back at him, still saying nothing. What *could* he say? Telling anyone about anything seemed only to get him into trouble.

'Oh, come on,' Steamarm chided. 'I'm just after a few facts here.' He squatted down so that his and Az's eye-lines were level. 'Are you really from up there? And if so, what's gone wrong? Why have you descended to this lowly region? Not for a holiday, I'd hazard. Are you a reject, maybe? Have they exiled you? Chucked you out because you don't conform to their high standards? Is that it? Or is this whole thing just a story you've concocted, a prank, and you're actually an ordinary kid from around these parts who's got it into his head that it would be funny if he claimed he's Ascended? A stupid thing to do, if you ask me. What could you hope to gain?'

Steamarm's gaze was steady and unblinking. Az lowered his eyes and concentrated on the man's chin. It had a cleft in it, like the chin of a hero in a novel. It was a masculine, chiselled, good-guy chin.

'If I'm wasting my time here, Azrael, just say so. Did I pronounce that correctly – Azrael? The Deacons have long been telling us that the Ascended have exotic names. And your surnames are your father's forename suffixed by 'son' or "daughter". Is that right? Is that how it works? Seems like a rather convoluted system to me. Must make life murder for your census takers, all those different surnames in one family. Do you even have census takers, I wonder. Come on, what's it like up there? Tell me a bit about it, Azrael. If you can.'

A chin like that ought to belong to someone you could trust, someone reliable. Not someone whose every word dripped with egotism and self-regard.

'You really should tell me now,' Steamarm insisted, 'because I'm starting to lose patience. If you're a liar, if this is all just some big hoax, I'll find out. Believe me, I will. I'm not one of these backwater simpletons like the Grubdollar family. You can't pull the wool over *my* eyes so easily. I'm a clever and some might say ruthless man. I'm also a man with precious little time to spare right now. So, if you aren't really Ascended, come clean and save yourself – and me – a heap of bother. If, on the other hand, you *are* what you say you are, and can prove it, then you could be very useful to me. You and I could even be friends. Understand? You could help me very much. Am I getting my point across?'

Yes, there were plenty of men who would give anything to have a chin like that.

'All right. I see.' Steamarm straightened up. 'So that's how it's going to be, is it? Fine.' He smoothed out the wrinkles in his trousers with a sharp downward brush of his hands. 'I'm going to give you an hour, then. One hour to think about things. After that, I'm coming back with one of my pals. You know who I'm talking about. You've met them. One of those big fellows who like to use their fists. *Then* we'll see how long you keep up this silent act of yours.'

He swept out of the room. The door slammed.

One hour.

Az drew his legs up to his chest, buried his face against his knees, and wished he was elsewhere.

CHAPTER 37

What To Do Instead Of Sitting On Your Backside All Day

'Da? Da?'

Den Grubdollar was slumped in a wicker chair, as he had been for the past couple of hours. He didn't glance up but he did give a grunt, to indicate that he was listening.

'Da, us has got to get out of here.'

'Oh really, Cass? Why'm that?'

Cassie moved closer to him, keeping her voice low. 'For one thing, us has got to get *Bertha* back. I been thinking, and I reckon those Humanists is going to use she to worm their way inside the Chancel. Them be going to do that this evening. Remember what Steamarm kept saying? "After tonight ..." It be the only reason I can think of for they taking her. With Martin or Fletcher driving ...' She corrected herself, remembering her father's edict about mentioning those two of her brothers. 'With you-know-who or you-know-who driving, them could get through the gates easily. Deacons on guard duty'll recognise their faces. Won't look at they twice. Meantime there'll be a bunch of Humanists hiding in *Bertha*'s loading bay. Them can be smuggled in that way, and then when them's inside the Chancel them can take over the place. I doesn't think the Deacons will put up much resistance. All a bit soft and weedy, be'n't them, from all that fine living. I mean, them'll try but it won't be a fair fight.'

Her father considered this, then nodded slowly.

'So?' he said. '*Cackling Bertha* be their ticket into the Chancel. So what? Why'm it up to we to stop they?'

'Not stop they, Da. I just wants she back, that'm all.

I doesn't want she to be used like that. Her's family. I know that sounds daft-headed but it be true. Her's one of us, an honorary Grubdollar, and it be'n't' right for they to drag she into their Humanist shenanigans.'

Den studied his daughter. His mood at present was aggrieved and distracted, and his face betrayed that but little else.

'You said, "For one thing,"' he said. 'Be there a second thing?'

'Um, yeah. I reckons we should go get Az back too.'

'Beg pardon?'

'The boy. The Ascended One. Az.'

'I know who you be referring to. What I doesn't know is what you be on about. Az? What's us want he back for?'

'Da, it'm thanks to we that him's now a prisoner of them Humanists. I's no idea where them's got he or what them's after from him, but it be'n't' proper that us let they have he.'

'Weren't *us* that did that, lass. Weren't you and me. Were ... them who us be'n't mentioning.'

'All the same, him were in our care, him were our responsibility, and us let he down.'

'If I recall rightly, you was all after selling he to the Deacons.'

'Well, changed my mind, I has. Thinking about it, I reckon that it weren't proper to do that and that it *be* proper to rescue he now.'

Cassie's father looked inward for a while.

'Right,' he said, 'let's just I get this straight. You thinks us should somehow break out of here, somehow find where *Bertha* be, somehow get she back, then somehow find where Az be and someone get he back too. That about the long and short of it, lass?'

'Just about, yeah.'

'Lot of "somehows" there, you don't mind my saying.'

'I never said any of it were going to be simple, Da. But what else is us going to do? Sit here all day on our backsides, prisoners in our own house?'

For the first time since the Humanists had invaded his

home, Den's gloomy demeanour showed signs of brightening. He even almost smiled.

'Well, when you put it like that, lass …'

CHAPTER 38

Breakout

The Humanist guarding the three Grubdollars was a professional layabout called Colin Amblescrut.

He belonged to a family who were famous in Grimvale for many things, a fondness for booze being one of them, work-shyness being another. Mainly what the Amblescruts were noted for, however, was their failure to produce offspring who might be described as in the least bit intellectually developed. Indeed, there was a saying in the region: 'I may be dumb but at least I be'n't an Amblescrut.' Generation upon generation of Amblescrut youth had passed through the local education system without leaving a mark, apart from the odd scar or two on their fellow pupils. That, of course, was another notorious family trait: bullying. The Amblescruts took a particular pride in their liking for bullying and their proficiency at it. Bullying was their legacy, something handed down from parent to child, one might say dished out by parent to child. When they weren't doing their best to avoid earning an honest living, Amblescruts – alone or in packs – roamed about looking for victims to pick on. It whiled away the time between pub opening hours.

Alan Steamarm had left this particular Amblescrut in charge of the Grubdollars precisely because of his thuggish denseness. He would do the job he was assigned to do, unthinkingly, unquestioningly. Amblescrut was also the one person Steamarm felt he could spare, out of the squadron of Grimvale Humanists he had gathered around him. If he was going to leave behind one of the tools in his box, so to speak, then it might as well be the bluntest.

Truth was, Amblescrut was nursing a bit of a hangover today, after the pub session with Steamarm last night, where he had out-drunk everyone else by a margin of several pints. So his already far-from-sharp wits were further dulled by dehydration, a swirling stomach and a sore head.

This, in the event, would work very much to the advantage of Cassie and her father.

'Excuse me,' said Cassie, rapping on the inside of the bedroom door.

'Hmmh?' said Amblescrut, stirring from the bleary doze he had fallen into.

'I said excuse me.'

'What you be wanting?'

'My brother. The one in here, him that got knocked out. Him's taken a turn for the worse. Started bleeding.'

The note of panic in her voice sounded real enough. What Amblescrut couldn't know was that this was because it stemmed from a genuine sense of urgency.

'Bleeding?' he said.

'From his ear. That'm a bad sign. Someone needs to get he to a doctor.'

Colin Amblescrut cogitated very, very hard on this news. His thought processes were moving like porridge, not only slow but hotly painful as well. Bleeding? No, that was never good, was bleeding. Specially not from the ear.

Of course, it might be a trick.

Being who he was, Amblescrut was always on his guard for tricks. He had the bully's natural paranoia. He felt that anyone smarter than he was must be out to get him – and since there were few people who *weren't* smarter than he was, that meant just about everyone was out to get him. Which was why it was usually better to get them first.

'I be needing to see,' he said, 'with my own eyes. I be'n't just going to take your word for it.'

'Fine. Only, be quick about it. Him's losing blood fast.'

Amblescrut went in search of a weapon. He wasn't about to enter the bedroom without some kind of hitting implement in his hand that would give him an edge. He remembered Den Grubdollar earlier on, fighting like a human cyclone. Grubdollar was old, and Amblescrut was both younger and stronger than him. Still, he knew it would be foolish to go in there unarmed.

He found a poker by the fireside in the lounge. Nice, stout lump of wrought iron. He gripped it in one hand and slapped it into the palm of the other.

Ouch.

But good.

'Right,' he said through the bedroom door. 'You and your da go to the far corner of the room and stand there facing the wall, backs to I, hands on your heads.' This was what they did at Grimvale police station when opening the cells to let detainees out. Amblescrut, having been arrested by the local constabulary on numerous occasions for drunk and disorderly behaviour and causing affray, was more than familiar with the procedure. 'I be opening the door a crack, and if I doesn't see you both standing there like I said, I's shutting it again straight away, and it stays shut and never mind your brother. Straight up?'

'Straight up.'

He waited a moment, hearing footsteps on the floorboards. Father and daughter were doing as asked. And why not? Amblescrut was used to getting his own way. When he made demands, people listened, and woe betide them if they didn't.

He turned the key, pressed down on the handle, and eased the door open.

First thing he saw was the young Grubdollar brother lying on the bed – and yes, there was blood trickling from his ear, and spots of blood on the pillow too.

Next thing he saw was that the other two Grubdollars hadn't gone to the far corner as instructed.

In fact, they didn't appear to be in the room at all ...

... unless they were hiding to the left of the door, out of his line of sight.

A cleverer man would have made this deduction more or less instantly, and hurried to take the appropriate countermeasures.

Not Colin Amblescrut, alas.

The sight of the blood had unnerved him, and then there was the fact that he had definitely heard footsteps, and the footsteps had got quieter, just as though they were moving away. But then what he had neglected to take into account was that footsteps could be made to *seem* as though they were moving away if the people generating them simply remained in one spot and trod more and more softly. An elementary ruse that wouldn't have fooled a child but *had* fooled him.

The door was yanked from Amblescrut's grasp. Next instant, he was being struck from the side with something large and heavy. He crumpled to the floor, the poker clattering out of his hand. He levered himself up onto all fours and scrambled to retrieve the weapon. Before he could reach it, he was struck again, this time squarely on the crown of his head. He went down but immediately got back up. It took a lot more than a couple of blows to fell an Amblescrut, particularly if the target was the head. Unusually thick skulls, the family had. More bone than brain, it was said.

The heavy object crashed down on his spine, flattening him.

For a third time he rose up.

He heard Den Grubdollar curse and say, 'What'm it take to stop the bugger?'

'How about this, Da?'

At the periphery of his vision, Amblescrut saw the girl pick up the poker – *his* poker – and toss it to her father.

Ah, he thought. *This'm going to hurt.*

He did his best to get himself upright before Den had a chance to wield the poker effectively. But he knew he wasn't going to manage it in time. There was a tragic, even poetic inevitability to the situation. By fetching the poker, he had brought this on himself.

He heard the poker swing. It made a sort of thrumming, humming *whoosh* through the air.

Then there was a lightning-like flash.

Followed by utter dark.

CHAPTER 39

No Either-Or

'I said, didn't I? I said us'd need something more substantial than that.'

Den indicated the wicker chair which he had used to thump Colin Amblescrut three times before having to resort to the poker. The chair was now looking rather sorry for itself. A dent had been gouged in the back of it, one of its legs had broken off, and another leg was hanging on by a splinter.

'You got he, that'm the main thing,' Cassie replied. She was winding a piece of cloth around her hand in order to bandage up the small gash in her palm which she had inflicted with the blade of her father's straight razor. The blood for Robert's ear had had to come from somewhere, and it was sensible that Cassie should be the source. Her father needed both hands unimpaired so that he could tackle Amblescrut. 'Now, let's tie he up before him comes round.'

They bound the unconscious Humanist's wrists and ankles with a length of strong cord from the storage area downstairs. Then, for good measure, they dragged him between them to the broom closet in the hallway, bundled him inside, and propped the door shut by shoving a kitchen chair at an angle up beneath the handle.

'Amblescruts,' said Den, shaking his head. 'Put three of they together, you still wouldn't have a whole brain.'

With a *tsk*, he turned away from the closet. All at once he staggered and let out a gasp.

'Da! What'm up?'

'Nothing.' He grimaced, clutching his side. 'Just overdid it, maybe, a little. Pass in no time, for sure.'

The pain did pass, but still Cassie insisted that her father sit down and let her examine him. She probed his chest and abdomen carefully with her fingers.

'*Aiiichh!*' her father hissed, as she found exactly where it hurt.

'Cracked a rib,' she diagnosed. 'Likely as not it happened when you'm got punched, and bashing Amblescrut made it worse. Da, you'm not going anywhere in this state. You won't barely manage to walk a hundred metres. I be going out after *Bertha* on my ownsome.'

'Uh-uh, lass. Face them Humanists without me to protect you? No way.'

'It be'n't no either-or, Da. You'm hurt too bad to be doing any protecting. Besides, somebody's got to stay here with Robert. Can't just be leaving he all by himself.'

'I reckoned a neighbour might—'

'Da.' Cassie scowled at him sternly. She had never loved him more and never before realised how vulnerable he could be. He was looking old. 'Be'n't often that I's the one what tells *you* how things is going to be, but that'm what I's doing right now, and no dispute. I'll find *Bertha* if I can, and if those Humanists is there when I finds she, I be dealing with they somehow. On my ownsome, a girl, there be less chance of fisticuffs breaking out than if I be turning up with my Da, who, let's face it, has a temper of him wouldn't shame a wild boar. Maybe I'll manage to get somewhere using subtlety and female wiles, and maybe not, but whatever happens, at least this way it be far less likely that anyone ends up injured.'

Den regarded his daughter. He had never loved her more and never before realised how grown-up she could be. She was looking old.

'Very well, lass,' he said with a sigh, and winced. Even sighing hurt. 'But you be careful, all right? Don't take any stupid risks.'

'Yes, Da.'

On impulse, Cassie leaned forward and gave him a peck on

the cheek. Long after she had left the house, Den Grubdollar was still stroking the spot where she kissed him, with a faraway look in his eyes.

CHAPTER 40

The Hunt For Cackling Bertha

To track down a murk-comber even in a smallish place like Grimvale (population: 5,500) was not as straightforward a task as it might seem. There were four families with a licence to trawl the Shadow Zone for Relics, and a couple of professional businesses as well, so the sight of a murk-comber trundling along the streets was not an uncommon one. Added to that, there was the fact that the Humanists had taken *Bertha* in the early morning when most people were still fast asleep in bed. It was unlikely that there were any eyewitnesses to her departure, and even if someone heard her rumble past their house, they wouldn't necessarily know which way she had been heading or even be curious enough to draw back the curtains and take a look.

In Cassie's favour, a great big thing like a murk-comber would be very difficult to hide. It wasn't something you could just stash in your backyard under a tarpaulin or park out of sight down a side-alley. You'd need somewhere large, ideally an enclosed space or a place with stacks of equipment or raw materials to provide cover. A stockyard, a warehouse, somewhere like that.

And, logically, if you were going to drive your hijacked murk-comber to the Chancel later, you would want a site reasonably close to your destination, for convenience sake. You would probably choose a location either on or not far off one of the main roads into the Shadow Zone.

Based on this line of thinking, Cassie concluded that the Humanists would be keeping *Bertha* at one of the mines or lumberyards at the northern edge of town. Which narrowed down the field of search slightly, although not by a huge amount. There were two lumberyards and several coalmines all in close proximity to one another in that area, as well as a slate quarry and a couple of factories. What was she going to do, check them *all* out?

Well, yes. That was just what she was going to do. It was the only option open to her.

Cassie knew the countryside around Grimvale well. This had been her playground as a child. She had roamed far and wide through the forests and hills and was familiar with every back-route and every trail. She made her way up to a high ridge which ran parallel to the main road north out of town. It was hard going in places. The ground was sodden with rain. Ankle-deep mud sucked at her feet, trying to liberate her of her boots.

Once she had gained firmer ground she headed for one of the many clear-felled areas of forest. A swathe of treeless slope gave her an unimpeded view down to several of the industrial premises that were strung alongside the road.

There was the Filkshaw and Hawserdean Timber Mill, with its pyramid piles of tree trunks waiting to be sawn into planks, the piles laid out in a grid pattern like a miniature city.

There was the mine known as the Black Lake Lode, so named not because of any nearby body of water but because the seam of coal which the first prospectors had discovered there was so deep and broad that a lake was the only thing they could think of to compare it to, although it turned out to be even bigger than that, a seemingly limitless subterranean sea of carbonaceous rock.

Next door lay a rival mining concern, the Consolidated Colliery Collective. This was a communally-run enterprise where the workers were called stakeholders and where there was no disparity between the wages paid to labour force and management. Everybody earned the same basic salary, plus productivity bonuses.

The CCC had long been a hotbed of Humanist activity. It was there that the first pickets had been set up, there that the embargo on supplies to the Chancel was initially declared – and so it was on there that Cassie focused her fullest attention. In the leaden noonday light, gazing down across the expanse of dead stumps and spindly tendrils of new-growth, she surveyed the site. She observed miners – stakeholders – wheeling cart-loads of freshly dug rubble out of the mouth of the mine. They deposited the contents onto conveyor belts, which fed into a large corrugated-iron building where the stuff was sorted by hand and sent up either of two distributor escalators. From the summit of one escalator, lumps of pure coal rained down; from the summit of the other, lumps of excess material, slag. Side by side, two conical heaps grew, respectively glossy black and drab grey.

There was a notable lack of urgency in the way everyone was working. A go-slow was in force at the CCC, as it was almost everywhere else. The pit was operating at 50% of full capacity, turning out enough product to cater to the needs of paying customers but no more. The extra coal that would normally have been donated to the Chancel was not being mined, and the trucks that would have transported it there were consigned to their sheds, not needed for the time being.

Unable to spot *Bertha* amid the coal heaps and slag heaps, Cassie homed in on the truck sheds. She saw that a couple of trucks were parked in front. Why leave them outdoors, she wondered, when they weren't being used? Surely it would be better to keep them safely garaged, out of the elements.

Then she knew.

It was instinct as much as anything, a prickle at the nape of her neck, a tingling in the pit of her stomach.

Of course.

There was no direct evidence to corroborate her suspicion. It was perfectly possible that the trucks were parked outside because someone was planning to work on their engines or else they were old and decrepit and were going to be taken away and broken down for parts.

But she knew.

It was as though *Bertha* was calling to her from her place

of concealment. Cassie had spent so much of her life in, on, around or under the murk-comber that she truly believed some kind of link had been forged between the two of them. Yes, *Bertha* was a machine, an inanimate thing. But she was so much more than that, too. Cassie knew her inside out, intimately. She knew her every mood, her every whim. When the Humanists made off with her, it was like having a beloved pet kidnapped. Worse – a close relative.

Bertha was family, just as Cassie had said to her father. She was like a maiden aunt, portly, sometimes cantankerous, with a hearty appetite and a wicked laugh, who worked hard and took care of all her kin, and asked only for a little care and kindness in return.

And she was down there in those sheds, taking up space normally occupied by the two trucks.

Cassie was sure of it.

Absolutely sure.

So sure that, without any further ado, she set off down the side of the ridge at a run.

CHAPTER 41

Crunch Time

The larder door opened. Az's hour was up. In came Steamarm, accompanied by Lawrence Brace. The latter seemed even larger and more hulking than before, an absolute giant of a man, with hands the size of dinner plates. Az saw that he was missing a finger. He hadn't noticed this earlier. The little finger on his left hand had been sheared off clean to the knuckle in some accident or other. Brace knew about pain, then. The receiving of as well as the inflicting of.

Az gulped. There was a constriction in his throat and a terrible dryness in his mouth. Up in the world he came from, that dream realm where the Airborn lived, it was hard to conceive of an adult ever deliberately harming a child. Down here, he didn't think the same rules applied. The ground was altogether a more brutal place.

Over the past hour he had had plenty of time to think. He had seesawed back and forth between defiance and submission. He had vowed not to tell Steamarm a thing, and to face the consequences. Then he had decided to give in and tell him everything. What had he got to lose? Then he had decided against *that*. Come what may, Steamarm wasn't getting a peep out of him. And so on. Back and forth, back and forth ...

Now it was crunch time, and he had to make a choice, fast.

'Azrael,' said Steamarm. 'Here we are again. So, are you ready to co-operate?'

'Please don't,' said Brace with a cruel leer.

Az's solution to his dilemma was a compromise: get in some defiance first, then submit.

'You're very brave,' he said. 'Two grown men threatening a teenager. You must be very proud of yourselves.'

'Oh, an attempt to make us feel ashamed!' said Steamarm. 'Well done, nice try. The fact is, Azrael, I have a calling, a cause that to me is far more important than the wellbeing of any single individual, be they adult or child. I don't care what I have to do in the name of that cause. Anything and everything is allowed if it gets me closer to my goal. Do you see what I'm driving at? I know no guilt, no shame. You can't appeal to my better nature because I don't have one.'

'What about you?' Az said, turning to Brace. 'You're the one who's actually going to … to beat me up if I don't co-operate. How does that make you feel?'

Just a flicker of hesitation before Brace replied, 'Good. I be fine with that.'

'Really?'

Az knew that to tell if a person was unsure, you looked at the eyes. Whatever the mouth was saying, if the person didn't believe it then the eyes would not stay still.

Brace's eyes were darting to and fro.

This was a bluff. Brace was here only to intimidate Az. Steamarm had no intention of ordering him to use his fists.

'I'm not in much of a talking mood right his moment,' Az said, with a hint of gloating. He folded his arms. 'I think I'll just sit here and enjoy the solitude, and you two can go pluck yourselves.'

Steamarm looked him up and down, appraising him. A slow smile spread across his face.

Then he took two quick steps forward and whacked Az across the face, backhand.

Az crumpled to the floor and came up again pressing a hand to his cheek. It felt like it was on fire. Tears of pain filled his eyes, smarting. He couldn't stop them. His head reeled.

'You weren't listening, were you?' Steamarm said through clenched teeth. 'I made myself very clear. Anything and everything is allowed. So let's try once more, shall we? We'll start from the very beginning. Are you or are you not an Ascended

One? Simple question. Yes or no? And I want the truth. No mucking about.'

The shock of the blow faded. Az's head settled. He felt his cheek starting to swell. The pain became less fiery but no less unpleasant.

Dully, miserably, he nodded. *Yes*.

'There,' said Steamarm. 'There we go. An honest answer, I'd say. Now we're getting somewhere. So, tell me more. Fill me in on the whole thing. Why, where and how. Leave nothing out. This ought to be quite enlightening ...'

CHAPTER 42

Inside The Shed

There were skylights in the shed roofs, and Cassie, keeping to the high ground at the rear of the Consolidated Colliery Collective, peered down through each, one after the other in a row. She moved stealthily, staying low, following the line of the sheds. The skylights were grimy, hadn't been cleaned in ages. At best she glimpsed dim outlines through them, silhouetted segments of vehicle, here the top corner of a driver's cab, there the tailgate of a flatbed. She was beginning to lose heart, fearing her instinct had been wrong.

Then, unmistakably: *Bertha*. Her rounded contours. Her turret and nacelles. Her big behind.

Cassie had to suppress a yelp of triumph.

She scrambled down the last section of mountainside; clambered over a tallish chainlink fence that was there mainly to keep forest animals out; scurried across a strip of open terrain; gained the shelter of the back of the sheds; pressed herself flat against the corrugated iron siding; took stock.

There was a taste in the air. She had noticed it a little while ago, but it had been faint then. Now it was strong. A slightly singed, oxidised taste that was nothing to do with her proximity to a coal mine. She knew what it meant.

A storm was on its way. Brewing up there in the clouds. Soon to be breaking.

All the more reason to keep moving, get this over and done with swiftly.

The sheds were arranged in threes, with narrow alleys running between each group. Cassie padded down the length of the nearest alley and peeked round the corner. Two miners were coming towards her, ambling along. They had evidently just finished a shift down the pit, to judge by their soot-smudged faces and forearms. Emergency breathing-apparatus packs were strapped to their backs. The masks and air-nozzles dangled from their belts, bouncing in time to their strides.

Cassie snatched her head back. Had the miners seen her? She didn't think so. She shrank into the alley's shadows, hearing the men's footsteps getting closer, their big workboots clumping.

She caught a snippet of conversation as the miners drew level with the alley mouth:

'Half the effort, same wages. Don't mind if this go-slow go on for ever!'

'But with them Deacons out of the picture, it'll be same amount of work as before, double the income. Look at it that way.'

They tramped past, lost in musings on a better future.

Cassie peeked out again. The miners were soon out of sight. The coast was clear.

She darted out from the alley and tiptoed past the broad, open entrance to the first shed. *Bertha* was in the next shed along.

There!

Cassie nipped in through the entrance and took another breather, hunkering against a toolbench. *Bertha* bulked in front of her, filling the shed with her presence, almost to the rafters. Her floodlight arrays seemed to be grinning.

'I be pleased to see you too,' Cassie whispered.

As far as she could tell, nobody was guarding *Bertha*. She took a couple of steps towards the murk-comber, thinking that the tricky part was over and from here on things were going to be plain sailing. She would climb in, start the engine up, and drive off. Once she got rolling, nothing and no one could stand in her way.

'Cass?'

She whirled round.

'Fletcher.'

Her brother had appeared from behind *Bertha*. He was carrying a large adjustable spanner. His hands were piebald with grease stains.

'What the hell is *you* doing here?' he said.

'Coming to take back what don't belong in this place,' Cassie replied, 'what else?'

'*Bertha?*' Fletcher hefted the spanner, weighing things up. 'Don't think I can let you do that, girl.'

'Yeah? Be that so?' She took another step in *Bertha*'s direction.

Fletcher moved to intercept.

'Come on then, Fletch,' Cassie said, squaring up to him. 'Let's see what you'm made of. Hit I with that spanner. 'Cause that be what it'm going to take to stop I. You'm going to have to deck me.'

'Cassie . . .'

'What?' she snapped.

'Please don't be like this. Just back off. Go on home. Don't make it hard for I.'

'Hard? Give me one reason to make it easy! Fletch, look at what you and Martin's done. Stolen *Bertha*. Got our Da and Robert beaten up – who be both all right, thanks for asking, though neither of them's exactly what you might call chipper.'

'I didn't—'

'What? *You* personally didn't beat they up? No, but you might as well have. And you's helped split our family in two. Proud of yourself for that? Well? Eh?'

Fletcher shifted his feet uncomfortably. 'Cass, it be'n't so simple as you make out. This stuff, what us is up to, us Humanists, it'm important. It'm about more than just family or *Bertha* or any of that. It'm about . . . a brighter tomorrow. For everyone. And maybe, in time, you'll come to realise that. Da too. When the dust's settled, maybe you'll both understand.'

'I tell you what I understand, Fletch,' Cassie said, tight-lipped. 'I understand that you'm just spouting that old tosh

169

what Alan Steamarm says. And I understand that Martin believes in it but you not so much. You want to because he does. You admire Martin. Of course you do. All of us do. Him's our big brother. Us has always looked up to he. And you'm closer to he than anyone 'cause there be only a year in age between you, while me and Robert, us has always been the babies. But you'm got to ask yourself, be this honestly what *you* want? This your own true dream? Or is you just going along with it to please Martin? 'Cause that be no reason for doing anything, just to please someone else.'

Again Fletcher hefted the spanner, gripping it tight as though it had all of a sudden grown much heavier. A V-shaped furrow appeared between his eyebrows.

'That be'n't it. That be'n't why I ...'

Her words were having an effect. He was probing inside himself, searching for his true feelings.

Finally, after what seemed to Cassie like an age, he said, 'She be misfiring a bit.'

Cassie blinked. 'Eh?'

'*Bertha*. She be misfiring. I been having a fiddle with her distributors. But I reckon some of her pipes is clogged too. Coke build-up.'

'They not have wire brushes here? What kind of mechanics they got working in this place?'

'Oh yeah, they got brushes. I were going to get round to it next. Clean off them spark plugs as well.'

'She still be roadworthy, though?'

Fletcher gave his sister a shy, sly wink.

'Roadworthy as ever, lass.'

CHAPTER 43

A Stranger To Storms

'One step at a time, Azrael,' said Steamarm. 'So you were born wingless, you say?'

'Deacons tell we,' said Brace, 'anyone who attempts to build a flying machine, him'll get Reconstituted without wings as a punishment.'

'Yes, that old superstition.' Steamarm gave a sneering laugh. 'Another little lie designed to keep us in our place. And of course the Deacons make sure that when a flying machine from above comes crashing to earth, the wreckage gets whisked off into their Reliquaries before anyone has the chance to get a good look at it. They wave a fistful of money at whoever finds it, and it's gone, never to be seen again. So the knowledge of how to make the damn things is kept from us. It's all about the Deacons preserving their position, hanging on to power, subduing the rest of us ... Sorry, started speechmaking there. Do carry on, Azrael.'

'What else do you want to know?' Az said, numbly.

'Anything. Everything. Let's try: why you're here.'

Az remembered his cover story, made up on the spot to dupe Cassie. It seemed a gossamer-thin confection now. It surely wouldn't hold up to Steamarm's abrasive scrutiny.

Still, he had to give it a go.

'I ... I came to be among my own kind,' he said. His cheek, where Steamarm had hit him, began throbbing more painfully, as if to remind him of the price of incurring the man's wrath. He forged on regardless. 'I wanted to see if I could belong here. You know, fit in, sort of thing. Like I couldn't up there.'

Steamarm leaned back, studying Az. He pursed his lips and tapped a forefinger against them.

Unconvinced.

'No,' he said. 'No, I don't reckon that's it. You want to know what I think? I think you were *sent* down here.'

'No, I wasn't, I came of my own accord. I—'

'Azrael.' Steamarm barked the word. 'It's very courageous of you to lie, when you know what the consequences are. It's also very stupid. It doesn't get anyone anywhere, and it only delays the inevitable moment when you *will* tell me the truth. So let's cut the nightsoil and get right down to it. Spare us all a lot of unnecessary unpleasantness. You're a spy, aren't you?'

Az was a fraction of a second late in denying it, and that fraction of a second was all Steamarm needed to know that he had struck gold.

'Not a guess on my part, just a piece of logical deduction,' Steamarm explained. 'Who better to send to investigate when the supplies from down here get interrupted? Who better than someone who looks like one of us? Even if he is just a kid.'

Az considered trying to protest again, telling Steamarm he had got it wrong. But there was no point.

He felt dispirited but at the same time oddly relieved. He didn't have to keep up a pretence any more, however flimsy it was. That burden had been lifted from him.

What next, though? Just how much information about the Airborn world was Steamarm going to try to pump out of him?

'Now,' the Humanist spokesman said, 'I'm told by the elder Grubdollar sibling, Martin, that you were very sick when they found you. They feared a case of rattle-lung at first, but it wasn't that. You were nauseous, right? Dizzy? Had difficulty breathing?'

Az nodded, puzzled by the turn the questioning had taken.

'Interesting. And this state of feeling rotten lasted for roughly twenty-four hours?'

'Thereabouts.'

172

Steamarm turned to Brace. 'Remind you of anything, Lawrence?'

'Miners,' came the reply. 'Apprentice's bends.'

'Quite. Apprentice miners experience similar symptoms for their first few days on the coalface, especially if they start off working deep underground. Gradually they adjust. Their bodies acclimatise.'

Steamarm turned back to Az. 'But we shall say no more. This is of no concern to our young friend here. Not yet, at any rate. From you, Azrael, I think I require a little strategic intelligence now. For instance, your leadership. Who, exactly, commissioned you to come down here?'

'Her name is Serena, Lady Aanfieldsdaughter,' Az said, 'and she is a great and wise woman.'

'She runs everything?'

'More or less.'

'A matriarch. Formidable, I should imagine.'

'She's a proper leader, not a longwinded, self-satisfied buffoon,' Az said.

Steamarm's right hand twitched, but he decided to be amused.

'I should like to meet this wonderful person someday,' Steamarm said. 'Apparently I could learn a thing or two from her. And perhaps I could teach *her* a thing or two in return.'

Just as he was saying this, there was a flicker of dazzling light at the window, followed a few heartbeats later by a deep, grinding rumble from above.

Az looked round in alarm. What was that?

'You seem startled,' said Steamarm. 'Just a spot of thunder. Surely you've heard thunder before.'

'"Thunder"?'

'Ah, an unfamiliar word. And "lightning" too, I suppose.'

Az shook his head to show that both terms were new to him.

'Really you do come from another world, Azrael. That flash of light, that rumble, they signify that a storm is coming. But of course, up above the clouds you don't have storms, do you?

You're not affected by them. We down here, on the other hand, are. Sometimes severely. We get flooded, there are fires … All sorts.'

The electrostatic discharges in the clouds – those noiseless flickers of light – meant little or nothing to the Airborn. It was an event that happened far below, beneath notice. On the ground, however, it was obviously a matter of great importance.

There was another flash, and it filled the larder with a stutter of brilliance, making the shadows leap and writhe. The rumble that came after was like something vast being split asunder.

Lightning. Thunder. Mist. Rain.

All at once Az felt horribly, gut-wrenchingly homesick for the bright, sunlit, calm place where such ugly weather conditions were unheard of.

He was never getting back there. Not now. Once Steamarm was finished with him, once he had drained all the usefulness out of him, he wasn't simply going to let him go free, was he? No, either he was going to keep him here in the larder indefinitely, leaving him to rot, or …

Or dispose of him. In a more violent fashion.

Az felt a plunge inside, not unlike the horribly unforgettable sensation of plummeting through space with those copper wings on his back three years ago.

'Let us continue, shall we?' Steamarm said. 'Now that we've established you're a stranger to storms. I think we should turn our attention to defence matters. Specifically, what kind of military arrangement, if any, might one expect to find up in the realm of the Ascended Ones? Is there a standing army? Maybe some kind of aircraft-borne wing of the armed forces?'

'Wing!' said Brace, with a chuckle.

'Oh yes, a pun. Totally unintentional, I might add.' Despite that, Steamarm looked impressed by his own wordsmithery. 'Well, Azrael? Come on, I asked you a question. Don't start the silent act again. That would be a shame. We were getting along so nicely.'

Once more there was a rumble from outside.

Thunder again?

Az thought so, until he realised that it hadn't been preceded by a snap of lightning. And it wasn't a short, sharp burst of sound; it was continuous.

Continuous, and growing louder.

And louder.

'What the …?' Steamarm looked around, perplexed.

So did Brace.

Suddenly a shadow loomed in the tiny window, casting the larder into darkness.

Next instant, the outer wall collapsed, erupting inward in a cascade of mortar and stones.

CHAPTER 44

Murk-Comber Versus Cottage

It hadn't been thunder, of course. Rather it had been the roar of a 500-horsepower engine propelling fifty tonnes of caterpillar-tracked vehicle at a sedate but remorseless speed across Lawrence Brace's back garden, straight towards his cottage.

The collision of murk-comber with external wall made both vehicle and building shudder. But only one of them suffered any harm.

And it wasn't *Cackling Bertha*.

Within seconds of the impact, Cassie leapt nimbly out from the loading bay and hurried towards the cottage. Meanwhile Fletcher threw *Bertha* into reverse, pulling her back to expose the large, jagged hole she had punched in Brace's home. Debris scattered from her nose. Chunks of plaster and stone tumbled to the ground, to be crushed beneath her treads.

'Az! Az!' Cassie stumbled across rubble and peered into the dark of the larder. 'Az, be you there?' She wafted away swirls of rising dust. 'Az?'

Lightning briefly whitened the world, and in its illumination Cassie made out three figures in the larder. Two were sprawled together, pinned by a fallen set of shelves, with an avalanche of crockery all around them. They were lying still. The third figure was slumped in the opposite corner, and was stirring.

'Az, that you?'

A cough came from the third figure, then a muffled 'Yes'.

'Up you get. Come on. Us is here to rescue you. You OK?'

Az got shakily to his feet. 'Think so.'

'This way then. Hurry.'

Az tottered towards her. There were fragments of mortar and plaster all over him, and his hair was whitened by dust. She noticed a couple of small cuts on his face, and a bruise-like swelling on his cheek. His eyes were glazed with shock.

'How ... I didn't think ... Why ...'

'No time for gab. Explanations later. Get yourself into *Bertha*.'

Cassie shoved him out through the hole and round to the side of the murk-comber. He clambered inside the loading bay, and Cassie jumped in behind him and hit the switch to shut the hatch.

She snatched up the speaker tube.

'Us is in, Fletch. Give she loads!'

Bertha let out an almighty cackle of delight and accelerated in reverse across the back garden, ploughing a fresh set of track furrows.

CHAPTER 45

A Heart-Rending Loss Of Marrows

Not long after, the two men left in the larder groaned and began to move.

Brace was the first to come to his senses fully, and as soon as he perceived that he and Steamarm were lying under a set of shelves, he set about remedying the situation. With a huge grunt and a flex of his shoulders he shunted the shelves off them, then he swiped away shards of broken crockery to clear an area of floorspace. He hauled himself upright, bent, and helped Steamarm to his feet. Tentatively, the two men made their way out through the hole, emerging into the open air.

'My house.' Brace surveyed the damage, his mouth down-turned mournfully. 'Look what them did to my house. D'you know how much that'm going to cost to fix? And my garden. Them drove straight over my vegetable patch. My precious veggies! My poor marrows!'

Brace was very partial to a marrow and very proud of the ones he grew, which he believed to be the largest and best in all of Grimvale. The sight of them smashed to a pulp by the murk-comber's treads was almost too much to bear. His eyes moistened.

'Never mind that,' said a still-dazed Steamarm. 'They've taken something I need, and I want it back.'

'You mean the boy?'

'No, not the boy.' Steamarm swore soundly through clenched teeth. 'And when everything was going so well, too! They'll regret it, though. You don't mess with Alan Steamarm and get away with it.'

'The murk-comber,' Brace said, belatedly realising what

Steamarm's 'something I need' referred to.

'Yes, the bloody murk-comber. *My* murk-comber. But it's all right.'

Suddenly Steamarm's voice was preternaturally calm; his face viciously determined.

'Yes, it's all right. They've got it now, but it won't be theirs for long.'

CHAPTER 46

Steamarm's Further Ambitions

'Figured you needed saving,' Cassie said. 'And being as it were our fault you ended up captured in the first place, it were up to we to get you out.'

'But your brother who's driving,' said Az, 'isn't he one of them? A Humanist?'

Cassie gave a wry shrug. 'Fletch and I had a bit of a chat. I set he straight on a couple of things. Got he to see sense. It were lucky, though, that him were alone when I reached *Bertha*. Martin were around at the pit but off having a bite of lunch. If *him'd* been in the shed, I wouldn't have stood a chance and I wouldn't be here now. Martin's a dyed-in-the-wool Humanist, while Fletch... Well, him were open to persuasion, put it like that. And him knew where you'm being kept, and so here us is.'

Az eyed her by the glow of the single, low-output bulb that lit the loading bay yellowly. The pair of them were swaying to and fro in time to the ponderous sway of *Bertha*'s progress, like dancers in some strange, non-contact waltz.

'I don't know what to say, Cassie.'

'"Thanks" would do, but actually I reckon this makes things even. Now all us has to do is return you to the Chancel so's you can get back up where you belong.'

'You'd do that for me?'

'Barring disasters, us can get you inside as far as the Relic sorting-house area. After that, you'm on your own. Think you can find them elevators again?'

Az wasn't at all certain, but he said yes.

'There you go then,' Cassie said. 'Done and dusted. Now,

you'm really all right? What did our good friend Mr Steamarm want with you anyway?'

'Hard to say. He kept asking these random questions, wanting to know about our leadership, military capability and so on. He didn't get very far before you came crashing in. I don't think he learned very much.' This last statement was one which Az hoped, rather than felt, was true.

'Hmm,' said Cassie, musing. 'Sounds like ... No, him wouldn't. Would him?'

'Wouldn't what?'

Instead of answering, she grabbed the speaker tube.

'Fletch? After you lot was going to take over the Chancel, what then? What were your man Steamarm planning next?'

'Occupy it,' came the reply. 'Kick out the Deacons.'

'That'm it?'

'Far as I know.'

'No phase two?'

'Not that anyone told I about.'

Replacing the tube on its hook, Cassie said to Az, 'Maybe him was just being nosy. I mean, who wouldn't want to interrogate a real, live Ascended One if them got the chance?'

'But maybe not,' said Az slowly. He was catching her drift. 'What if Steamarm's ambitions aren't limited to occupying the Chancel? He mentioned our "flying machines", as he called them. And there was also some stuff about apprentice miners and "bends", although I can't say I completely followed it. You think he's planning an invasion, don't you? He's going to lead the Humanists up into the Airborn world.'

Cassie's frank, perturbed expression told Az that was precisely what she was thinking.

'So why hasn't he said anything about it to your brother? Surely he wouldn't keep his fellow Humanists in the dark about something as major as that.'

'Him might, especially with them who'm some way down the pecking order, like Fletch. So as not to alarm they. Telling they from the start that them's going to be mounting an attack on the Ascended Ones – it'd put a lot of they off. Them'd think it a step too far. But wait till the Chancels has fallen, and while everyone's flush with victory, tell they *then*, and him's considerably more likely to get they to go along with it.'

'The Humanists would really do that? Go up into the sky-cities?'

'I don't know, Az,' Cassie said, slightly testy. 'I be'n't one of them, be I? Also, Deacons say it'm impossible. Us can't survive up there. But judging from what Steamarm were asking you, all them things he were curious about, I'd say him be thinking about it.'

'A co-ordinated assault,' Az said, 'and nobody up there will be expecting it.'

'Them will be,' Cassie said, 'if you'm able to get there and give they a warning.'

Az squared his jaw and nodded. 'You're right. That's what I'm going to have to do, warn them. Straight up.'

Cassie peered at him askance.

'What?' he said. 'Why are you looking at me like that?'

'You said "straight up".'

'No, I didn't. Did I?'

'Yeah, you did.' She half smiled. 'How long you'm been here? Couple of days. And already you's picked up some of the lingo.'

Az half smiled back. 'Yeah. I *has* done and all.'

'Hey, watch it.'

'So, how long till we reach the Chancel?' Az's relief at being rescued was starting to ebb away as he considered the prospect of another run-in with the Deacons.

'An hour or so. *Bertha* be'n't the fastest thing on the road, but her's sure to get you there in the end.'

'What shall we do in the meantime?'

Cassie waved a hand. 'Want to take a tour?'

'Of the famous *Cackling Bertha*? Love to.'

CHAPTER 47

A Matter Of Perspective

They wriggled through *Bertha*'s crawl-ducts and up and down her ladders. Cassie showed Az each of the observation nacelles in turn, and the roof turret, and finally took him up to the driver's pod. There, they crouched behind Fletcher, and Az watched, fascinated, as the second eldest Grubdollar brother manipulated the control sticks, guiding the murk-comber along the streets of Grimvale. Rain had begun to fall in heavy drops, spattering the windscreen. Fletcher engaged the wipers and switched on the headlamps. Lightning flickered every now and then, forking white through the inky blackness of the clouds. Each time, a thunder crackle resounded soon after.

Outside, Groundlings hurried through the rain, seeking shelter. Some huddled in doorways or under shop awnings. A few were carrying a protective device which Cassie told Az was called an *umbrella*. It was like a portable, foldable canvas roof, and it kept you from getting wet.

Soon *Bertha* was out of the town and beetling along through a forest. The trees were tall and thick-trunked, giants compared with the tended, coppiced courtyard trees Az was used to. Even in the Airborn's parks there was nothing as towering as these evergreens, nor was there such a profusion of undergrowth. The Airborn favoured lawns and tidiness. Nature, in the sky-cities, was tamed and contained. It had to be. Down here, on the other hand, it had no confines. It proliferated wherever and whenever, without limits.

Even so, Az noted that there was something about the trees' foliage, a droopiness, a lack of vitality, that implied they grew tall only through great effort. Poorly nourished by the thin, cloud-filtered sunlight, it cost them everything they had to become as big as they did. Their needles were a yellowy green, nothing like the deep, vibrant, sun-drenched pine greens he was familiar with. Lichen covered their trunks, and moss, too, in thick, spongy blobs – parasites that thrived in the damp conditions.

At Cassie's suggestion, Fletcher took a detour, leaving the main road and heading off along a side road. The side road was windy and narrow and slowed them down, but, as Cassie explained, it meant they wouldn't be travelling past the Consolidated Colliery Collective, which was where the Humanists had been keeping *Bertha*. She didn't think it a good idea to parade the murk-comber in front of the noses of the people they had recently retrieved her from.

'Them wasn't too happy when us left,' she said to Az. 'Had to drive out through the front gate, and them picketers couldn't get out of our way fast enough. Scattered they like skittles, us did.'

'Them used some very colourful language,' said Fletcher, chuckling at the memory. 'Some even threw stones at us. Bounced off *Bertha*, of course. Doubt her barely felt it. But those people won't be any too happy to see we again, that'm for sure. Didn't make no friends there.'

'Plus, Martin's probably got they mobilised and setting up roadblocks, knowing him. Speaking of which, d'you think Martin'll ever talk to you or I again, Fletch?'

'Doubt it, lass.' Fletcher gave a rueful laugh. 'Maybe twenty years from now we'll get a "hello" out of he. Maybe. Martin be the type to hold a grudge all right.'

'Sorry to turn you against he.'

'Weren't *he* specifically, Cass. Was all of they. You just re-minded me where my priorities lay. It were that and your poor hand.'

Cassie glanced at her bruised, verm-bitten hand.

'I looked at that,' Fletcher said, 'and remembered how you saved I the day before yesterday. Helped make sense of things, a bit. Truth be told, I were beginning to feel a bit queasy about it all anyway, not least when I saw they hitting Da. Didn't think it would come down to choosing sides, but it did, and I's glad I chose the right one.'

'Yeah, you did.' Cassie patted his shoulder – with her good hand.

'How about you, Mr Ascended One?' Fletcher said to Az, craning round. 'You'm going to be glad to get back home, I reckon. Tell you, life down here be'n't always this dramatic. You should come down another time when it'm calmer. You'll see us is an all right lot really.'

'I may take you up on that offer,' Az said. It didn't sound convincing even to himself.

They rejoined the main road at a point beyond the northernmost of Grimvale's industrial premises. Shortly, the landscape began flattening out, the mountainous terrain giving way to foothills and eventually a plain.

'The Shadow Zone,' Cassie announced.

Az leaned forward, peering even more attentively through the windscreen. The clouds were still black and rifted with forks of lightning, as though intermittently shattering. But ahead, there was a darkness that was deeper than that caused by the storm, a dreary, tenebrous gloom.

The last time Az was in the Shadow Zone it had been night and he had, moreover, been in no fit state to take stock of his surroundings. Now he saw a barren, broken expanse of landscape where scant vegetation grew and any that did was either low and mossy or tough and spiky. There were boulders and rough hillocks, and silvery flashes of waterway. Far, far in the distance Heliotropia's support column was visible, rising sheer into the clouds, finger-thin. In the low light Az could just make out the cluster of buildings at its base, the Chancel. Somewhere up above lay the sky-city itself, he knew, but there was no way you could get any sense of how it looked or even its size. It was visible only by the shade it cast through the clouds, the roughly circular penumbra that left several dozen hectares of the world below in perpetual eclipse.

'It's an impressive city,' he said in hushed tones, 'and yet down here you have no idea of that. All you get is what it isn't.'

'Yup, that about sums it up,' said Cassie, with more than a touch of irony. 'What us gets down here is what you lot up there be'n't.'

'Oy-oy.'

Fletcher was frowning up at a large convex mirror that was mounted to the left of the windscreen. There were two of these mirrors in the driver's pod, and if Az didn't miss his guess they reflected images conveyed from *Bertha*'s aft end along tubes via a system of lenses. Rearview mirrors with knobs on.

Fletcher turned to check the right-hand one.

'Oy-oy,' he said again, more emphatically this time.

'What'm up?' said Cassie. From any angle except from the driving seat the images in the mirrors were opaque; it was hard to make out what they were showing.

'Us is being followed. Two coal trucks. No, three. And them's gaining fast. Don't think the drivers is after checking our union accreditation, either.'

CHAPTER 48

The Low-speed Chase Begun

The coal trucks all bore the insignia of the Consolidated Colliery Collective – three C's, one inside the other. They were unladen and being driven at top speed. There was no question that they could catch up with *Bertha*, who couldn't manage more than 30 kph at full throttle. The question was, what were they going to do when they did?

'Steer off-road,' Cassie urged Fletcher. 'Them won't be able to follow.'

'Thought of that already, girl. If you take a look around, you may notice it'm too rocky out there. Us'll get stuck. First possible turning-off point be a good couple of kilometres ahead.'

'Block they, then. Get in the middle of the road.'

Fletcher eased the right control stick forward a notch. 'Think one of they will still be able to pull alongside. *Bertha's* broad but maybe not enough.'

'What do they want with us, Cassie?' said Az.

'Best guess? Stop we. Run we off the road if they can. Anything, so long as they gets *Bertha* back.'

'Run us off …? But we could be killed!'

Cassie's smile was grim. 'Not sure as that be too much of a worry for they.'

The leading truck swiftly closed the gap between it and *Bertha*, until its front bumper was less than a metre from her left-hand track. The driver nosed forwards into the space between *Bertha's* flank and the edge of the road. Fletcher steered the murk-comber in that direction, narrowing the available room. The truck driver braked, falling in behind once more. As Fletcher straightened out *Bertha*'s course, the driver attempted the manoeuvre a second time. He was deterred again by the lumbering bulk of *Bertha* veering into his path.

The second truck arrived and took up position on the opposite side of the road. Using the mirrors, Fletcher nudged *Bertha* in front of it so that there was no way through. This, however, meant that the first truck now had a clear run. The driver seized his opportunity, gunned the engine, and accelerated past *Bertha* before Fletcher could swing back over to prevent him.

Now there was one truck in front, one behind, and the third zooming up to join them.

'Pull over,' Az advised. 'This is no good. Give them what they're after. It's all about me. Getting me to the Chancel. That's not worth risking your lives over.'

'What'm you talking about, boy?' said Fletcher. 'This be'n't about you. It'm about *Bertha*. And I'd sooner crash she in a ball of flames than let they have their way with she.'

'Fletch's right,' Cassie agreed. 'Took he long enough to realise it, but better late than never. No way is those Humanists having she. Besides,' she added with a tight smile, 'look at the size of what them's driving compared with *Bertha*. I don't know how them hopes to stop she with just trucks. Her weighs about five times as much. Them'd have to be crazy to—'

The truck in front braked sharply.

'Hold on!' shouted Fletcher.

Bertha rolled onward and collided nose-first with the truck's rear. There was a deafening screeching *smash*. The truck was shunted forwards, its tyres lost traction on the wet road, and it went careering this way and that till the driver regained control.

'Reckon him won't try that again in a hurry,' Cassie said.

'Let's hope not,' said Az.

The third coal truck at last joined the fray. All Fletcher could see in each of the mirrors was a driver's cab, a windscreen with the wipers working furiously, and a radiator grille with the three-C's logo embossed on it. The drivers themselves were hard to make out, blurry faces that appeared briefly each time the wipers cleared the windscreen before becoming lost again in the rain. He wasn't liking the fact that *Bertha* was boxed in, at the centre of a triangle of trucks. Even if the trucks were no match for her in terms of bulk, they might still be able to do some damage, enough to disable her. And as the somewhat foolhardy driver in front had just demonstrated, the Humanists were prepared to try anything to get her to stop, even at risk of their own lives.

The third truck suddenly veered sideways, slamming its wheel arch against *Bertha*'s caterpillar track. One of the sticks jumped in Fletcher's grasp but he regained control quickly.

The truck repeated the assault. The impact resounded through the murk-comber's frame.

'Him's a loony, that bloke,' Cassie said. 'Likely as not him'll kill himself, if him's not careful.'

'No, not a loony,' Fletcher said, coldly. He was staring hard at one of the mirrors. He had at last got a clear view of one of the drivers. 'It'm Martin.'

'Martin?'

'Him's the one ramming we. Because him knows. Knacker one of *Bertha*'s tracks, and her'll be crippled. Her'll stop dead.'

Cassie bent, trying to get a glimpse of the truck driver in the mirror. 'You'm sure it be he?'

'I know our own brother's face, girl.'

One more time, the truck hurled itself at *Bertha*. As it hit, its wheel housing was ripped away by the force of the collision. Metal twisted and tore. The truck slewed off the road, bumped and jerked crazily on the roadside rocks, and then, more through luck than anything, bounced back onto the tarmac and carried on driving. One of its front wheels was now uncovered, exposed by a section of missing bodywork.

And part of the section of missing bodywork was entangled in *Bertha*'s track, being rolled around between the track links and the running wheels. This had been Martin's plan. If the shred of metal became caught—

It did. It jammed between two of the wheels.

All at once, *Bertha* began to skid.

CHAPTER 49

The Low-speed Chase Continued

Fletcher did everything he could to manage the skid. It happened with dreamy slowness, for *Bertha* never did anything in a hurry. Her front started to turn, sliding round in the direction of the tread that had seized up. Her rear end followed, lumbering outwards. Fletcher hauled back on one stick to counteract the rotation, but with minimal effect. *Bertha* had momentum, plenty of it, and all of it was going into the skid.

As for Cassie and Az, there was little else they could do but find something in the driver's pod to hang onto, and hang onto it tight.

Now *Bertha* was sideways on the road, still skidding. She was almost graceful in this moment of loss of control, ballerina-like as she pirouetted. Anyone watching from a safe distance might have been enchanted by the smoothness, the stateliness with which the sizeable vehicle spun.

She continued to turn, while the three trucks kept pace with her, as though this was all some prearranged formation exercise. *Bertha* had nearly about-faced when, through an abrupt stroke of good fortune, the piece of coal truck bodywork snapped loose from the wheels, pinging out onto the road. All at once, her jammed track was working again. Fletcher sensed it through the sticks and took the appropriate action. He had only one choice, if he wished to keep going at any speed. He lined *Bertha* up on the road and wrenched both sticks into reverse.

Bertha was still rolling. The three trucks were still with her, having failed to stop her yet. The only difference now was that *Bertha* was going backwards.

Through her windscreen, the two pursuing trucks were clearly visible. And yes, Cassie could see Martin at the wheel of one of them. The other driver was one of the Humanists who had invaded the Grubdollar's house that morning, one of the ones whose names Cassie didn't know. And beside him, in the passenger seat, was none other than Alan Steamarm.

A very angry-looking and unhappy-looking Alan Steamarm.

Cassie blew him a sarcastic kiss.

In return, Steamarm sneered.

'Perhaps you could stop flirting and start doing something useful,' Fletcher admonished her. 'Driving backwards like this be'n't easy. Why not find some way of messing they up like them tried to mess we up, eh?'

'What d'you mean?'

'Well, doesn't us have a javelin launcher on board?'

'You don't want me to—'

'Take out a tyre, that'm all.'

Cassie grinned. 'Fletch, genius!' She dived out of the driver's pod.

'What about me?' Az asked Fletcher. 'Can I help somehow?'

'Go aft to one of the rear observation nacelles. Tell I if I'm getting too close to the edge of the road.'

'No problem.' Az, too, dived out of the pod.

In the roof turret, Cassie primed the launcher and swivelled it round. Her priority, she decided, was the truck in front. She should clear the road.

The truck was perhaps thirty metres ahead. She drew a bead on it with the launcher's sights. What was it that Da said? Aim slightly high. A javelin never travelled in a dead straight line. There was always an arc to its flight.

She curled a finger round the trigger and squeezed. With a sharp propulsive hiss the javelin shot towards the truck's back wheel ...

... and missed, hitting the road with a spark and spiralling away.

'Bugger!'

Ordering herself to keep her nerve, Cassie reloaded, primed the launcher again, and aimed.

She was about to shoot, but the truck hit a pothole and leapt out of the sights.

She centred the tyre again in the sights, then raised the launcher fractionally.

'You're mine,' she said. 'Pop!'

The javelin whistled across the distance between *Bertha* and the truck.

The tyre exploded. One instant it was there, inflated, full; the next it was just so much loose, shredded rubber.

The truck immediately went into a long, shuddering deceleration, throwing out fragments of tyre behind it. A moment after it came to a complete halt, diagonally across the road, *Bertha* went barging into it.

With so much weight behind her, *Bertha* wasn't going to be hindered by a mere truck. It was no obstacle whatever. She shunted it along for a hundred metres or so, pushing it up at an increasingly oblique angle, until the truck, as if deciding it had had enough of this undignified treatment, keeled over and tumbled off the road, rolling, bouncing, crunching onto the rocks, where it came to a standstill, upside down.

Bertha trundled past it, as did the remaining two trucks. Seconds later, one door of the overturned truck flipped open and the dazed driver hauled himself out.

'Good shot!' came Az's voice over the speaker tube.

'Yeah, lass, not bad,' said Fletcher. 'Now how about them other two?'

Cranking on a lever, Cassie spun the turret round. She grabbed a fresh javelin from behind her, slotted it in, and sighted on the coal truck Martin was driving.

No, she couldn't. In spite of everything, she couldn't fire on her own brother.

She swivelled her aim onto Steamarm instead.

No qualms about javelining *his* vehicle.

Suddenly: 'Left!'

Az, yelling urgently.

'We have to go left!'

Cassie felt *Bertha* start to turn.

'No, *my* left, not yours!'

Bertha lumbered the other way.

Cassie glanced out. They had reached a section of the road that had been carved into the side of a small hill, the last such hill before the Shadow Zone plain began. The ground fell away to the right in a steep slope some ten metres deep, a gradient of loose earth and gravel. On the left rose a bank of similar size and composition. It was like this for the next half-kilometre.

Slight subsidence meant that the road surface was very uneven and the camber more bowed than it should be. Additionally, the road started to curve round a bend here, following the contour of the hill.

In other words, it was a tricky stretch to navigate in *Bertha* even when you were going forwards and at a sensible speed.

Fletcher was tackling it in reverse and at full throttle.

No wonder he hadn't answered Az. He couldn't be bothering with the speaker tube. He had his hands full just keeping them on the tarmac.

Well, Cassie was in a position to give him assistance. She locked the javelin launcher back on her target: Steamarm's truck.

Martin, however, had other ideas.

CHAPTER 50

The Low-speed Chase Concluded

Martin stamped on the accelerator, ramming *Bertha* with his truck just as Cassie loosed off the javelin. The launcher jerked sideways and her shot went wild. The javelin lodged itself in the bank, quivering.

Another, unintentional, consequence of Martin's action was that *Bertha* was knocked slightly off-course. She was close to the bank already and the impact was just enough to shove her against it. She scraped the bank and rebounded with force, swerving slowly and inexorably across to the other side of the road. Her right-hand track left the tarmac and dug into the top of the slope. Earth and gravel churned out sideways.

Cassie could feel Fletcher fighting to keep *Bertha* steady. The murk-comber was shuddering and juddering. If she came off the road and went sliding down the slope, she would flip up when she hit the bottom and somersault end over end. Cassie had a stark vision of this happening. Everyone on board would be tossed around like beads in a baby's rattle. None of them would survive, and *Bertha* herself would be so much scrap metal.

Az was yelling frantically into the speaker tube, but to Cassie his words were meaningless gabble. His voice was just part of a tumultuous background cacophony, along with *Bertha*'s cackle – anxious now – and the gruelling grind of gravel beneath her treads.

Inside, Cassie was weirdly calm. For seconds that seemed like minutes, she waited for the sudden sideways lurch that would mean *Bertha* was doomed. It was all she could do, wait. Wait, and wonder how much it would hurt when the moment of death came, and who would turn up for her Ceremony of

Ascension. And what would become of Az? If an Ascended One died down here, could he or she Ascend? Did it work like that? It was an intriguing conundrum.

Then *Bertha* began to level out. Fletcher had her under control again. Both of her tracks were safely on tarmac, and the road was straightening now, and the slope on the right was gradually getting shallower.

When the slope was gone altogether, they would be properly in the Shadow Zone. At that point they could leave the road, striking out across the rugged open terrain where the coal trucks could not follow them.

Martin knew this. From the turret, Cassie saw him bring his truck in close, evidently contemplating one final assault.

He thought better of it. He eased off on the accelerator and the truck fell back.

She understood why. Just now, he had nearly killed his brother and sister. He had meant only to knock Cassie's aim off but he had come close to causing a disaster. No way did he want their deaths on his conscience. For all the differences between him and them, they were still family.

Alan Steamarm, on the other hand, had no such compunctions. Cassie saw him give Martin's retreating truck a furious stare. Then he gave an order to his driver, his gesticulations clearly saying that the driver should do what Martin had failed to earlier and snarl up the murk-comber's track with a bit of truck.

The driver steered close.

Fletcher, at that very moment, realised his chance to get away had come at last. He turned *Bertha* sharply. There was bumping, bouncing, thudding, thumping. Cassie was tossed around in her seat, so violently that she banged her forehead on the launcher handles.

Then they were moving away from the road. Fletcher had driven off it backwards, and now they were reversing across the raw terrain of the Shadow Zone. He must have felt confident that Steamarm would not pursue them any more, because he reduced *Bertha*'s speed to a crawl.

Steamarm, though, was not about to give up so easily. His truck braked, then ventured off the road in first gear.

'I don't believe it,' Fletcher said into the speaker tube.

'Don't believe what?' Az replied. 'What's going on?' Az was at the back of *Bertha*. He couldn't see the road.

'Steamarm thinks him can still catch we,' Cassie said. 'Him won't get far, though.'

If a vehicle could look tentative, that coal truck did. It resembled someone wading into icy cold water. The driver got all four wheels off the road, then pumped the accelerator experimentally. The truck lumbered forwards, and hit a snag. One of the front wheels rolled into a cleft, the kind of thirty-centimetre fissure in the ground that *Bertha* could pass over without even noticing. The driver shifted into reverse and, after several false starts, pulled out. With great care he navigated around the cleft – and promptly got a wheel stuck in another one.

Fletcher brought *Bertha* to a complete halt, putting her into neutral. 'This should be funny.'

The truck escaped the second cleft, but now there was a series of small boulders to be got around. The truck had a high wheelbase and good suspension but it couldn't ride a rock field the way a murk-comber could.

In all, the truck managed to struggle forward for a grand total of twenty metres before Steamarm admitted defeat and told the driver to turn around. Getting back to the road was another epic effort, and the truck almost didn't make it.

On the road, Martin was waiting. He had known better than to attempt what Steamarm had attempted. Steamarm climbed out of his truck and went over to Martin for a conference.

Az poked his head up through the turret entrance. 'Mind if I join you? I'm obviously missing out on some good stuff.' He clambered in. 'So what's up? Why aren't we moving any more?'

'Because us is safe, for now,' Cassie said.

'I must say, I thought we were goners back there.'

'You wasn't the only one.'

'I can laugh about it now.'

'But you was screaming like a girl earlier.'

Az looked sheepish. 'Yeah. Sorry.'

'Don't worry. Least you'm man enough to admit you was scared.'

Martin left his partly mangled truck, and he and Steamarm walked to the roadside. Martin looked towards *Bertha* and waved both arms in the air, the gesture of someone who wished to parley.

'What you reckon, Fletch?' Cassie said into the speaker tube. 'Go out for a chat?'

'Tempted, but I be'n't sure Martin has anything to say to I that I wants to listen to. Besides, us has the advantage here. Foolish to waste it.'

'My thoughts exactly.'

Martin's hands fell to his sides in disappointment as Fletcher started *Bertha*'s engine up. Fletcher brought the murk-comber around, beat out a cheeky toot-toot on the horn, and trundled away.

'That'm that then,' Cassie said to Az. 'Next stop, the Chancel.'

CHAPTER 51

Escape From The Chancel: The Blanks In *Az's* Memory Filled In

The Chancel boasted four entrances positioned equidistantly around its perimeter fence, one for each of the main roads that came in across the Shadow Zone. The entrances were fortified and patrolled. There were barriers, gatehouses, and even retractable ramps in the road which could be operated hydraulically to stop a vehicle from going in or leaving.

The Deacons took their security seriously. Or, to put it another way, they were very keen on protecting what was theirs.

The perimeter fence itself was a lofty steel stockade, crowned with outward-curving spikes. Looking at it, Az marvelled at the fact that he had escaped from the Chancel at all. He had no recollection of getting over such a fence.

'That'm because you didn't,' Cassie told him. 'I be guessing you went *through* it.'

'Through it? How?'

She showed him. Fletcher was making a detour around a shallow lake, crossing it at the far end where it dispersed into a series of streams and rivulets which ribboned out in all directions. *Bertha* splashed through them like they were mere puddles.

The lake's other end touched the Chancel's perimeter, and it was there that a water outflow pipe penetrated the fence, disgorging its contents into the lake in a pale brown cascade.

'You went out with the cleaned-up sewage,' Cassie said. 'Must have. That'm why you was so wet when us found you.'

This corresponded with Az's patchy memories of his last

few moments inside the Chancel – the sewage treatment tanks, the rushing channel. He congratulated her. 'Brilliant detective work there, Miss Grubdollar.'

'Thank you.'

'So can't I get back in the same way?'

'Not unless you be a damn strong swimmer, and I's thinking you'm not. Actually, I doubt even a strong swimmer could get in that way. Doubt a fish could.'

'Fish?'

'Animal that— Never mind. Nope, only possible way in be by the front door, so to speak.'

'The Deacons'll let us in?'

'Don't see why not, us being in a murk-comber. And then, for afterwards, I's got a plan. Tell me, how big be your shoes?'

'How big?' Az was taken aback. What did the size of his shoes have to do with anything? 'I don't know. Medium large.'

Cassie studied his feet. 'Them look to be about the same as Robert's.' She hoisted herself out of the launcher seat. 'Let's go down to the loading bay, see if I be right.'

CHAPTER 52

A Sticky Moment With The Chancel Guards

Fletcher pulled up at the Chancel entrance. Cassie had anticipated that the guards in the gatehouse would simply raise the barrier and wave *Bertha* through, as normally happened. *Bertha* was a regular visitor. There was no reason for them to be suspicious.

But she was wrong. The barrier did not go up. Instead, the retractable ramps shot up behind and in front of *Bertha*, bookending her. She was trapped in place. Then the two guards emerged from the gatehouse and came striding over. The guards were ordinary Deacons, but armoured and armed. They had helmets on, breastplates over their robes, pikestaffs in their hands, handcuffs attached to their belts. One of them used the tip of his pikestaff to rap on *Bertha*'s hatch.

Cassie motioned to Az: *get out of sight*. Az hurried up the nearest ladder. Then Cassie hit the lever for the hatch. As it opened, she greeted the guards with a beaming grin.

'What'm up, gents?'

'Afternoon,' said one of them. 'Haven't seen you Grubdollars here in a while.'

'That be because us has been having a run of bad luck. Not finding anything.'

'What a shame,' the guard said, although from the sound of it he couldn't have cared less. Both he and his colleague were looking past Cassie, scanning *Bertha*'s interior.

Cassie knew these two. They were familiar faces to her. They were never friendly but they were usually a lot less frostily formal than this.

'Something you'm after?' she asked.

'No. No. It's just that we had a security breach here the other day.'

'Oh?'

'Yes. Someone got in who shouldn't have. A kid. So now we're under orders to check every vehicle that arrives, in case of stowaways.'

'Not that a lot of vehicles *are* arriving right now,' said the other guard.

The first guard nodded. 'Doesn't help that we're all a bit jumpy anyway, what with the Humanists and all that.'

'Ruddy Humanists,' Cassie said, encouragingly.

'Yes, quite. The Archdeacon is very concerned about them. Hence, extra vigilance. You can never be too careful. Even when dealing with the Grubdollars and *Cackling Bertha*. Where's your father, then?'

'My Da?'

'Yes. He not with you today?' The guard gestured up towards the driver's pod. 'I see your brother, but there's nobody in any of your observation nacelles. Is it just the two of you?'

'And have you had an accident lately?' the other guard asked. '*Bertha*'s got a few new scrapes and dents, front and back.'

Cassie thought fast. The two Deacons were becoming too inquisitive for her liking.

'Yeah, would you believe it? Da had a prang with her yesterday. Him's OK but still puckered up about it. Said him didn't feel like coming out today. And Robert, him's come down with a touch of something. A cough. Don't think it'm serious, not rattle-lung or anything. And Martin … Martin be looking after the pair of they at home.' How fluently she could lie, when she needed to. 'So that'm why it be just me and Fletch. And we found a Relic! Them'll be green with envy back home when us tells they about that.'

The guards didn't show any sympathy about her family's misfortunes, but at least they seemed to believe her. Perhaps it was the word 'Relic' that did it, reminding them that as well as protect the Chancel they were there to welcome valuable artefacts in.

'Relic, eh? Where is it?'

'Oh, it'm a small thing. Stowed somewhere up top, it be. I could go and get it for you if you like ...'

'No, no, won't be necessary.' The guards gave the loading bay a final once-over, then glanced at each other, satisfied. Shouldering their pikestaffs, they marched back to the gate-house. A moment later, the ramps slammed flat and the barrier began to rise. *Bertha* rolled forward.

Cassie heaved a sigh of relief. She was glad she'd had the foresight to make Az hide. If the guards had spotted a stranger on board *Bertha*, there would have been all sorts of trouble.

And so the guards let in the very same kid who'd caused the security breach less than forty-eight hours ago.

CHAPTER 53

Difficult Farewell

All Relics were delivered to a sorting-house round at the eastern side of the Chancel. It was a large barn-like building with a rounded, ribbed roof, echoingly spacious inside. You drove your murk-comber in, parked, and showed your Relics to a Deacon, who assessed their worth and, if he wanted them, handed over a money chit which you took to another Deacon behind a barred window in a kiosk in an alcove. He exchanged the chit for cash. Since there was no strict itemised tariff for Relics, the transaction was sometimes open to negotiation. If the Deacon on duty was one of the more compliant ones, you could haggle with him.

The deacon on duty today *wasn't* one of the more compliant ones. Deacon Leavenscale was a hard bargainer, with an uncompromising, take-it-or-leave-it attitude. Cassie's father called him the tightest man he had ever met. 'Any tighter,' Den said, 'and him'd squeak when him walked.'

Cassie, however, couldn't have been more pleased. For Deacon Leavenscale, in addition to being extremely miserly, was extremely nearsighted. He wore spectacles with lenses like magnifying glasses, and in spite of this still had to hold an object up to his nose to see it clearly.

'I's known verms with better eyesight,' she said to Az. They were still inside *Bertha*, Cassie getting ready to exit.

'I take it verms are blind.'

'Spot-on.'

'So you think this gives me a chance?'

'You'd have to be pretty clumsy not to be able to sneak past Leavenscale.'

'I *feel* pretty clumsy in these clodhoppers.' Az indicated the boots he was wearing, which were the ones Robert used to go exploring outside *Bertha*. They were big, hobnailed, mud-encrusted things that came halfway up the shins. Az's own shoes, which Cassie was now holding, were delicate, almost slipper-like, in comparison.

'Them mayn't be as dainty as yours,' Cassie said, 'but them's a damn sight more practical.'

'By my people's standards mine *are* practical shoes. They're made specially for me by a cobbler. I walk a lot more than the average Airborn, so I need something tough on my feet.'

Cassie laughed, somewhat ruefully. 'Well, you'm going back up there now, where toughness be'n't all that necessary. Back to your old life.'

'I know.' Az hadn't thought he would feel anything except glad to be leaving the ground and its denizens. He was surprised to discover that this was going to be quite a difficult farewell after all. 'Listen, Cassie ...'

Fletcher came shinning down into the loading bay from the driver's pod. 'You seen? It'm Leavenscale!'

'Yes, Fletch, us knows.'

'Blind old Leavenscale. Man wouldn't know where his own bunghole were if you gave he a mirror and a lamp and told he to ...'

Fletcher's voice trailed off as he realised he was intruding on a sensitive moment.

'I'll, um, I'll just go and, er, do this thing over here,' he said, and ducked into a crawl-duct.

Az looked back to Cassie. He groped for what to say. 'You've risked so much for me. I appreciate that. No, "appreciate" doesn't begin to cover it. Thanks to you I'm alive, and thanks to you I've got this chance of warning my people about the Humanists. Don't think I'll ever forget that, because I won't. I ... I don't know if it's possible that I can come back down. I'd like to think I could, but ... you know.'

'Come back down!' Cassie exclaimed. 'Why would you *want* to?'

'Well, er, to visit. Say hi.'

'Oh. I see. Sorry, I just couldn't think of a reason why you'm be considering making the journey here twice. Bad enough once. But you mean, like, a social call.'

'Yes.'

She understood then that Az wished to be friends with her, and perhaps more than friends. In a fumbling, roundabout way he was asking if she would like to see him again. Yet he must know that what he was suggesting was impractical, if not downright absurd. He must know someone like him and someone like her couldn't be anything more than footnotes in each other's life. He'd said what he had said because he had to say it. He'd had to get it out of him. But in a minute or so from now, he would be gone and there was never any chance they would lay eyes on each other again. Once Az was up where he belonged, among his own kind, he would quickly be reabsorbed into their way of life. For all his protestations, he *would* forget her.

And Cassie didn't mind that.

Did she?

She had rescued him, after all. She had put herself on the line for him. Was it just because she felt guilty? Because her sense of what was right had obliged her to? Or was there more to it?

Had she saved him because he needed saving, or because *she* needed to prove something to him by saving him?

Cassie confronted these thoughts in the space of a couple of seconds, then banished them. She was a pragmatic girl. She had little room in her for fanciful notions. She dealt in possibilities only, not impossibilities. In her next life, winged, Ascended, she would have all the time in the world for wondering and dreaming. Until then ...

'Not going to happen, be it, Az?' she said. 'I mean, let's be realistic. Social call? You come down here to see I? About as likely as me going up there to see you.'

'Yes. Yes, of course.'

'Besides, us may have ruined things for the Humanists in

206

Grimvale, but there'm other townships and other Chancels. This situation be happening everywhere, not just here. Sooner or later, probably sooner, there'm going to be strife. Your people against mine. Sky against ground.'

Punctuating her point, thunder rolled distantly, making *Bertha* vibrate.

'Not sure it can be avoided,' she went on. 'And I doesn't think there'll be much socialising going on then, if you see my meaning.'

'It can be avoided,' Az said resolutely, 'if everyone's prepared to negotiate. And I'm certain my people will.'

'Then you'd better hurry and get up there and tell they what'm going on, so's them can sort out their bargaining position.'

'Yes. You're right.' Az was disappointed, but her commonsense talk had blown through him like a sharp breeze, clearing his head. 'Well then. Pleasure to have met you, Cassie Grubdollar.'

'Likewise, Az Gabrielson.'

'Thanks for everything. And … and goodbye.'

'Goodbye to you too.'

They shared a handshake. She noted how soft his skin was. He noted how firm her grip was.

The handshake lingered.

Then Cassie disengaged her fingers from Az's and reached for the hatch lever.

CHAPTER 54

Distraction Techniques

'Hmmm,' said Deacon Leavenscale.

Fletcher winked at Cassie. They both could tell that it was a very positive *Hmmm*. Az's shoes intrigued him.

'Yes, I've no doubt they're authentic,' he said, holding one of the shoes so close to his nose it looked as if he was sniffing it. Distorted by his spectacle lenses, his weak grey eyes bulged like two mushrooms. 'The quality of the stitching tells me that, as does the nature of the leather. Tanned bird hide has its own peculiar pliancy and grain. I can't say I've seen soles quite as thick before, but perhaps it's a new fashion. But a pair. That's the remarkable thing. A *pair* of Ascended shoes. That's rare. Usually it's just the one.'

Cassie had taken a quick glance over her shoulder in *Bertha*'s direction. Realising that Leavenscale had stopped talking, she snapped her head back to face him.

Az had not made his move yet.

'Yeah, us was surprised about that too,' she said.

'Very surprised,' Fletcher chimed in. 'But, you know, us be'n't the sort to question what fate brings.'

Deacon Leavenscale laid the shoe carefully beside its counterpart on his desktop.

'Water-damaged,' he observed, 'and somewhat battered. That lowers their value.'

'Oh come on!' Fletcher said, genuinely indignant. 'It'm pissing down with rain outside. How's them *not* going to be water-damaged? Not to mention them fell who knows how many kilometres. When be the last time you saw a Relic that'm in a tenth as good condition?'

'True, true. It would, however, be remiss of me not to point out any flaws.'

Cassie sneaked another look over her shoulder. She glimpsed Az lurking just inside *Bertha*'s hatchway, poised to climb out. She took a stealthy step to the right, so that she was blocking Deacon Leavenscale's line of sight to the murk-comber. He might be a myopic old geezer but that didn't mean that his attention would not be caught by a distant blur of movement. She wished they could have parked *Bertha* the other way round, with her hatch on the far side, but the set-up in the sorting-house was such that this was impossible. There was a one-way system, from which you pulled off into angled parking bays that were clearly demarcated by white lines on the floor, with your hatch side exposed. There was no deviating from this arrangement.

At least there were no other murk-combers here at the moment, and consequently nobody present who was sharper-eyed than Deacon Leavenscale. The other Deacon, tucked away in his alcove kiosk, was in no position to see anything that went on in the main part of the sorting-house.

In the north-west corner of the building there was a swing-door, next to which were lined up the trolleys used for transporting larger, heavier Relics to the Reliquary. The door joined the sorting-house to the rest of the Chancel. Az had to make it there unobserved. He could do it, as long as he was careful.

Cassie sent him an encouraging thought: *You'll be fine, Az. Just take it nice and easy.*

Leavenscale bent his head, lowering his face to the shoes for another examination.

Az would not have a better chance than this to get going. Cassie turned and made a surreptitious flapping gesture to him.

Az nodded, taking the hint. He put one foot out from the hatchway, then other, and slithered to the floor.

'Miss Grubdollar?'

She spun round. 'Yes?'

Deacon Leavenscale blinked up owlishly at her. 'You seem ... preoccupied. Is there something the matter?'

'The shoes,' Fletcher interjected quickly. 'What do you think them's worth?'

The Deacon turned his head. 'What? Oh, too early to say. I'll need to study them some more.'

'Rough estimate, though.'

'I do not give "rough estimates", Mr Grubdollar,' the Deacon said sternly. 'You know that.'

'Go on. Nearest round figure.'

'Young man, do not try my patience. I will not be hurried. And moreover ...'

Leavenscale began to lecture Fletcher on how the assessment of Relics was a highly specialised art that required practice and time. As he blathered on, Cassie canted her head to one side. By straining her eyeballs as far round in their sockets as they would go, she was just able to see Az at the periphery of her vision. He had sensibly frozen stock-still when he heard the Deacon addressing her. Now he began moving again. He crouched low as he went, pressing himself against *Bertha*'s side. He had fifty metres to cover to get to the swing-door, some distance, but between it and him there was a line of large concrete blocks which formed a cordon that ran almost the whole way. If Az stayed behind the blocks and kept his head down, he could follow them as far as they went, scurrying from one to the next, then make a final dash.

He must not be seen, though. There was a button on Deacon Leavenscale's desk which operated a bell to summon assistance from the Reliquary, which was in the adjacent building. The bell doubled as an emergency alarm. If Leavenscale spotted Az, he could hit the button and there would be other Deacons here in no time.

Az stole across the gap between *Bertha* and the nearest of the blocks. He vanished from view.

In front of Cassie, Leavenscale was still droning on about the skill and precision with which he judged the value of Relics. It had been a smart move by Fletcher to ask for a rough estimate. It had pricked Leavenscale's sense of pride, and now he was too busy setting Fletcher straight to notice much else.

'... so you allow me to do my job properly, Mr Grubdollar,' Leavenscale said, concluding his sermon, 'and I shall not tell you how to do yours.'

'Yup. All right.' Fletcher sounded contrite, but he was having to hold back a smirk.

The Deacon flicked a hand, as though swatting aside Fletcher's little blunder like a fly. 'Now then, a moment or two's peace and quiet, please, so that I may continue my inspection.'

He picked up Az's shoes again, one after the other, and turned them over and over. He held them by his fingertips, handling them delicately, reverently.

Meanwhile the shoes' original owner crept, block by block, towards the door. Thunderclaps shook the sorting-house every so often, making the rafters groan. This and the drumming of rain on the roof provided camouflage for any scuffing sounds Az inadvertently made.

At last Leavenscale lined up the shoes on his desk, with a nod of finality.

'One hundred notes,' he said.

It was a lot of money, although Cassie knew that another Deacon would have gone higher.

Leavenscale sat back, confident his offer would be accepted.

'A hundred and fifty,' Cassie said.

Leavenscale blinked. 'I do not haggle, Miss Grubdollar. The Relic market is a buyer's market only. I'm saying a hundred and there's an end of it.'

'Hundred and fifty.'

Her last furtive look-round had told her Az wasn't at the end of the concrete-block cordon yet. She had to keep Leavenscale's attention fixed on her and not let it stray anywhere else.

'One hundred,' Leavenscale said, pronouncing each syllable crisply.

'One fifty,' she replied, mimicking his pronunciation.

'Or nothing. That's the alternative, Miss Grubdollar. You can keep the shoes if you don't want my money.' Leavenscale looked almost pitying. 'Don't think I don't realise that your family has been having a hard time of it recently. Cash reserves must be running low, eh? The cupboard starting to get bare. Now, I'm told that if you boil shoe leather in water for long enough, you can end up with a palatable and perhaps even nutritious soup. So there's always that option, is there not? Or there's money, plain and simple. A far surer way of getting hungry bellies filled. Which is it to be?'

Cassie gulped hard. No question, the family could do with that hundred. They could pay off their debts and still have a tidy sum left over.

Get a move on! she urged Az mentally.

'You yourself said a pair be a rare thing,' she said to Leavenscale. 'In my book, rare equals expensive.'

'And in *my* book, rare equals whatever I say it equals. I'm going to give you one last chance, Miss Grubdollar. A hundred notes. That's it. If you yet again come back with anything but a yes, the offer is rescinded, our business is over, you go home, 'bye-bye.'

'Cassie ...' Fletcher said out of the corner of his mouth. His expression was pained. He was aware what she was up to, but he was envisioning all that ready cash, a thick sheaf of notes, wonderful folding stuff – seeing it there in his hand, in danger of being whisked away at any moment.

Az had reached the end of the cordon. Barely a half-dozen metres separated him from the door.

Cassie made a great show of rumination: scratching head, tapping feet, staring into space, humming. She was stalling for time, but she couldn't keep it up for ever.

Do it, Az!

If he didn't hurry up, she was going to have say it. Going to have to say no.

Do it!

Az was hesitating. She saw him peek round the edge of the block. Indecision was written all over his face.

Go!

'Miss Grubdollar? An answer.'

'Hundred it be,' Cassie said.

'Good. I thought you'd see sense.'

In the north-western corner, the swing-door squeaked. Cassie looked round. The door was closing, easing shut on its sprung hinges.

Az had made it.

Deacon Leavenscale was looking towards the door too. He squinted, frowned, then muttered something about draughts, and began filling out a chit.

It wasn't the best price she could have got, Cassie knew. Her father would have held out for 120 notes at least. But right now there were more important considerations than money.

Preventing a war, for example.

CHAPTER 55

The Reliquary

It was different this time, being inside the Chancel. Very different.

Last time, Az had been in a state of confusion and amazement. Dizzy, too. His head had been swimming.

Now he was clear-headed and suffused with a sense of mission.

Nothing was more important than reaching the elevators.

He proceeded along the corridor that led away from the sorting-house. Robert's boots were taking some getting used to. They felt like clamps on his feet. But apart from that he was in fine fettle, alert, ready for anything.

Almost anything.

Rounding a corner, Az came face to face with a pair of large doors. Each had a circular window inset into it, like a porthole. He knew he should move straight past the doors but he couldn't resist a quick glance through first.

His jaw dropped.

Beyond the doors lay a room, massive, but its massiveness was not its remarkable feature.

It was crammed. Crammed with stuff. *Stuffed* with stuff. From wall to wall, floor to roof, there were objects – objects on shelves, objects in cubbyholes, objects behind or under glass. The more Az looked, the fuller the room seemed. There wasn't a square centimetre that didn't have something in it, stacked, racked, piled up, or shoved in any old how.

Tiered galleries had been built to accommodate all the items, with a network of ladders affording access from one tier to the next. For all the apparent unruliness, there was organisation. Az saw labels on everything, and there were a couple of deskbound Deacons at work on ledgers, evidently in the process of cataloguing and cross-referencing. Other Deacons were dotted around the room, some on the ladders, many carrying clipboards and pens.

Az had a pretty good idea what this room must be: the Reliquary. It took him several moments, though, to adjust to the fact that its contents were bits and pieces which had fallen from above. Hearing about the Reliquary from Cassie was one thing, actually seeing it for himself quite another. Every item in the room was a scrap of what had once been Airborn property, an article that had been dropped from the sky-city overhead, come tumbling through the cloud cover, and wound up in the Shadow Zone, from where it was retrieved by the Grubdollars or by others in the same line of work.

The items included:

Clothing, some of it in shreds.

Tattered pages from books and newspapers.

Coins and paper money.

Hair combs.

Splintered twists of what must have been furniture.

Shards of glass.

Broken ornaments that had been pieced together painstakingly.

Cups, cutlery, crockery ...

Centuries of accumulated detritus, gathered and labelled, hoarded like wealth. This was a second Museum of Airborn History, an upside-down version, a secret chronicle of the race told through dropped morsels and forgotten artefacts.

Az himself had doubtless contributed to a similar collection, not here but at a Chancel beneath High Haven. Once he had let the wind take hold of a sweet wrapper and whip it away. Then there was that sock of his that had inexplicably gone missing. Perhaps the wrapper and the sock had ended up in a Reliquary like this one, reclaimed from High Haven's Shadow Zone and squirreled away like treasure.

Horrifyingly, the Reliquary didn't contain just *things*.

Az's roving gaze came to rest on a series of padlocked, glass-fronted cabinets that held bones. Human bones. Airborn bones. They were dry and browny-white, and were sorted and stored according to type. In one cabinet there were femurs. In another, what looked like upper wing radii. Worst of all, one cabinet was host to a stack of skulls.

People. People fell and were never seen again. There were accidents – aircraft collisions and suchlike. The victims plummeted helplessly into the cloud cover, dead or dying, unable to save themselves, doomed.

This was where their remains wound up.

Az wished now he hadn't stopped to look in. He would have been content to go through life never having seen the inside of a Reliquary.

In a moment's time, there would be another reason for him to wish he hadn't stopped.

CHAPTER 56

An Unfortunate Coincidence

Deacon Shatterlonger was not a happy man. Although it had not been his fault, he was nonetheless being held responsible for the security breach a couple of days earlier. Archdeacon Corbelgilt needed somebody to blame, a scapegoat to take his anger out on. Deacon Shatterlonger had been saddled with that role.

The fact was, no one knew how the boy had got into the Chancel and found his way into the cupboard in the Ascension Chapel. Perhaps he had stowed away aboard the bus which brought the mourners in, and somehow sneaked out as they were disembarking, then hurried ahead of them to get to the room before they did. However, parties of outsiders visiting the Chancel were monitored from the minute they arrived and were escorted every step of the way, in and out. There were head counts and roll calls. It was almost inconceivable that the boy could have slipped through unnoticed.

Nor could anyone figure out *why* he wanted to infiltrate the Chancel, unless, as Archdeacon Corbelgilt surmised, he was a Humanist spy. Understandably the Archdeacon was paranoid about Humanists at present, and the boy could well have been one, sent to eavesdrop on the Chancel's inhabitants and find out what effect the embargo was having on them. Shatterlonger had pointed out that the boy had seemed too nervy for that, too bewildered and skittish. And surely if the Humanists were going to choose a spy, they would go for a grown man, someone who could don a robe and pass himself off as a Deacon, rather than a boy in plainclothes. But there was no reasoning with the Archdeacon on the subject.

What had irked the Archdeacon above all else was Shatterlonger's failure to catch the miscreant. Shatterlonger acknowledged that he should have made good on the opportunity he had to seize him in the sewage treatment works. But who could have known the lad would do something as suicidally insane as jump into the outflow channel?

Now, anyway, Shatterlonger was in disgrace. Archdeacon Corbelgilt had given him a public dressing-down in front of all the Deacons and demanded penance from him. Penance entailed the shaving off of his hair, a diet of bread and water for a week, and one month spent carrying out the sort of duties that were expected of an initiate but not of a senior Deacon.

The loss of hair was tolerable (though his scalp itched and his head felt cold all the time). The subsistence diet was grim but also oddly bracing. What Shatterlonger really couldn't stomach was the demotion. Having been a favourite and a confidant of the Archdeacon, well in line to take over from Corbelgilt when he retired, he was now reduced to menial tasks such as doing the washing-up in the kitchen and helping out in the Reliquary.

Even once the penance was over, Shatterlonger would have to work hard to get back into the Archdeacon's good books and regain the status he had lost. In the meantime, he spent every spare moment fuming over the injustice of his punishment and musing on what he would do to the boy if he ever laid eyes on him again.

He was entertaining thoughts of revenge on the boy – physically abusive revenge – as he made his way towards the Reliquary to begin an afternoon shift there. Shatterlonger hated working in the Reliquary. Of all the aspects of his penance, it was by far the worst. He hated the dustiness of the place, and the fustiness of the Deacons who ran it. The Reliquary attracted a certain type of personality. Those who volunteered for full-time duties there were the sort of men who enjoyed indexing and numbers and bookwork. Librarian types. They had poor social skills and lax personal hygiene. Some of them loved being in the Reliquary so much, they seldom left it. They lived among the assembled Relics, constantly reshuffling and rearranging them and obsessively coming up with new ways to categorise them. They didn't see the Relics as Relics any more, as venerable reminders of the world above – they saw them as a large, complex taxonomical puzzle. Deacon Gnomoncast, for instance, the Head of Reliquary, had devoted the past decade of his life to establishing a precise set of formulae for the codification of carpet fragments, drawing up tables which ranged them according to size, colour, pattern, weave, texture, and so on.

A wasted decade, in Shatterlonger's view, although he would never have said this aloud to anyone.

Nearing the Reliquary, Shatterlonger felt his fires of revenge being stoked by the prospect of the coming work shift. It would be six hours of Deacon Gnomoncast and the others bossing him about, making him scuttle up and down ladders as though he was their personal dogsbody, and mocking his ignorance of their intricate classification systems.

He had, in fact, built up quite a blaze of vindictiveness inside as he reached the Reliquary doors.

And who should be standing there, peering in through the doors' windows?

Who but the source of his grievance.

The object of his violent revenge fantasies.

The boy.

Shatterlonger stopped in his tracks, overcome with disbelief. He had to blink several times to make sure his eyes weren't playing tricks on him.

It really was the boy. He wasn't imagining it. This wasn't some vision conjured up by his thirst for vengeance. Nor was it a hallucination brought on by a lack of proper food. The boy was right in front of him, gazing into the Reliquary, oblivious to his presence. He had survived his plunge into the outflow channel, and now here he was, large as life, a sitting duck, a gift, an offering from kindly providence.

Shatterlonger thanked his luck, clenched his fists, and charged.

CHAPTER 57

The Drawbacks (And Benefits) Of Robert's Boots

Something, some instinct, made Az turn at the very last second.

He recognised the Deacon who was bearing down on him at full tilt. The shaven head altered his appearance but the face was etched in Az's memory.

Shatterlonger.

Az sprang back from the Reliquary doors. He spun round and started to run ...

... and tripped over his own feet.

The boots! Robert's boots!

Even as he went sprawling to the floor, Az cursed his unfamiliar footwear.

Then hands grabbed him. He was hauled upright. Deacon Shatterlonger took hold of his shirtfront in one fist and bunched it tight. Knuckles dug into Az's throat. His collar began to constrict his neck.

'You have no idea what this means to me,' Shatterlonger said, breathing a blast of malodorous breath in Az's face. 'I never thought I'd get this chance. I'm going to make you suffer, you brat. I don't care who you are or why you're here. I'm going to make you wish you'd never been born.'

He slammed Az against the wall, knocking the wind out of him. Then he pushed upwards, and Az felt his feet leave the floor and his collar become even more constrictive. Suddenly it was getting hard to draw a breath.

Shatterlonger's eyes were insanely bright and joyful.

It was quite clear to Az that the Deacon intended to kill

him. He didn't know what he had done to make the man so mad, other than escape from him. It didn't seem to matter anyway. Shatterlonger was bursting with murderous rage, that was all that mattered. He was going to choke Az to death.

Az tried to speak. He wanted to remonstrate with Shatterlonger and plead for his life. But his larynx was being crushed. He couldn't get anything out of his mouth except a hoarse hiss.

Shatterlonger shoved him further up the wall, so that Az was looking down on him, so close to him that he could see the broken capillaries that crazed the whites of the Deacon's eyes. Around the edges of Az's vision there were exploding sparkles of light. There was a roaring in his ears.

A tiny voice inside his head urged him to do something now or else he would die. The voice, funnily enough, sounded a lot like Cassie's. It was just the sort of thing she would have said.

Do something.

But what?

Az registered the fact that his feet were dangling and re-membered that they were clad in heavy, hobnailed boots. The same boots which had caused him to trip had, he realised, the power to hobble someone else. All it needed was a good, hard kick.

Az kicked.

He didn't have the presence of mind or the coordination to aim. He kicked desperately, with all his might, hoping that his toecap would connect with Shatterlonger's knee, perhaps, or his thigh.

As luck would have it, he hit the jackpot.

Shatterlonger's face went white. His eyes rolled. A high-pitched whoop of pain escaped him. He dropped Az and his hands flew to his groin. Clutching himself there, he sagged to his knees.

Az, meanwhile, slid down the wall, holding his throat and wheezing.

For at least a minute neither of them could move. Az was having trouble getting air into his lungs. Shatterlonger was whimpering and swaying from side to side, racked with indescribable agony.

Finally Az managed to get himself upright.

He'd left it too late, though. Shatterlonger was starting to recover from the kick. As Az made to run past him, Shatterlonger reached out with an arm, barring his path. Az tried again, the other side. Again Shatterlonger blocked the way.

'You're mine,' the Deacon gasped. 'Little ... bastard. Mine.'

Az launched another kick at him but Shatterlonger managed to deflect it. Az realised there was no way forward.

He looked to his right.

The Reliquary?

A dead end, surely. He could hide in there, but he would still be trapped. And of course, the place was riddled with Deacons.

Back. That was his only option. Back the way he had come. Back into the sorting-house.

Maybe there was another route from the sorting-house into the Chancel.

It was a slim hope but it was all Az had.

He turned and lurched away from Shatterlonger.

The Deacon, hissing with pain, staggered to his feet and gave chase.

CHAPTER 58

Scuffle In The Sorting-House
(Grubdollars Against Deacons)

Cassie and Fletcher left the kiosk with their money and returned to *Bertha*. Their delight over the cash was mitigated by the sight of the murk-comber. This was the first chance they'd had to get a good look at her since the chase, and the recently-acquired dents and gouges in her bodywork gave her a bedraggled, hangdog look. To add to this impression, one of her floodlights had been broken during the chase. The empty housing dangled limply by a wire, like an eyeball that had been knocked from its socket and was dangling on the end of its optic nerve.

That's going to cost, Cassie thought. The Grubdollars could panel-beat *Bertha*'s bodywork back into shape themselves and give her a lick of paint where needed. This would set them back next to nothing. The floodlight would have to be replaced, however, and lightbulbs and lamp glass did not come cheap. Some of the 100 notes would have to go on that.

Cassie's thoughts turned to Martin, who was in part responsible for the damage to the murk-comber. She couldn't decide whether she felt bitterness towards him or regret. The bond between siblings was a strong one, so that when it broke, it broke painfully. She would find it hard to forgive him for all he had done. But then Martin, in turn, would find it hard to forgive her for her part in thwarting the Humanists' plans.

Maybe, just maybe, the two of them would be able to patch things up eventually. But Cassie knew things weren't ever going to be the same. Like a shattered bone that had knitted back together, their relationship might work again, but never as well as it used to.

Reaching *Bertha*, Cassie tossed Az's shoes in through the hatchway. She was about to climb in after them when she heard a commotion over at the swing-door.

She turned in time to see Az bursting through the door, with a Deacon in hot pursuit.

Az!?

Cassie experienced a surge of pure resentment. Not two minutes inside the Chancel, and already Az had got into difficulties and come running back out with his tail between his legs. After all this! After all they had gone through to get him here!

Then the Deacon chasing Az let out an almighty snarl and lunged. He caught him around the midsection. They both went crashing to the floor together, Az on his front, the Deacon on top.

The Deacon straddled Az and began cuffing him around the head. The man's face was a contorted mask of hatred. Cassie could not help but wonder what Az had done to enrage him so much.

She also could not stand by and watch him beat Az up.

Fletcher clearly felt the same way, because as Cassie set off to help Az, so did he.

Az retaliated, flailing behind him, trying to parry the Deacon's assault. But the Deacon was a maniac. He rained blows on Az's head with mounting ferocity. He graduated from loose-hand slaps to clenched-fist punches. He would have ended up concussing Az, or worse, if Cassie hadn't intervened when she did. She dived at him sidelong, grabbing his wrists. As the Deacon fought to make her let go, Fletcher joined in, hooking an arm around the man's neck. The Deacon gave an infuriated grunt as Fletcher and Cassie together dragged him off Az.

Meanwhile, a startled Deacon Leavenscale groped for the button on his desk and pressed it three times. Far off in the

Reliquary, a bell sounded. Three rings signalled an emergency in the sorting-house.

Between them, the two Grubdollars got the Deacon onto his back and pinned him down. Fletcher placed a knee on the man's chest while Cassie secured his legs. The Deacon bucked and squirmed beneath them but couldn't break free.

Cassie turned to Az, who was sitting up, looking stunned and battered.

'Go back in,' she told him. 'Now, while you can. Likely as not there'm more Deacons coming. Go! And don't screw it up this time.'

Her words galvanised him. Az stood and made his way back to the swing-door.

Leavenscale was still thoroughly perplexed by what was going on, but could not ignore the fact that a fellow Deacon was in trouble. He stumbled from his desk and went to assist Shatterlonger. He sized up the two Grubdollars and decided the sister was the weaker of the two, the easier to deal with. He took hold of Cassie by the shoulders and attempted to pull her off. Cassie lashed out, thumping him square in the belly. Leavenscale tottered back. His heel caught on the hem of his robe and he thudded backside-first onto the floor. Pain lanced up his spine. The impact also dislodged his spectacles, leaving him all but blind.

As he groped to find the spectacles, Leavenscale had time to regret getting involved in the fracas and regret even more picking on the girl. He would be nursing a sore coccyx for days. The rough stuff, he concluded, was best left to others.

Cassie saw Az arrive at the swing-door, just as the door flew open and a half-dozen Deacons barged through. In their pell-mell haste they went straight past Az, not seeing him. The way was left clear. Az ducked into the doorway.

The Deacons summed up the situation in the sorting-house at a glance. They swarmed over Cassie and Fletcher, over-whelming them with numbers. In no time, the two Grubdollars were no longer holding down the Deacon on the floor; they themselves were the ones being held down.

Az was still in the doorway. His gaze locked with Cassie's. Two of the Deacons were holding her by her arms.

Her eyes told him not to hang about. There was nothing he could do for her and Fletcher. He should just make sure that this sacrifice of theirs wasn't in vain.

He acknowledged it regretfully, and disappeared.

At the same moment, the Deacon whom Cassie and Fletcher had saved Az from rose to his feet with a roar.

'You!' he yelled, gesticulating at one of the Reliquary Deacons. 'And you! Come with me. The rest of you, keep a tight grip on those two.'

With that, he wheeled round and stormed off after Az. The two Reliquary Deacons followed.

Run, Az! thought Cassie.

She hoped he would be all right.

But she feared he wasn't going to make it to the elevators.

CHAPTER 59

Az's Run

As he sprinted headlong through the Chancel, it seemed to Az that he was fated to spend his entire life running away from Deacons. Even though this was only the second time that it had happened, there was a nightmarish repetitiveness to the event. The corridors he passed through looked the same as last time; they linked and diverged in the same labyrinthine fashion. And it was the same Deacon behind him, Shatterlonger, with another two Deacons accompanying him, just like before. Az began to wonder if he'd actually escaped the Chancel after all. Perhaps everything he had done since then – wandering the Shadow Zone, meeting the Grubdollars, being taken captive by the Humanists, getting away from them – had been in his imagination. This was still the same chase as the first one. He had just experienced some sort of delusional lull in the middle of it.

Nevertheless, on he ran, his arms pumping, his feet pounding, his breath coming in rasps. Sweat began to dampen his armpits and dribble stingingly into his eyes.

Once or twice Az thought he had managed to shake the Deacons off his tail, but then suddenly he would hear them again – the clatter of their footfalls, Shatterlonger's urgent cries. They were never more than one turn of a corner behind him. If he paused even briefly to catch his breath, within moments one of the three would spot him and alert the other two, and the chase would resume.

How long could he keep running? How soon before exhaustion overcame him and he simply couldn't continue another step?

Az had a feeling he was going to find out. Unless he reached the elevator chamber in the next few minutes, he was going to use up the last of his stamina and collapse. He couldn't maintain this pace for ever.

Then he was in a red-lit area. He was scared to believe it but his surroundings somehow did look familiar. These were corridors he had been down during his previous visit, he was sure. The elevator chamber was close by.

But where? Where?

With his destination seemingly so near at hand, Az redoubled his speed. He quested this way and that, making frantic left and right turns. He recalled the door with the lever handle, which led off from the monitoring gallery in the elevator chamber. If he could just find *that* ...

Another corridor. No such door.

Another one.

Now Az was aware of a burning sensation in his chest and a terrible bone-deep ache in his muscles. His legs were getting sluggish. Robert's boots seemed to weigh even more than before. Still he kept going, the exertion as much mental as physical. His body was close to conceding defeat. With his mind he forced it onward, telling himself to ignore the pain and the weakness he was feeling.

Shatterlonger and the other two Deacons were still hot on his heels. He could hear how tired they were. None of them was talking now. All three were panting hard. But they weren't giving up, so neither could he.

Then, dead ahead, as if by a miracle – the door! The door with the lever handle!

As he zeroed in on it, Az knew that it might be a different door, identical but the wrong one. It might open onto another room entirely, or onto a dead-end. In the time it took for him to struggle with the handle, the Deacons might catch up with him.

But he had no choice. This was it. All or nothing. He had to try it.

He grasped the handle, yanked down, put his shoulder to the door, pushed, fell through ...

The monitoring gallery!

Moments later, Az was on the gantry in the elevator chamber. The drone of machinery hit him in a torrent of sound. In front of him were the whirling cranes, the thump-whumping pistons, the trundling pallets, the whole fantastic, intricate, clockwork-like array of moving parts which he remembered so vividly from two days ago.

Two days? It felt more like two *years*.

There was no time to stand and gawp. Az bounded across the gantry and scrambled down the ladder. As he reached the bottom, three faces appeared overhead. It was Shatterlonger and the other two Deacons, peering down at him. Their cheeks were scarlet, their skin polished with perspiration.

'Stop!' Shatterlonger gasped out. 'Stop! You can't go any further. It's – it's not allowed.'

Az stepped back from the foot of the ladder. What was and wasn't allowed had no relevance for him at the moment. His only concern was getting to the elevators.

'Forbidden territory,' one of the other Deacons said, between wheezing breaths. 'Only by special dispensation. The Archdeacon. Essential maintenance.'

So the Deacons weren't permitted to go any further than the gantry unless something in the chamber needed repairing. Az was on safe ground.

He started to walk backwards with slow, cautious steps, mindful that parts of the machinery around him might fling themselves out unexpectedly and send him flying. The Deacons on the gantry were aghast at what he was doing.

'Stop,' Shatterlonger said again. It was almost pleading. 'Or you'll never Ascend.'

Maybe so. But Az had every intention of ascending in the literal sense. First available upward-bound elevator – he was taking it.

Shatterlonger wrestled with indecision. Finally he placed a foot on the top rung of the ladder.

'Shatterlonger, don't,' warned one of his colleagues.

'It's not worth it,' said the other.

'I can't let him get away.' Shatterlonger grasped the ladder uprights. 'Not after all this.'

'It'll be penance for a year.'

'Weekly self-flagellation.'

'A stay in the Contrition Cells.'

'I know,' Shatterlonger replied. 'Even so …'

He began climbing down, and there was nothing the other Deacons could do except look on, helpless.

Az knew his advantage was lost. He turned and staggered forwards, hurrying into the chamber. When he next glanced over his shoulder, he could see only the two Deacons on the gantry. Shatterlonger was no longer in view.

Az upped his pace. The frenetic mechanical tumult around him intensified, so he knew he was getting nearer the elevators. Then, there they were: some of them rising up the column, others coming down, their doors opening, empty pallets slotting in. Az had never been quite so grateful to see anything as he was those elevators. He was almost home.

Next thing he knew, he had collided with Deacon Shatterlonger.

He reeled back. The Deacon had popped up out of nowhere to obstruct his path.

'That's enough,' Shatterlonger said, voice raised in order to be heard above the background din. His face was haggard, his eyes wayward and wild. 'This ends here. You're coming with me.'

There was no way Az could let that happen.

Immediately to his left, he saw a set of rails. They ran towards the column base, but just before they reached it there was a junction and they fanned out into several subsidiary sets of rails. Each of these served a different elevator. Pallets rolled along the main set of rails and were distributed by a switching device to go down the subsidiary sets and feed into whichever elevator was ready and waiting.

Az took all this in at a glance. A pallet was approaching from behind him. He heard it hiss shimmeringly.

He knew, then, what he could do. *Must* do.

The move would have to be split-second perfect, though. If he stumbled or misjudged, he was likely to be mowed down by a heavy steel pallet travelling at speed. The result would be messy.

But he was worn out. His legs felt like rubber. Could he make it?

Suddenly Shatterlonger pounced, hands out like claws.

At the same time, Az sprang sideways.

He felt fingers brush his shirt. He seemed to be suspended in mid-air for hours. Then he landed awkwardly and was thrown over onto his side.

Propping himself up on all fours, he realised he had made the jump successfully. He was riding the pallet, and the pallet was racing away from Shatterlonger. The Deacon was frozen in a posture of bafflement, his arms embracing empty air. Shatterlonger couldn't seem to fathom how his quarry had evaded him *yet again*.

The pallet hurtled along the rails with Az aboard, clinging on. There was a moment of jolting and jouncing as it hit the switching device and was diverted down its allotted course. Then an open-doored elevator loomed like a hungry mouth. The pallet rammed inside. Az lost his grip and was bowled backward by the abrupt stop. He fetched up against the elevator's back wall, heels over head.

Upside down, dazed, he watched the elevator doors slowly slide shut. Through the narrowing gap he was treated to the sight of Deacon Shatterlonger clutching the air and stamping his foot in an ecstasy of despair.

Then, with a creak and a lurch, the elevator started to climb.

CHAPTER 60

The Taking Of RSE-2

Having lost *Cackling Bertha*, Steamarm returned to the Consolidated Colliery Collective in a foul temper. At the mine, he berated the picketers for failing to stop the Grubdollars when they made their escape bid with the vehicle. He knew that only a fool would stand in the way of a murk-comber rolling at full speed, but that wasn't relevant. He gave the picketers what-for, calling them cowards and incompetents. Afterwards, he felt better.

Martin came up to him when he had calmed down. He asked Steamarm if he had a back-up plan for getting into the Chancel. Steamarm, in a rare fit of honesty, admitted that he didn't.

'So what be them doing at the other Chancels?' Martin enquired. 'What'm going to happen there?'

'They'll be using brute force,' Steamarm replied. 'They'll ram the gates with trucks. Not elegant, not subtle, but probably effective.'

'Then why doesn't us do the same?'

'We could. I just prefer the murk-comber method. It has a greater guarantee of success, and there's less likelihood anyone on our side will get hurt in the process.'

'*Bertha* be'n't the only murk-comber in Grimvale.'

'I know.'

'Thought about commandeering one of the others?'

'I have,' said Steamarm. In fact, he hadn't. 'But I doubt there are any other murk-comber owners with Humanist sympathisers in their midst. I struck lucky when I met you and Fletcher. Well, *you*, at any rate,' he added bitterly.

'There doesn't have to be any sympathisers,' Martin said. 'There just has to be fewer of they than of we, if you get my meaning.'

Steamarm certainly did get his meaning, and in very short order he had rounded up a posse of Humanists. The same picketers he had yelled at half an hour ago he now coaxed and cajoled. Soon he had persuaded them to follow him to the headquarters of Relic Seeker Enterprises, a firm which operated not one but two murk-combers. The Humanists marched through the storm-lashed streets of Grimvale Township, assembled outside the Relic Seeker Enterprises building, and barged in. The firm's proprietor, Peter Lumplaid, looked up from his paperwork to find several burly, sodden miners filing into his office, dripping rainwater all over the floor. He spluttered indignantly, demanding to know the reason for this ... this *intrusion*. Steamarm strode up to Lumplaid's desk and explained in simple terms what he was there for. Lumplaid blustered, postured, but inevitably gave in. The alternative was to have his premises vandalised and himself roughed up, and he valued his property highly and his own health even more highly.

One of the Relic Seeker Enterprises murk-combers was out at work, but the other was inactive today because it was having a new carburettor fitted. The job was complete, and down in the garage the firm's mechanic was giving the engine a test-run. It chugged smoothly. The mechanic congratulated himself on his handiwork, then looked round to find his boss and a whole bunch of men he didn't recognise coming towards him across the garage floor. Within moments, his newly repaired murk-comber was pulling out, with none other than Martin Grubdollar up in its driver's pod. The mechanic didn't know which was worse: having the murk-comber taken from him, or seeing one of his firm's main rivals at the controls.

RSE-2, as the murk-comber was known, crawled to the Consolidated Colliery Collective with its loading bay full of Humanists. There was a brief stop as they gathered up weapons – sledgehammers, crowbars, lengths of chain, fence-posts, shovels – a formidable makeshift arsenal.

Other Humanists were there at the mine, having assembled at a prearranged time. They boarded three coal trucks, carrying weapons too. *RSE-2* set off, leading the way. The trucks followed in convoy, like baby ducks behind their mother.

As they drove towards the Shadow Zone Steamarm listened to his troops in the loading bay, growling, cheering, and singing songs. He was in the driver's pod with Martin but the men's voices were so loud he could hear them even up there. They seemed not just ready for conflict but eager for it. Their blood was up. Finally, after all this time, it was starting. The Deacons' rule was coming to an end.

Steamarm pictured it: a spasm of rebellion taking place all across the Westward Territories more or less simultaneously. In other counties and countries Humanists were mobilising, making their way to the local Chancels, just as here. Steamarm felt part of a vast mass-movement, connected by a web of solidarity to thousands of likeminded individuals. All of them had but one incentive, one goal – to overthrow the Deacons. It was a marvellous thought, and it brought a tear to his eye.

And after the Deacons, what next?

Next, the sky-cities and the Ascended Ones.

Not every Humanist deemed it wise, or even feasible, to follow the invasion of the Chancels with an invasion of the sky-cities. To Steamarm, however, the second step was a logical extension of the first. When the Deacons had been displaced there would be no more supplies at all for the Ascended Ones. The Ascended Ones would not take kindly to this and would react aggressively. *How* aggressively, no one could say. Steamarm, in the light of his conversation with Azrael, thought there would at least be some form of concerted counterattack – and in order to prevent it, he felt the Humanists should get in there first. Hit the Ascended Ones before they could hit back.

Other Humanist leaders were uncomfortable with such an idea and balked at it. They still believed the Deacons' claim that it was death for a living person to go up above the clouds. Steamarm himself was convinced this was not true, especially now that he had met Azrael. Azrael had proved that what could come down could also go up – as long as you had the right equipment.

So Steamarm was resolved to show everyone else the way. Once the Chancel here fell, he would lead his men up in the elevators and overrun the sky-city above. Having set an example in this manner, he was sure all the other Humanist groups would copy it. Sometimes people lacked the courage or the imagination to follow things through right to the very end and needed a pathfinder, a trailblazer, a man of vision – in short, someone like Alan Steamarm – to demonstrate what had to be done.

In spite of all the setbacks he had suffered today, Steamarm was confident of victory. He had no reason not to be.

As *RSE*-2 reached the Shadow Zone, the trucks behind halted. This was as far as they went, for now.

Steamarm looked ahead through the windscreen at the distant Chancel. Soon, oh so soon, the Deacons would be confronted by the might of a creed more powerful and meaningful than their own – Humanism. Their long and unjust reign was coming to an end.

It was going to be a great day.

CHAPTER 61

An Audience With The Archdeacon

Cassie and Fletcher were bundled unceremoniously along corridors and up and down staircases. Two Deacons were holding each of them by the shoulders. Shatterlonger led the way. Leavenscale shuffled at the rear, wincing with every step. He had a hand pressed to his lower spine.

Shatterlonger had said very little when he returned to the sorting-house, but the fact that he had come back empty-handed spoke volumes, as did the blank fury in his face. Cassie knew then that Az had got away, and she had good reason to think he had actually reached the elevators.

That didn't help Fletcher's and her situation any, but it did at least give her a glow of satisfaction inside. Whatever else happened now, Az's people had some forewarning of what was coming.

Several disorientating minutes later, she and Fletcher were thrust into a beautiful chandelier-lit room. The place was cluttered with antiques and artworks, such an abundance of wonderful objects that the mind almost couldn't take it all in. Everywhere Cassie looked there was something expensive and ornate to admire, be it a painting or a timepiece or an item of furniture. There was more wealth on display in this one room than could be found in all of Grimvale.

Everyone knew the Deacons were rich but Cassie had never really understood what that meant until now. It meant the Deacons could surround themselves with centuries' worth of accumulated treasures and live with this kind of luxury as a matter of course. Any time of day or night they could come in here and feast their eyes on wonders.

For the first time in her life, she envied them.

Shatterlonger instructed one of the other Deacons to pay a call on Archdeacon Corbelgilt and request an audience. The man returned shortly, saying that His Grace was on his way.

The corpulent Archdeacon swayed in, looking both serene and inquisitive. Deacons scurried to find him a chair, then helped him lower his bulky backside into it.

'Well?' Corbelgilt said, lacing his fingers across the mound of his belly, comfortably cradling his own girth. 'What is it?'

'Your grace,' said Shatterlonger, 'first of all I have a confession to make. I have strayed onto forbidden territory without your permission.'

'Forbidden territory? You set foot on the floor of the elevator chamber?'

Shatterlonger bowed his head. 'I did, and I humbly beseech your forgiveness.'

'Forgiveness doesn't come into it, Shatterlonger!' Corbelgilt's fleshy double-chin wobbled in outrage. 'It's a year's penance. You know that. What, are you some kind of glutton for punishment?'

'Not at all, your grace. I committed the sin in question because I was pursuing a certain boy – the same boy who interrupted the Ceremony of Ascension three days ago.'

'Indeed? I thought the lad was dead.'

'I assumed he was, but it turns out I was mistaken.'

'So where is he?' Corbelgilt scanned the room. 'You caught him this time, I take it. He didn't elude you again.'

'No. No, unfortunately, he … he did. But he's surely dead now, since he threw himself aboard one of the elevators. No one can make that journey and survive.'

Cassie allowed herself a quick, self-congratulatory grin.

The Archdeacon noticed it. He fixed her with his piggy little eyes. 'You, girl. Who are you?'

'She's a member of a murk-combing family,' Deacon Leavenscale piped up. 'The Grubdollars. And that's her brother with her.'

'I recognise the name. You looked pretty pleased with yourself, Miss Grubdollar. Care to explain why?'

Before Cassie could say anything, Shatterlonger stepped in. 'It's my belief, your grace, that these two are in league with the boy.'

'And on what grounds do you base this assumption?'

'During my initial pursuit of the lad today, they interfered. I had him pinned down and would have been able to subdue him if they had not prevented me.'

'Subdue?' said Fletcher. 'You was killing he, more like.'

'So you don't deny you are associates of this boy?' said Corbelgilt.

Fletcher looked at Cassie, hoping she would know how to answer the question.

'Your grace,' she said, 'all that happened was that us was in the sorting-house and saw a youngster getting clobbered by a Deacon. Our natural reaction were to help he, as anyone's would be. Picking on a kid like that ...'

'Balderdash!' exclaimed Shatterlonger. 'You held me down deliberately so that he could get away. I'm not stupid, girl. I saw you look at him. You knew him. You were helping him. Deacon Leavenscale will back me up. He was a witness to the whole event.'

'Erm, I must admit I didn't see a great deal.' Leavenscale pointed at his magnifying-glass spectacles. 'I'm not so keen-eyed at the best of times, and there was a lot going on, it was very confusing ...'

'Even so, I know what *I* saw,' said Shatterlonger, adamantly. 'Your grace, I'm sure the Grubdollars are lying, and I beg your leave to detain them and interrogate them so that I can get to the bottom of the matter. If the boy was, as you yourself have surmised, a Humanist spy, and these two are in cahoots with him, that would make them Humanists too. They could therefore have intelligence that could be useful to us.'

'Or you *wish* that to be the case, Shatterlonger, hoping it might mitigate your penance,' said Corbelgilt. 'Yours does strike me as the behaviour of a desperate man, someone who will say anything in order to get himself out of trouble.'

'I be no Humanist,' muttered Cassie.

'Quiet, girl,' said the Archdeacon. 'I'm not talking to you. On the other hand, Shatterlonger, there might be some merit in your claims. With that in mind, I consider it fair and reasonable that the two of them should be detained for a period of time.'

'You can't do that!' said Fletcher.

'My boy, I am Archdeacon of this Chancel and I can do whatever I want.'

'But – but us just *stopped* some bloody Humanists from getting in here. Us just foiled their plan. So us be'n't Humanists ourselves! How can us be? Don't stand to reason.'

'Really? Foiled a Humanist plan?' Corbelgilt sounded dubious. 'And how did you achieve that? Actually no, I'm not interested. Doubtless you'll spin me some cock-and-bull story, and I haven't got time for it. No, my decision is made. Deacon Shatterlonger, your second penance is deferred for now, and you will be exempted from it altogether *if* you can prove these two knew the boy and are Humanists. That's all. Good day.'

He tried to stand, only to find himself wedged in the chair. Resignedly he raised his arms and waited for a couple of Deacons to come to his aid. With grunts and groans they hauled on him until finally he popped free like a bung from a bottle. Then the Archdeacon waddled out of the room with as much dignity as he could still muster.

'Nice try,' Shatterlonger said to Fletcher. 'But a bit far-fetched, don't you think? If I was going to dream up some little fib to get me off the hook, it wouldn't be as preposterous as "we stopped the Humanists". It'd be something a lot more plausible.'

'But it'm true. Tell he it'm true, Cass.'

'Yes, of course it is,' said Shatterlonger with a sarcastic leer. He turned to the other Deacons in the room. 'All right, you lot, you heard His Grace. I believe we need to find somewhere to put these two. What do you think? The Contrition Cells?'

He looked back at Cassie and Fletcher.

'Not the cosiest of accommodation,' he said, 'but better you than me, eh?'

CHAPTER 62

The Contrition Cells

A rivet-studded iron door, bolted on the outside, with a spyhole at eye-level. A bare wooden bunk. A latrine bucket. A recessed ceiling light that burned no brighter than a candle.

This was what a Contrition Cell was like.

And then there was the heat. Sweltering heat. The air was so stiflingly, broilingly humid that the walls were slick with condensation, and Cassie herself, in a very short time, was slick with sweat.

She measured out the cell in paces: it was ten by five. She sat on the bunk and got jabbed in the thigh by a splinter. She put an eye to the spyhole but saw nothing. It was covered on the other side by a hinged shutter.

After that, there was nothing else she could think of to do, so she went and stood in the middle of the cell. Just stood. Not moving. Conserving energy. She didn't feel so hot and bothered if she stayed still.

'A Deacon spends time here to ponder on the error of his ways,' Shatterlonger had told her, shortly before slamming the door shut. 'If he has sinned or been disobedient, a spell in a Contrition Cell will soon sort him out. I'm hoping it will have the same effect on you and your brother. Now, how long should I leave you before you're ready to confess everything? How long do I think you need? Quite a while, I should imagine. Quite a while ...'

How long was 'quite a while'? Cassie dreaded to think.

'Cass ...?'

It was Fletcher, very faint. He was in the next-door cell.

Cassie moved to the wall, putting her mouth close to it. 'I be here, Fletch.'

'This'm a pretty pickle us is in, straight up.'

'I know.'

'Why'm it be so hot in here?'

'Us is close to the furnaces, is what I reckon.'

'Infernally hot. I don't know how long I can stand it.'

'You'm going to have to. Just stay calm.'

'All right, I'll try. Though I reckon I be half-baked already.'

A little later, Fletcher spoke again. 'You think I should admit to they that I *be* a Humanist? Might save we, you never know. It'm the truth as well, sort of.'

'If it comes to that, I'll say I be one too. But let's hope it don't come to that.'

'Funny that us did help the Deacons and them wouldn't believe it.'

'It'm called irony, Fletch.'

'Irony. That be when it hurts to laugh about it, right?'

'Something like.'

A little later again, Fletcher said, 'Think Da be missing we?'

'Not yet, but when us doesn't come home tonight him will. Then him'll move mountains to find out what'm happened to us.'

'Can him help we?'

'I hope so. Someone has to.'

There was another period of silence. Then: 'Cass?'

'Yeah?'

'I be frightened.'

'Don't you worry, Fletch. Just keep quiet and still and think cool thoughts. Us is going to be OK. Trust I. Us is going to be OK.'

Even as she said this, Cassie wished she felt half as certain as she sounded.

CHAPTER 63

Infiltration

The storm was reaching a climax as *RSE-2* pulled up at the Chancel's south gate. Rain was sheeting down, and the thunder-cracks came so thick and fast that barely had one finished rumbling before the next began.

Ramps shot up at either end of the murk-comber. Steamarm had not anticipated this. But it wasn't a disaster. His plan would still work. Everything else was on his side, even the weather.

A guard came out of the gatehouse and ran, hunching, over to *RSE-2*. He rapped on the hatch, and when it opened he leapt inside to get out of the rain. He looked around the loading bay and saw a dozen hostile faces peering back at him. He saw hands gripping implements – tools, shovels, that sort of thing – which glinted in the lightning flickers. He had just enough presence of mind to bring his pikestaff forward ...

... then he was flat on his back, out cold.

The other guard, who remained in the gatehouse, saw none of this. Apart from anything else it was hard to see more than five metres through the driving rain. He waited for his colleague to return and give the all-clear to let the murk-comber in. Soon enough, a robed figure emerged from *RSE-2* and loped back to the gatehouse. The second guard placed his hand on the lever, ready to lower the ramps. Then he sensed something was amiss. He scrutinised the other man's face. The truth dawned. Someone else was wearing his colleague's robe.

Too late. The impostor's pikestaff whistled through the air, haft first. The guard slumped from his chair, unconscious.

Ramps down.

Barrier up.

RSE-2 trundled through the gate.

Martin steered unerringly towards the sorting-house.

Meanwhile, at the very edge of the Shadow Zone, a Humanist with a telescope observed that the murk-comber had got inside the Chancel perimeter. He gave a signal, and the three coal trucks restarted their engines.

In the sorting-house, *Cackling Bertha* still occupied the frontmost parking spot. Martin drew in alongside her. *Bertha* looked abandoned. Her hatch was wide open.

'Why'd Fletch and Cassie come here?' he mused aloud.

'Obviously to send their Ascended friend home,' Steamarm said.

'Yeah, that'd make sense. Damn it, though. Trust they to be here when the trouble starts.' A bad thought occurred to him. 'You reckon them's told the Deacons about our plans?'

'I doubt we'd have got this far if they had.'

'Good point.' Martin killed the engine. 'Alan, promise I one thing. No one harms my bro and sis.'

'I can't make any guarantees, Martin. In the thick of battle ...' Steamarm left the rest unsaid.

'Well, at least let me have first crack at they. If anyone be going to wring their necks it should be I.'

The Deacon on desk duty was a Reliquary junior who had been drafted in to replace Deacon Leavenscale. The junior Deacon had missed all the commotion earlier. He had been deep in the bowels of the Reliquary at the time, carrying out a survey of Ascended handkerchieves (the lace-trimmed ones were in the process of being subdivided into men's and women's, and sub-subdivided into used and unused). He regretted not being on hand to witness Deacon Shatterlonger getting into a fight with a couple of murk-comber folk. Life in the Chancel could sometimes get very boring, and the junior Deacon often longed for diversions and a bit of excitement in his life.

Little did he realise he was just about to get more excitement than he could ever have wanted.

Out of *RSE-2* stepped a large man. The junior Deacon was not experienced enough to know whether or not the fellow was a longstanding employee of Relic Seeker Enterprises. However, the man smiled as he approach the desk, and the junior Deacon was reassured. He smiled back.

Thwack!

The Deacon did not see the punch coming. Nor did he see the kick that followed. Nor the several kicks that came after the first one. He rolled up in a ball on the ground until unconsciousness finally, mercifully, claimed him.

Humanists piled out of *RSE-2*. Some went to the main entrance, others to the swing-doors, taking up positions there.

Martin was second-to-last to leave the murk-comber. Steamarm stepped out last of all. He checked his watch. Just about now the coal trucks would be nearing the south gate, where the Humanist in Deacon's clothing was waiting to wave them through.

Tick-tock, clockwork. Everything was going smoothly.

One of Steamarm's men came up, hauling the Deacon from the money kiosk behind him.

'It be just the two of them in here, be'n't it?'

'That's correct.'

'So what should I do with he?'

'D-don't hurt me,' stammered the Deacon.

Steamarm gave the Deacon a cursory once-over, then nodded to the Humanist. 'Hurt him. Just a little.'

He stalked off, leaving the Deacon to his beating.

The sorting-house had been secured. Within minutes the trucks appeared, and men clambered off the back, shaking rainwater from their hair. In all there were about seventy Humanists now inside the Chancel. Somewhere on the premises a hundred or so Deacons were roaming, oblivious to the danger they were in, utterly unsuspecting.

No big speech now, Steamarm thought. He was sorely tempted to give one, but there was no need for it. The Humanists were champing at the bit, eager for action. Why delay it any longer?

He kept it concise. 'Gentlemen,' he said, 'tonight we make history. Tonight we change the world.' He waved an arm. 'Off you go! Leave no Deacon standing.'

With a guttural massed roar, the Humanists swarmed towards the swing-doors, brandishing their weapons.

CHAPTER 64

Home

Az staggered out of the elevator and fell to his knees. The journey up through the storm had been a rocky ride, to say the least. The elevator shaking like a demented thing. The wrench of tormented metal. A tang of ozone. The thunderclaps like the planet splitting in two.

But home! He was home at last!

He could have kissed the floor of the supply-arrival depot. But instead he simply knelt there, grateful to be alive.

There was a *whoosh* of wings – a sound Az had once feared he might never hear again. He looked up, expecting to see the depot supervisor or a supply-arrival volunteer. But the person touching down gently in front of him was none other than Aurora Jukarsdaughter. Lovely, lovely Aurora Jukarsdaughter, smiling like a creature in a dream.

'You made it back,' she said. 'We knew you would.'

As she escorted him out of the depot, Az asked where everybody had got to. The depot was empty, the hover-lifters sitting idle, no one at work.

'We closed the place down temporarily,' Aurora said. 'No supplies were coming up anyway, so we invited all the volunteers to take time off. We didn't even need to invoke Silver Sanctum authority, just told them they'd be alerted when supplies resumed.'

'They didn't find that suspicious at all?'

'I don't think so. Mr Mordadson told the supervisor to pretend there was a technical fault. As a cover story it seemed to do the trick. As far as the volunteers are concerned, any excuse not to have to work is a good one.'

'And then you waited for me.'

'We decided we'd give you a week. Your brother, Mr Mordadson and I have been taking it in shifts, keeping watch over the elevators.'

'You were *that* sure I'd come back.'

'We were. Mr Mordadson especially. In fact, he was all for giving you longer than a week.'

'Really?'

'Oh yes. You may not realise it but that man has great respect for you.'

'Could have fooled me.'

'Didn't he give you that warning? When you went down?'

'"You're not alone."'

'He wanted to prepare you, so that it wouldn't come as a complete shock if … Well …'

'If I found people down there,' Az said. 'Which I did. He could have just told me straight out, though, couldn't he?'

'Not with Michael and the administrator within earshot. Besides, "straight out" has never been Mr Mordadson's way.'

'You can say that again. So everyone at the Silver Sanctum knows about the Groundlings, right?'

'Let's save the questions for now,' Aurora said. 'First things first, let's reunite you with your brother. Then, after that, we can go over everything you've seen and done.'

She took Az to a hotel, the Heliotropia branch of the Acme Inn chain. Michael was staying in a room on the fifth floor.

When he opened the door, Michael took one look at Az and said, mock-irately, 'You're late.'

Then he hugged him so hard, Az thought his spine was going to snap.

CHAPTER 65

How The Deacons Came To Be

The news of Az's safe return to Heliotropia reached Lady Aanfieldsdaughter by carrier dove, which was the method used to transport all confidential Silver Sanctum communiqués. A dovecote official brought the message straight up to her as soon as it arrived, shortly after first light. Lady Aanfieldsdaughter, still in her nightgown, unrolled the little slip of paper which had been coiled around the bird's leg and spread it out between the thumb and forefinger of both hands. The handwriting was tiny and cramped. She recognised it as Mr Mordadson's nonetheless, and as she read, a frown eased from her face. Muscles which had been tense with anxiety for the couple of days relaxed somewhat. It was a small ray of hope. Az had made it back.

She was glad, and relieved. She had not slept well recently. On her desk was a letter drafted during the small hours of the night before last, a particularly wakeful night. The letter was addressed to Az's parents and began, 'Dear Mr and Mrs Enochson, It is with the sincerest regret that I must inform you ...' She had put off sending the letter, and now, thankfully, would never have to. Worry had a weight. Now that it was lifted from her, Lady Aanfieldsdaughter felt several kilograms lighter.

However, there was a P.S. to Mr Mordadson's message:

Situation on the ground is in flux and potentially un-favourable. Will report to you in person ASAP.

Lady Aanfieldsdaughter knew this meant the Silver Sanctum's

worst fears were realised. Mr Mordadson was a master of understatement. When he said the situation was 'potentially unfavourable', he was actually saying 'we're in real trouble'.

For so long, Lady Aanfielsdaughter had been afraid the day would come when the Groundlings rebelled. In fact, she had dreaded it ever since she learned that the Groundlings still existed. She recalled Asmodel, Lord Urielson revealing the truth to her all those years ago, soon after she arrived at the Silver Sanctum and he took her under his wing. 'My dear,' he said, 'our entire society relies on the continued toil of those neglected folk beneath us. Were it not for them and the sweat of their brows, we would not survive. So far, without trying, without even realising, we have retained their goodwill. Let us hope that we can carry on doing so indefinitely.'

He then explained to her about the Deacons. In the period immediately following the Great Cataclysm and the building of the sky-cities, an elite class of engineers came to prominence on the ground. This was all a matter of record, part of an established oral history kept alive in the Silver Sanctum and passed down through generations of politician. The engineers ran things at the base of the columns. They oversaw the input and distribution of supplies. The job provided them with wealth and comfort, not to mention influence and power. Gradually they realised they should make the most of their position and at the same time ensure it for the future. To this end, they devised a cunning and cynical scheme. They decided to control not just the goods that people brought but the hearts and minds of the people themselves. So they began insisting that they could offer life after death. They, and only they, could guarantee that everyone's souls went up into the sky-cities, in much the same way that timber, coal and suchlike did.

It was a scam but an effective one. It was the promise of a reward which the engineers themselves never had to honour. Nobody could prove that the afterlife they were offering was a falsehood, and everybody was desperate to believe it was true. The engineers spun a yarn about rebirth above the clouds, and did it so brazenly and persuasively that their fellow Groundlings swallowed it whole. Over the centuries since then, little had changed except that the engineers took to calling themselves Deacons and their scam developed into a religion, with all the trappings and ritual that that entailed.

'But that's appalling!' Serena Aanfielsdaughter exclaimed. She was young then, and idealistic, not worldly wise. Everything Lord Urielson was telling her shocked her to the core. 'They're using others. *Exploiting* them. That's wrong.'

In answer, Lord Urielson merely shrugged. 'Perhaps, but if so then we are guilty of the same crime. It's beneficial to us that the Deacons maintain their hold over the rest of their kind. They are the buffer between the Groundlings and us. Should they fail in that role ...' He flourished his wings with a dramatic flap, loud as a whipcrack. The action spoke of explosiveness and finality.

Lady Aanfielsdaughter flinched now, still able to hear that startling, ear-splitting *snap* even after all this time, so indelible was the impression it and Lord Urielson's words had made on her. She looked back on the conversation as the moment when she lost her innocence. She paid a price for entry into the Silver Sanctum, and the price was this knowledge.

Forty years on, the consequences implied by that wing-flap had never seemed more possible or more imminent. Lady Aanfielsdaughter had ended up in charge of the Airborn race at a pivotal time in history, when there was a risk that the centuries-long status quo was about to be overturned. Fate had decreed that an immense responsibility had fallen on her shoulders. She was facing the biggest crisis any Airborn leader had ever faced.

Was she up to the task?

Lady Aanfielsdaughter hoped so, and believed so.

But at the back of her mind lurked the fear that, ultimately, there was little she could do to alter the course of events. All she could do was manage the situation to the best of her abilities, while accepting that there was a very good chance that the Airborn race was doomed.

CHAPTER 66

Az The Ambassador

None of these concerns showed on Lady Aanfielsdaughter's face when, a short while later, she welcomed Az into her office, along with Michael, Mr Mordadson and Aurora. She betrayed not the slightest trace of distress or unease as she shook Az's hand warmly and told him how delighted she was to see him again. She was every inch the confident, charismatic politician. No one could have guessed the thoughts and fears that simmered within her.

'Look at you,' she clucked, eyeing Az's dishevelled clothing and his various scrapes and bruises. 'You've been through it, haven't you?'

'You could say that,' Az replied. 'It was ... interesting down there.'

'Interesting!' Lady Aanfielsdaughter laughed. 'I suspect it was a great deal more than interesting. Fill me in.'

Over the next hour, Az did. He described the descent in the elevator, the machinery he had found below, his encounter with the dead body, then the Deacons, the Ceremony of Ascension ...

As his tale unfurled, Lady Aanfielsdaughter grew more and more remorseful. She had known Az might run afoul of the Deacons, but she could never have foreseen the other tribulations he would have to endure. Nearly getting eaten by 'verms'. Being held captive and threatened by the Humanists. Being pursued by them. Managing to get back to the elevators by the skin of his teeth. Even the journey back up to Heliotropia had been a fraught one.

'Somehow, though, I knew I was going to be all right,' Az

said. 'It would just have been silly otherwise. To go through all I did, only to die in the elevator on the way up? Wasn't going to happen.'

This was not the same boy Lady Aanfieldsdaughter had sent off on a mission scant days earlier. He was stronger, she could tell, and wiser. He was also sadder. He had undergone the same change she had when Lord Urielson told her about the Groundlings, the same loss of innocence. It was haunting him, as it had haunted her. *She* had done this to him.

She said, 'It's only fair that I come clean and say we knew about the Groundlings all along.'

'Yes, I did gather that,' Az said.

'Me, I'm still finding the whole concept hard to get used to,' said Michael. 'But right now, frankly, it doesn't bother me.' He scrubbed an affectionate hand through his brother's hair. 'This is all I'm bothered about.'

'Trust me, I share your sentiments, Michael,' said Lady Aanfieldsdaughter. 'And Az, while I'm coming clean with you, I should mention that the sickness you experienced wasn't wholly unexpected either.'

'Oh yes?'

'Yes. It's been theorised that there's a marked difference between the air pressure up here and down on the ground. The air up here is thinner, with less oxygen, and our Airborn lungs have evolved to cope with that. Down on the ground, the air is denser and oxygen much more richly available, and as a result your respiratory system became overloaded. That's why you felt the way you did. It took a day or so for your body to acclimatise.'

'But you didn't warn me beforehand.'

'We didn't know for certain. It was just a theory, an unproven, untested one. You have every right to be annoyed with me, Az. I sent you down there completely uninformed, and you may think you deserved better.'

'I think,' Az said, in measured tones, 'that you must have had your reasons.'

'That's true. You see, I needed you to be a blank slate. You had to go down without prejudices or preconceptions, so that you could form your own opinions, clear-eyed. Also, if you did run into trouble with the Groundlings, it was better that you had innocence and honesty on your side. Guile doesn't come as second nature to most of us, and I don't think the Groundlings would have appreciated you trying to hoodwink them. I think they would have seen through it very quickly.'

'Then I was supposed to be a sort of ... ambassador? Is that it?'

'Well put. Yes. A dual-purpose ambassador-cum-spy, but more the former than the latter. Ambassadorship was your ulterior motive. Even though you didn't realise it, you were representing your race. You were intended to be the Groundlings' introduction to us, a way of easing them into an understanding of who we are, to show them that in many respects we're just like them.'

'Then I didn't do a very good job of it. Seems like most of them either wanted to use me or beat me up, or both.'

'Unfortunately, yes. But that wasn't your fault. Any of it.'

A shadow flitted across Az's features. 'Not even me blabbing to the Humanists about the sky-cities and everything? That wasn't my fault?'

'Az,' Michael said, 'I thought we settled this on the way over here. Two grown men were threatening to hurt you. You couldn't do anything except give them what they were after.'

'Agreed,' said Lady Aanfieldsdaughter.

'Mind you,' Michael added, 'if I ever get my hands on that Steamarm fellow ...'

'Join the queue,' said Mr Mordadson.

Lady Aanfieldsdaughter noted the remark. It seemed that relations between Az and Mr Mordadson had shifted since the last time she saw them. Her emissary appeared to have become very protective of Az. Az, in turn, seemed less resentful and mistrustful of the man. He had thawed towards him.

Mr Mordadson, she thought, *I hope you're not turning into a big softy in your old age.*

'In my view, I made a big mess of things,' Az said.

'In *my* view,' said Lady Aanfielsdaughter, 'you're a hero. Nothing less.'

Az didn't seem convinced. 'So what now?' he said.

'I was hoping you might have some suggestions.'

Az puzzled it over. 'We have to assume most of the Chancels, if not all of them, have been occupied. We also have to assume the Humanists are getting ready to make the next move, raiding the sky-cities. So we should put defences in place in the supply-arrival depots.'

'You truly believe the Humanists are going to invade?'

'If there's a leader like Alan Steamarm in every region, then yes, I do. Steamarm is ambitious and avaricious, and I don't think he'd have risen as far as he has if the other people at his level weren't the same. Birds of a feather flock together, and all that. So, sooner rather than later, they're going to be coming up. Probably Steamarm first, but the rest will follow. But there's something else.'

'What?'

'Lady Aanfielsdaughter, I probably shouldn't ask this, but – what the heck. You owe me one, I think.'

Lady Aanfielsdaughter raised her eyebrows, but then nodded. 'If it's a reasonable request, I'll do what I can.'

'I want to go back down.'

CHAPTER 67

Overstepping The Mark

Everyone looked surprised, even Mr Mordadson, who was in the habit of not revealing his emotions except through those smiles of his, and usually not even through them.

Back down? After Az had only just returned? *Eh?*

Az ploughed on, ignoring the astonished stares around him. 'The girl who helped me, Cassie Grubdollar – when I left her, she and her brother were in the clutches of the Deacons. That's bad enough, but if the Humanists have got into the Chancel, then the two of them are in double trouble. I wouldn't be talking to you now if it wasn't for them. I have to go back down and help them.'

'No,' said Lady Aanfieldsdaughter, shaking her head. 'I'm sorry, Az, but it's out of the question.'

'You said you'd do what you can.'

'If it was a reasonable request. It isn't. It's madness. I understand your attachment to these particular Groundlings. You did well by them. However, I simply cannot sanction another trip down for you, especially with war brewing.'

'You say "attachment" like they're pets or something. Cassie and Fletcher are my friends, Lady Aanfieldsdaughter, and they nearly got themselves killed helping me. What's more, they weren't helping just me, they were helping me, you, everyone in this room, the whole Airborn race. I hate to think what Deacon Shatterlonger's doing with them right now, or if not him then Alan Steamarm. We *have* to go down and get them out of there.'

'There are far more pressing concerns, Az.'

'Are there, Lady Aanfieldsdaughter?' said Az, snidely.

'Az,' Aurora cautioned, 'remember who you're talking to.'

Az knew he was out of line, but he was too fired-up to care.

'I'm not asking for much, just four or five Alar Patrollers to go with me and—'

'Four or five Alar Patrollers!' Lady Aanfielsdaughter snorted. 'Why not a dozen? Why not a hundred? In fact, take the lot, Az, so there's no one left to defend the sky-cities. And while you're at it, why not take Troop-Carrier *Cerulean* as well? Honestly! Have you even thought this through? You go down with some Patrollers, and then what happens? They reach the ground and experience the same low-altitude sickness as you did.'

'Not if they're only there for a short while.'

'And as if that's not enough of a disadvantage,' Lady Aanfielsdaughter went on, 'they'll be facing Groundlings in their own environment. I doubt wings will be much help on the ground. They'll probably be a hindrance, actually.'

'It might give them the element of surprise. It might even—'

'No, Az.' Lady Aanfielsdaughter wafted an imperious hand. 'That's all there is to it. No.'

Az opened his mouth to speak, but a withering look from Lady Aanfielsdaughter silenced him. He realised he had gone too far. In his bad-temperedness he had overstepped the mark and had alienated the one person who could have helped him. All was lost. Cassie and Fletcher were on their own and there was nothing he could do about it.

A soft cough came from behind him.

'Excuse me, milady, but might I put forward a suggestion?'

Lady Aanfielsdaughter switched her gaze from Az to Mr Mordadson. Her haughty expression faltered just fractionally.

'There might be a way in which we can combine helping Az's Groundling friends with forestalling a Humanist invasion,' said her emissary. 'Kill the proverbial two birds with one stone.'

Lady Aanfielsdaughter seemed as though she was about to

tell him to shut up, but then, instead, she gave the tiniest of nods. 'Go on.'

'Something your ladyship said a moment ago has given me an idea. Would you permit me to elaborate?'

After a long pause, the answer came: 'Very well.'

Mr Mordadson flashed a smile and began to speak.

CHAPTER 68

Moving Mountains

The previous afternoon, Cassie had told Fletcher that their father would 'move mountains' to find out what had happened to them, but even as she said those words, Den was having difficulty moving even himself. His broken rib felt like shattered glass inside his chest, grinding excruciatingly if he so much as breathed the wrong way. He would have asked a neighbour to fetch a doctor for him, but Robert was still unconscious and he refused to leave his son unattended for even a few minutes. He kept hoping Cassie would come home soon, and nursed this hope throughout the day and well into evening.

At that point Robert came round, groggily asking for a drink of water, which his father brought him. Not long after, Colin Amblescrut came round too, in the closet on the landing. Immediately, he started whining. Den told him to shut up but it was no good. Amblescrut begged to be untied and let out. He promised he would behave. He was sorry, so very sorry, for everything he had done to the Grubdollars. He didn't like being trussed up like this. He didn't like small, dark spaces either. In fact, he hated them. He would do anything in return for being released – anything.

Den ignored him. He was far more worried about Robert, not to mention Cassie. Where had the girl got to?

But Amblescrut continued to whine, and then started to groan, and then sob, and Den realised he was in earnest. Amblescrut really was frightened of the dark and of confined spaces.

Unwillingly, against his better judgement, Den freed him.

He did it holding the poker in one hand. 'For insurance,'

he told Amblescrut, as he bent down and sliced through the Humanist's bonds with a kitchen knife. 'One wrong move and you'm getting a second bump on that thick noggin of yours to match the first one. And don't think I won't use this knife on you either, if I has to.'

Amblescrut was so relieved to have been freed, he looked as if he might kiss his liberator.

'Oh, thank you, thank you!' he cried. 'You'm a good man, a kind man, a decent man.'

'That I may be,' said Den. 'I'm also a man wondering how you can stand getting yourself in police custody so often if you'm so claustrophobic. Don't it make you stop and think every time you be about to get into a fight? "Maybe I shouldn't, 'cause I hates being cooped up in dark cramped places, like police cells."'

Amblescrut heaved a morose, self-pitying sigh. 'Never be thinking too clearly, be I? Not at the actual moment when I get into trouble. That be on account of I may have had a pint or two first. And then next thing I know, I wake up the morning after feeling pretty rough, find I's been banged up in a tiny cell, and scream the whole police station down till them lets me out. I be'n't too proud of that. Any of it.'

'Nor should you be,' said Den. 'Well now, remember you promised you'd do anything for I in return for your freedom? I'm holding you to that promise. So here be what I want …'

Amblescrut left the house ten minutes later, meek as a lamb, and returned shortly with a doctor. The doctor bandaged up Den's chest tightly, so that the rib would stay put, and pronounced that Robert was fine and would make a full recovery.

Amblescrut was sent out again, having proved by his doctor-fetching mission that he could be relied on to do what he was asked to. This time, he went in search of news. Specifically, he was charged with the task of discovering where Cassie was and what the Humanists were up to.

He was gone for quite a while. The thunderstorm raging

outside began to abate and had eased off completely by the time he came back.

The information Amblescrut managed to glean was that the Humanists had taken over the Chancel and that Cassie was believed to be there with them, along with Fletcher and Martin.

It was now nearly midnight, at the end of a long, weary day for everyone. Den nevertheless could not rest, and set about figuring out how to get into the Chancel and find his daughter. In this, he enlisted the aid of Colin Amblescrut yet again. By now Colin had become a sort of faithful hound. Like a dog, he had developed an admiration and a fear of Den Grubdollar that made him docile and obedient. Den, after all, had the power to hurt him and throw him into closets. Colin was keen to please his 'master', even if it meant acting against the man to whom he had previously pledged allegiance, Alan Steamarm.

For his part, Den did not like having Colin Amblescrut as an ally. He didn't trust the man any further than he could throw him (which, with his busted rib, was not far at all). However, as long as the fellow was scared of him, and as long as he didn't get drunk in the next few hours, he would serve his purpose. After that, he would no doubt revert to being the shiftless layabout he normally was.

So, while he could, Den was determined to get all the use he could out of Colin Amblescrut.

And not just out of Colin but out of the whole wastrel Amblescrut clan.

CHAPTER 69

The Amblescrut Army

That was how, at dawn the following morning, Den and Robert Grubdollar embarked on their rescue mission in the company of several dozen members of the extensive Amblescrut family.

During the night, Colin had gone round the Grimvale region and rousted cousins, uncles, aunts, nephews, siblings and step-siblings out of bed. Some of them he had bribed with promises of a beer down the pub later. Others he had boxed around the ears till they agreed to help. It was a crude but effective recruiting programme.

As daybreak suffused the clouds with a silvery glow, an Amblescrut army gathered in the Grubdollars' courtyard. They were a motley, shambolic bunch, hardly the kind of team Den would have selected for the job if he'd had any choice in the matter. They ranged in age from early teens to late sixties, although many of the younger ones had led such careless, dissolute lives that their bodies were prematurely old and had the wrinkles and sags more commonly found on the bodies of grandparents. Some of them were mangy, some were toothless, some sported all sorts of inexplicable bumps and knobbly bits here and there on their persons, and at least three of them had an extra finger on each hand. They came from outside town, the majority of them, from shacks up in the mountains and smallholdings deep in the woods, from remote spots where they led their aimless, self-contained Amblescrut existences with little disturbance. They had got here in a fleet of pick-up trucks and jalopies, now parked in the street outside – rusty, patched-together vehicles which seemed scarcely capable of staying in one piece, let alone being driven.

Together the Amblescruts looked, to a large extent, as though they couldn't quite figure out *why* they were there, other than that cousin/nephew/brother/stepbrother Colin had muttered vaguely about the Chancel and getting into a fight, which in itself was a good reason. A fight was always an attractive proposition to an Amblescrut, and a fight inside the Chancel had an especially exotic allure.

So this puzzled but expectant crowd of relatives waited in the courtyard, murmuring among themselves and smoking pipes and home-rolled cigarettes, till Colin emerged from the Grubdollars' house along with Den Grubdollar and one of the Grubdollar sons. Then it was explained to them in very simple terms what they would have to do. The principle was straightforward enough. They were to gatecrash the Chancel and tackle all the Humanists inside. When one of the family, a third cousin of Colin's, asked why, he was told that he didn't need to know why. All any of them needed to know was that the Humanists were the bad guys.

'But be'n't you one of they yourself, Colin?' another family member called out, scratching her whiskery chin.

'I *were*,' came the reply, 'but I be better now.'

That seemed to clinch it. If the Humanists were the enemy, so be it. If one Amblescrut was against the Humanists, every Amblescrut was. End of story.

Engines coughed and revved. Exhaust pipes blurted out great sulphurous farts of fumes. Suspension springs creaked with the weight of people clambering aboard. Gears crunched. Threadbare tyres squealed for grip on the road surface.

The Amblescrut army, led by Den Grubdollar, with Colin as his lieutenant, got on the move.

CHAPTER 70

Meanwhile, At The Chancel ...

... the Humanists were solidly entrenched.

It had been a rout, as Steamarm had predicted it would be. The Deacons had put up some resistance but not much. Overnight there had been a series of skirmishes throughout the building, each of which had ended with the Chancel's robed residents either surrendering or being beaten into insensibility. The Deacons had simply never countenanced being attacked in their own lair. They hadn't foreseen such a possibility. Over the centuries they had grown complacent, confident in their own security, sure that the world outside needed them so much and was in such awe of them that they would never be unseated. They had been wrong.

Even Archdeacon Corbelgilt, for all his anxieties about the Humanists, hadn't quite been able to believe that a day like this would come. He admitted as much to Steamarm when he was dragged into Steamarm's presence by a couple of Humanists. With his robe torn and his golden-arrowed mitre askew on his head, Corbelgilt cut a sorry figure. His shoulders were hunched abjectly and his voice quavered as he said, 'This ... this cannot be happening. After so long, so many hundreds of years, so many generations of Deacons, so much respect paid to us ... this isn't right. You've damned us all. Don't you realise that? You've upset the proper order of things and now we shall never Ascend, any of us.'

'Maybe *you* won't, Archdeacon,' Steamarm replied, 'but I certainly intend to.'

The Archdeacon didn't understand the remark, but then Steamarm hadn't intended him to. He snapped his fingers, indicating that Corbelgilt should be taken away. All of the Deacons, captives and casualties alike, were being held prisoner in a residential section of the Chancel. Archdeacon Corbelgilt was hauled off to join them, still protesting his disbelief.

That was late last night. This morning, Steamarm went on a tour of the Chancel, surveying his new domain. Everywhere he went there was jubilation and roistering. His men were making free with the Chancel's bountiful supplies of food and luxuries. Steamarm smiled fondly, indulgently, at their antics. Let them celebrate. They'd earned it.

Then he learned, to his dismay, that the Chancel had not been as comprehensively overrun as he had thought. A Humanist came to him with the report that a handful of Deacons had avoided capture and were still holding out, down at the Contrition Cells.

Irked, Steamarm hastened down there to find out what was going on.

There was only one door that led to the Cells and it was a massive thing of iron and rivets, thick as a brick. A half-dozen Deacons had barricaded themselves behind it and were refusing to come out. The door showed signs of Humanist efforts to break it down or pry it off its hinges. There were fresh scuffs, scratches, dents and gouges all over it. Yet it still stood in place, essentially unharmed, and several sweat-soaked Humanists were gathered around it, frowning, with hammers and crowbars hanging uselessly from their hands.

Steamarm approached the door, loosening his shirt collar. The heat in this part of the Chancel was ferocious! He banged the door with his fist and demanded to speak to whomever was within.

For a while there was no reply. Then a muffled voice said, 'Who's this?'

'My name is Alan Steamarm. I'm the leader of this group of Humanists, and I suppose you could say I'm the new owner of this Chancel. Who are you?'

'Deacon Shatterlonger, and while I live this Chancel will *never* be yours.'

'Big talk, coming from someone stuck like a rat in a hole.'

'It's no idle threat, Mr Steamarm.'

'Oh come off it!' Steamarm sneered. 'What do you hope to do from in there? Clearly there's no way in or out except via this door. You're our prisoner, Deacon Shatterlonger, and somehow you think you can still interfere with our plans?' He barked a laugh to show what he thought of *that* idea.

'I have something in mind,' Shatterlonger said.

'Do you? How interesting. Perhaps you're going to chant a few prayers to your precious Ascended Ones, get them to come down and save you. Is that it?'

'Do not mock my beliefs, Humanist.'

'I'm not mocking. Well, OK, I am a little bit. But honestly, I'm intrigued too. What cunning stratagem have you devised to turn the tables against us?'

'You'll find out soon enough.'

'Tell me now and spare me the suspense.'

'This conversation is finished. Farewell, Mr Steamarm.'

Nothing further was heard from behind the door. Steamarm called out Shatterlonger's name a few times, but to no response.

He turned to his fellow Humanists. 'That was a bit rude, wasn't it?'

'You think him's actually up to something?' one of the Humanists asked.

Steamarm shook his head. 'No. No, I think he's bluffing. Madly. He can't face the fact that he's been beaten and his cushy lifestyle is over, so he's deluded himself into thinking he still has a way of fighting back. It's pathetic, really.'

'So you wants we to just leave he and those other Deacons in there?'

'Of course not. We can't have any of them unaccounted for, and more importantly we can't let defiance go unpunished. I want them out. Ideally alive, but if not, dead will do.'

'And how you'm proposing to get they out? Us has tried our damnedest to bust in. That door be rock-solid.'

'There's a truck about to depart for the Consolidated

Colliery Collective to bring back certain supplies,' Steamarm said. 'I'm going to ask the driver to pick up a few small extras as well.'

'Extras? Like what?'

Steamarm beamed broadly, looking as if he could hardly believe his own ingenuity. 'You're a miner, correct?'

The man nodded. 'I be.'

'What do you do when you come across an immoveable object down the pit?'

'You mean like a rock or a big old wall of limestone or something like that? Something that'm in our way? Blow it up, of course.'

'And here we have a rock-solid door ...'

All of the Humanists began to nod, catching Steamarm's drift.

'Those few small extras I'm referring to?' Steamarm said. 'Dynamite, my friends. Sticks of dynamite.'

CHAPTER 71

Death By Dehydration

In her Contrition Cell, Cassie had been able to build up a picture of what was going on around her. It wasn't a pretty picture at all.

She knew the Humanists had invaded and taken over the Chancel. That came as little surprise. She knew how determined they were. Even without *Bertha*, they had found a way in.

What came as a surprise was when a number of Deacons had retreated here, to the Cells. She had heard their voices out in the corridor all night, and also dim scrapes and thuds which she presumed were the sound of the Humanists trying (and failing) to break in through the main door to the Cells to get at them.

What the Deacons hoped to achieve by burying themselves down here, she had no idea. Fletcher was as perplexed by it as she was.

'Nothing here but these Cells,' he said, 'and we.'

Fletcher claimed, however, that there was activity in the Cell next to his, on the other side from the one Cassie was in.

'Them's bashing and scratching away in there,' he said. 'I can't make it out clearly but them's working at *something*, straight up.'

Cassie had a bad feeling about it. Truth be told, she had a bad feeling about the entire situation. She and Fletcher were trapped, there were Humanists pounding away outside, Deacons beavering away inside, and no sign of her father coming to help ... what on earth was there to feel good about in any of that?

She was also desperately thirsty, and somehow that was the most worrying thing of all. She had sweated so much that her clothes were soaked through, and now she seemed to have no moisture left in her. There was an itchy, salty crust all over her skin. Her tongue felt dry and heavy, and a headache was starting to throb behind her eyeballs. She would have killed for a sip of water, and there was none to be found. She had tried licking off some of the condensation on the walls but the taste was repulsive and she would have had to lap up several square metres' worth even to begin to slake her thirst.

You could die of dehydration, she knew that.

It was a horrible thought, being slowly parched to death in this oven-like Cell, perspiring till she expired. It was the kind of thought which, if you weren't careful, could drive you crazy and make you start to scream and rave.

For some reason, Cassie's mind drifted to Az. She imagined him, up with the Ascended Ones, up among his own, safe and content in the cool, cloudless world of the sky-cities. Happy up there. Carefree.

Then she imagined him thinking about her.

And then she imagined him being not so happy, not so carefree.

And then, just like that, she knew he was coming back down. It wasn't a hope, it was a conviction, a certainty.

Az was not going to leave her here.

Perhaps it was delusion. Perhaps dehydration was making her believe things which had no basis in reality.

Still, deep down, in her gut, Cassie *knew*.

Az was on his way.

CHAPTER 72

A Rearguard Action

Deacon Shatterlonger had not forgotten that he had two prisoners in the Contrition Cells. Nor had he forgotten that he had been intending to interrogate Cassie and Fletcher Grubdollar this very morning. By now, after a night spent baking in the Cells' relentless heat, they should have been eager to tell him everything. Done to a turn, like turkeys. Crisp and ready to be carved.

The only problem was, Shatterlonger just didn't care about them any more. Other events had got in the way. Even the fact that the Grubdollar siblings had mentioned a Humanist invasion was of no concern to him. They'd said they had foiled it, but then it had happened anyway. This somewhat invalidated their claim and suggested, moreover, that they might actually have had some involvement with the invasion. They had concocted a lie about foiling it so that the Deacons would remain off-guard, while in truth they were part of it all along.

At any rate, it didn't matter now. The Grubdollar siblings were old news as far as Shatterlonger was concerned. He was focused on one main goal, namely making sure that the Humanists did not get the chance to enjoy their victory for long. He understood that he and the handful of men with him were the only Deacons left free in the entire Chancel. He understood, too, that it was lucky he had had the presence of mind to take refuge in the Cells not long after the invasion started. The moment he laid eyes on the Humanists as they came barging through the building, Shatterlonger had known the Deacons were facing superior forces and would be overwhelmed. The Humanists were larger, fiercer, tougher, and armed. Resistance, though noble, would be futile.

Hence he had taken the decision to retreat to the Contrition Cells. Along the way he had collected several Deacons, persuading them to accompany him. It wasn't an act of cowardice. The Cells were a defendable position, thanks to their stout main door with its many bolts and heavy lock. They were a good place from which to fight a rearguard action.

The reason for this was simple. The Cells were bang next door to the Chancel furnaces. The furnaces themselves were not a defendable position, since the chamber that contained them was accessible by a number of entrances and covered too large an area for a half-dozen men to guard effectively.

However, if the wall between the Cells and the furnaces was breached, then the furnace chamber could be entered that way. Someone could sneak in without the Humanists realising. Someone could then tamper with the furnaces, doing something to them which would force the Humanists to flee the Chancel in terror of their lives.

Breaching that wall was what the Deacons were up to right now, and had been up to all night long. In the Cell adjacent to Fletcher's, they were hammering and chiselling at the brickwork with a variety of makeshift tools: planks from a bed, the lip of a latrine bucket. They were even using bare fingernails to scrape away the mortar between the bricks.

It was painful, bloody, exhausting work, made still worse by the heat. Yet the Deacons, urged on by Shatterlonger, kept at it. They realised this was their one and only hope of ridding the Chancel of the invaders.

In the wall at the back of the Cell they had managed to gouge a hole a metre in circumference and nearly half a metre deep.

It wouldn't be long before they broke through to the other side.

CHAPTER 73

Travelling Out, Travelling In

Steamarm saw off the truck that was bound for the Consolidated Colliery Collective. The driver was Lawrence Brace, who had come to think of himself as Steamarm's second-in-command, although in truth Steamarm didn't see it that way. As far as Steamarm was concerned, all the Humanists he led were alike, an undifferentiated mass of footsoldiers. One in particular didn't stand out from the rest.

Brace steered through the Chancel gates and out across the Shadow Zone, tingling with a sense of purpose. He was on his way to collect dynamite from the mine. He understood that the explosives were going to be used to dislodge some Deacons who refused to surrender. The idea of blasting Deacons with dynamite was amusing, in a ghastly way.

However, the original and main purpose of his journey to the CCC was one that mystified Brace somewhat. Steamarm had told him to bring back as many emergency breathing-apparatus kits as he could lay his hands on. These were the cylinders of compressed air which every miner wore on his back in case of a release of poisonous fumes down the pit. Sometimes, when digging or drilling, miners hit a pocket of firedamp, that mix of deadly gases which could kill a man in seconds. The breathing-apparatus kits gave you a couple of hours of oxygen, and you could survive as long as you fitted on the mask quickly enough. The kits could also help if you got trapped by a cave-in and began to run out of air in the enclosed space.

What could Steamarm want so many of them for?

If Brace had been paying close attention during Steamarm's

interrogation of the Ascended boy, Azrael, he would have realised the answer. And if Brace had really been a second-in-command, Steamarm would have *told* him the answer.

Well, the reason would be revealed soon enough, Brace decided. In the meantime he was happy simply to have a special job to do and to know that his leader trusted him enough to do it. Moreover, he was so keen on doing the job right that, for the time being, his mind was distracted from the matter of the sad fate of his homegrown marrows and the big hole in his cottage. That was a good thing, because Brace was still pretty sore about all the harm done to his property.

Hurtling along the road towards Grimvale, Brace crossed a bridge that spanned a narrow gully.

Had he looked down at that moment, he might have seen people hunkering in the gully, in the shadow of the bridge. But he was going too fast and his thoughts were elsewhere.

When the truck was long past the bridge and had become a mere dot on the horizon, the people in the gully began climbing out.

First of them to reach the top of the slope was Den Grubdollar. He scanned ahead. The Chancel lay less than two kilometres distant.

Robert appeared by his side. 'How long to get there, d'you reckon, Da?'

'Twenty minutes. Half an hour at most.'

'Still don't see why us is having to walk it. Would've taken no time by vehicle. Why'd us have to leave all them cars and trucks way back there at the edge of the Zone?'

'I told you,' said his father. 'The indirect approach. Us turns up in a convoy of backfiring old rustbuckets, it'm going to raise the alarm. The Humanists'll know us is coming long before us arrives. There be a better chance of we getting inside by sneaking up on foot.'

Robert cast an uneasy glance around. 'And then there be the verms ...'

'Verms won't attack we, long as us is in a large crowd. Them's cowardly things and only goes for strays and singles.'

'Best listen to your Da, Robert,' said Colin Amblescrut, puffing from the effort of hauling himself out of the gully. 'Him's a brainy and sensible bloke, him is.'

Robert said nothing. Nor did his father, who simply waited till all the Amblescruts were up beside him. Then, with a loft of his hand, he set off across the plain, and his ragtag army straggled after him.

CHAPTER 74

Troop-Carrier Cerulean

She sailed out from Prismburg, stately lady, last of her line. For the past few decades, pleasure trips were all she had been used for, brief jaunts from her berth, circular journeys out, round and back in, none of them longer than a couple of hours. These kept her in working order, and the money from the paying passengers went towards maintaining her. She was costly to run. There had to be some way of making her earn her upkeep. So every day, she took tourists out, and airship enthusiasts, and nostalgia buffs, and anyone who had an interest in history or military hardware. She floated into the blue with these people in her belly, her propellers whirring, her graceful bulk bobbing in the jetstream currents, and showed them what she could do.

Once, she had fought in combat. She had manoeuvred against enemy airships. She had sent out boarding parties and siege squadrons. She had braved cordons and collisions.

But that was another time, a less settled time, when trade disputes between sky-cities were commonplace and when the smallest difference of opinion could trigger armed conflict. The Airborn had put all that behind them when the Pact of Hegemony was signed. They had taken the collective decision to embrace peace, and had entrusted the Silver Sanctum with full responsibility for preserving that peace.

There were still trade disputes, of course, and other disagreements, but nowadays they were resolved at the Sanctum. Such matters were arbitrated on by the wisest and best among the Airborn. The Silver Sanctum's decrees were law, and the other sky-cities abided by them.

In a sense, then, Troop-Carrier *Cerulean* had been summoned towards the very place which guaranteed her obsolescence.

Except, now she was needed again. This wasn't any tourist outing. People were on their way to rendezvous with her, important people who wanted her and her crew to carry out a vital mission.

One of those people was Az Gabrielson, a boy who had longed all his life to fly in *Cerulean*.

CHAPTER 75

Martin's Unease

Martin Grubdollar found triumph to be a hollow feeling. It wasn't how he had imagined at all.

For one thing, the Chancel had fallen so easily. The Deacons were hardly any opposition. Throughout the night Martin had seen them cower before the Humanist onslaught. He had watched them behave like mice in a darkened room when you turned the light on, scurrying for cover or else just freezing on the spot and trembling in panic. The Humanists had attacked savagely, weapons flailing. Some of the Deacons had retaliated, but in vain. Most had curled up and allowed themselves to be pummelled and battered. Blood had been spilled, bones fractured. It had turned Martin's stomach. He could still hear, echoing in his memory, the cries of helpless pain and the pleas for mercy which had gone unheeded.

Why hadn't he joined in? Staunch Humanist that he was, he loathed the Deacons and all they stood for. Why hadn't he gleefully laid into them the way all his colleagues had? Why had he held back, stayed on the sidelines, looked on but not participated? Why had he started to feel sorry for the Humanists' foes and guilty for being involved in the violence against them?

These were questions Martin was still asking himself this morning, and the answers troubled him.

Everywhere he went now in the Chancel, he found Humanists vandalising and ransacking, or else evidence that they had vandalised and ransacked recently. There were men in the Reliquary, going through the shelves and smashing anything that could be smashed. In the library and the communal areas, pictures had been torn off walls, furnishings had been slashed and ripped, wooden tables had been reduced to kindling, and valuables that were small enough to fit in pockets had been pilfered (Martin saw empty display cabinets and Humanists bragging about their finds). A wine cellar had been plundered, and a few very drunk men were yelling along corridors, chanting victory slogans. In the kitchens, food was strewn about. Humanists had raided the Deacons' larders and feasted, and when they'd had their fill and couldn't eat any more they had chucked the leftovers around, just for the fun of it.

It was as if a herd of animals, not people, had stampeded through the place. Martin was not expecting that the Humanists should act in a civilised fashion during their takeover of the Chancel, but such a level of mindless barbarity was shameful and unnecessary. With every fresh example of destructiveness he came across, his unease deepened.

A further worry was that he hadn't seen Cassie or Fletcher all night long; hadn't even caught a glimpse of either of them.

Martin didn't know what to make of his brother's defection or his sister's efforts to derail the Humanists' plan of attack. As he had told Steamarm, he wanted to wring their necks. Yet at the same time, they were Fletcher and Cassie, blood-relatives, kin. Fletcher had always adored Martin, looking up to him as only a younger brother could, while Cassie was the baby of the family, the little girl Martin had felt protective towards all his life. He was stung that the two of them had turned against him. Hatred of them seethed within him – and yet the hatred would not have been nearly so strong if he didn't still love them too.

So where had they got to?

Now that the Chancel was securely under Humanist control, Martin made it his priority to track down his brother and sister. He searched every section of the building purposefully and methodically. The Chancel was truly a vast place. Fletcher and Cassie could be almost anywhere. But little by little Martin began narrowing down the possible locations, determined that he would get to them and confront them.

At one point his quest led him to the elevator chamber, and for a while he stood on the gantry, stupefied. The roar of the machinery, the turning of huge cogs, the slotting in and out ...

Then a thought occurred to him. Maybe Fletcher and Cassie had got on an elevator. Maybe they weren't in the Chancel at all. Maybe the Ascended boy had convinced them to go up with him above the clouds.

Martin dismissed the idea. They wouldn't be that stupid, would they? Go up in the elevators and die?

He resumed his search. Cassie and Fletcher were still somewhere in the building, he was sure. And when he found them, how he dealt with them would depend entirely on his mood. Either he would escort them to *Bertha* and tell them to get back home, or he would give them a piece of his mind and perhaps a few kicks in the rear end as well. Or he'd do both things.

Family!

Was there ever, Martin wondered, anything quite as confusing and exasperating as family?

CHAPTER 76

Breakthrough

In a section of wall in the furnace chamber, low down near the floor, a brick began to move. It shuddered, protruded by a centimetre, then by two centimetres, and all at once shot outwards. It landed on the floor with an almost musical *clink*, one corner of it snapping off.

In the aperture left behind, a pair of eyes appeared. They were Deacon Shatterlonger's. They scanned from side to side, checking if the coast was clear. As far as Shatterlonger could tell, there was no one in the chamber, not a Humanist to be seen.

Over the course of a couple of minutes, the gap left by the missing brick was widened. More bricks were knocked out, along with chunks of mortar. Soon there was a hole large enough for someone to crawl through. A short tunnel now connected the furnaces to the Contrition Cells.

Out from the tunnel came Shatterlonger on all fours. He straightened up, brushed dust and dirt from his robe, and looked around him. Definitely no Humanists in sight. They hadn't thought to post a guard here. Well, why would they? As far as they were concerned the Deacons in the Contrition Cells were stuck there with no way out. They hadn't reckoned on the possibility of them burrowing through to freedom like this.

But that didn't mean a Humanist might not by chance come along in the next few minutes. Shatterlonger knew he must work quickly.

The air in the furnace chamber was so hot, it was difficult to breathe. Covering his nose and mouth with a handkerchief, Shatterlonger crossed the floor.

The furnaces resembled a series of big brick beehives. Each rose to the ceiling and was crowned with ducts and flues. The flame glare from their inspection windows cast everything in a leaping orange light. Shadows stuttered and danced, making it difficult at times to see where he was going. The chamber was a world of brightness and darkness, two extreme opposites at war with one another. Shatterlonger trod carefully.

The furnaces weren't there just for burning the bodies of people Ascending. They were power. They provided the Chancel with heat and light, things that were needed at the epicentre of a Shadow Zone even more than they were needed anywhere else. The furnaces boiled water in pipes, which evaporated to steam, which turned turbines, which generated electricity, which ran everything.

At present, thanks to the Humanist embargo, the Deacons had been obliged to tap into their reserves of coal and other combustible material. The furnaces were still going full-tilt, therefore.

For Shatterlonger's purposes, that was perfect.

He reached a steel pipe which ran vertically from floor to ceiling, the size of a dinner plate in diameter. It had a wheel fitted to it at waist height – an air intake valve.

Shatterlonger started turning the wheel clockwise. It moved stiffly, stubbornly, with a protesting squeal. He kept turning it, grimacing with the exertion. Eventually the wheel hit a point when it could go no further.

There were several other identical pipes and air intake valves all around the chamber. Shatterlonger did the same with each of them, rotating the wheel till it could be rotated no more.

On a free-standing console in the centre of the room was a row of pressure gauges. As Shatterlonger went around the chamber turning wheels, the needles on the pressure gauges began to move. One after another, they slowly edged round from the green zones which denoted safety to the red zones, which were marked DANGER.

CHAPTER 77

Subtlety And Extreme Violence

Near the Chancel's southern gate, the Amblescrut army halted, regrouped, and debated their next move.

'Leave this to me,' said Colin Amblescrut, who was crouching behind a low ridge along with his relatives and Den and Robert Grubdollar. They had been observing the Humanist who was on guard duty, and Colin was convinced he could take the man down. 'Him be'n't exactly the beefiest fellow I's ever seen, and if I uses a combination of subtlety and extreme violence ...'

He was off before anyone could stop him. Den tried to object but it was no use. Colin leapt out from hiding and strode across the ground between the ridge and the gate with his arms swinging and an air of supreme self-assurance. Den was convinced that the self-assurance was misplaced. He had no doubt that Colin could manage *extreme violence*. It was the *subtlety* part of the plan that worried him.

'Oy-oy!' Colin called out. 'Be that you, Digby Sandwill?'

The Humanist in the guardhouse looked up, somewhat startled. 'Colin? What'm you doing all the way out here? Last I heard, you was back in town keeping watch over that murk-combing lot, the Grubdollars.'

'Change of plan. Fancied a bit of a stroll, I did. Stretch my legs.'

Behind the ridge, Den put his head in his hands. *Fancied a bit of a stroll!* Who would be dumb enough to fall for that?

Digby Sandwill, apparently.

'Oh? Well, I suppose it'm not a bad day for a walk. But you's come a long way, straight up.'

'Felt like seeing how things was going at the Chancel. Obviously it'm all gone well. You lot managed to take over the place, even without I.' Colin chuckled broadly.

'Yeah, it were pretty straightforward in fact.' Sandwill stepped out from the guardhouse. Colin was now less than five metres away. 'So, somebody else be looking after the Grubdollars then. I mean, you didn't leave they all by themselves, did you?'

'Of course not.'

'So who? Who'd you leave with they?'

Sandwill was not quite *that* dumb after all, then. He was peering at Amblescrut with a half-formed frown of suspicion, and he knew his question had caught the other man on the hop. Colin did not have an answer ready.

'Maybe you should tell I what'm really going on, Colin.' Sandwill raised the weapon he was carrying, a pickaxe handle. ''Cause something here just don't smell right.'

Den, listening to all this, knew that drastic action was called for. Otherwise the efforts they had made to reach the Chancel and get inside undetected would be in vain.

He popped his head up from behind the ridge.

'Digby Sandwill!' he yelled. 'Your mother be a monkey and your father has bandy legs and nothing hanging between!'

Sandwill spun round angrily, looking for the person who had insulted his parents.

Colin spotted his chance and seized it, just as Den had hoped he would. With Sandwill momentarily distracted, he was able to launch himself forwards and snatch the pickaxe handle away.

Then he clouted Sandwill with it, once, twice, three times, till the Humanist was battered into submission.

'See?' said Colin, as his family filed out from behind the ridge and headed for the now-unguarded gate. He tapped the side of his head. 'Not just a pretty face. I be smart too, in my way.'

Den resisted the urge to groan.

CHAPTER 78

Mid-Air Rendezvous

They met with Troop-Carrier *Cerulean* at a prearranged rendezvous point some forty kilometres west of the Silver Sanctum. They flew there in two small planes, with Lady Aanfielsdaughter and Mr Mordadson in one, Michael, Aurora and Az in the other. Each plane was piloted by a Silver Sanctum employee.

Az was first in their plane to spot *Cerulean* on the horizon. The great airship, with her pale blue balloon, was almost perfectly camouflaged against the sky. Az, however, was keeping his eyes peeled, and when he spied a distant, ellipse-shaped blur, he knew – just *knew* – that it was her. The long grey shadow she draped across the clouds below confirmed it.

They drew alongside her. *Cerulean* was enormous, bigger than Az could ever have imagined. He thought of the scale model he and his father were building. It could have fitted a million times over into the space the real *Cerulean* occupied.

The planes matched their speed to *Cerulean*'s and nipped in under her hull. Docking clamps were ready, like open jaws. They latched onto the planes' wings, and the pilots cut the engines. Now they were the airship's passengers, clinging to her belly.

Overhead, hatches slid open and rope ladders unrolled. One after another, Lady Aanfielsdaughter, Mr Mordadson, Aurora, Michael and Az clambered up.

A crew member escorted them along the keel catwalk which ran the entire length of *Cerulean*'s balloon, some 300 metres in all. Above, hundreds of gas cells were held in place by an intricate weave of struts and taut wires. The cells were made of rubberised canvas and bumped and swayed against one another, buffeted by the airship's progress. Together they held just over a million cubic metres of helium, providing over 200 tonnes of gross lift. Below the catwalk were the cabins where, in times of war, as many as 500 troops could have been quartered.

Down through an opening, the Silver Sanctum contingent entered the control gondola. There, they were greeted by Captain Qadoschson, a straight-backed, trim-bearded man with eyes that were pouched in wrinkles – eyes that had spent many a year squinting at bright, far horizons. He snapped a salute to Lady Aanfielsdaughter, as did his seven-man crew at their stations. All of them wore military dress uniforms which were smartly pressed and historically accurate right down to the Prismburg Air Force insignia badges sewn to the jacket sleeves. Captain Qadoschson had a gold-braided peaked cap on his head and impressive gold epaulettes on his wing arches. He looked like a veteran of countless wars, even though he had never seen a day's combat in his life.

'Milady,' he said, 'it's an honour to have you aboard.'

Lady Aanfielsdaughter returned the compliment. 'And I'd like to commend you and your crew for volunteering to take part in this expedition and for taking to the air at such short notice. You are all of you aware how risky a venture this is, and yet you've come without hesitation.'

'When the Silver Sanctum calls, one must answer.'

'Even so. You realise there's a good chance we may not make it back alive?'

Captain Qadoschson looked around the gondola, catching the eye of each crew member in turn. 'I speak for all of us when I say that we're ready to do whatever is necessary and face whatever dangers lie ahead. My understanding is that this is a matter of the utmost gravity and that the future of the Airborn race may depend on us.'

'Your understanding is correct.'

'Then we must do what we must do, milady. No question.'

'Thank you, captain,' said Lady Aanfielsdaughter. 'And now

I'm going to hand over to this young man, Az Gabrielson, who is going to brief you fully on the situation and tell you what we can expect to find when we descend below the cloud cover. Az?'

Michael nudged Az from behind, and Az took a step forward and cleared his throat. He still could not believe that he was actually aboard *Cerulean*. It felt like a dream. Someone had taken his fondest wish and granted it. If only he could have been here under pleasanter circumstances.

The crew members were staring at him, as was Captain Qadoschson, all of them waiting for him to speak.

Az found his voice. 'It's like this,' he said, and started to explain.

He told them about his journey down in the elevator, about the Chancel, the Deacons, the Humanists ... He could tell from the crew's sceptical expressions that they didn't believe him, but he kept going and gradually the scepticism turned to cautious acceptance and then to full acceptance.

He then outlined the state of affairs down at the Grimvale Chancel, or rather at the base of Heliotropia's column. He stressed that he had no way of being absolutely sure about what was happening down there but he strongly suspected that the Humanists were in control of the Chancel and were soon going to be taking the elevators up, assuming they hadn't done so already.

Finally, he described the unpleasant physical symptoms which everyone was going to experience once the airship was below the cloud cover. The dizziness crept up on you slowly and was tolerable in the short term. With luck, they weren't going to be near ground level for long, so at worst they would feel mildly unwell, as if they had a stomach bug or a dose of 'flu.

'And that's the point at which you take over from me,' said Captain Qadoschson. 'You've experienced this ... this "ground-sickness" before, so you're likely to be hardened to it. If I'm incapacitated by it, you're the one who should take command of the ship.'

'Let's hope it doesn't come to that, sir.'

'But it may, so you'd best pay close attention to everything I say and do, just in case.'

'I think I can manage that,' said Az.

'Then let's start now.' Captain Qadoschson turned and barked out orders to his crew. 'All engines full ahead. Helmsman? Hold her steady on this course. Trim-master? Bring her nose up two degrees. Flight engineer? Keep an eye on the balloon pressure readings.'

With a low, keen murmur of power, *Cerulean* picked up speed.

CHAPTER 79

Aside

Mr Mordadson drew Lady Aanfielsdaughter to one side for a private conversation.

'Milady, it's still not too late. Take one of the planes back to the Sanctum. Please. It makes me uncomfortable, having you here.'

'Why, Mr Mordadson? Because I'm a woman and this is men's business?' She spoke the last two words sarcastically. 'It's not like you to be so gallant.' This, too, was sarcastic, but teasing as well.

'That's not it at all, milady. Otherwise I would be recommending that Aurora go with you, and I'm not. To put it bluntly, I'm expendable. The airship's crew, Aurora, Michael, Az – we're all expendable. It doesn't matter what happens to us. You, on the other hand, as one of our highest-ranking government officials, are not expendable. We cannot afford to lose you.'

Lady Aanfielsdaughter looked serene. 'I appreciate the concern, but I'm not going to run off and leave you now. What kind of leader would I be if I didn't take an active role in proceedings? Besides, I bear some responsibility for this crisis. If I hadn't sent Az down, perhaps the Humanists wouldn't have got it into their heads that they could come *up*. So I'm going to see things through to the end, come what may. It's only right and proper.'

'Well, I tried,' said Mr Mordadson, slumping his wings.

'And a very noble effort it was too. I have to admit to another reason for being here, though. I'm curious.'

'Curious, milady?'

'To see the ground. Aren't you? Finally to see with my own eyes what it looks like. I feel as if I'm about to break some great taboo, trespassing where I don't belong. It's been a long time since these old bones of mine felt quite so ...'

'Excited?'

'Yes, that's the word for it. It seems inappropriate, but yes, I *am* excited.'

Mr Mordadson offered a vague smile. 'Me too. Although apprehensive as well.'

'Do you think this idea of yours is going to work?'

'Milady, I can't say.'

'Do you think the Groundlings are ready for us?'

Some certainty entered the smile. 'Long past ready, I'd say.'

CHAPTER 80

Steamarm And The Suspicious Steam

The first intimation Steamarm had that things were going awry was a sound. Something like a moan, albeit not one made by any human throat, it was so faint as to be only just at the threshold of his hearing. It seemed to come from everywhere and nowhere. It seemed to emanate from the Chancel itself, from the walls, the windows, the floors. It lasted only a brief time, there and gone in an instance, but after it had faded the atmosphere in the building was distinctly different. Something had changed, something small but vital.

Steamarm cocked his head and listened. The sound did not repeat itself.

Feeling unnerved, he went to the nearest window and looked out. He was in the apartment that belonged to the Archdeacon himself. It was a sumptuous set of rooms located high up, with a view of a large portion of the Chancel and, beyond, a wide southward expanse of the Shadow Zone.

Outside, Steamarm could see several of the furnace chimneys, as ever pouring dark smoke into the air. Next to one of them he noticed a vent which was sending up a furiously rippling white plume of steam. He frowned. That was odd. He was sure that last time he looked, no steam had been coming out. He hadn't even realised the vent was there until now.

Did this have anything to do with the sound a moment ago?

Before he could ponder the possible connection, Steamarm's eye was caught by movement outside. There were people down by the Chancel perimeter, on this side of the fence, not far from the southern gate. They were edging along in a line. He counted thirty of them, perhaps more.

They were too far away for him to make out their faces, but he knew they weren't Humanists. The way they were moving told him that: hunched over, treading softly, looking furtively around them as they went.

Someone had just invaded his Chancel!

Steamarm let out a growl of indignation and rushed out of the Archdeacon's apartment to round up Humanists.

Whoever the incomers were, he would make sure they got a very hostile reception.

CHAPTER 81

Under Pressure

In the furnace chamber, Deacon Shatterlonger beheld what he had done, and was pleased.

The other Deacons had joined him from the Contrition Cells and were on lookout at the chamber's entrances. They would warn him if anyone was coming.

A short while earlier, a deep, resonant moan had told Shatterlonger that the turbine system was starting to feel the strain. He imagined that steam vents all over the Chancel were wide open and doing their best to relieve the pressure. But the air intakes to the furnaces were fully open and the pressure was still building. The gauges indicated that. The needles were nudging remorselessly into the red zones.

It was awesome. He could feel the mounting power through his soles, through the floor. It trembled up his legs, flowing into his whole body, flooding through his veins. He was un-leashing something incredible, a force with enough destructive potential to flatten the entire Chancel. The turbines were old and had, moreover, not been designed to operate at maximum output for any length of time. If pushed to the extreme, they would surely overload and break down. Then there would be unchecked steam coursing through the system, though aged and breakable pipes. Meanwhile the furnaces would continue to burn at temperatures far higher than their structural toler-ances allowed. In other words, there was every chance of some kind of significant explosion.

Of course, it wouldn't come to that. Shatterlonger had no intention of allowing the overload to go beyond the critical stage. He wanted to put the wind up the Humanists, that was all. He wanted to scare them into quitting the Chancel.

But in order to do that they had to be prepared to believe that he *would* blow up the Chancel.

And if it came down to it, if he had to, really had to, he would.

CHAPTER 82

Into The Cloud Cover

Soon – far sooner than Az had anticipated – Heliotropia was visible from the forward viewing windows. *Cerulean* was not only graceful in flight, she was surprisingly fast. It helped that Captain Qadoschson understood the jetstream currents and knew how to take advantage of them. He had kept the airship at whatever altitude and whatever bearing would give her added velocity in the right direction. The jetstreams interleaved, running this way and that at different levels, and sometimes all it took was a 100-metre increase or decrease in height to go from struggling against a headwind to coasting along with a tailwind. *Cerulean's* balloon acted like a sail. With a favourable following wind she could achieve speeds far in excess of anything a solely propeller-driven aircraft was capable of.

Az kept an eagle eye on everything Captain Qadoschson did, remembering it for later in case it was needed. *This, truly, is flying*, he thought. Compared with a plane, *Cerulean* was quiet, she was smooth, she slid through space as though cleaving the air open before her.

He was exhilarated. She was everything he had imagined, and more.

The sight of Heliotropia brought Az out of his reverie, reminding him that this wasn't some pleasure cruise he was on.

'Commence descent,' ordered Captain Qadoschson.

The mood in the control gondola became perceptibly tenser as *Cerulean's* nose dipped and she sank towards the clouds.

'This will get rocky,' Captain Qadoschson announced to his passengers. 'Best find something to get hold of.'

Az grabbed the brass handrail which ran all the way around

the inside of the gondola, bolted to the bulkheads. He saw Michael, Lady Aanfielsdaughter and Mr Mordadson do the same. Aurora did not. Instead, touchingly, she groped for Michael's hand and gripped it. Michael gripped back.

Az looked away, pretending he hadn't witnessed this. Michael wasn't the type who voluntarily held hands with a woman. He wasn't that kind of boyfriend. Az sensed that his brother had fallen very hard for Aurora and that he had at last met someone who wasn't bowled over by his good looks and cool job, who was in many ways his equal and in several ways his superior. Michael had, in other words, met his match.

There wasn't time to muse on this, however. The cloud cover loomed. It seemed to be rushing up to greet *Cerulean*, a rising field of torn white and grey. It looked solid, as though there would be an impact when the airship reached it, a devastating crash.

Nobody had ever done this before – willingly flown into the clouds.

At that moment it seemed to Az that they were attempting something insane.

'Steady does it,' said Captain Qadoschson. 'Steady.'

His voice didn't quaver in the slightest. His apparent nervelessness astonished Az. What self-control! Only the faint pulse of a tendon at the corner of his jaw betrayed the fact that Qadoschson was as anxious as everybody else on board.

Now filmy wisps of vapour surrounded the control gondola, and *Cerulean* began to buck and shake. Az could imagine her as a living creature, balking at the prospect of going where she clearly ought not to. He felt like patting the handrail to reassure her. He had never before quite understood how people could regard a vehicle or any kind of machine as a sentient being, the way Cassie regarded *Cackling Bertha*, for instance. It had seemed absurd and sentimental to him.

Not any more.

Cerulean immersed herself deeper in the clouds. Everything outside went pure white, then darker white.

This was it. No going back now.

Suddenly the airship lurched sideways.

'Helmsman! Correct her course!'

The helmsman counter-steered, spinning the large brass conn wheel. *Cerulean* resumed her original heading.

'Flight lieutenant. Readings?'

'All nominal, captain. Propellers working at ninety per cent of full thrust. Engine temps good. No red-lining.'

'Excellent. Notify me of any fluctuations. Trim-master? I think we're skewing a few degrees from true.'

'Aye-aye, captain. Fixing it.'

Az could tell that none of these commands was strictly necessary. Captain Qadoschson was keeping his crew's minds on their jobs so that they wouldn't have the leisure to think about anything else.

Cerulean plunged.

'Air pocket!' yelled one of the crew.

Az felt his stomach rise into his throat. At the same time, all the blood in his body seemed to rush to his feet. From several people in the gondola came an involuntary cry, almost as if the air was being shoved up out of their lungs. Wings flared to help maintain their owners' balance.

'Keep her nose up! Keep her nose up!' the captain ordered. 'More power to the forward props!'

Az clung to the handrail, fearing he would be thrown to the ceiling otherwise.

Then, as if nothing had happened, *Cerulean* settled.

There were white faces around the gondola. Even Aurora looked a paler shade of brown.

'We're all right,' said Captain Qadoschson. 'It was just a pressure drop. Happens even above the clouds. We probably fell about two hundred metres.'

'Two hundred and fifty, captain,' said the navigator, eyeing his instruments.

'Thank you, Mr Ra'asielson. Two hundred and fifty in a few seconds. An alarming sensation, but—'

Something seemed to strike *Cerulean* from outside, making her twist around her horizontal axis. The floor became a slope.

Everyone leaned. Az found himself being squashed against the wall, the handrail digging into his side.

'Adjust! Adjust!'

'Trying to, captain!'

The slope steepened. *Cerulean* was pitching, slowly turning onto her side.

'Cut starboard props! Rotate port props to forty-five and down!'

'Sir ...'

'Do as I say!'

Engines whined. The whole of *Cerulean*'s structure creaked and groaned. A mighty force had a grip on her and was rolling her over, rolling, rolling ...

But the captain's countermeasures started to take effect. Slowly, strenuously, with so much effort that she seemed she might pop her own rivets, *Cerulean* righted herself.

There were relieved sighs all over the gondola, except from Captain Qadoschson.

'I don't think that's all you can do,' he said, addressing the cloud cover. 'Let's see what else you have in store for us.'

What came next was a bout of turbulence that rocked the airship from end to end, gusts of wind hurling themselves at her from a hundred different angles at once.

Overhead, in the balloon, there was a loud, sinister snapping *twanggg*.

'It's nothing,' Captain Qadoschson announced. 'Just a wire breaking. We've lost wires before. It's no big deal. Plenty of others to keep everything in place.'

The turbulence continued, and the clouds outside were getting darker and darker, the light in the gondola dimmer and dimmer.

Captain Qadoschson called for an altitude reading.

'Can't be much further,' he said. 'How thick are these clouds anyway?'

Cerulean fought her way onwards and downwards through the shocks and buffeting. Minutes passed during which not even her captain spoke. The crew members manned their stations in grim silence, the occasional twitch of wings betraying edginess and uncertainty. Outside the windows there was nothing but roiling, impenetrable greyness. Time slowed. To Az it began to feel like the turbulence would go on for ever. There would be no end to this tempestuous abuse. They had entered a kind of perpetual twilight existence, an eternity of shaking and gloom. He remembered this feeling from when he was in the elevator, this sense of being removed from reality, of being trapped in timelessness. They were nowhere, belonged nowhere, were going nowhere ...

And then, just like that, without warning, they were out of it.

The clouds were gone.

They were in clear air.

And below was the ground – the rough, rocky contours of the Shadow Zone.

And ahead, a little to starboard, lay the Chancel, that collection of jagged and bulbous buildings clustered at the column's base.

Cassie, Az thought, *I'm coming.*

CHAPTER 83

Cracks In The Coalition

The task of rounding up Humanists to repel the invaders did not go well.

What Steamarm had thought of as high spirits earlier, he now began to perceive was rowdiness. What had appeared to be jubilation was actually wanton, thuggish glee. His foot-soldiers were out of control. They were dispersed across the Chancel, doing pretty much as they pleased. A few were still more or less behaving themselves – the ones guarding the captive Deacons, for example. Most, though, were treating the fall of the Chancel as an opportunity to run amok. It hadn't been enough to take out their resentment of the Deacons on the Deacons themselves. They had to exact revenge on the Deacons' property as well. The result: a spree of looting and damage.

What prompted his realisation that things were degenerating into chaos was the discovery of several Humanists lying slumped in a corridor, dead drunk, snoring. The temptation to kick them was so strong Steamarm was almost blinded by it. In the event he didn't succumb. He left the slumbering men where they were, unharmed, and went in search of someone a bit more sober. He knew he had to reassert order, and quickly. He must rein his men in, or else.

'You there,' he said to the next lot of Humanists he found. They were in the Chancel library, systematically taking books off shelves and ripping the pages out of them. 'What's the meaning of this?'

The men looked up from the snowdrifts of torn paper around them. Their eyes had a strange, glutted gleam, like the eyes of children who'd indulged in too much cake at a birthday party.

'Just having some fun, that'm all,' said one of them.

'Being thorough,' said another. 'Be'n't fair that the Deacons has all this nice stuff. Reckon them can do without it from now on, like the rest of we.'

'Besides,' said a third, 'this all originally belonged to folk like we. Deacons blackmailed it out of they in funeral tithes. Them doesn't deserve to own it.'

'This is not what we came here for,' said Steamarm firmly.

'Be'n't it?' said the first Humanist. 'Well, maybe not you, Alan, but it certainly be what *I* came here for.'

There were low cheers of agreement all around.

Alan, thought Steamarm. *He called me Alan.*

He was disturbed, not so much by the use of his first name as by the way the man had said it. There had been no respect in it, nor even a kind of friendly *dis*respect. He had said it coldly and antagonisingly, in a belittling tone.

Steamarm began to wonder if he had made a serious miscalculation. He'd thought the Humanists were relying on him to rally them, to lead them, to help them achieve their aims. But what if they had merely been using him all along, without even consciously knowing they had? Could it be that, to them, he was just a convenient figurehead rather than an actual leader? Could it be that he had far less power over them than he thought?

Inconceivable!

And yet ...

'Listen,' he said, with all the authority he could muster. 'I've spotted some people outside. I don't know who they are, but they've found a way onto the premises and I doubt their intentions are good. We have to see them off.'

The Humanists glanced at one another. Steamarm could scarcely believe that the idea of a fight did not appeal to them, and yet here they were, having to think about it. He reasoned that they had got a lot of aggression out of their systems over the course of the night. They hadn't yet worked up an appetite for fresh violence.

Or was he genuinely losing his grip? Were these men loyal to only one thing, their basest instincts?

'Who'd be coming to kick we out of here?'

'Seems daft. Deacons don't have friends out there.'

'You'm sure it be'n't more of our lot, come to see how us has got on?'

'Yes, I'm sure,' said Steamarm. 'Pretty sure. No, sure.'

'Don't sound it.'

'I'm sure. Straight up I'm sure.'

'Oh, "straight up", eh?' All of the Humanists chortled at Steamarm's attempt to sound like one of them. 'Well, if you be "straight up" sure, then who's us to argue?'

'So you'll do it then?' Steamarm had to struggle to keep the exasperation out of his voice. 'You'll see these people off?'

'If that'm what you want, Alan.'

This pattern was repeated elsewhere in the Chancel. It took Steamarm far longer than he would have liked, and was far more effort than he had anticipated, to gather together enough Humanists to confront the invaders (whoever they were). The situation was in danger of falling completely to pieces, and he pinned his hopes on the act of repulsing the invaders serving as the catalyst that would bring the Humanists back in line. For perhaps the first time in his life Steamarm was doubting himself. It was a feeling he did not relish in the least.

CHAPTER 84

A Building With Rattle-Lung

After hours of fruitless searching, Martin wound up in the bowels of the Chancel. He had looked everywhere else. By a process of elimination, Fletcher and Cassie had to be down here. Unless, that was, they were wandering around the Chancel too and he kept missing them. Which was possible but unlikely. If they *were* on the move, his path and theirs would surely have crossed by now. No, Martin was convinced that wherever they were, they would be staying put, lying low.

So he was left with just this one area to hunt through, the sweltering lower reaches of the building. The air smelled rank and humid here, and Martin was aware of a deep, vibrant rumble which pulsed around him, sometimes growing to a tormented roar then dwindling again. He could not identify the sound or pinpoint its origin, but he could tell it was not healthy, not the sound of things functioning well. It resembled the laboured breathing of someone in the throes of rattle-lung, that rasping, hiccupping inhale/exhale which Martin knew only too well. When their mother had been dying, the whole family had had to listen to her making that noise in the bedroom, night and day. It had filled the house and become the stuttering rhythm of their lives. Of all of them, only Cassie had remained oblivious to it, but then she had been too young to understand what it meant. She had been upset, but only because no one would let her into the bedroom to see their mother. She'd had no idea why she wasn't allowed in there and had thrown tantrums. She hadn't been able to connect the horrible wheezing and gasping that came from the room with the fact that she was being kept away from Ma. Infant innocence had protected her from the truth.

Now the Chancel seemed to be suffering from its own case of rattle-lung, and Martin wished he wasn't reminded of his mother. A building with a terminal illness? Not good. A sudden quake erupted all around him. He had to grab a wall to steady himself. The quake ebbed away, but the irregularly throbbing rumble continued.

Not long after that, Martin arrived at the furnaces.

He realised two things as he approached the furnace chamber. One was that he had finally found where the sound was coming from. This was its source. The very air around him seemed to churn with the noise. The flagstones underfoot trembled with it.

The other thing he realised was that there were Deacons still on the loose. It seemed impossible. He had been under the impression that they were all corralled somewhere upstairs. But he caught sight of a flash of robe in the entrance to the chamber up ahead and heard a muffled cry: 'Someone's coming!'

Martin quickly debated what to do. He ought to alert Steamarm. But that would take time, time he couldn't spare. Not with this worrisome rumble going on …

He made his decision and continued forwards. Maybe it was just two Deacons at the most. He could handle two Deacons. And they might have some idea of his siblings' whereabouts.

'Humanist!' yelled a voice ahead of him.

Martin halted.

In the entrance, a tall, lanky Deacon appeared. He had a shaven head and a weird kind of wildness in his eyes – the look of someone whose sanity had started to break loose from its moorings. Martin vaguely recognised him, but then he knew the faces of quite a few Deacons and had a hard time telling them apart sometimes. The robes made them all look alike.

'Don't come any further,' said the Deacon. 'Go back. Go back and tell your leader, tell Alan Steamarm, that he should leave the Chancel now, while he has the chance. All of you should. Tell him he doesn't have long. The furnaces are over-heating and the turbine system is exceeding safe limits. He has perhaps just minutes before the entire Chancel is blown to smithereens.'

As if to underline the Deacon's remark, another short quake reverberated through the surrounding brickwork. The electric lights flickered. Dust sifted down onto Martin's head.

Martin raised his hands in a peacemaking gesture. 'Look, I don't want any trouble,' he said. 'I don't even much care if you want to blow this place up. I be looking for my brother and sister, Fletcher and Cassie Grubdollar. That'm all I want. Do you know where them might be?'

The Deacon peered at him appraisingly. 'Ah yes, a Grubdollar. Thought I saw the family resemblance. Well, I shan't lie. Your brother and sister are here, right here, not fifty metres from where we're standing. Right in harm's way. So you run off and find Alan Steamarm – and run quickly, mind – and if you reach him in time and if he vacates the Chancel immediately, then maybe, just maybe, I'll shut down the furnaces and we won't die, all of us, your brother and sister included.'

'Or maybe,' said Martin, starting forward, 'I'll just go past you and get they.'

The Deacon did not look too happy about this, but the wildness in him reasserted itself, fuelling his courage.

'I'm not alone, you know.' He nodded over his shoulder, and Martin noticed at least three other Deacons lurking behind him. 'There's several of us and only one of you.'

Martin didn't falter. 'My bro, my sis. Them's all I be after. Get out of my way.'

'And if I don't?'

Martin's answer was to snarl and break into a run.

CHAPTER 85

Fight In The Furnace Chamber

Martin charged headlong into the furnace chamber, ramming into the shaven-headed Deacon and sending him flying.

Two other Deacons set upon him, but Martin butted one sideways with an elbow and brought the other one down with a kick to the groin. Another Deacon grabbed his shirt collar. Martin spun round, twisting out of the man's grasp. He took hold of the Deacon's head with both hands and yanked down, at the same time bringing one knee up. Knee and nose collided, and there was a crunch of breaking cartilage and the Deacon let out a shrill, girlish shriek.

Martin turned, to find yet another Deacon in his way. This one was bulkier than average, with a bit of muscle on him. He looked as though he might put up more of a fight than the others.

Martin, however, was in a reckless, rushing whirl of action. His heart was racing, the blood pounding in his ears. The only way to win here was to be brutal and relentless. Without a second thought he crossed the gap between him and the Deacon and started punching. A straight shot to the midriff, another to the jaw. The Deacon punched back but without the same force or accuracy. His blows glanced off Martin's shoulder, scuffed the side of Martin's head. Martin drew his right arm back and landed a piledriver in the Deacon's midriff. The Deacon doubled over, clutching his belly, heaving for breath. Martin brushed him aside and continued on his way.

There was a howl from behind him that sounded more animal than human. Martin turned in time to see the shaven-headed Deacon sprinting straight at him. He managed to get his arms up in defence, then the Deacon hit him and together they went hurtling across the floor. Martin struck something spine-first. Next thing he knew, searing heat flared across his back, and with the heat, pain. He had been shunted up against a steam pipe and it was burning him through his clothes.

He flexed away from the pipe but the Deacon shoved him into it again. There was heat again, and pain, and Martin smelled scorching cotton. He gritted his teeth and arched his back and wrestled with the Deacon and strained, and eventually managed to thrust both of them away from the pipe once more.

The shaven-headed Deacon recovered his balance and went for Martin, hoping to push him against the pipe a third time, but Martin was ready for him now. He used the Deacon's own momentum against him. As the man lunged, Martin grabbed his robe and swung him round. The Deacon slammed sideways into the pipe. Martin didn't hesitate. He clamped a hand over the Deacon's ear, shoved the other side of his face onto the pipe, and held it there.

The Deacon's scream was horrifying. Worse, though, was the sizzle that his skin made as the pipe cooked it, and the stench that came off it, sweet and meaty and all too similar to the odour of bacon frying.

Nevertheless, Martin kept the Deacon's cheek pressed against the pipe, even as the man clawed at Martin's hand and lashed out at him desperately. Martin's lips peeled back in a grimace of disgust, but he had to do this, he had to do whatever it took to defeat the Deacon, because that was the only way he was going to be able to get to Fletcher and Cassie.

Finally the Deacon went limp and Martin let go. The Deacon collapsed to the floor in a dead faint, leaving a patch of fluid on the pipe which bubbled stickily. Martin stepped away, feeling sickened. Bile rose in his throat, and he bent over and vomited.

When he had finished he wiped his mouth with the back of his hand, then turned and looked at the other Deacons. Their faces were ashen, their mouths agape in shock. One of them had thrown up too. He could see they weren't going to give him any more trouble now. The shaven-headed Deacon was their ringleader, and they had watched how Martin had dealt with him. Also, they were still reeling from the punishment they themselves had received from him. The fight was over. Martin had won.

'Where be them, then?' he demanded. 'Cassie, Fletch. Where'm you keeping they?'

A trembling finger pointed him in the direction of a ragged hole in the chamber wall.

Martin set off towards it at a run.

CHAPTER 86

Outdoor Brawl

The clash between the Humanists and Den Grubdollar's Amblescrut army took place outdoors on a patch of ground between the Chancel and the perimeter fence. The fight went on for only a few minutes, but while it lasted it was fierce and most of the time it seemed an even contest, each side as likely to triumph as the other.

It began as a dozen over-zealous Humanists rushed out from the Chancel brandishing their weapons and yelling a wordless battlecry. They took one look at the opposition, realised they were outnumbered three to one, and turned tail and fled back inside.

The Amblescruts naturally gave chase. In spite of Den shouting at them to hold back, they charged forward yelling a battlecry of their own, which was a mix of phrases such as 'Get they!' and 'Bash their heads in!' with a sprinkling of crude insults thrown in. They piled through the doorway from which the Humanists had emerged, but then found themselves suddenly at a tactical disadvantage. They were in a passageway that was wide enough for two people to stand shoulder to shoulder, but no more than two.

This equalised things, and the Humanists knew it. They turned and confronted the Amblescruts. A pair from each side grappled in the narrow space. Meanwhile all the other Amblescruts were telling one another to retreat, get back outside, it was a bottleneck here, no good for anyone. Everyone was giving orders, no one obeying. It took some time for them to begin shuffling backwards out of the passageway, and four of them didn't make it, bludgeoned senseless by the Humanists.

Humanist reinforcements arrived in the interim, so that the battle which then took place was between forces of more or less equal strength. Humanists charged the Amblescrut army from two directions at once. Some came from the passageway, the rest attacked the Amblescruts from the rear, having exited the Chancel via the sorting-house nearby. The Amblescruts were caught in a classic pincer movement, but to their credit they collected themselves and fought back valiantly and effectively.

The two sets of combatants milled and mauled. For a time, Den could not tell which side was winning and sometimes could not even tell his forces apart from the enemy. From a distance, an Amblescrut and a Humanist looked similar, and when they were all in a throng like this they merged together, becoming an amorphous mass of people. Whose hammering fist was that? Whose flying foot? There were no uniforms here to make distinguishing friend from foe easy.

That was one reason why he didn't get embroiled in the fray himself. The other was that his cracked rib was agony. Despite the bandaging it had been giving him grief all the way across the Shadow Zone, and now he could scarcely move his upper body without a burst of pain shooting across his entire torso. He knew, to his chagrin, that he was useless for fighting. All he could do was call out to his troops, encouraging them. He made sure that Robert stayed by his side and did the same. Robert was too young to get mixed up in this kind of carnage. He kept asking to be allowed to join in, and his father kept forbidding it.

Luckily the Amblescruts *could* tell friend from foe. Family member recognised family member, even amid all the chaos and confusion. It was almost instinctive.

Luckily, too, they didn't require much help. The addition of Den to their ranks wouldn't have made much difference. Although surprised by the Humanists' double-pronged assault, they soon had the measure of the enemy. They soon had quite a few of the Humanists' weapons as well, which they wrested from their hands and immediately used against them.

Gradually the Humanists' strategic advantage was whittled away. They began to cede ground. They dispersed into small, separate pockets of men, losing unity. The Amblescruts clung together in larger groups. The battle broke down into a series of skirmishes, with two or three Humanists harrying a half-dozen Amblescruts and being soundly repulsed. Along the way there was attrition. Humanists limped off to the sidelines, some of them with broken limbs, some with deep gashes that would not stop bleeding. Several had to be carried off, concussed. Amblescruts likewise retired hurt from the battlefield, but in smaller numbers. It became a kind of running tally, a means of determining which way the fight was going. The side with the greater amount of casualties must be losing, and it was increasingly obvious that, in this instance, the Humanists were that side.

The Humanists had been weary to begin with, and they had won an easy victory over the Deacons, which had made them overconfident. The Amblescruts, by contrast, had come to the fight fresh and keen, and were considerably more skilled in the art of hand-to-hand combat than the Deacons were. Given those factors, the outcome should never have been in doubt, but Den remained unsure of success right up until the moment he realised that the Humanists were surrendering. Startled, he looked around and saw that everywhere, almost as one, they were throwing down their weapons and haggardly raising their hands. They had had enough. He then saw Amblescruts start to dance and cheer. The truth still didn't quite hit home until Robert tugged at his arm and said, 'It'm over, Da. Them did it. Them brainless hillbillies actually did it!'

'Best not call they that, boy,' Den replied in a growl. 'Like it or not, them's our friends now. Best get used to being a little more respectful to they.'

Colin came swaggering up and offered Den a jokey, exaggerated salute. 'General Grubdollar sir, I be pleased to report that us has engaged with the enemy and kicked their arses. What'm you wanting we to do now?'

'Round the Humanists up and put they somewhere safe.

Then find out what them's done with the Deacons. Meantime, I'll be looking for Cassie.'

'Very well.' Colin snapped another salute and marched off to rejoin his rejoicing family.

'Haven't seen Martin or Fletcher anywhere, Da,' said Robert, surveying the defeated Humanists. 'Reckon them's inside the Chancel too?'

'Maybe. Not much bothered right now. Cassie's the one I be worried about.'

'You still mad at they?'

'Your brothers? I be waiting to have cause *not* to be. Now Robert, listen carefully. You stay here. You'm in charge now. Make sure them Amblescruts doesn't do anything too stupid.'

'*That'll* be hard.'

'Robert ...'

'Sorry, Da. OK, I get it. I be in charge. You'm going off to rescue Cass. Good luck.'

'Thanks, boy.'

So saying, Den set off towards the Chancel. Meanwhile, just around the corner ...

CHAPTER 87

The Blue Cigar

Lawrence Brace drove through the southern gate unchallenged. He was puzzled that there was no longer anyone on duty in the gatehouse as far as he could see (but then he could not see the unconscious Humanist whom Colin Amblescrut had dragged *behind* the gatehouse). The barrier itself was wide open, which also puzzled him, but he came to the conclusion that Steamarm must have decided that such security measures weren't necessary any more. And why would they be? The Chancel belonged to the Humanists now. Who would be foolhardy enough to want to break in?

Brace was feeling hugely pleased with himself as he steered the truck towards the Chancel buildings. He had obtained everything Steamarm had asked for: 50 breathing-apparatus kits and a box of 20 sticks of dynamite, with fuses. He looked forward to being showered with praise by the Humanist leader for having completed the errand so promptly and efficiently.

And lo and behold, here was Steamarm now, running to meet the truck. Brace had to admit that Steamarm didn't look like someone who was ready to shower praise. He looked agitated and panicky. Nevertheless Brace halted the truck, applied the handbrake, rolled down the window and waited to be congratulated on a job well done. Something of an optimist, was Lawrence Brace.

In the event, Steamarm charged straight past the truck's cab, barely giving its driver a second glance. He undid the tailgate and leapt up onto the flatbed where the items from the mine lay. He snatched up a breathing-apparatus kit, then opened the box of dynamite and began stuffing the sticks into the waistband of his trousers. By the time Brace had got over his bewilderment (and disappointment) and climbed out from behind the wheel, Steamarm had jumped down to the ground again and was hurrying back to the Chancel.

'Alan!' Brace called out. 'Alan? Alan, what'm up? Where you going? Alan!'

In reply, all he got was: 'They can't have won. Can't have. And they can't have it. It's mine. The Chancel is mine. I'll show them. I'll bring it down. Down around their miserable heads.'

Brace didn't think Steamarm was even speaking to him. Steamarm was speaking to himself. *Ranting* to himself.

Scratching the top of his scalp, Brace wondered what was going on. He had been away for a little over an hour. How much could have happened in such a short space of time?

The answer to that question, of course, was a lot.

But before Brace had a chance to find this out, something else happened – something which made him forget all about Steamarm's peculiar behaviour, something so extraordinary it had him wondering if he himself was starting to go a bit crazy.

A gigantic blue cigar came down from the sky and exploded with light.

CHAPTER 88

Five Minutes Earlier

On board *Cerulean*, Az observed the fighting at the Chancel, using a telescope that Captain Qadoschson had passed to him.

'What do you make of that?' the captain had asked, indicating the swarm of tiny, distant figures.

What Az made of it was that a third faction must have become involved in the takeover of the Chancel. There weren't any Deacons down there amid the mêlée. He could see no dark robes. It seemed to be Humanists versus ... whom? Az couldn't say. He couldn't even hazard a guess. A rival set of Humanists? That didn't feel like the right answer.

He confessed his ignorance. 'But it's good that they're out there in the open, because then our dramatic entrance will have more impact,' he said. 'And I think we should get on with it, too, before things spiral any further out of control.'

Captain Qadoschson gave a nod of assent. 'Let's take her down then, men,' he said to his crew. 'Two hundred metres above ground level should do it. How are we all faring? No ill effects yet?'

The crew members took it in turns to say they felt all right.

'Lady Aanfielsdaughter?'

'Fine so far, captain. Yourself?'

'I must admit, I'm a little bit light-headed. But it could just be the excitement, the unfamiliar situation ...' He fanned his face with his cap, then resumed supervising the airship's descent.

Mr Mordadson appeared beside Az at the front of the control gondola.

'And how about you, Az?' he enquired. 'Everything OK?'

'I want to get down there. I want to find Cassie.'

'I know. Patience. We must stick to the plan. We're about to change the world for ever. That's not a thing you can rush.'

'Do you think the Groundlings will be frightened by us?'

'You'd be a better judge of that than me. You've met some of them.'

Az thought. 'Maybe they'll be frightened at first, but then they'll be intrigued. Glad, even. Finally to have actual contact with Ascended Ones, to meet them in the flesh ...'

'To see that, wings aside, we're just like them.'

'And they're just like us.'

Mr Mordadson aimed a smile at Az, and for once the smile included his eyes as well as his mouth. Behind the crimson spectacles, his eyes sparkled. It was a revelation. Briefly, while the smile lasted, Mr Mordadson seemed like an ordinary, normal, approachable person. He seemed like someone you could even *like*.

Az's feelings must have been clear on his face. 'There's more to me than meets the eye, Az,' Mr Mordadson said. 'I'm not as I appear. All my life I've done hard things, made hard choices, but invariably it's been for what I believe are the best reasons. I don't set out to be a nice person, I've never felt that life is a popularity contest – but I know right from wrong, and that's my overriding imperative, always to do what's right. *This* is right, what we're about to do. And for that' – Mr Mordadson lowered his voice – 'for that, Az, I have you to thank.'

'What? Me?' Az was no longer surprised, he was astonished.

'You, for wanting to save this girl. You, an Airborn, befriending and defending Groundlings. You, proving that our two races can and should coexist, that it's high time the division between us was ended. You've pointed the way, Az. People of your own race may have looked down on you because you don't *look* Airborn. But to me, you're everything an Airborn should be. As a matter of fact, you're one of our best.'

Before Az could even think of a response, Mr Mordadson added, 'But if you tell anyone I said what I just said, I'll deny it. I do have a reputation to uphold.'

He drifted off, leaving Az to question whether his own ears were working properly. Had Mr Mordadson really just called him 'one of our best'? It must be the low altitude. Either it was addling Az's brain or Mr Mordadson's.

'Approaching two hundred,' the navigator announced.

Captain Qadoschson acknowledged this, somewhat wanly. 'Very well. Flight engineer? Ready with the lights. Divert all surplus power to them. Done? Then on my mark ... Three. Two. One. Now!'

The flight engineer threw a series of fork-switches in rapid succession, and all at once, inside and out, *Cerulean* was ablaze. Floodlights within her balloon, searchlights attached to the hull of her gondola, running lights on her nosecone and tailfins, all burst into brilliant life. The glow lit up the ground below and was reflected in sparkles off the Chancel's windows. Az saw Groundlings recoil in astonishment, craning their necks and shading their eyes. He tried to imagine how *Cerulean* must look to them, floating majestically towards them like some gigantic blue lantern. He prayed they wouldn't panic. Panicking people could turn hostile. The purpose of turning on the lights was simply to draw attention to *Cerulean*'s presence. This was the crucial moment. This was the fulcrum on which Mr Mordadson's idea teetered. If the Groundlings stayed calm, if they were fascinated by the sight of the airship rather than alarmed, then the plan stood a decent chance of succeeding. The Airborn would make a good first impression.

If not, then all was lost.

CHAPTER 89

First Contact

Humanist and Amblescrut peered upwards, side by side. There were gasps of amazement and muted murmurs of concern. People who a few minutes ago had been locked in conflict and had only just separated themselves into winners and losers, now stood united in awe. They watched the huge array of lights in the sky loom closer, squinting against the radiant dazzle. They perceived that this was manmade, a vehicle, some kind of aircraft. But weren't such things prohibited? Hadn't the Deacons decreed that aircraft were forbidden to exist anywhere except above the clouds? So what was one of them doing down here? Who could have built it and be piloting it?

Soon the aircraft was directly overhead, and the downdraught from its propellers set people's hair swirling and kicked up a thin cloud of dust. An urge passed through the crowd like an electric current. *Run. Scatter. Take cover.* But it was overwhelmed by a stronger urge, to stay put, to wait and see what the aircraft did next, to learn who was inside.

They didn't have to wait long.

A figure emerged from amidst the lambent blue glow that was at the heart of the phenomenon. To the crowd below it was a small dark silhouette, approximately human-shaped. A second figure joined it, then a third. Were they attached to the aircraft somehow? Descending from it on ropes?

No. No, the figures were moving away from the aircraft sideways, independently. Four of them. And they were people, yes, but they were more than that. Look how they moved. They were hovering, circling. They were coming down. They were like birds.

They had wings. People with wings.

Ascended Ones!

Now the crowd's consternation became a mutual buzz of excitement. Amblescrut turned to Amblescrut, Humanist to Humanist. In an instant, injuries were forgotten. So were animosities. Some Humanists found themselves sharing amazed looks with Amblescruts, and the other way round. Their expressions spoke eloquently. Ascended Ones? Here? Now? How could this be?

Down the Ascended Ones came with their wings outstretched, feathers splayed to create drag and slow the descent. Down, till the Grimvale residents on the ground could make out their individual physical details. There was a man with crimson spectacles. There was an elderly, elegant woman. There was a younger, dark-skinned woman. There was another man, also young. And in the arms of that man there was—

'Az!'

It was Robert who shouted this.

Az turned in the direction the shout had come from. Though he had only had the briefest of meetings with the youngest of Cassie's three older brothers, he recognised him nonetheless.

'Robert,' he replied.

Robert ran forward through the crowd, while the Ascended Ones covered the last few metres to the ground. Just as they touched down, the aircraft lights were doused and the Shadow Zone's habitual gloom returned. The aircraft spun slowly and pulled away, to take up position just outside the Chancel perimeter.

Robert reached the Ascended Ones. Az slipped from the arms of the man carrying him and greeted Robert.

'I owe you a pair of boots,' he said. 'I forgot to bring them back with me. Sorry.'

Robert frowned. 'Eh? What boots?'

'Never mind. How are you doing? Have you recovered from that knock on the head?'

'Got a bump there the size of a steamed pudding, feels like, but otherwise I be all right.'

Az scanned the crowd. 'So tell me what's been going on.'

Robert gave a hollow laugh. 'What hasn't? But maybe first you should tell *we* about these friends of yours.'

'Ah yes.' Az got ready to make introductions. He sensed the significance of the occasion. It had fallen upon him to officiate at the first-ever formal encounter between Airborn and Groundling. For the moment his own personal desire, to find out about Cassie, had to take a back seat.

No sooner had he opened his mouth to speak, however, than there came a loud, ominous groan from the Chancel, followed by a flare of fire from one of the chimneys.

'That didn't sound good,' said someone in the crowd.

CHAPTER 90

Ground-sick

Flames continued to shoot up from the chimney. The groan repeated itself.

'What was that?' Az asked.

'No idea,' said Robert, with an anxious glance at the Chancel. 'But Da be in there, and Cassie too. And Fletch, Martin ...'

'Then introductions can wait.' Az turned to his brother and the other three Airborn. 'Mike? I think you should move off to a safe distance. All of you. Whatever's going on in there, it sounds pretty serious.' He then turned to the crowd of Groundlings. 'In fact, I think everyone should evacuate the area. Now.'

The residents of Grimvale Township were still coming to terms with the presence of Ascended Ones in their midst, but they weren't so astonished that they couldn't see the logic in what Az was saying. Colin took charge, repeating the suggestion about evacuating. He had recognised Az as the wingless Ascended One whom the Grubdollars had been looking after (and whom Alan Steamarm had kidnapped from them). Any friend of Den Grubdollar was a friend of Colin Amblescrut.

'Come on,' he said, 'everybody head for the southern gate.'

Galvanised into action, people started to move. The uninjured helped the injured to walk. The crowd made its way in a shuffling, straggling mass towards the gate.

Az, meanwhile, set off towards the Chancel, with Robert in tow.

'Hey!' Michael took off, soared over Az and Robert, and landed in front of them, barring their path. 'Where do you think *you're* off to, Az? You just said we had to get to safety.'

'I said *you* did, Mike. *I'm* going in there.'

'Inside?' Michael frowned incredulously. 'That's crazy.'

'Maybe, but so what?'

'Look, I appreciate that you ...' Michael shook his head. For a moment his eyes seemed to lose focus. His brows knitted. 'Uhhh, that was odd.'

'It's the low altitude. It's starting to get to you,' Az said.

'No, it isn't.'

'Bit of dizziness? Buzzing in your ears?'

Michael nodded.

'Told you. You're getting ground-sick. You have to go back to *Cerulean* while you still can, you and Lady Aanfieldsdaughter and everyone. And I have to go in and get Cassie. That's all there is to it.'

Michael began objecting, but a second dizzy spell washed over him. The colour drained from his face.

'OK,' he said, reluctantly. 'But if I had any choice ...'

'I know,' said Az. 'Look, don't worry, I'll be out again in no time.'

'You damn well better be.'

CHAPTER 91

A Grubdollar Thing

Cassie could hardly believe it when the door to the Contrition Cell flew open and there was Martin standing there, looking ruffled but stoic. All at once she forgave him everything. She threw her arms around him, thinking he was the best, the handsomest, the bravest big brother a girl could have. Martin returned the embrace, hesitantly at first, then warmly.

'I still be mad at you, you know, Cass,' he said. 'Just because I came looking for you don't change anything.'

'And I still be mad at *you*,' she replied, hugging him tighter.

They let Fletcher out of his cell. He whooped with joy at being free, then became somewhat sheepish as he remembered that he had helped Cassie steal *Bertha* behind Martin's back and had betrayed the cause which his older brother held so dear. Then he realised that frankly all he cared about right now was that he was no longer trapped in a confined space being torturously slow-roasted, and he whooped with joy again.

'If you'm finished defeaning we, Fletch,' Martin said gruffly, 'maybe us could have a stab at getting out of here.'

'What'm the big hurry, Martin?' said Cassie. 'Be it something to do with all that grinding and shaking that'm been going on? Been scaring me half to death, that have.'

'It'm the furnaces, Cass. Deacons have sabotaged they.'

'What! Why?'

'Why d'you think? To destroy the place. If them can't have the Chancel, no one can.'

'Well, who be stopping they? Be'n't your lot trying to?'

'Not as far as I know.'

322

'Why not?'

'To put it plainly, things has got a little unruly around here. Which be all the more reason for us to leave, while us still can.'

Cassie nodded, but then shook her head.

'No?' said Martin. 'You don't agree?'

'No. Reckon us has something else to do.'

'Such as?'

'Not liking the sound of this,' said Fletcher, who had found a pitcher of water and was busy gulping it down. He handed Cassie the pitcher, and she drank deeply and gratefully.

'Us is bang next door to the furnaces,' she said, wiping her mouth. 'Therefore it'm up to we to do some *un*sabotaging if us can.'

'Don't be daft,' said Martin. 'It'm none of our concern.'

Fletcher agreed. 'Yeah. Let's just make for the exits like Martin says. What do you care if the Chancel get blown up, Cass? Be'n't as if the Deacons has been our best friends or anything. I don't know if you remember, but them's the ones as shut you and me up in these cells.'

'Think about it,' said Cassie. 'There be a sky-city directly up above. Helio-something-or-other. If the Chancel be demolished, the column might be demolished with it, and if that happens then down comes the sky-city with a ruddy great crash. Not only will Deacons die but Ascended Ones will die too.'

'Oh. Yeah. Well, I see your point.'

'Plus, there be all sorts of folk in this building at present, not just Deacons. Us can't go rushing out, not when us is in a position to try and save everyone.'

Martin regarded his sister with a blend of admiration and despair. 'Cass, where'm it come from, this need of yours to always do what be proper?'

'It'm a Grubdollar thing, Mart. Us all has it. Even you. Just takes a bit longer to come out in some of we. Now, the furnaces. How's us best getting there?'

Martin wavered, but then, with a resigned sag of the

shoulders, showed Cassie and Fletcher the cell he had come in by.

'So that be what Shatterlonger and the rest was up to all night,' Fletcher said when he saw the hole in the back wall. 'Burrowing away like moles.'

Without any further ado, Cassie ducked down to enter the hole.

Next moment, the floor leapt underneath them, as if a giant foot were delivering a mighty kick from below. The three Grubdollars were sent sprawling. A massive rolling shockwave of sound followed. For several seconds it felt as if the world was tearing itself asunder around them.

It passed. Cassie staggered to her feet, as did her brothers. Their ears were ringing.

Another, no less massive eruption came, knocking them flat again.

This time when they got up, not only were their ears ringing but their eyesight seemed to have been affected as well. Everything had gone hazy. It took them a moment to realise that this was due to the vapour that was billowing into the cell through the hole, filling it like a fog. It was a mixture of smoke and steam, and smelled oily and burnt.

'Cass,' Fletcher said, then repeated it as a shout because his voice sounded hopelessly muffled to him: 'Cass!'

'Yes?'

'Don't suppose *that* just changed your mind about all this, did it?'

Cassie shook her head with a grimace of determination.

'Didn't think so.' Fletcher coughed. The smoke and steam had begun to irritate his throat. 'Oh well, let's get cracking then.'

Cassie groped to find the edges of the hole, then lowered herself in.

CHAPTER 92

A Trouserful Of Dynamite

'Steamarm!' roared Den. 'Alan Steamarm!'

The Humanist leader halted in his tracks.

'Where'm you off to, you scumbag? Running away like a lily-livered coward, looks like. Now why'nt that surprise I?'

Slowly Steamarm turned to face him. They were at an intersection between four passageways. Steamarm had been heading along one of them, Den the other. The moment he spied Steamarm crossing in front of him, Den had felt a sudden and uncontrollable upsurge of anger. Now he stalked towards Steamarm, fists clenched, teeth tight. The pain from his rib was temporarily forgotten, obliterated by his loathing of this man who had barged into his home, hurt his youngest son, stolen his murk-comber, done who-knew-what with his daughter ... and that was just the tip of the iceberg of his crimes. The fact that Steamarm had a breathing-apparatus kit strapped to his back was, at this particular moment, of no concern. Den was intent on exacting retribution. Everything else was incidental.

By rights Steamarm should have been trembling in his boots. The sight of Den bearing down on him in a passion of fury would have been enough to make almost any man quail. But in fact Steamarm seemed weirdly unperturbed. If his face showed anything, it was annoyance. He looked peeved to have been interrupted on his journey to wherever he was going.

'What?' he said testily. 'Just what it is you want from me, Mr Grubdollar? I've a lot to do. State your intent, then leave me to get on with things.'

'State my ...?'

'Sorry, not plain-spoken enough for you, was I? Tell me what you're after. And make it quick.'

'I be after *you*, Steamarm,' Den said, halting in front of him. 'That be my "intent". I be after your head on a plate.'

'Oh really?'

'Yes oh really. I be after my girl Cassie as well, but now as I's come across you, I be looking forward to settling a few scores with the fellow who's mucked my life around so much this past couple of days. Maybe you'm seen how things has gone outside. Us has taught your Humanist chaps a lesson. Now it'm my chance to do the same to you.'

Steamarm studied Den's raised fists with a kind of weary contempt.

'Violence,' he said. 'That's how you solve everything, isn't it?'

'On the evidence I's seen, it'm how *you* solve everything.'

'Violence is merely a tool, a means to an end. It's not a way of life with me as it is with some people.'

'Weren't a way of life with me till you happened along.'

'Mr Grubdollar ...' Steamarm flung open the flaps of his jacket, revealing the top of his trousers. 'You're just not getting me. Look. Do you honestly think I'm scared of you beating me up? Do you honestly think I'm in any way bothered that some lumpen Grimvale no-account has "a few scores to settle"?'

Den gaped. At first he thought Steamarm wanted to show that he was wearing some kind of corset, which would have been bizarre in itself. But then he saw that the corset was in fact sticks of dynamite wedged between Steamarm's waistband and shirt. There were at least ten of them, protruding up like a set of slender, uneven brown teeth.

He was lost for words.

'Yes,' said Steamarm. 'As you can see, I've far bigger fish to fry. So if you'll kindly let me be on my way ...'

At that moment, two loud detonations occurred in swift succession. The first sent both men lurching to one side. The second sent them lurching to the other. It was as though the

Chancel was being twisted one way, then the other, with appalling force.

On the second detonation, Den collided sideways with a wall. It was a tragically perfect mishap, since his ribcage took the brunt of the impact and, despite the bandage, his fractured rib was flexed inward. The agony was excruciating and all-consuming, like a flare of white light filling him from head to toe. He sank to the floor, almost weeping with the pain. By the time he regained any level of self-awareness, Alan Steamarm and his breathing-apparatus kit, not to mention his dynamite corset, were long gone.

CHAPTER 93

Inferno

Fires blazed. Smoke swirled. Steam hissed in jets. The furnace chamber was a nightmare of flame and heat and turmoil. The three Grubdollar siblings moved cautiously through it, groping their way like blind people. They *were* blind, almost. The smoke stung their eyes, forcing them to wipe them constantly and blink hard. Breathing was also a problem. At Martin's suggestion they tore off strips of shirt and wrapped these around their noses and mouths. Even so, they coughed and choked.

'Look for some kind of shutoff,' Cassie said. 'There'm got to be regulator controls or the like, something the Deacons opened which us can close.'

Martin nodded, but he himself was looking for a Deacon. Any Deacon would do. He could grab him and ask him to explain how to damp down the runaway furnaces, *force* him to if necessary.

But there were no Deacons around, and he could only assume they had fled the chamber once the explosions started. Even the shaven-headed Deacon, the one he had burned, was nowhere to be seen. Shatterlonger. That was his name, Martin remembered now. He guessed that the other Deacons had gathered Shatterlonger up and helped him to get out of there, leaving the furnaces unguarded. It wouldn't have occurred to them that anybody would be so foolish, so insane, as to enter the chamber and try to undo what they had done.

This guess was almost correct. Most of the Deacons had indeed fled the scene. One, however, remained behind.

Amid the seething smoke and steam, a single baleful eye was

watching the three Grubdollars, staring out from a mangled face. The eye's companion had been baked in its socket and now, with its sightless yellow iris, resembled nothing so much as a cross-section of a boiled egg. The skin around and below was a rippled, glistening mess, wet with blood and lymph. The corner of the mouth on that side was tightened, pulled into a lopsided leer.

This distended, asymmetrical visage belonged, of course, to Deacon Shatterlonger, and ugly though it was, its ugliest part was the remaining good eye, which blazed with pure, undiluted loathing. All the hurts and humiliations Shatterlonger had suffered, not just recently but ever, were condensed in that eye. If emotions were visible things then the Deacon's hatred would have manifested as a beam of sheer malevolence, shooting in a straight line from his cornea to the trio of Grubdollars.

He tracked them stealthily, matching their steps with his, biding his time, waiting for the right moment to attack. From the moment he had laid eyes (or rather, eye) on them, it hadn't even bothered him to ask himself why they had re-entered the furnace chamber. All he knew was that he would have his revenge on the older brother for what he had done to his face. He would have his revenge on all of them.

When the three Grubdollars halted, Shatterlonger halted too. He heard them debating what to do. They had come to a stop next to one of the air intake valves, and the girl, Cassie, was suggesting to her brothers that this might be what they were after.

'That look like a ventilation pipe to you?' she said.

'Hard to tell in all this smoke and mess,' said Fletcher. 'There'm some sort of valve wheel there, straight up. But who knows if it be'n't to shut down the steam vents? If so, turning it'd only make matters worse.'

'Us has to do something,' his sister urged. 'And fast.'

'If it'm a steam pipe, it'll be hot. Touch it.'

'You touch it.'

Shatterlonger couldn't bear it. The Grubdollars, if they could finally make up their minds, might follow up Cassie's hunch about the wheel, and then he would be defeated. He couldn't let that happen.

His hands became claws, and with a cry of 'Nooooo!' he lunged towards the three siblings.

CHAPTER 94

Sacrifice

Martin turned in time to see the figure of Shatterlonger come hurtling out of the smoke. Without thinking he dived to meet the oncoming Deacon. They collided hard. Shatterlonger fell backwards but grabbed Martin's shirt as he did so, dragging Martin down with him. They crashed to the floor in a heap. Martin capitalised on the fact that he landed on top. He pinned Shatterlonger with his left hand and started thumping him with his right.

'Let's see if I can't make both sides of your face match, Deacon,' he growled as he punched Shatterlonger's unburnt cheek again and again.

Shatterlonger just took the blows, laughing. Laughing horribly. Insanely.

'What?' said Martin, pausing in his onslaught. 'What'm so funny?'

'Keep wasting your time on me.' The Deacon's voice was slurred, his distorted mouth unable to shape words properly. 'It doesn't matter what you do to *me*. I've got nothing to lose any more. This place can come down around our ears for all I care.'

'How does us stop it? Tell I!' Martin demanded.

'No.'

Martin struck him, viciously.

Shatterlonger just laughed again.

'Want I to take out that other eye of yours?'

'Threaten all you like. You'll not get any help from me.'

As Shatterlonger said this, however, he flicked a look with his good eye towards the air intake control.

It was an involuntary reflex, and it gave the game away. Martin, following the line of the glance, understood. Cassie was right. That valve wheel *was* the way to shut down the furnaces.

But before he could relay the information to her and Fletcher, his opponent acted. Martin's momentary distraction gave Shatterlonger an opportunity. He reached up, grabbed Martin's wrists, and thrust him off. Martin rolled over and came up onto his feet. Shatterlonger got to his feet too and closed in. He threw himself at Martin and began propelling him towards one of the furnaces, intent on scorching him on the hot brickwork and finishing the job he had started on the steam pipe during their earlier fight. Martin resisted, digging his heels in. The two men grappled, the one pushing, the other shoving back, their hands clasping and flailing. It was like some ghastly dance, a clumsy, desperate minuet of violence.

Fletcher moved in to help. His brother had lost the advantage and could do with a hand. Martin, however, saw him coming and shouted at him to back off.

'I can handle he,' he gasped. 'That wheel. Turn it. It'll do the trick. And there be others. I saw they when I were here the first time. You and Cass find they and turn they as well.'

Cassie wasn't convinced that Martin could handle the Deacon as he claimed. The injured Shatterlonger was possessed by madness, and that made him far more dangerous than he might otherwise have been. In his lunatic rage he was growing more and more feral with every moment. He raked fingernails at Martin's face. He even tried to bite him. Spittle flecked his lips and chin. It was all Martin could do just to hold him at bay.

'Don't just stand there gawping,' Martin yelled. 'I mean it. Turn that wheel or us is all goners.'

Cassie overcame her hesitation and grabbed the wheel. Anticlockwise was always the direction for shutting off taps and the like. She started hauling on the wheel with both hands, rotating it that way. At first it didn't want to move, but then bit by bit it budged. Fletcher stepped in to add his strength to hers, but she shook her head.

'You heard what Mart said. Other valve wheels. Go find they.'

Fletcher threw a last look over at his brother. Martin and the Deacon were still locked in their savage clinch. The strip of shirt over Martin's mouth had fallen away. His teeth were bared, just like Shatterlonger's, and clenched tight.

With a shoulder-shrug, a gesture of hapless resignation, Fletcher headed off into the smoke.

Cassie kept up her battle with the wheel, turning and turning it with all her might. She could hear grunts and gasps from several metres behind her, the sounds of the ongoing, tooth-and-nail struggle. Someone screamed, and she had a horrible feeling it was Martin. The wheel seemed to go round for ever, like an eternal punishment, a task without end. And what if it was all in vain anyway? What if it was too late to prevent all the furnaces from exploding?

The wheel halted. It could go no further.

Cassie spun round.

What happened next would remain etched in her memory till she died.

There was Martin. There was the burned Deacon. They were silhouettes in the smoke, outlines of men, with the furnace behind them. They were still wrestling for advantage, Martin bleeding from where a flap of skin had been torn from his forehead, Shatterlonger with his ruined face looking like something that should not be alive ...

Then fire erupted around them, engulfing them, and with the fire came a noise so loud it was like the world splitting in two.

Cassie was blown off her feet. When she staggered upright, there was no more Martin, no more Deacon, only their afterimages seared onto her retinas, two blue ghosts, hovering there, frozen in conflict, soon starting to fade ...

During the next few minutes of her life Cassie felt like a passenger in her own body. She moved around the furnace chamber, finding valve wheels, rotating them mechanically and methodically. Her ears were ringing. She was oblivious to the smoke, the flames, the piles of rubble on the floor, the general chaos. It didn't matter. Nothing mattered. She was tiny and insignificant. There was nothing to do but this: shut down the furnaces. There was nothing else to think about. If she thought about anything else, she would collapse in a sobbing heap. She was numb all over. She turned the wheels. Turned the wheels. Around her the pressure build-up perceptibly started to subside. The smoke thinned. Flames dwindled. The chamber's groans subsided.

She came across a control console and watched needles on gauges creep out of the red. She stared at them, understanding what this meant but not caring, not even caring that she understood.

Fletcher appeared. He was grey-faced, bloodshot-eyed.

'Cass, back there ... I saw two ... two bodies. I thought it were you and Martin, but ...'

He realised she knew. Their brother was dead.

They clutched each other, clung to each other, while the furnace chamber gave a last few rippling sighs and settled back into something like its usual operational rhythm, an uneasy and damaged beat which nonetheless conveyed a sense of things functioning again, still producing power. From the intact furnaces heat radiated once more, managed heat, the kind of heat which in the past had consumed countless bodies and sent their smouldering atoms spiralling up to the skies. Close to a gaping hole in the side of one of the furnaces that weren't intact, two charred corpses lay, joined in an embrace, flesh fused to flesh. Smoke drifted from them and was drawn by convection into the hole and up into the furnace chimney, up through the chimney, up and out into the open air. In a thin, almost invisible thread it continued to rise towards the clouds. In this way, together, wisps of Martin Grubdollar and Deacon Shatterlonger ascended, and Ascended ...

CHAPTER 95

A Sore Loser

Az and Robert almost collided with Den Grubdollar coming the other way. Robert's father was moving in a gingerly fashion, supporting himself on the wall with one hand.

He was annoyed to see Robert inside the building. 'Didn't I tell you to stay with them Amblescruts?' he growled. Then he looked at Az and his eyes widened. 'You? Why'm you still down here?'

Az quickly filled him in. Before he could finish the explanation he was interrupted by an immense *boom* which reverberated through the Chancel corridors. He just managed to keep his balance, as did the two Grubdollars.

'Third one of they,' Den said dourly. 'I be'n't liking our chances much. And then there'm that Steamarm and his dynamite.'

'What?'

'Just had a run-in with he a few minutes ago. Steamarm's got enough explosive attached to his body to take out half this building. Got a miner's breathing kit on his back too, for some reason. Haven't a clue what him wants *that* for.'

Az's face went hard. 'Oh no. He can't. Surely not.'

'Can't what?'

'Steamarm's going up.'

'Up where? Up how?'

'Up to Heliotropia, Mr Grubdollar. The sky-city at the top of the column. He's going to take the elevator up there.'

'What for? Wait, you don't think ...'

'I do.'

'Bring down a whole sky-city? Could he do that?'

'If he has enough of this dynamite stuff, and if he sets it off at the top of the column, just underneath the city ... it could work.'

'But surely him'll die on the way there.'

'This miner's breathing kit – it's designed to supply you with air, right?'

'Right.'

Az saw it all. Steamarm's talk of apprentice's bends, Lady Aanfielsdaughter's description of the differences in air pressure above the clouds and on the ground ...

'Has he gone mad?' he wondered aloud.

Den weighed up the possibility. 'I saw his face. Spoke to he. Not mad, I don't think. Him just doesn't like losing. Doesn't like it one little bit.'

'So, because he's such a sore loser, he'll kill tens of thousands of people? Not to mention himself, more than likely.'

'Reckon so.'

Az went from incredulity to purposefulness. 'Robert. Mr Grubdollar. Keep looking for Cassie.'

He turned and started to run back the way he and Robert had come.

'Az!' Robert yelled after him. 'What are *you* going to do?'

'What do you think?' Az replied over his shoulder, not breaking stride. 'No one's destroying a sky-city if I can help it.'

CHAPTER 96

Taking Command

Out in the open, Az signalled desperately to *Cerulean*. He jumped up and down and fanned his arms above his head, praying that Captain Qadoschson or someone was keeping lookout and would spot him.

Someone did. A winged figure emerged from the airship and swooped towards the ground in a steep, breakneck dive, halting at the very last moment.

'You haven't found her then,' said Mr Mordadson.

'We've got to go up,' Az said. 'In *Cerulean*. Now.'

'Captain Qadoschson is extremely unwell. I don't think he—'

'Then I'm captain. Take me up there. There's no time to waste.'

'At least tell me why the great urgency.'

Az did in as few words as possible. In response, Mr Mordadson snatched up a crowbar that was lying nearby, left behind in the wake of the Humanist/Amblescrut battle. Then, with his other hand, he grabbed Az by the wrist and took off. Az was yanked into the air. The ground fell away beneath him. Mr Mordadson soared, his wings beating furiously. He was a much stronger flyer than Michael. The extra weight of his living cargo scarcely seemed to trouble him.

Moments later they were aboard *Cerulean*. In the control gondola, everyone was in various states of physical discomfort. Worst off was Captain Qadoschson, who was lying on the floor, moaning and looking very sorry for himself. Aurora was tending to him, although she herself seemed ready to keel over. Michael was putting on a brave face, as was Lady

Aanfieldsdaughter, but in neither instance was it particularly convincing. The crew were still manning their stations but several of them would clearly rather have been lying down like their captain.

Of all of the Airborn present, only Mr Mordadson appeared unaffected by ground-sickness. Az suspected he was feeling as bad as anyone but refused to show it, such was his self-control, his iron willpower.

'Listen up,' Az said to the crew. 'We need to climb, and fast. We also need to get as close to the column as we can. Lives are at stake. There's no time to go into detail. You'll just have to trust me on this.'

The crewmen regarded him doubtfully. This kid, this wingless kid, was giving them orders? Some nerve.

'Do as he says,' came a weak voice from the floor. Captain Qadoschson rolled his eyes in Az's direction, then back at the crew. 'You all know how to fly her, and I believe Az has a feel for her. Whatever he asks of you, give it to him. That *is* an order.'

The crewmen exchanged uncertain glances. Then one of them nodded, and another offered a soft 'Aye-aye'.

'Then let's go,' said Az. 'Trim-master? Thirty-five degrees.'

'But that's—' The trim-master bit his lip. 'Thirty-five it is, aye-aye.'

'Engineer? Full thrust, all props.'

The flight engineer threw open the throttles.

'Helmsman? The column.'

The helmsman whirled his conn wheel.

Az looked round at the column and the elevators falling and rising on its circumference. Steamarm was in one of the ones going up. Az was sure of it. But which one?

It wasn't relevant just yet. What *Cerulean* had to go was gain height and reach Heliotropia before Steamarm did.

Could the airship outpace the elevators?

Az didn't know. All he knew was that she must, otherwise the sky-city was doomed.

CHAPTER 97

Race Against Disaster

When they hit the cloud cover, *Cerulean* was going so fast that for a time it was plain sailing. The turbulence couldn't seem to get a grip on her. She sliced cleanly through.

Then there was an almighty shudder and abruptly her nose began to lift. The floor of the control gondola, already at quite an angle, steepened severely. One of the crew lost his footing and went skidding backwards, fetching up against the gondola's rear wall with a thump and a burst of feathers. Everyone else clung on for dear life to the nearest fixture.

'Level her out!' Az demanded.

The trim-master replied that he was trying to, but if they hadn't been at 35° to begin with …

'Az,' croaked Captain Qadoschson. 'She mustn't go tail-down. She'll drop like a stone.'

Az had a brainwave. 'Ballast,' he said to the flight engineer. 'The rear ballast tanks. Are they full?'

'Yes.'

'Jettison them. The lot.'

'But we'll be less stable after.'

'There might not be an after if we don't jettison them now.'

The flight engineer threw the requisite levers. Sluicegates opened at the rear of *Cerulean*'s balloon and ballast water poured out in gushing, twisting streams. Seconds elapsed during which Az believed his drastic tactic hadn't succeeded. Then, with aching slowness, *Cerulean*'s aft end started to rise; the angle of the control gondola floor became steadily less acute.

Az allowed himself a moment of satisfaction, but only a moment. The ascent wasn't over yet, and there could be any number of further challenges to deal with.

Cerulean battled on up through the clouds, until finally, with what seemed like a leap of exultation, she broke free. Brightness – the glorious brightness of the Airborn realm – surrounded her. Everyone on board experienced a lift of the spirits, however ill he or she was feeling. They had missed the sun. They hadn't realised till now just how much they had missed it.

Ahead, the column filled the viewing windows. Az ordered the helmsman to bring *Cerulean* alongside the column and keep her there while they continued to rise. 'Stay within fifty metres. Closer if you can.'

'Fifty, aye-aye.' The helmsman puffed out his cheeks, none too happy. Fifty metres was perilously close to the column. A stray gust of wind might catch the airship sidelong and send her crashing into the column, with fatal consequences for all. But he didn't cavil. As Az had said, lives were at stake. The helmsman chose to treat the exercise as a test of his skills, one he didn't dare fail.

'Mr Mordadson?' Az said. 'Are you all set?'

Grimly Mr Mordadson hefted the crowbar.

CHAPTER 98

Hard Choices

Holding the handrail, Az looked out through the viewing windows as Mr Mordadson winged his way across from *Cerulean* to the column. Az had done his part. Now everything depended on Mr Mordadson.

Briefly Az recalled his first encounter with the Silver Sanctum emissary less than a week ago. He remembered his initial mistrust of the so-called school inspector and his subsequent dislike of him when Mr Mordadson threatened his father. How things had changed. Now, all his hopes were pinned on Mr Mordadson. Everyone's hopes were. He alone stood between Heliotropia and its destruction.

As Mr Mordadson neared the column, Az thought that he looked pitifully small, dwarfed by the column's thickness and height. At the same time, metaphorically speaking, Mr Mordadson's stature had never seemed greater.

Mr Mordadson alighted on top of one of the rising elevators. Steadying himself with outstretched wings, he bent and inserted the tip of the crowbar between the doors. Straining with effort, he pried the doors apart. The elevator was empty. Mr Mordadson took to the air and circled round the column to the next rising elevator.

He tried three elevators in succession, without any luck. Az had time to doubt his own belief that Steamarm was riding up in one of them. He began to think he had misinterpreted the evidence and that Steamarm had something else in mind, some entirely different ploy. In which case, this desperate journey, with all its attendant risks, would have been in vain, and Steamarm would almost certainly pull off whatever lethal stunt he was attempting.

But the fourth elevator Mr Mordadson tried was occupied.

Lady Anfielsdaughter had joined Az at the viewing windows. So had Michael. Both were starting to recover from their ground-sickness. Az, however, was unaware they were even beside him. He was focused, with every fibre of his being, on what was happening outside.

He watched Mr Mordadson lever the doors apart, and there was Steamarm, crouching inside the elevator. He was wearing a sort of funnel-shaped mask. The mask covered his face completely, with two glass discs to see through. A flexible tube led from the front of it to a metal cylinder on his back. He looked inhuman with this device on, featureless and grotesque, not even a Groundling any more but something else, something less.

In his left hand he was holding what looked like a short length of wood. Az took this to be the dynamite. There were more such sticks around his waist. In his other hand was a match. Steamarm must have heard Mr Mordadon land on the roof of the elevator. He had had sufficient time to light the match. He now applied it to the dynamite fuse, which started to fizzle brightly.

Each of the next five seconds felt about a minute long.

One – Mr Mordadon somersaulted forwards into the elevator.

Two – in a single fluid manoeuvre he rolled out again, dragging Steamarm with him.

Three – he launched himself and Steamarm out into space.

Four – in a flurry of wing flaps, he put distance between them and the column.

Five – he continued to speed away from the column, with Steamarm twisting and writhing beneath him but still clutching the dynamite.

Then, with little ceremony, Mr Mordadson let go of the Humanist leader.

Steamarm fell. He fell with his arms flailing, frantically beating at the air, as though he thought they were wings, as though he himself could fly. He fell head-first, the dynamite fuse sparkling all the way like a star. By the way his mouth was wide open, you could tell he was screaming.

Hard choices, Az thought.

That was what Mr Mordadson had said. That was his philosophy.

Watching Steamarm plummet, Az understood exactly what he had meant. This was the right thing to do. It wasn't the kind thing or the moral thing. But it was the right thing. All those lives in jeopardy, set against the life of this one man.

Steamarm reached the cloud cover and vanished from view.

A split-second later, light blossomed within the clouds, a burst of brilliance, like a flicker of lightning, appearing and disappearing. After a short pause, a *bang* could be heard, faint and brief.

That was all.

That was the end of Alan Steamarm.

Hovering, Mr Mordadson looked down, then looked up towards *Cerulean*. He shook his head, adjusted his crimson spectacles on his nose, and with heavy wingbeats began making his way back to the airship.

CHAPTER 99

The Beginning

It was simply a continuation of what had been started, but not everyone was in favour of it. A couple of the crewmen grumbled. Hadn't they been through enough already today? A sharp rebuke from Captain Qadoschson soon brought them into line. He wasn't fully recovered but even so he could tell that what Az was proposing was worth doing. Lady Aanfieldsdaughter agreed, and that settled the matter.

So they descended again. They endured the cloud cover and the fresh onset of ground-sickness. *Cerulean* revisited the Chancel.

There, the situation had calmed. The Chancel buildings were no longer on the brink of tearing themselves apart. That particular threat had been negated, and Az quickly found out how and by whom. He also found out at what cost.

Cassie was softly weeping. Tears spilled down her cheeks, cutting trails through the smudges of dirt that covered her face. Fletcher was similarly distraught. Both of them looked tattered and battered. Bit by bit Az learned that Martin was dead, along with Deacon Shatterlonger. Martin had died buying time for Cassie and Fletcher to save the Chancel from Shatterlonger's sabotage attempt.

The member of the family hardest hit by Martin's death was his father. Den Grubdollar was in a state of shock, gazing into the middle distance, his face a mask of remorse. It wasn't simply that his eldest son was no more. He was remembering all the disputes they had had, the rows about Humanism, the rift that had yawned between them over the last few months. They would never be reconciled now. Neither would have a chance to apologise and mend fences. In the end Martin had been a hero and had done something which would have made his old man proud, but this was no consolation. It had come too late. Den was left with only regret and bitter self-recrimination.

Az felt awful for intruding on this family tragedy. He wondered if it would be best to postpone what he wished to do, or even abandon the idea altogether.

But then Cassie said, 'What did you come back down for anyway?'

'You,' he answered, simply.

She sniffed back tears and tried to smile. 'Yeah, I reckoned you would. And that thing over there ...' She gestured towards the airship.

'That's *Cerulean*. She's my *Cackling Bertha*, I now realise.'

'She'm big. Makes *Bertha* look like a slip of a girl. That'd please *Bertha*.'

Even in her grief Cassie was able to make a joke. This instilled Az with renewed confidence. Cassie's strength gave him strength.

'Look,' he said, 'I know this is hardly the time, but there's something I'd like to offer. To everyone.'

'Go on,' said Cassie.

The offer was made. It was accepted.

Three dozen Groundlings were gathered together. Their numbers were drawn from the ranks of the Humanists and the Amblescruts, the uninjured ones, any of them who was still in reasonably healthy condition. The offer was also extended to the Deacons, who had been released from the Chancel apartment where they had been imprisoned. They turned it down point-blank. It was wrong. Blasphemous. The Humanists and Amblescruts, by contrast, were only too keen.

They were all equipped with breathing-apparatus kits, which were conveniently to hand because of course Lawrence Brace had collected a truckful of them from the Consolidated Colliery Collective. The chosen Groundlings were then escorted to *Cerulean*. The airship was brought down groundscrapingly low, and they climbed aboard her using the rope ladders.

Cassie volunteered to come too. Az told her to stay with her family. She needed them right now, and they definitely needed her. But she said this was an opportunity she couldn't pass up, however sad she was feeling. She *had* to go.

With the Groundlings distributed among her troop cabins, *Cerulean* took to the air.

One relatively unbumpy flight later, she was above the cloud cover and rising towards Heliotropia.

It was unavoidably a short visit. The breathing-apparatus kits had a limited supply of air. *Cerulean* circuited the sky-city, and the masked Groundlings looked out from the cabin portholes.

In the control gondola, Az stood with Cassie, herself masked. Cassie didn't know whether to stare at Heliotropia or at the Airborn people in the gondola with her. She confessed to Az at one point that she had an irresistible urge to touch someone's wings. She wanted to know what they felt like. Az summoned Michael over and made him extend one wing to her. She stroked the feathers wonderingly. They were soft but real. They confirmed this was no dream. Then she turned back to Heliotropia and resumed gazing at it through the eye discs of her mask.

Az tried to see it as she was seeing it. Heliotropia was not the loveliest of the sky-cities. It was no Prismburg or Pearl Town or Silver Sanctum. It was gaudy and overblown, suited to its role as a tourist resort but not refined or monumentally spectacular the way those other cities were. Even plain old High Haven had more class.

Still, it stood proud in the air. It brushed the firmament. It towered against the sun. It spread its immense, hotel-covered 'petals' in all directions. And there were crowds of Airborn in it and around it, winging between the buildings, sporting over the rooftops.

Not Ascended Ones. That was not how they were to be regarded. Just people with wings.

346

Cassie and all the other Groundlings were being shown the sky-city for that reason. So that they could return home and say, *We've seen the world above the clouds, and it's a beautiful place but it's just a place and the people who live there are just people.* They could tell everyone that, and word would start to spread.

There were tricky times ahead. Lady Aanfieldsdaughter and the others at the Silver Sanctum would have much to do. There would have to be negotiations and careful diplomacy. Establishing a new form of relationship between Airborn and Groundling was not something that could be achieved overnight. The Airborn still needed their supplies from the ground, and with the Deacons' authority much diminished, if not utterly eliminated, that meant a brand new system would have to be put into place. Lady Aanfieldsdaughter and Mr Mordadson were already conferring about this quietly in one corner of the control gondola, discussing the shape of the future.

That was none of Az's concern. He was content that Lady Aanfieldsdaughter would do her best. She would try, and if she failed it would not be for lack of diligence or patience.

For now, taking Cassie and the other Groundlings on this trip to see Heliotropia was what counted to Az.

He felt Cassie fold her hand through the crook of his elbow. She squeezed his forearm. He wished he could see her face properly, but even just through the eye discs of the mask he could tell she was glad to be there with him. Not happy, because she couldn't be happy, not so soon after Martin's death. But glad.

Heliotropia shone in the sunlight, like a beacon.

Cerulean's Groundling passengers stared amazedly.

The world was changing.

It was a beginning.